Barbara Murphy went into advertising before she switched to publishing, as a secretary to the editor of *Home Notes* and *Modern Woman* magazines. She lives in Hampshire with her husband and two children, and a keen member of a local music and drama group.

FIVEPENNY LANES

At first glance, Fivepenny Lanes appears to be a sleepy, tranquil country village. But it is an altogether different scenario behind closed doors, for someone has taken a dislike to certain members of the community. Vicious anonymous letters begin to circulate the village; letters full of scandalous allegations which have already led to the revered headmistress to be announced unfit to teach, and the curate to be hounded from the village. James Woodward, the piano-tuner, has remained a silent witness — until now. For he is beginning to suspect who is behind the lies, and before any more lives can be destroyed, including his own, the culprit must be revealed . . .

Books by Barbara Murphy
Published by The House of Ulverscroft:

JANEY'S WAR

BARBARA MURPHY

FIVEPENNY LANES

Complete and Unabridged

ULVERSCROFT
Leicester

First published in Great Britain in 2000 by
Inner Circle
London

First Large Print Edition
published 2001
by arrangement with
Judy Piatkus (Publishers) Limited
London

British Library CIP Data

Murphy, Barbara, *1928 –*
    Fivepenny Lanes.—Large print ed.—
    Ulverscroft large print series: general fiction
    1. Anonymous letters
    2. Country life—England—Hampshire
    3. Large type books
    I. Title
    823.9'14 [F]

ISBN 0–7089–4450–7

Published by
F. A. Thorpe (Publishing)
Anstey, Leicestershire

Set by Words & Graphics Ltd.
Anstey, Leicestershire
Printed and bound in Great Britain by
T. J. International Ltd., Padstow, Cornwall

This book is printed on acid-free paper

For Philip and Julia —
because I am proud to be their mother.

Acknowledgements

Very few books can be written without some help and advice on research. I am very grateful to the following for pointing me in the right direction:

Rev Gary Philbrick
Father Jamie McGrath FMM
HCC Social Services Department
HCC Roads and Transport Department
Royal Hampshire Museum
Royal Marines Museum
Marc Paronio
Southampton University

And, as always, the staff of Hythe Library.

John Sutherland is not the piano-tuner of this book, nor do any of the events or characters relate to him. However, he has tuned my piano for more than thirty-five years, which gave me the idea for the story. He also helped with the background details of his training. Thank you, John.

My thanks also go to my agent, Judith Murdoch, for her patience and support, and to Judy Piatkus, for 'making my day'.

1

Nobody was quite sure how the village acquired its name. At the hub stood a signpost, with five fingers pointing towards Winchester, Southampton, Romsey, Salisbury and Andover. Rumour had it that at some time in distant history there had been a penny toll on each lane — it seemed a likely explanation. Just at the moment, though, the proprietor of the Fivepenny Lanes Tea-Shoppe was more concerned about the lack of pennies plopping into the till.

Mary Fitzgerald was a handsome woman with hair the colour of copper-beech leaves and green eyes always ready to crinkle into a smile. As for her voice, the softly lilting accent was straight from the land of shamrocks and the little people. Even the fact that, like the ducks, she was slightly above her ideal weight, did not stop admiring glances from men and envious ones from women. Every so often she would try a new diet from a magazine, until the lure of her own mouth-watering cakes proved too much for her willpower. Clearing the table after her one and only breakfast customer, Mary glanced around the empty café — and worried.

Normally, she was not of a worrying nature, and the quaint little thatched tea-shop couldn't be in a better position, right opposite the pond and village green. The sort of location that had tourists scuttling around with handfuls of high-tech photographic equipment. Then, after they had ducked under the olde English doorway and, if they were short of stature, missed the oak beams lined up like ancient missiles, they invariably bought a postcard or two, 'just in case'. The brass bell over the door was superfluous, as entry was usually announced by a yelp of pain, strong language, and barely suppressed mirth from those already sipping their tea and watching out for the next hapless victim.

At least, that had been the scenario until the new stretch of motorway had shunted coaches away from the narrow lanes and fords leading to the village. Now the shop bell tinkled less frequently, there were fewer hapless victims with bruised heads and the postcards faded in the sunlight. As a result, the quarterly returns on the VAT forms for September made depressing reading. And there were other reasons, more serious and personal reasons, that kept Mary pacing her bedroom floor at night, wondering whether she could carry on. But who would want to buy a tea-shop, even ye olde desirable tea-shoppe, in October?

If only there was someone she could talk to. She could phone her sister in Ireland — but Maeve would get angry, probably pack her shillelagh and fly straight over, full of threats to sort him out. What Mary needed was a friend who was not too closely involved. Someone she could trust. Someone who wouldn't gossip. There wasn't anyone she could think of who was caring and wise. Only her Holy namesake, and she was already on the hotline to the mother of God, night and day.

The sound of a car changing gear interrupted her

thoughts and she crossed to the window to watch the gunmetal Sierra carefully circle the war memorial. A light toot acknowledged her presence, then the car steadily climbed the hill on the Romsey Road, leaving Mary with another thought. The piano-tuner was one of the few good men left in this unholy world. Always pleasant, and never a word out of place. He'd given her good advice about the insurance — and he'd be here for lunch. Cloth in hand, thought in mind, she paused. Could she? Why not?

'Christ almighty! What have you been up to?'

Mary jumped at the voice. So engrossed had she been in her thoughts, she hadn't noticed her assistant wheeling her mountain bike round to the back. 'Sharon, dear,' she gently admonished. 'I wish you wouldn't take the Lord's name in vain.'

'Sorry.' The girl still stared at the visible damage to Mary's face. 'But that's a real shiner. And don't tell me you walked into a door.'

'No.' Mary had her answer prepared. 'But wasn't I the fool to try to take a short cut from the upstairs landing? Might have made it if it hadn't been for the newel post getting in the way.' It was the nearest explanation to the truth, and nobody needed to know how she had come to be lifted off her feet in the first place.

Sharon shook her mane of unruly hair. 'Those stairs are diabolical — death-traps,' she said, wisely. 'Just like the bloody beams.'

Mary flashed another reproving glance.

'Well that's nothing to what the blokes say when they're seeing stars.'

3

'And didn't I put up a sign to warn them? They just have to be more careful with these old buildings.'

'You're the one who needs to be careful, Mary. That's the second bad fall you've had lately.' Sharon looked as though she was about to say something more, then changed the subject. 'Just saw old Fanny Partridge in the Post Office. Yapping away, as usual.'

'Sharon! It's not kind to talk about our customers like that. It can't be much of a life for her, with her mother always complaining, and her father unable to speak at all since the poor man had his stroke. Miss Partridge enjoys a little chat with her friends in the village.'

'Well, she gave me a right earful when she saw I'd had my hair streaked green. Practically called me a Jezebel.' Chuckling, Sharon went on, 'Said it would serve me right if I caught my death through going around half-naked.'

Mary could imagine Miss Partridge's sniff of disapproval at the sight of the girl's psychedelic pedal-pushers and skimpy vest, which left little to the imagination. 'Oh, dear. Was that really what she said?'

'More or less.'

Anxiously, Mary asked, 'And what did you say to that?' Mary knew Sharon's tongue could be a little too smart for her own good at times.

'I just smiled sweetly and said young people didn't feel the cold and it would be yonks before I'd be needing thermal underwear in October.' Still grinning, Sharon went on, 'I nearly told her to put that in her pipe and smoke it, but stopped myself

4

just in time.' She traced a halo shape above her head with her finger.

'Good.' Mary couldn't resist a smile at Sharon's saintly expression. 'I'd better be getting her tray ready.'

'No rush. She's going home first to let the piano-tuner in. Said by the time her mother got to the door, any visitors were long gone — ' Sharon paused. 'Doesn't he usually come here first?'

'Yes, but he's had to change his timetable today. He'll be up at the Dower House now, so Miss Partridge won't need to cycle too fast.'

Sharon pulled a face. 'He'll be ages by the time Madam shop-until-you-drop Burridge has finished showing off. Wonder what she's bought this time.' Without waiting for an answer, she took the tray from Mary and headed towards the kitchen. 'Better make myself look decent, I suppose.' Over her shoulder she called back, 'Any coaches booked?'

'One in about half an hour. The only one today, I'm afraid.'

Sharon's loafers squeaked as she turned. 'You sit down and make the sandwiches. I'll do the running around. And don't make so many as yesterday. Those ducks are getting too fat on our leftovers.'

'Yes, ma'am.' Laughing, Mary raised her hand in a mock salute. She would miss Sharon's sense of fun as well as her kind heart. And she knew she should warn the girl that she might be out of a job before long, but hadn't the heart to wipe the smile from that pretty face.

By the time Mary had finished making sure no smidgen of air could sneak under the clingfilm wrapping and curl the edges of her sandwiches, Sharon had several trays of cups and saucers at the ready, the coffee machine hissing gently and boiling water waiting to spurt into the huge teapot. Then she buttered a huge quantity of scones — quicker to have them ready buttered for coach parties — and topped up the bowl of sugar on each table. Now that she had changed into a neat turquoise overall and braided her multi-coloured hair with a ribbon, she looked respectable enough to satisfy even Miss Partridge.

Suddenly, the peace was shattered by screaming brakes, and they stared out of the window as the Sierra took the sharp corner from the Romsey Road at high speed and whizzed past the café and up the hill towards Southampton.

'Wow! I've never seen him drive like that before,' Sharon said.

Mary agreed. 'Perhaps he'll be dashing home to get a new string or something?' But she didn't believe her own explanation. 'He can't have had time to tune Mrs Burridge's and Miss Partridge's pianos.' A tiny frown creased her brow. 'And didn't he say he'd have his lunch here before tuning mine?'

Sharon pulled a face. 'I wouldn't hold your breath. He had a face like thunder. Ah — here they come.'

The window darkened as a huge coach slowed, ready to disgorge its passengers. Quickly filling the teapot, Mary murmured, 'Let battle commence.'

All thoughts of the piano-tuner were put from Mary's head as the advance party of elderly customers crowded through the door, jostling with each other for window tables, and yelling to be served immediately.

'Just a moment. You'll all get served, don't worry.' Sharon nodded towards the rear of the shop. 'The loo is through there — and plenty more seats in the garden.' Moving through the tables, she held the tray high above the grasping hands. 'Please don't take the cups from the tray — someone will get scalded — and I don't want it to be me.'

Mary smiled at the coach driver as he sat near the counter. She knew, and he knew, that he was always served last. If he dared to finish his tea quickly, some of the old dears would panic in case the coach went without them, might even storm behind the counter and help themselves.

Refilling the coffee machine, Mary recalled that she had planned to confide in the piano-tuner. Oh, well, that would have to wait. But she wondered what on earth had happened to make him drive like a bat out of hell. Had he heard bad news from home? He had one of those mobile phones. Or could it be anything to do with Susan Burridge up at the Dower House?

Sighing, Mary whispered a hasty little prayer to the Holy mother, that the dear man was all right.

2

The Dower House was close to the gate leading to the Brigadier's estate. Or rather, what had once been the Brigadier's estate, but now belonged to his nephew, Ralph Beresford-Lawson. The late Brigadier had never married, but his mother had preferred the Dower House to the Manor, said it was cosier, and lived there for the last twenty years of her life, surrounded by her splendid collection of antique furniture and silver. When she died, the Dower House remained empty, its rooms smothered in dust sheets, until the Brigadier, failing in health, agreed to sell it to Percy Burridge, who was perfectly happy to order embossed notepaper with the new address, *Cranleigh Manor Dower House*, in order to please his wife. Susan Burridge liked the finer things of life. She had always been a magpie, collecting Capodimonte porcelain, Swarovski crystal, pieces of amethyst and topaz, garden statues; whatever might be fashionable, until she tired of them, gave them away, and moved on to the next collector's item. But the handsome pieces of furniture already in the house sparked a different kind of interest to Susan, who pleaded with her husband to buy them from the old boy. Before long, she became addicted to TV programmes like the *Antiques Road Show*. The difference was that, this time, she really loved the things she collected. Loved, almost to the point of obsession. Every penny that her husband made went into the auction salerooms. Fortunately for her, Percy Burridge was a devoted husband, who would give his wife the moon if he could get hold of someone at NASA. Even after thirty-something years, nothing was too good for his Susan, although he had asked her to hold back before buying that grand piano — the recession was hitting the building trade hard and the heated swimming pool had set him back a pretty penny.

Swirling the whisky around her glass, Susan stared moodily across the huge pool, copied from something she had seen in an article about California. A few crisp autumn leaves drifted across the surface of the water, but no matter. The gardener could clear them tomorrow. The late morning sun became trapped on her side of the patio and, wrapped in a towelling robe, she stretched her smoothly tanned legs along the lounger, deep in thought. The thoughts were cunning, devious, and intended to maim. Percy was in London. Their future depended on the outcome of his business meeting, which was bound to go on for hours, so she had plenty of time to plot and plan. It really didn't matter what she said, or implied, as long as Percy believed her, and as long as that wretched man was hounded from the village. Who did he think he was, anyway? He was only a piano-tuner.

Raising her glass, she tossed the remains of her drink down her throat, then took the crystal tumbler indoors for a generous refill from the decanter of old malt whisky, adding a dash of dry ginger ale. Mrs

Graham always raised her eyebrows when Susan asked her to pour a whisky and dry ginger. Susan knew the woman thought it *infra dig* to add anything other than a little water to such a quality malt. So what! The woman was only a housekeeper, but had airs of grandeur, like the old biddies up at the Manor. They had been in service all their working lives, and would remain in service, always at someone else's beck and call, until they retired, or died.

Placing the glass on a silver coaster to protect the inlaid drum table, Susan appraised the drawing room. Every piece of furniture had been carefully sought and purchased, and she loved them with a passion deeper than she would have believed possible. The other things she had collected over the years were very nice to show off, but easy to discard, whereas the antiques were a part of her life she couldn't do without. No matter what happened to Percy or the business, she would always have her treasures. And now, at last, she had a grand piano.

Relaxing, she sank back into the leather chair and smiled. Not bad for the daughter of a bricklayer, born and raised in a humble terraced house. But Susan had always aspired to greater things. Not for her the continuing existence in a back street of Leeds. It might have been good enough for her father and grandfather, but it certainly wasn't good enough for Susan. Even though she hadn't passed the eleven-plus, there were other ways of avoiding the humdrum life that was her mother's chosen lot.

Closing her eyes, she remembered the day that Percy Burridge had opened the door to a different world, and she had realised that she could be part of that world — if she played her cards right.

★　★　★

It was the first time that Susan Wallace had been to the races. She wasn't particularly keen on horses and thought betting on them was stupid — she'd seen what had happened to the family evicted from number fourteen. But when Mr Dewhurst said there was a spare seat on the coach to Doncaster and would she like to join them, she smiled her sweetest smile and said, 'How very kind. I'd like that.' She'd been working hard at toning down her accent and speaking nicely without being too la-di-da.

Mr Dewhurst was a regular customer at Grimshaw's Building Supplies and often talked to Susan while she made up his order. He had a small building and decorating business. Mainly working on house repairs and extensions. Nothing much to shout about, but he never seemed short of cash. His eldest son worked in the business with him and tried to chat up Susan at every opportunity. She didn't encourage Brian Dewhurst. He was short-sighted, painfully thin with a protruding Adam's apple and — most important — completely lacking in ambition. But it wouldn't hurt to go to the races with him. After all, what better way to meet someone else? Someone with ambition. Not a no-hoper punter, but someone who went to the races for relaxation. An owner perhaps? Or a high-flying business man entertaining equally high-flying clients?

Percy Burridge was neither of these. But he was ambitious. Like Susan, he thought gambling was a mug's game and, like Susan, he had gone to the races hoping he might meet someone who could be of benefit to his future. Certainly he was not looking for a wife, or even a girlfriend. But fate has a strange way of playing tricks.

She was in the bar when it happened. The male Dewhursts had disappeared in the direction of the Tote and Mrs Dewhurst had gone in search of the ladies' room. Sipping her first ever glass of Babycham, and trying to look as though it was something she did every day, Susan studied form. Not the horses, but the affluent-looking men, and their women. She knew she didn't have the kind of looks that presented glamour, but it was their behaviour she wanted to emulate. One or two were horsy types, enthusiastically marking their cards and obviously well versed in racing know-how. They wouldn't be much help. But the cool blondes with their slightly supercilious smiles and perfunctory nods punctuating the conversation, those were the ones who slotted into the little groups with complete confidence. Behind her, Percy Burridge, glass of whisky in one hand, pack of cigars in the other, backed his way through the thirsty mass surrounding the bar, straight on to a collision course with Susan.

'Sorry, mate — ' he began, then stopped as he turned and saw Susan looking down at her beige Crimplene dress, glistening with the contents of her glass. 'Oh dear, I am sorry, lass. Let's go over there so we can see how much damage I've done.' He nodded towards a nearby table where he deposited his glass and cigars.

Outwardly, Susan managed to keep a calm expression, but inwardly she was seething as she dabbed ineffectually at her dress with the tiny scrap of lace-trimmed cotton from her handbag. The clumsy lout had the broadest Yorkshire accent she'd ever heard, and she wished he'd go away and leave her alone.

'Here, mop yourself up with this, while I get thee another drink.' He produced a huge white handkerchief. 'That scatty little thing is useless.' He looked at her glass. 'Same again? Or would you rather have a brandy?'

About to refuse, she looked up at him and immediately changed her opinion. This man might be clumsy, but he wasn't a lout. A little below average height, and with rugged looks that reminded her of the Welsh actor, Richard Burton, he had an attractive smile and an air about him that she recognised. Like Susan, this man was travelling in one direction — upwards.

She smiled graciously as she took his hand-kerchief. 'A Babycham would be very nice, thank you.'

Covertly watching him as she dried her hands, Susan admired the mature way he caught the bartender's eye and ordered a refill. Brian Dewhurst had taken ages to be served with the first glass.

'There we are, lass.' The man placed her glass alongside his whisky and took a card from his wallet. 'Reckon that dress will need cleaning. Just let me know how much and I'll refund it.' He raised his glass to her. 'Good health — hope I've not spoiled your day.'

'No. Of course not. It was an accident.' She took a sip of her drink, then looked at his card. *Percy Burridge — Builder of Quality Houses.* Percy! He didn't look a bit like a Percy. More like a Ted or a Bob. Should she demur a little about the dress? 'And I'm sure the stain will wash out — ' she began.

He shook his head. 'You take it along to cleaner's first thing,' he insisted. 'Happen they'll know best how to deal with it.'

'Well, thank you — if you're sure.'

His blue eyes were piercing in his somewhat weather-beaten face and his gaze was frank and open. 'Haven't seen you here before,' he observed with a smile. 'What brings a lass like you to the races?'

Rather than make a fool of herself, she decided to be honest. 'Actually, it's my first visit. A client of my employer invited me to join his party.'

'And left you all alone in the bar?'

'They've only gone to place a bet.'

He nodded, then said. 'Reckon you work in an office. Secretary, or summat like that?'

Briefly she hesitated before she nodded. His address was in Castleford, it was unlikely that he knew Sam Grimshaw.

'Well, you'll never be out of a job, that's for sure.' He drained his glass and replaced it on the table.

This was the point where he would say goodbye and go on his way, Susan realised. And she couldn't think of a single thing to say to keep the conversation going.

'Ah, there you are, Susan! Thought we'd lost you.' Mr Dewhurst appeared out of the crowd, a pint of ale in his hand. 'And I can't find the missus — ' Noticing her companion, he stopped, then grinned. 'By heck, if it isn't Percy Burridge. Haven't seen thee since you were just out of school. You'll remember my lads?' Brian and his younger brother, Norman, nodded. 'And here's the wife. I was about to send out a search party.'

Mrs Dewhurst laughed raucously. 'It's all right for you men, you never have to queue like we do.' She looked at Susan. 'Sorry to leave you all on your own, love.'

Susan practised one of the little nods.

Handing his wife her gin and lime, Mr Dewhurst said, 'Look who's here, Doris. Young Percy Burridge.'

'Well, I never!' She stared at him. 'You look as though you've gone up in the world a bit since we last saw you. Didn't follow your dad down the mines, then?'

'Not likely!' He grimaced. 'His mine's closed down, anyway, and he's been thrown on the scrap-heap with his mates — and their coughs.'

'Happen you did the right thing, Percy. So what are you doing?'

'Building houses, Mrs Dewhurst. Can't fail with houses. People will always need somewhere to live.'

'Aye, that's true enough.' The people sitting at the next table began to leave. 'Let's sit down for a bit.' she suggested. 'These shoes are killing me, and we can catch up on the gossip.' With a sigh of relief, she sank on to the nearest chair. 'Stanley, have you

15

introduced our guest to Percy?'

Percy Burridge smiled. 'Reckon I introduced myself. Bumped into the lass and made a right mess of her pretty dress.'

Mrs Dewhurst's mouth dropped open. 'Oh, Susan! I hope your mother knows how to wash these new synthetics.'

'Mr Burridge has very kindly suggested I have it cleaned.'

'That was the least I could do. And how about calling me Percy? I know I'm a bit older than thee, but I'll not be drawing pension for a while.'

Susan wondered whether it was ethical at this stage, but the others laughed and he seemed to take it for granted, so she didn't argue.

'At least you didn't insist on your lads being named after you,' he said to Mr Dewhurst. 'Eldest son has always been Percy in our family. When Grandad was alive there were three of us: Old Percy, Percy, and Young Percy!'

Susan asked, 'What name would you have liked, if you'd had a choice?'

He thought for a moment, then said, 'Don't rightly know. Perhaps John. Or Edward. One thing I know for sure, if I get wed, I'll not name my son after me.' He smiled. 'Susan's a grand name. You wouldn't want to change that, would you?'

She'd thought about it often enough, wanting to call herself Vivien, or Lauren, after the film stars. But if he liked the name Susan . . . 'No, I don't want to change it, although I don't like being called Sue, or Susie.'

Various names were discussed, then Percy turned

16

to Mr Dewhurst. 'So you know Susan through her boss?'

'That's right. I've been dealing with Grimshaw's since I started up.'

'Sam Grimshaw? With the yard back of railway station?'

Oh, heck! Susan thought. Now he'll find out I'm not a secretary at all, just the girl who works in the warehouse. But luck was on her side.

'That's the one,' Mr Dewhurst said. 'And he thinks the world of young Susan. She's been there since she left school, but I reckon a nice lass like that could do better for herself.' He picked up his empty glass. 'Same again, everyone?'

While Brian went off to collect his winnings, and Norman helped his mother to select a horse from her card, Percy slid into the chair next to Susan. Quietly, he asked, 'Do you reckon you could do better for yourself?'

Her reply was just as quiet. 'Mr Grimshaw is a very nice gentleman, but I don't see myself staying in the same job for the rest of my life.' She shrugged. 'So if something better comes up — ' She looked at him over the rim of her glass, wondering if he might know of a firm that had a vacancy.

'You're right, Susan,' he said. 'The days of staying at the same place until retirement are over. That was something I couldn't make my dad understand.' He leaned a little closer. 'How would you feel about working for me?'

She was so surprised, she almost spilt her drink again. 'For you?' She regained her composure and lowered her voice. Instead of asking, 'Doing what?'

17

she said, 'In what capacity?' It sounded more like a secretary than a warehouse assistant.

He didn't laugh. 'I'm building some fancy houses over at Morley, but looking out for more work all the time.' He glanced at his watch. 'In fact, I'm meeting an architect here later on who might have something for me. So I need someone to work in the show house at Morley.'

'Do you mean showing the house to prospective buyers?'

'Aye, that sort of thing. And keeping the paperwork in order. Typing letters. Phoning and so on. Should be right up your street.'

It was right up her street, except that her typing was more of the two-fingered variety when she addressed the odd envelope. Still, Susan Wallace was willing to learn.

Percy was still talking. 'A mate asked me to take on his girlfriend, but she was useless. Careless with the petty cash, no dress sense whatsoever and smoked like a chimney. When I got complaints about her language I had to give her the sack.' He smiled. 'I want someone with a bit of class. Someone like you, Susan. I'll pay well for the right girl. What do you reckon?'

What did she reckon! Susan Wallace was already wondering when she could start and whether it would be easier to travel by bus or train, but she stared thoughtfully into her glass for a moment or two longer. She could enrol at the Technical College for typing classes and practise like mad in her dinner hour. How long would it take to be reasonably proficient?

Eventually, she said, 'I will have to speak to Mr Grimshaw, and give him time to replace me. Perhaps I should give him a month's notice?' Percy frowned, so she quickly said, 'Just a suggestion but, in the meantime, if you could cope with the paperwork, I would be quite happy to man the show house for you at weekends, or during the evenings. I presume that is when most of your prospective buyers would be looking around?'

He stared hard at her for a long moment. Then the corners of his eyes crinkled and he murmured. 'You'll do, lass. You'll do.'

★ ★ ★

It didn't take long for Susan to make herself quite indispensable to Percy Burridge. She developed a pleasant telephone manner, kept careful records, improved her typing, and refused to be provoked by the occasional loud-mouth who complained about the price of the houses. Instead, she politely pointed out that good workmanship was worth paying for and that the Burridge houses would long outlive the jerry-built ones. Percy was delighted when complimented on the efficiency of his new assistant and noted that she was rapidly learning the jargon and technical descriptions of the building trade.

Their relationship was very much on a business basis, and not once did he invite her out in a social context until the day the last house on the Morley estate was sold, when he suggested a celebration meal. Susan dressed with even more care than usual that evening, and brushed her light brown hair until

19

it gleamed. Percy had said he wanted to make her a proposition, and she wondered . . .

When she discovered that the proposition was strictly business, she was disappointed, until she realised just what he was suggesting. He had two new projects in the pipeline and wanted her to take charge of the one at York, acting as his negotiator, and she would receive a commission for each house sold, on top of her basic salary.

'Some folks might think you're a bit young for such a responsibility, but you've got a good business head and I think you could handle it. Point is, what do you think?'

Having worked out a few rapid sums in her head, Susan was in no doubt that she could handle it — but she didn't want to appear too eager. It might seem immature. Slowly chewing on her fillet steak, she eventually said, 'Based on my experience at Morley, and with your help, I'm confident I could handle it, Percy, and I'd like to thank you for the generous offer. However — '

'What's the problem?' He looked concerned.

'Not a problem, Percy. Just one or two things that occur to me.' She dabbed at her mouth with her napkin and continued, 'I've been thinking of taking a course of business studies at the Tech, but it would mean time off — and the fees are not cheap.'

He mulled over this, then nodded. 'I could manage to cover you for one day a week, and foot the bill. It's good business to have someone at college, learning proper-like, and I can claim for it against taxes. Anything else bothering you?'

'Only the journey. It's going to take longer and

cost more.' She hoped he might offer to pay her fares, and was completely unprepared for his next suggestion.

'Aye, I'd thought of that, and come up with a solution. Have you ever thought of learning to drive?'

For a moment she gaped at him. Then she said, 'Often. But where can someone like me get the money for driving lessons, let alone buy a car? Nobody in my family drives, and you're the only person I know who has a car.'

'I'll pay for driving lessons, and give you a bit of extra practice like.' He'd saved the best bit till last. 'And if — no, *when* — you pass your test, I'll buy you a little company car.' Pushing back his chair, he grinned broadly. 'No one can say that Percy Burridge doesn't treat his staff right.'

Breathlessly, she smiled back. 'I don't know what to say, Percy. You're so generous.'

'It's a good investment, Susan. All I ask is that you sell those houses as quickly as possible, so we can move on to the next project. Reckon me and thee will make a good team.' He clicked his fingers at the waiter. 'A bottle of champagne — best you've got.' Then he smiled at Susan. 'The best deserves the best.'

★ ★ ★

The following year, Susan was successfully selling Burridge houses near Halifax — and Percy had another proposition. Over after-dinner coffee and mints he told her he was seriously considering moving down south. Dismayed, she gazed at him, wondering if this was the end of her dream.

'How far south?' Her voice was just a little tremulous.

'Wherever growth market is best. There's a plot of land going in Hampshire that would suit. Between Winchester and Southampton. Handy for folks who work in London. That's where the brass is, and that's where I want to be.' He deftly clipped the end of his cigar.

Although she longed to ask 'What about me?' Susan had learned the value of silence, so she waited while Percy lit his cigar.

For the first time since he had started speaking, he looked at Susan. 'Have you ever been down south?' he asked.

She shook her head.

'Reckon your dad will let you come with me next weekend? I'd like your opinion on the place.'

He didn't elaborate any further as to her role in the project. And she didn't ask. Her father made a few anxious sounds then went back to his newspaper, and her mother warned her to keep her room locked, then got on with the ironing. A little late for her mother to be concerned, Susan thought, remembering the incident with Dennis Rivers not long after she started work at Grimshaws. That had been warning enough, after allowing herself to get drunk at a Christmas party and believe a good-looking travelling salesman when he said he wanted to marry her. She wouldn't have minded so much if it had been a mind-blowing experience. But Dennis, for all his experience, had been more interested in satisfying his own sexual desire as quickly as possible than in making it a momentous occasion for the girl he'd seduced, and headed back to London before she could find out if it would be any better second time around. So Susan, being a practical girl, decided to withhold her favours from any other men until her wedding night. Not for her the disgrace of having an illegitimate child, like some of the girls she'd known at school.

★ ★ ★

Percy Burridge was the perfect gentleman. He'd booked two rooms with their own private bathrooms, on different floors of one of the best hotels in Winchester. There would be no gossip to mar the reputation of his assistant. As they drove the seven miles to the village of Fivepenny Lanes, Susan commented on the glorious reds and golds of the trees, and when she gasped with pleasure at her first glimpse of the village centre, he smiled. Perhaps it wouldn't be too great a hardship for the lass to uproot herself from Leeds.

He parked the Jaguar outside the church and led the way along the narrow footpath at the back until they came to a large, fenced off field.

'This is the place, Susan,' he said, pointing. 'Should be able to get close on fifty houses there with decent-sized gardens — and there's access on to the Salisbury road over the far side. What do you reckon?'

Trying very hard to be businesslike, she studied the field and nodded. 'It's an attractive location,

Percy,' she said. 'And not many trees to be felled.'

'I'll keep that chestnut in the centre. It's a good shape and will make a focal point with the houses fanning out from it.'

'Good idea.'

'To start with, I'll have a caravan on site, but when all the houses are sold, I'll move into the show house.' He watched her face for a reaction, and was not disappointed.

'Percy!' she cried. 'Are you planning to stay down here?'

'Aye. There's other building plots for sale not too far away, and this would be a good place to live, don't you reckon?'

'Well, yes. It's a beautiful area. But — ' She hesitated. 'What about the new project in Harrogate?'

'I was hoping you would take care of that one, Susan?'

'Yes, of course. And do you have another one to follow? Up north, I mean.'

He shook his head. 'If this site makes as much brass as I expect it to, I'll not be looking for any more work in Yorkshire.'

'I see.' Susan looked as though that was far from the truth. 'Do you have any plans for me — or will you be giving me the sack?' Her voice was low.

'Ruddy heck, no! I was hoping you might consider — ' He puffed fiercely on his cigar before he continued, 'The countryside is not as grand as Yorkshire, but quite agreeable-like. It would mean leaving your folks, of course, but, would you consider coming down here later on?'

Her face brightened a little as she asked, 'As your negotiator?'

'No.' It was not often that Percy Burridge was ill at ease. He didn't dare look at her face as he quietly said, 'As my wife.'

★ ★ ★

Their wedding was given prime coverage in all the Yorkshire newspapers, with photographs of Susan in her beautiful Empire-line dress and Percy resplendent in his hired suit and top hat, and reports of their hotel reception for seventy guests. In his speech, Mr Wallace said he was proud that his only child had done so well for herself, and Mrs Wallace wept and told Percy's father that she didn't know why their offspring should want to live so far away. She'd heard that the southerners were a miserable lot who never popped into one another for a cup of tea and a chat. Not at all like the friendly neighbours she had in Leeds. Mr Burridge senior agreed and said young Percy had always thought himself a bit above his brother and sister. He'd offered to let them have one of his houses a bit cheaper, but what would the likes of his family be doing in a posh neighbourhood? Better to rent and let the landlord have the problems. As for going abroad on honeymoon! He and the wife had a good enough time with a couple of days in Scarborough. But that wouldn't do for young Percy. Oh, no.

★ ★ ★

By the time they flew in to Majorca, Susan had worked out a believable reason to explain the loss of her virginity. Percy must be fairly experienced at his age, but she knew he would expect his bride to be completely innocent. So she told him she had once had a minor operation for some female problems, which had resulted in her hymen being ruptured. She had a certificate somewhere to prove it, she said, looking suitably embarrassed, and offered to show it to him on their return.

Percy swallowed the story, hook, line and sinker, and promised to be very gentle with her. To her surprise and delight, he was a remarkably good lover, and by the time she packed for the return flight, Susan's sexual instincts were well and truly awakened. She couldn't believe her luck. Not only had she landed a successful and ambitious man who adored her, but she was falling in love with him.

As he carried her over the threshold of the show house, Percy told Susan to close her eyes. When she opened them again, she thought she was dreaming. Every piece of furniture was exactly as she had chosen from the brochures, except one. A beautiful, brand new piano.

'Oh, Percy! I've always wanted a piano.'

'I know, love. Your dad told me you had lessons when you were little, but the piano you had at home wasn't much good.'

'Fancy you going out and getting this.' She kissed him. 'I can't get over it!'

'Well, I know nowt about pianos, so I asked the chap who tunes the one at the golf club, and he suggested this one. Said Chappell is a good make. Hope he's right.'

She lifted the lid and tried a few notes. 'It's lovely,' she enthused. 'But it could do with tuning.'

'Aye. The man said it would, after the journey. So I booked him in for next Wednesday. He's a nice young chap. A bit on the quiet side, but seems to know what he's about. You'll like him.'

3

'Only the piano-tuner.' The familiar words echoed inside his skull, nipping nerve ends like a terrier snapping at his heels. Hostile words. Wounding words. And it was the way she said it. Such contempt in her voice. The arrogance of the woman! His foot pressed harder on to the pedal until the whine of the protesting engine reminded him that a one in six gradient should not be climbed in top gear. Changing down, he crested the summit and pulled into a lay-by.

After a few minutes, his hands relaxed on the steering wheel and he leaned back against the headrest, trying to put the words from his mind.

He should be used to it by now. Whenever he telephoned or called, someone in the background was told, 'It's only the piano-tuner.' Probably the milkman, postman and dustman felt the same. All lumped together as doing a necessary job but of little consequence in their lives — unless they didn't turn up. What was wrong with being a piano-tuner, anyway? Someone had to do it, and it was a highly skilled job. Apart from Susan Burridge, they didn't mean to be hurtful, but it would be nice if they remembered his name. Only one person had ever said, 'It's Mr Woodward, dear. He's come to put our piano back in tune for us.' But then the Reverend Hugh Jenkins was a man who practised his Christian principles, and he loved to discuss the eisteddfod and the works of Bach while the Obermeier was being brought back into pitch. Apart from the Reverend Jenkins, most people asked him again for his name when writing a cheque — even the old Brigadier had always called him 'Woodson' and constantly had to initial his corrected cheques. Still, at least they didn't bounce, which was more than could be said for some.

Usually, being known as 'only the piano-tuner' was a minor irritation, but today the barb had struck deep, and it could have unpleasant consequences. He would have to go back and carry on with his other appointments, but he really didn't know what to do about the Dower House. If only there was someone he could talk to. Someone who would be discreet, and give him some sensible advice.

Stepping from the car, he eased the tension in his neck muscles, his attention taken by a blackbird singing in a nearby tree. How exquisite, he thought, seconds before the bird swooped towards him, deposited a dollop across the gleaming paintwork of his Sierra with a triumphant squawk, and flew on towards a promising line of snowy washing billowing in a cottage garden.

The aptness of his muttered 'Shit!' struck him as he lifted the hatch and pulled out a plastic box, neatly packed with everything he might need in an emergency. He began to laugh, a little bitterly at first, then almost hysterically, at the irony of the situation.

'I'm glad you thinks it's funny!'

He turned towards the sharp voice. Across the road, a woman waved her arm furiously towards a

29

sheet, now splattered liberally with the blackbird's personal calling card.

'I wasn't laughing at you, madam.' He pointed to his car.

She came towards her fence for a closer view, her shoulders shaking in silent mirth. 'Oh, dear,' she sighed, wiping her eyes. 'You've got a right load of it there. Want some water?'

'Thank you. That would be most kind.'

While the woman went back into her cottage, he carefully laid his Harris tweed jacket on the passenger seat and rolled up the sleeves of his white shirt. Not a very practical colour, but James Woodward preferred to look businesslike and always carried a brown linen coat to protect his clothing if he had to crawl around on dusty floors, like the school assembly hall. By the time the woman returned, he was neatly covered up. She watched as he squirted a little car wash into the water, her glance taking in his olive cords and conservative tie. 'You look like an agricultural rep,' she commented. 'But you'd never keep the car that clean around the farms.'

Rinsing the sponge, he attacked an obstinate spot. 'True,' he agreed. 'Actually, I'm a piano-tuner.'

'Is that so?' She contemplated his words. 'Nice to be working for yourself. Able to choose when you works. Not having to live in a tied cottage, like my Ted.'

'I like it.' He didn't explain that you had to work the times dictated by clients, or there wouldn't be sufficient money to pay the mortgage. And no holiday or sick pay. She wouldn't understand.

She nodded towards the village. 'Bet there's not many pianos in the posh estate. They all has those keyboard things these days.'

'I've one or two regulars there, as well as the school and the village hall — although I've just been told they're getting rid of the old upright and buying a little electric organ instead.'

'I'd heard rumours.'

'Apparently, the youngsters would prefer it.'

'Our Gary would. Not that he goes there much. More likely to find him in the Cup and Stirrup.' She shaded her eyes against the sun. 'Where else does you go then?' she asked.

'Anywhere there's a piano to tune or repair. Hotels. Clubs. Ships.'

'Ships? Do you have to go to sea?'

'No. But I do have to go down to the docks whenever they berth, even late at night.'

'You don't live round here, do you?'

He shook his head. 'Bramblehurst. In the New Forest.'

'That's a tidy way.'

'This is about the furthest I go. The motorway has made it easier. When I started out I had to cycle on the old road. Must have been close on twenty miles.' He smiled at her across the roof of the car. 'I was younger then, of course. And fitter.'

The woman smiled back. 'We had a piano once. One of those with candlesticks on the front. A blind chap used to tune it. Lived over Michelmersh way. Expect you knows him.'

'Mr Headingly? Died a few years ago?'

'Never knows his name. We just calls him the

piano-tuner.' She cleaned her teeth with her tongue. 'When the old boy pops off I told our Gary he ought to give it a go. You don't need no training or equipment, do you? Only a tuning fork.' She didn't wait for an answer. 'But Ted said it ain't a proper man's job. So they both sweats their guts out on the farm, with only a rusty old Escort to show for it.' Shaking her head, she sighed. 'Gary could have had a nice car like yours. And I wouldn't be scrubbing cow dung off two lots of clothes, week in, week out.' She scowled at the washing line. 'Better put that lot in to soak again, I suppose. Bloody birds.' Crossing the road back towards her cottage, she called out, 'Leave the bucket by the gate when you've done.'

'Right. Thanks for the water.' Deep in thought, he washed, dried and polished until his face reflected in the surface. Only a tuning fork! No training! If only she knew. Seven years it had taken him to learn the trade.

His first set of tools had set him back fifteen pounds. A lot of money in those days. Deducted each week from the pittance he received. He couldn't afford a proper fitted box, so his father had given him a battered little cardboard suitcase to strap onto the back of his bike, a piece of oilcloth protecting it from the elements. Now he carried a handsome custom-made case, the large array of tools secure in their slots. Ruefully he glanced at the set of brand new strings lying on the back seat, specially ordered from Germany. Two hundred and fifty pounds they had cost, and he wasn't sure he'd get his money back. He wouldn't have minded so much if someone had phoned to cancel the order.

Drying his hands, he gazed back towards Fivepenny Lanes. From his high vantage point, he could see the pond, the green, the thatched cottages, all looking exactly the same as when he first saw them — must be close on forty years ago. Any changes were subtle, like the general store combining with the Post Office and newsagents, and the art gallery replacing the little hairdressing salon. The housing development over on the Salisbury Road was still just a dream on Percy Burridge's blueprint in those days. Leaning on the stile, 'the piano-tuner' vividly remembered that autumn day when he had paused to get his breath back, leaning his bicycle against this very stile.

★ ★ ★

James Woodward was just twenty years old, but he needed a brief rest after pushing his heavy bike over the crest of the hill. The stile was just the job. He made sure his suitcase was secure on the carrier. Didn't want to lose anything before he arrived at the village with the funny name. Fivepenny Lanes. Wonder where that came from? That must be it, down the other side of the hill. He could see the steeple of a church, over towards the Andover road. The Vicarage shouldn't be too hard to find.

He couldn't help grinning like a Cheshire cat at the thought of it. After three years in the workshop, then two more as apprentice to the improver, accompanying him on his rounds, Mr Fielding had finally agreed that James was now an improver himself, and could go out on his own. And here he was, on his first solo assignment. He could see the school on the Winchester Road, but no sign of a village hall. Have to go down and ask.

James was freewheeling down the hill at full pelt, whooping with the sheer exuberance of youth, when he saw the village hall. Half-way down, lying back a little from the lane. He'd just passed it! As soon as his hands locked on the brake levers he knew it was a mistake. Climbing out of the ditch and brushing soggy leaves from his coat, his first thought was for his case, and he wished he'd tied it up with a thicker piece of string as he searched every nook and cranny for his precious tools. Then he wondered if there would be a toilet round the back of the hall where he could tidy himself up.

No such luck. The caretaker was waiting at the door, bunch of keys in his hand, sour expression on his face.

'They should have warned us they were sending an apprentice,' he complained.

'I'm not an apprentice — well, not exactly. I'm an improver,' James tried to explain.

'Is that what you're called?' The caretaker eyed James from top to toe. 'Looks like you could do with a bit of improving yourself.'

'Sorry . . . came off my bike down the hill.'

The man nodded. 'You're not the first. Don't suppose you'll be the last.' He turned and went into the hall. 'Gents is over on the left.' He found the key he was looking for and unlocked the ancient upright piano. 'Just hope you know what you're doing. The parish council won't be very happy if you muck it up.'

As he listened, tightened and tuned, James realised that the piano needed refelting and new strings, but decided not to make too much of an issue about it just yet. The caretaker stood over him the whole time.

Next on his list was the school. No real problems there, although the headmistress also hovered with an anxious expression, as though not sure such a young fellow could know what he was about.

His arrival at the vicarage made him aware of his insignificance in the vast scheme of things, even in the patch of God's world inhabited by one of His personal representatives. The housekeeper opened the door, looked a little surprised, and ushered him into the hall. When a voice from an inner sanctum whispered, 'Who is it, Mrs Lofthouse?' she briskly answered, 'Only the piano-tuner, Reverend, nothing for you to be bothered about. I'll keep an eye on him.'

Denting his confidence even further, she smiled politely at James. 'No offence, but you are new, and you are, well, shall we say, much younger than we had anticipated.' She led the way into the inner sanctum, explaining in a hushed voice, 'The piano was left to the church some years ago by one of the parishioners. I'm afraid it is rather out of tune as the blind gentleman hasn't called for a while. The choir-master often complains, but the Reverend Simpkins has no ear for music.

The rector was of indeterminate age, plump, pale and hairless. It was difficult to know his height, or the colour of his eyes, as he remained on his knees in a dark corner of the room, his lips silently

35

moving. He didn't raise his head, or look at James.

It wasn't easy to ignore the lowered bald pate so close to the piano. Each note played seemed an intrusion into the aura of prayer, but it wasn't until the middle C was being tightened that a sudden burst of anguished sound filled the room. Startled, James thought he had trodden on an unseen cat, but no. It was the Reverend Simpkins, wailing the twenty-second Psalm as only those who are utterly tone deaf can wail. James fought to regain his composure, but lost the battle as the rector reached the line, 'O My God, I cry in the day-time, but thou hearest not.'

Covering his mouth with his hand and avoiding eye contact with Mrs Lofthouse, he choked, 'Could I use your toilet, please?'

It was some time before James was able to rejoin the housekeeper in the hall. Judging by the expression on her face, she was also finding the toneless chanting rather difficult to handle. 'I should have warned you not to play middle C,' she murmured. 'The Reverend takes it as his cue — but he shouldn't be too long.'

After a few more moments of unbearable caterwauling, a blessed silence descended upon the house once more and James was able to finish his task.

★   ★   ★

And so it was for the next two years. Each April and October, James cycled valiantly up the hill, freewheeled down into the village, a little more carefully, and tuned three pianos. His other appointments were closer to Southampton, but he still found that owners of valuable pianos did not consider an 'improver' would really know what he was about. They hovered. They questioned. They watched every move. But they found little to complain about.

Then came the day that could no longer be put off. The day he cleaned and packed away his precious tools, said goodbye to his family, and went into the army. James was one of the last National Service conscripts. The guys were OK, but when he was posted overseas, he hated the humid Asian jungles, the poverty in India, and the whining music, so tuneless to his sensitive ear.

It had been strange at first, returning to civvy street, having to make his own schedules, instead of being told what to do every step of the way. He was treated differently, too. More respect. The newest apprentice even called him, 'sir'. And the manager confided a little background information on the company. That was when James began to rethink his own ambitions for the future. His great ambition had been to be like Mr Fielding, but did he really want to be the manager of an esteemed piano shop if the fear of losing his job was going to be more important than the customer's needs? Poor Mr Fielding was no longer a well man, and everyone said the job was making his nerves bad.

An October howler lashed rain into James's face on his first post-army trip to Fivepenny Lanes, but a puncture forced him to turn back. While she hung his saturated trousers and socks to dry, his mother told him she'd saved every penny from the money he'd sent home.

'Why don't you buy one of those little Vespas or Lambrettas, James? And some good protective clothing. That cape and sou'wester has definitely seen better days.' She frowned thoughtfully. 'You'll need a proper helmet as well, dear, in case you fall off.'

A week later, equipped with L plates, and his tools in a plastic box, he set off again for Fivepenny Lanes. This time he recommended that the piano in the village hall would sound so much better and keep in tune longer if some of the strings were replaced. The caretaker said he would pass the information on to the chairman of the parish council. And this time, the headmistress said, 'The other young man was quite good, but I always felt you understood our piano better. Nice to see you back.' Then she went about her duties, leaving him alone in the assembly hall.

Finally, he parked his scooter in the drive of the vicarage and rang the bell. To his surprise, a different lady answered the door. Had she replaced Mrs Lofthouse?

'Bless you, no, my love. It's the Reverend Hugh Jenkins who lives here now, and I'm his wife, see.' Her voice had an exquisite lyrical quality.

'Ah, I understand.' He could have hugged her, so pleased was he that he didn't have to dodge middle C any more. 'What happened to the Reverend Simpkins? Do you know?'

'Oh,' she breathed, standing aside for him to enter. 'The poor man became a little too — ' She

38

paused to consider. 'I think devout is the best explanation. Don't get me wrong, mind. It's not that I'm against devotion to the Lord, but the poor Reverend Simpkins spent so much time on his knees, he rarely completed his sermon in time, and never visited any of his parishioners. When he finally forgot to turn up for someone's funeral, it was suggested that he might be happier in a Holy Retreat, and now he's in Suffolk.'

Hopefully, far from any music-lovers, James thought.

The Reverend Hugh Jenkins was overjoyed to find such a splendid boudoir grand piano in his new home. 'There was always music in the valley,' he explained, then went on, 'I'd dearly love to stay and have a chat, but I have to finish an article for the parish magazine. Perhaps next time?' He paused by the door. 'You haven't met my daughter, have you? No, I thought not. Sings like an angel, does my little Megan.'

Five minutes later, his little Megan leaned across the piano. 'The piano-tuner, is it?' she crooned, allowing a lock of raven-black hair to fall across her rounded cheek, her clinging top and mini-skirt revealing that this sixteen-year-old beauty could hardly be described as 'little' in any department.

Unable to find his voice, James nodded, willing his eyes not to stare in the direction of Megan's cleavage. He was unsuccessful.

'Live in the village, do you?' Her honeyed tones hung between them as again he searched for a sound.

The one he found was more of a croak than a 'No'.

Enormous dark eyes studied him as she murmured, 'Pity,' stressing the 't' in the pure diction of the Welsh. Then she reached across in front of him to the fruit bowl on top of the piano, selected an apple, and perched on the arm of a chair, exposing even more of her shapely legs.

Oh, God! thought James, removing the fruit bowl, photographs and crocheted cloths so that he could open up the top. Oh, God! How can I concentrate on my work with this — this temptation — this delicious creature under my nose. And what about Katherine? She'd be horrified if she knew what I was thinking. Oh, God!

4

The street leading down to the docks was colourless, dingy, and flanked by the ugliest of Victorian warehouses, one of which had been converted into a makeshift hostel for homeless men. Canary Wharf and St Katherine's Dock might have been glamorised into desirable residences, but further east many of the streets were still as mean as those described by Charles Dickens. The basement store room which served as an office for the hostel had only a tiny window, level with the narrow pavement, for illumination. Pulling herself up by the bars, Megan Taylor felt more like a prisoner than a chaplain's wife but, by twisting her head and ricking her neck, she eventually found what she was looking for. A patch of blue sky. Suddenly, she felt so homesick it hurt, and tears welled up into her dark eyes. This wasn't her home. This was only the place where she lived. Home was 19 Susan Close. Percy Burridge had named the Close after his bride, later to become Megan's best friend, until . . .

Closing her eyes, Megan pictured a pond inhabited by hungry ducks, a row of thatched cottages, and a triangle of green grass with a five-fingered signpost. Memory took her a short distance along the lane towards Andover, where the steeple of All Saints Church rose high above the village and the old Vicarage nestled among the trees. Megan smiled as she remembered her teen years, playing tag with her brothers in the wilderness of a garden, waving to her father as he pondered over his sermon, her mother busy in the kitchen, scolding her children for bringing mud in from the garden, but always with a smile on her face. And singing. There was always music to be heard at the Vicarage. Although they had planned to go back to Wales when they retired, the Reverend Hugh Jenkins and his wife were content in the village and when Megan fell in love with a student, who later became the curate of All Saints, their happiness was complete.

Now look at them! All of them. Her devastated parents existing, not living, in a monstrous tower block in the east end of London. Nigel — consumed with guilt — having to mop up, slop out and feed a miscellany of the homeless and hopeless, knowing he had little chance of being granted a better living. Their children scattered around. It was so unfair. What had they done to be so punished? Why had Susan . . . ?

Opening her eyes, Megan let go of the window bars and blew her nose. No use keep going over the same ground, girl, she admonished herself. It's happened, and there's nothing you can do about it. Anyway, what had she come into the office for?

She opened the log book lying on the desk and picked up a pen. Old Jock had just been taken into hospital, and one of the young lads had said he was off on the road again, so records had to be updated. Each record telling its own tale of despair and loneliness. Then she must get two sets of clean bedding. One for Jock's bed — and she really must have a word with the doctor to see if anything could be done about the new arrival's incontinence. The date on the page caught her eye. 9 October. 'Oh!' A tiny sigh escaped as she again looked up at the window.

'Megan?' Nigel stood in the doorway. 'Are you all right, dear?'

'Yes. Yes, of course, my love.' Swiftly she recovered her composure and smiled. 'I was only thinking about the piano-tuner.'

'The piano-tuner?' A puzzled frown crossed Nigel's thin face.

'He's due today. I just hope Miss Partridge will keep my piano well tuned. Beautiful it is, when it's well tuned.'

Nigel gazed at his wife for a moment, a pained expression on his face. Then he put his arms about her and murmured, 'You will have a piano again one day, my love. And things will get better — I promise.'

Wryly, she smiled up at him. 'Well, they can't get much worse.'

'Have faith, Megan. We mustn't lose our faith.'

'I know.' She kissed him gently on the lips. 'And as long as we have our faith, and each other, that's the really important thing. Now, off with you while I sort out the bedding.'

After she had remade the two beds and dumped the soiled sheets in the reconditioned washing machine, praying that it wouldn't break down again, Megan gathered together the few pathetic bits and pieces that Jock had brought in with him. A mouth organ, an almost empty packet of cigarettes, and a creased and crumpled snapshot of a young woman in an ARP warden's uniform. His mother? Sister? Girlfriend? It seemed odd to think of the toothless old vagabond ever having a love life, but he had been young once. Perhaps he had even been good-looking?

Straightening up, she caught sight of her reflection in the mirror above the washbasin. She had been good-looking once. And sexy. All the village boys had lusted after her. And the piano-tuner. Megan chuckled softly as she remembered his expression when he first set eyes on her. Went a bit red at first, and fiddled around with the piano, but still managed to ogle from time to time when he thought she wasn't looking.

He wasn't bad-looking in those days, either. Not handsome, like Stewart Granger or Robert Taylor, but better looking than the spotty youths who hung around the Blacksmith's Arms puffing their Woodbines and pretending to be all grown up. He must have been about twenty-five then, which gave him an air of maturity that appealed to a sixteen-year-old schoolgirl. In fact, she'd quite fancied him as soon as she walked into the sitting room, and she was pretty sure he fancied her. Perhaps it was just as well that her brothers had come hurtling into the room from the garden. Clutching the tiny plastic bag holding Jock's sole possessions, Megan sat on the edge of the bed — and remembered.

★　★　★

Thomas and Geraint Jenkins never talked. They yelled. Constantly and loudly. Megan was sure they didn't know how to speak normally. Before she could bawl at them to go back outside, her mother hurried into the room, looking for the cause of all the noise, and finding her sons tugging fiercely at each end of a model car.

'Boys! How can the piano-tuner hear what he's doing with all this racket going on. No, I don't want excuses. I want you out in the garden. You can give me that toy first, and that will be an end to the argument. Megan girl, have you given the message from the big house?' she asked.

'I was just about to, when the boys came in,' Megan simpered, then wandered out of the French windows, but remained close enough to overhear the conversation between her mother and the piano-tuner. She bent over to break off a dahlia, knowing full well that he was following every movement, mesmerised.

'You mustn't mind Megan,' her mother said. 'She's at that age.'

Ruddy cheek, Megan thought. It's mother who's at *that* age, not me.

'Now, where did I put that piece of paper?' her mother asked herself. Searching amongst the clutter on the bureau, she went on. 'The Brigadier asked me only last Sunday if I could recommend a good piano-tuner. It seems he has inherited a rather unusual grand piano. Very old, I do believe.'

★ ★ ★

45

As James pop-popped his way along the curving drive to Cranleigh Manor, he couldn't take his mind off Megan Jenkins. If ever a young lady was destined to end up in disgrace, it was the vicar's voluptuous daughter. He sniggered to himself as he thought up rhyming couplets about her, along the lines of *There was a young lady from Gloucester*. But nothing seemed to rhyme with Fivepenny Lanes. Then he shook his head. What on earth was he doing, fantasising about a girl like that. She was probably still at school, and he was practically engaged. Definitely spoken for.

As he came out of the last curve into the circular turning area, he was so stunned by the size of the house that he stalled the Vespa. It wasn't a house. It was a stately home. All latticed windows and turrets and things. And the gleaming Daimler, complete with chauffeur. Wow! That was when he made up his mind that one day — one day — he would buy a car and whatever it was, even if it was only a little Austin Seven or one of the new Morris Minors, he would polish it until it gleamed, just like this one.

For some moments he stood there, quite transfixed. Then he looked down at his less than gleaming, second-hand vehicle. He couldn't park it by the side of the Daimler. It would look ridiculous.

The chauffeur's window slid silently down. 'Can I help you?' he asked. He had a Hampshire accent, pronouncing the 'I' as 'oi', and seemed quite friendly.

'I have an appointment with Brigadier Beresford-Lawson, but I'm not sure where to leave my scooter.'

'Prop it by the steps for now, then ring the bell.'

'Thanks.'

James climbed the impressive steps to the massive front door, and pulled the black iron ring. It was like something out of an old Boris Karloff movie, with measured footsteps sounding across a hard tiled floor. When the door was opened, James half expected an ancient retainer to raise a bony finger and beckon him inside, but the man looking down his nose was just as daunting.

'Yes?' he enquired. His voice was deep and resonant.

'Brigadier Beresford-Lawson?' James stammered slightly.

'No. My name is Johnson. I am the butler.' He raised his eyebrows ever so slightly. 'May I enquire your name and business?'

'Woodward. James Woodward.' James drew himself up to his full five feet ten inches and a bit. 'I telephoned earlier and was asked to call.'

'Ah, yes. The piano-tuner. The Brigadier did inform me that you would be coming. You couldn't give him an exact time, I understand?'

'That's right. I had to call at the school first and sometimes it takes a bit longer than others, depending on what the kids — the children — have been up to.'

'I see.'

James thought it highly unlikely that Mr Johnson the butler did see. He looked as though he had never had any contact with children; had probably been born middle-aged with a disdainful air and avoided the pathway through childhood.

The butler looked over James's shoulder. 'Would that be your — vehicle, sir?' he enquired.

'Actually, yes. The chauffeur said I could leave it there.'

'Did he indeed?'

There would be words later with the chauffeur, James was sure.

'I think it might be better if you were to take it around the corner to the staff entrance, sir. If you wouldn't mind? You will notice where the live-out staff park their bicycles. I will inform the Brigadier that you have arrived, and Mrs Henshaw, the housekeeper, will show you the way to the drawing room.'

With another glance in the direction of the chauffeur and the very slightest of nods, the butler closed the door. James grimaced as he glanced at the chauffeur, who had been watching the little scene with amusement.

'Don't worry about Johnson,' he said. 'His bark is worse than his bite. He's just a bit protective about the old boy. Won't let anyone near him without a rock-solid appointment.'

More nervous than ever, James wheeled the scooter around the gravel path to the side door. Mrs Henshaw, the housekeeper, was a brisk lady in a neat uniform.

'I'm James Woodward,' he began.

'The piano-tuner? The Brigadier did mention it. Please step inside and I'll inform the butler that you have arrived.'

'Actually, I've already seen Mr Johnson.'

'Johnson. We call him Johnson. Not Mister.' She

held out her hand. 'If you would give me your helmet and coat, sir, I'll take you through to the drawing room. No doubt Johnson will have informed the Brigadier of your arrival.'

Every inch of Brigadier Beresford-Lawson proclaimed that here was a military man. Tall, straight-backed, with a bristling moustache and clipped style of speech, he was straight out of a First World War recruitment poster, but his firm handshake and courteous manner soon put James at ease.

'The piano belonged to my mother, Woodson. Recently moved into the Dower House. Finds it more comfortable than the Manor. But this has been the family home for three centuries you know. I'll be here till I'm carried down to the churchyard.' His chuckle was gruff. 'Mother can't play any more. Damned arthritis. Don't play myself but like to listen.' He raised the lid. 'No idea what it's like. Haven't been able to get anyone to come out here. Jolly glad I mentioned it to the new vicar. If anyone would know anything about music, it should be a Welshman, what!' This time he laughed out loud.

The Broadwood grand was badly neglected and would need more attention than mere tuning, but James was sure he could restore it to its former glory. As he spread his tools out on his cloth, the Brigadier became interested.

'Mind if I stay, young man?'

As if James could refuse!

'Fascinated by watching craftsmen at work. Always have been. No good at anything like that myself.' The Brigadier poured himself a man-sized brandy and settled comfortably in a huge leather armchair near the piano. 'I'll not be in the way here, will I, Woodson?'

'No, sir.' James wondered if he should correct the Brigadier about his name, but decided to leave it for now. At least he didn't talk the whole time, just asked an intelligent question now and again. James needed to concentrate very carefully. It was not often that he was given the opportunity to work on such a beautiful instrument as this, and he wanted to make sure it sounded wonderful when he had finished.

It did. As he finished playing a Brahms waltz, James glanced at the Brigadier, who smiled and nodded his approval.

'Mother used to play that,' he reminisced. 'I remember Nanny bringing young Richard down from the nursery to listen. My brother, you know. Quite a bit younger than me. Shot crossing the Rhine in forty-five. Never saw his son. Damned rotten show.' He stood up. 'Richard used to play a bit. Ralph takes after him. He'll be pleased to hear it in tune again. Nice tone.'

'I'm glad you're satisfied, sir, but I wondered — ' James hesitated.

'Go on, Woodson. Go on.'

'I have studied French polishing and wondered if you would like me to — ?'

The Brigadier stared thoughtfully into his glass, then asked, 'Got much experience of it, young man?'

'No,' James answered truthfully. 'But it's an area that interests me greatly, and I was always top of the

50

class. It would improve the piano greatly, sir.'

'Hmm.' The Brigadier pondered a little longer.

'I know it's a valuable instrument, sir, and I would be very, very careful. I promise.'

The Brigadier looked him straight in the eye. 'Very well. You are insured, of course?'

'Yes, sir. Although nothing could ever replace such a handsome instrument.' He lightly touched the discoloured wood. The action seemed to please the Brigadier, who smiled and nodded.

'Exactly, Woodson. My point exactly. Come into the study and we'll make an appointment. One day next week suit?'

It was the finest job James had ever carried out. Took nearly all day, but when he'd finished, the rosewood gleamed, and the Brigadier beamed.

'First-class job, Woodson. First-class. Ah, yes. Wrong name. Sorry.' He initialled the corrected name on his cheque. 'Could have a little soirée now we have such a splendid piano. Young Ralph might be tempted to visit. Never know.' He handed over the cheque and shook hands. 'I'll have a word with the bar steward at the golf club. They've got one of those miniature pianos. Doesn't seem like a pukka job to me, but I seem to remember the barrister fellow playing some rather good jazz on it. He's probably got a proper piano at home. I'll mention your name.'

James didn't mind if the Brigadier did mention the wrong name. He was flying on cloud nine.

★　★　★

51

True to his word, the Brigadier told the golf club members about the first-rate job the young piano-tuner had done on the Broadwood. When James next called, he was handed two business cards.

'Groves is the club manager. Henderson is the QC. He's at his London place just now. Difficult murder case I believe. Said to phone him any weekend. Usually comes back here for a bit of peace and quiet.' The Brigadier searched a desk drawer. 'And there's a new member. Bridges, I think his name is. Builder. Planning one of those new housing developments. Near the church. Caused a few murmurs from some of the villagers. Called a meeting, you know. Told them the golf club wouldn't have accepted him if he was one of those cowboy chappies. Can't have jerry-built rubbish on our doorsteps.'

It occurred to James that Cranleigh Manor's doorstep was some distance away, so it wouldn't affect the Brigadier, anyway.

'Bridges assures me that he's aiming for what he calls the junior executive market. Got his card here somewhere.' The Brigadier found what he was looking for. 'Ah. Wrong name again. Bit of a weak spot, I'm afraid. Burridge — Percy Burridge. Northern accent. Bluff fellow. Know where you stand with his type.'

★　★　★

It was a surprise to find Mr Burridge living on site in a caravan, the first few houses at the footings

52

stage, the show house only partially completed, and no sign of a piano.

'Aye, it's a bit of a muck heap right now, but it'll be grand when it's done. Landscape gardens. Fitted kitchens. Tiled bathrooms. The likes of thee won't be able to afford the brass.' The builder's grin softened the words, and his rugged face, as he went on. 'There'll not be much change from six thousand.' He spread a plan on the table. 'Cast your eyes over that. Are you married?'

'Next year, if all goes well.'

'Is that a fact? Well, all the best, lad. Getting hitched myself as soon as this lot is off my hands and we can move into the show house.' He produced a snapshot from his wallet. 'That's my Susan. Fine-looking lass, you'll agree.'

James took the photograph. The girl was a bit like the fresh-faced girl-next-door type that Doris Day played so well. Looked considerably younger than her fiancé, though.

'Attractive young lady,' he agreed, handing back the snapshot. 'I hope you'll both be very happy.'

'No doubt about that, lad. I'd do anything for my Susan, and she knows it.' He smiled. 'Although what she sees in an old fogey like me, I'll never know. There's some back home reckon I'm cradle-snatching. She's hardly twenty, and I'll not see thirty-four again.' He replaced the photograph in his wallet. 'But I've still a few years in hand to make my first million by the time I'm forty.' It was said in a matter-of-fact manner, without bragging. 'I've made a bit of brass from a couple of projects up north, but reckon this is where the real money

53

is. In upmarket houses.'

James nodded, then asked, 'About the piano, Mr Burridge?'

'No doubt you were wondering when I'd come to the point.' The builder laughed. 'Trouble is, when I start talking about my Susan, I get carried away. But point is, I want to buy her a piano for a wedding present. She used to play a bit and said once that she wouldn't mind taking it up again. So I thought — ' He chuckled and looked enquiringly at James.

'Tremendous idea. I'm sure she will be delighted.'

'Aye. Happen she will. So I was wondering, like, whether you could help me out.'

'Of course. We have quite a few back in the shop. Would you like me to drop in some brochures? Or perhaps you would prefer to come along and see Mr Fielding, the manager?'

'Brochures will do fine. I'll pick out one or two I like the look of and you can tell me if they're any good. To tell the truth, I know nowt about pianos and I've not got time to leave the site for a bit.' His handshake almost bruised James's fingers. 'But reckon I can leave it up to you.'

5

Once the coach driver had finished his third cup of tea and taken a packet of cheese sandwiches with him, Mary and Sharon set about washing up, sweeping up and tidying up.

'Just look at this,' Sharon observed, as she gathered up a badly stained tablecloth. 'Some of them are worse than kids.'

'I know.' Mary glanced across the road to where the coach was parked in the bus lay-by. 'And would you believe, they're still squabbling with the driver over who should sit where.' She continued stacking cups on her tray. 'Still, at least there were no complaints.'

'Only the old know-it-all who said his wife could make a dozen scones for the price we charge for one.'

Mary smiled. 'If you have a gentleman surrounded by lady friends, he's bound to be showing off a bit, whether they're seventeen or seventy.'

'Well, I soon put him straight. Told him his wife didn't have to pay the rent and rates, electricity and gas, not to mention wages, out of her housekeeping money. And what about the winter, when the coaches stopped coming, but the bills didn't?' She smoothed a clean cloth across the table. 'He soon shut up when the ladies began to titter. Even his wife joined in, poor old cow.'

'Sharon! I know you mean well, but you really

shouldn't argue with the customers like that.'

'But he made me so mad. They don't see all the hours you slog away here. *And* we don't get the passing trade we used to.' She paused. 'The way things are going I reckon we'll both be signing on at the Job Centre before long.' She raised her eyebrows questioningly.

'I don't know, Sharon, dear. I really don't know.' Mary sighed. 'Tomorrow I'm off to Winchester to see the bank manager. I expect it's down on my knees I'll be, asking for a bigger overdraft.' She grimaced. 'Although I'm not at all sure I want to.'

'I know what you mean, Mary. It's horrible asking favours off people like that. They're so snooty, some of them.'

'No, it's not that. Mr Winslow is a really nice gentleman. It's just that — '

'What?'

Mary wondered how much she should explain to the girl. Perhaps now was the time to start preparing her, before too much gossip spread.

'Well, Michael is getting a wee bit restless. The job he's working on right now is almost finished, and he's talking about moving on.'

'Where?'

'I'm not sure. He's heard of some building work going in Essex.'

'But Miss Partridge said there's going to be another housing estate on the Brigadier's land. That would give him a few more years.'

'It's only a rumour, Sharon. Nothing for sure.'

'Do you want to move to Essex?'

'Not really.'

'Then tell him to get stuffed! Let him go and you carry on here. He can have those nuptial visits at weekends.'

Mary laughed out loud at the girl's frankness. She didn't even know if Michael would want her, anyway. And she certainly wasn't sure if she wanted him. Not after last night.

'It's not that easy, Sharon. We put everything we had into this place. The first few years were tough enough, but this year — I'm not sure we've made enough to keep it going through the winter, even if I do get another loan.'

'So, you're cash-strapped. Then let's put our heads together and see if we can think up some new ideas to bring in more dosh. Proper hot lunches and puddings instead of just jacket potatoes in the microwave. Fish and chips, rabbit pie and roly-poly pud. The coaches would roll up.'

Mary shook her head. 'We'd need someone else in the kitchen, and a chip fryer. It would cost too much. And the George and Dragon do things like that, anyway.'

'True.' Sharon nodded, then her face brightened. 'What about take-aways? Pizzas and so on. There's not much this side of Winchester. We could advertise. Do a bit of grovelling tomorrow and see what the old boy in the bank says.'

'Actually, he doesn't look much older than you, Sharon. Or perhaps it's me that's getting old.'

'Rubbish! My mum's old, and she's years younger than you.'

Mary chuckled. 'And I thought it was me that was Irish,' she said.

'You know what I mean. Look at your hair. It's gorgeous. And you've got a smashing skin. I've seen the way some of the blokes in here look at you.'

'Away with you, now. God willing, I'll be reaching the big five-O next birthday, and Michael is always telling me I'm too fat.'

'You're not too fat. You're — ' Sharon eyed her employer up and down. 'Cuddlable is the word I'd use. And Michael doesn't appreciate you.'

Perhaps the child is right, Mary thought ruefully as she carried the tray through into the kitchen. Sharon followed her with the dirty tablecloths and picked up a tea towel.

'How old were you when you got married?'

'Just seventeen.'

'Wow! That's two years younger than me. Were you pregnant?'

'No I was not! I was a good Catholic girl who waited for her wedding night. It was different then. Especially in Ireland.'

'But how the hell do you know if he's any good at it if you don't sleep together first? And if you find out he's not, it's too bloody late. They won't let you divorce, will they?'

'No, and quite rightly so. Vows should be binding. And sex isn't the only thing that matters in a marriage, child.'

'Maybe not.' Sharon's grin was mischievous. 'But it's a lot of fun, in or out of marriage.'

'Oh, away with you.' Mary pulled the plug out of the sink and dried her hands. 'That's the last, thank goodness. Will you keep an eye on the place while I pop upstairs? I need to make out a list for the cash and carry.'

The shopping list completed, Mary sat at the dining table a little longer, staring at the wedding photograph on the sideboard. Her mind went back to that day. She'd not only been a virgin, but a complete innocent. As Sharon would say, she had no street cred at all. Michael was her first real boyfriend. She'd had eyes for no one else once she'd met him. Wasn't he the most handsome man there'd ever been? Out of his teens, and so sure of himself. Cocky, Maeve had called him.

Mary smiled as she recalled the day she'd gone to Dublin with Maeve. She needed a smarter outfit than her school uniform before she started looking for a job, so Mam had agreed they could go in on the bus on their own, Maeve being older and all. Maeve was studying at the teacher's training college, but Mary wanted to work in an office, so she'd enrolled for the commercial course in evening classes. The two girls were reading a poster advertising a skiffle concert, and wondering if they could possibly manage to go.

'Mam will go spare,' Mary said.

'We could phone her and say we've met some friends and want to stay on for the evening.'

'And wouldn't that be a bare-faced lie, Maeve? I'd have to tell Father O'Brien at confession, and I'd die. Simply die!'

'Oh, don't be such a baby. It's only a little white fib.'

'We'd never be out in time for the last bus.'

'Yes we would, if we missed the end. Go on.

59

It would be such fun.'

'Oh, I'd love to. But I couldn't look Mam in the eye if we fibbed.'

'Yes you could. I'd do all the talking. What do you say.'

'I don't know, Maeve. I really don't — '

That was when Michael appeared on the scene. He'd been standing behind them all the time, listening.

'Why don't you toss for it?' he suggested. 'Here, you can use my lucky coin.'

Both girls spun round, and Mary gasped. It was a hot summer's day and Michael was wearing working trousers and a sleeveless vest, which showed off his brown shoulders and muscles to perfection. His friend, Diarmid, was almost as handsome and he smiled rather shyly at Maeve. For once, Mary's sister was too startled to argue. She just called heads, and heads it was. The young men already had tickets for the concert and, before the sisters knew what was happening, they'd arranged to go together.

They only just managed to scramble on to the last bus home, and Mary never was sure whether Da' believed Maeve's story of having met two friends from college, but the two young men were soon regular visitors to the family home. Diarmid was quite content to wait until Maeve had finished her training before asking for her hand in marriage. Not wanting to be a builder's labourer for ever, he was studying to be a surveyor. But Michael charmed his way around any objections to Mary being too young, and they were married within a year.

The wedding had been just as she'd dreamed, with Da' looking proud, Mam in tears, and her school friends giggling and whispering, 'Isn't Mary Dolan the lucky one to have been swept off her feet by such a gorgeous man?'

Diarmid had quite a collection of records, and the bridal couple had led the evening's dancing by waltzing to 'Moon River', rock and rolled to the Beatles singing 'She loves you, yeh, yeh, yeh', and smooched to Burt Bacharach's 'Magic Moments'. When Michael nuzzled into her neck and murmured, 'Time can't erase this memory, my darling Mary,' she thanked the blessed mother of God for her happiness. And when they'd said their goodbyes before climbing into the taxi for Dublin, Michael had assured her father that his daughter would never lack a roof over her head or food in her larder so long as Michael Fitzgerald was alive. And that was true. He was a worker, prepared to go anywhere there might be a job. What he hadn't made clear was what he intended to do with the rest of his wages.

Three months after they came back from their honeymoon, Dr Riley confirmed that Mary was pregnant. Michael strutted like a peacock. Mam was overjoyed. Even Da' was pleased with the idea of being a grandfather.

Oh, yes. Those were their magic moments. There was no doubt that nineteen-sixty-four was the happiest year of her life.

★　★　★

Forcing herself back to the present, Mary eased her bruised backside off the chair and left her precious memories upstairs. Down in the café, Sharon was cleaning out and refilling the Gaggia, and a solitary customer sat in her usual seat by the window, where she could observe everything that occurred on or around the village green. Buttering a scone with precise movements, eyes darting, bird-like, up and down the road, making sure that not a soul popped into the village store without her knowledge. A tiny lady, grey hair barely visible under a sensible hat — nobody had ever seen her out of doors without a hat, felt in winter, straw in summer. Miss Partridge. Spinster of this parish and likely to remain so.

Miss Partridge had lived for sixty years on her father's farm two miles along the lane pointing to Winchester, and there wasn't much she didn't know about the inhabitants of Fivepenny Lanes. For forty-five years she caught the early morning bus into Winchester and hung her hat and coat tidily in the staff room of the public library and, when she retired, Miss Partridge gave her parents an ultimatum. She would care for them, but not in the draughty old farmhouse with only a cold water tap and a zinc bath dragged into the kitchen once a week. The farm must be sold and a more modern house bought. One nearer the village, with central heating and a proper bathroom. After she had heard that the curate's house on the new Burridge estate would shortly be coming onto the market — not surprising after that bit of bother — they moved into number 19 Susan Close. Miss Partridge had developed the habit of taking her sit-up-and-beg bicycle from the garage each morning, cycling the short distance to the village, and ordering a pot of tea and a scone with butter, no jam, thank you. From there she could top up her endless supply of information and pass on any titbits she thought necessary. As with most close-knit communities, an abundance of gossip bounced to and fro between café, Post Office queue, doctor's waiting room, village hall, mobile hairdresser, and every one of the six public houses.

'Good morning, Miss Partridge.'

Tearing her gaze away from the window, the spinster acknowledged the greeting, her stare taking in the discoloration around Mary's eye. 'Good morning, Mrs Fitzgerald. Sharon told me about your nasty tumble. Have you made an appointment to see the doctor?'

Smiling, Mary wondered who was the biggest spreader of news, Miss Partridge, or Sharon? 'Oh, that won't be necessary, not at all,' she said. 'It looks worse than it is.' Changing the subject, she said, 'I believe Mr Woodward has changed his schedule today. Has he tuned your piano yet?'

'Oh, yes.' Miss Partridge sniffed. 'And quite out of sorts he was, too. Didn't want to talk about the curate at all. Barely gave me a civil answer to any of my questions.'

'Did he say if he was coming here next?'

'I did ask him, but he muttered something about catching the Post Office before they closed.' She turned back to the window.

Mary followed her gaze across the pond. Ah, yes. There was the Sierra, parked outside the general store. He must have returned to the village while she was upstairs.

Miss Partridge continued to talk. 'He'll be in at any moment, I expect. Then he has to go to the school. And I believe he has to make a return visit to the Dower House as well.'

'Oh?' Recalling his hasty departure from the village, Mary was curious.

'I confess I was more than a little surprised myself.' Miss Partridge daintily lifted the teacup to her lips. 'And — it may be my imagination, but I strongly suspect that something occurred at the Dower House.'

'What makes you say that, Miss Partridge?'

'Just a feeling, Mrs Fitzgerald. Just a feeling.' Miss Partridge pursed her lips and made a little sound, probably a sniff, then went on, 'But I am certain that something has upset him, and I think you will agree that I am right when you see him.'

As Mary returned to the counter, she wondered, not for the first time that day, what had happened to disturb James Woodward so.

6

Standing in the queue at the Post Office, James mulled over the events of the morning. He knew he would have to go back to the Dower House, but he was not looking forward to another confrontation. Whatever was the woman thinking about? And after all these years. He remembered so well the day he had first met her, when he arrived to tune her piano, a wedding gift from her husband.

★ ★ ★

The Chestnut Grove housing development looked exactly like the artist's impression that Percy Burridge had proudly shown to James the previous year. Colourful flags emblazoned with the words *Burridge Better Homes* led the eye towards an attractive layout of chalet-style houses with integral garages and open-plan landscaped gardens. The starkness of the stonework was softened by newly planted weeping willows or flowering cherries and a perfectly rounded chestnut tree formed an impressive backdrop, partly concealing the uncompleted Phase Three section which backed on to the churchyard.

'Every one sold,' Mr Burridge announced as he ushered James into his own home. The show house was the largest, the grandest, and the first house inside the entrance. 'My flagship,' he went on. 'You should see the Sunday drivers U-turning to take another look. Not many new houses as fine as this around these parts.' He opened the door into a spacious lounge with a beaten copper hood over the electric fire. 'And they want to know where they can get one just like it.'

Removing the lid from the keyboard, James asked, 'And where would that be?'

'Nowhere.' Mr Burridge grinned broadly. 'This was custom-made for my Susan. There'll not be another quite like this one. But, having said that — ' He left the room briefly and returned with a rolled up plan, which he spread out on top of the piano. 'I'm hoping to get planning permission soon for this little lot. Not quite as big as Chestnut Grove but a grand location. Over by King's Somborne. Happen you'll know it.'

'Oh, yes. Very nice area.' James listened politely while Mr Burridge explained each detail of the plan, the gas-fired central heating, separate cloakroom downstairs, utility room with plumbed-in washing machine and dryer. Meanwhile, the piano remained untuned, and James knew he would be late for his next appointment if he didn't start work on this one soon. Surreptitiously, he slid his hand underneath the plans and began to remove the collection of wedding photographs displayed on top of the piano. Mr Burridge was so immersed in his descriptions he didn't seem to notice, until his attention was distracted by the sound of a car turning into the drive.

'Ah, here's Susan now. Better give her a hand.'

As Mr Burridge opened the front door, James

quickly rolled up the plans and lifted away the front panel of the piano. Then he glanced out of the window. The young bride in the photograph was reaching into the back of her brand new Mini Traveller for a large cardboard box.

'Let me take that, love.' Percy Burridge's booming voice was clearly heard. He peered into the vehicle. 'My word, looks like you've cleared out every shop in Southampton.'

Mrs Burridge's voice was indistinct, but she was obviously curious about the Vespa parked in the drive, because her husband laughed. 'It's only the piano-tuner. Had you forgotten he was coming?'

After she had dumped a large quantity of plastic shopping bags in the kitchen, Susan Burridge came into the lounge. She was one of those clear-skinned fortunates who tan evenly all over and she still had a honey-coloured glow from Majorca. Although not pretty by conventional standards, she had a petite, trim figure and her glossy hair was cut into a neat bob with a fringe.

'Sorry I wasn't here.' Her hazel eyes smiled steadily at him. 'I asked for Spode china on our wedding present list and needed to top it up to make a complete dinner service. Then I saw so many other things we needed — ' Her accent was much softer than her husband's, but still hinted at her Yorkshire origins. 'But Percy never complains,' she went on, taking her husband's arm. 'He's right good to me. And I'm that pleased with the piano.'

'Nothing's too good for my wife.' Mr Burridge beamed, then glanced at his watch. 'Ruddy heck, I'd better be going!' he said. 'I've a meeting with the planning people in half an hour. What have I done with the blasted plans?'

'Here they are.' She picked up the roll of plans from the glass-topped coffee table. 'The documents are on my desk. And there were three enquiries first thing. I've logged them into the pending file.' She kissed his cheek. 'Hurry back, I'll keep my fingers crossed.'

'What would I do without you, Susan?'

After he had left, she silently watched James for a few minutes, then stood up. 'I'm going to make myself a cup of coffee,' she said. 'Would you like one?'

'Thank you. Two sugars, please.'

She brought in a small tray with two bone china mugs and a plate of chocolate-covered biscuits, then sat munching one for a while, her brow furrowed in thought. 'I suppose you don't teach?' she asked.

'I beg your pardon?' He tightened another string.

'The piano. I'd like to have lessons again.'

'Oh, I see. No, I don't teach, and I don't know anyone who does in this locality, I'm afraid.' He paused. 'The headmistress in the village might be able to help, or you could ask at the library in Winchester.'

'You wouldn't ask for me, would you? I'm a bit busy just now, helping Percy with the business, and you know all the right people. I'd be very grateful.'

James was also a bit busy just now, and the last thing he wanted was to go hunting for a piano teacher. But she was new to the area and her husband had put some business his way, so he could hardly refuse.

'I'll see what I can find out.' He went back to his task. 'Will you be moving over to King's Somborne if the plans are passed?'

'Goodness, no!' She put the mugs back onto the tray. 'This is the best place to run the business from. Percy put in an extra room so we can use the house as an office. Did he tell you I was his personal assistant in Yorkshire?'

'Er — yes. He did mention something.'

'He's made me a director of the company now.'

'That's nice for you.'

'Aye.' She bit her lip as though the word had slipped out. 'And not just a name on the letter-heading, either. I handle all the business side.' She picked up the tray. 'In fact, I'm not sure how Percy will manage when I take some time off.'

James raised his head and looked at her. Her smile was not coy, but it brought a slight colour to her cheeks. 'We want to have a child straight away. You've probably noticed that Percy is older than me, so no point in hanging around.' Her gaze went to the picture window with its view of the chestnut tree. 'That's another reason why we want to stay here. Fivepenny Lanes is the perfect place to bring up a family.'

Susan Burridge is a very capable, down to earth young woman, James thought. The perfect wife for Percy Burridge. Not beautiful enough to turn heads, like Katherine, but comely. The sort of girl most parents hope their sons will bring home. Grandma would probably call her wholesome.

Homeward bound, James day-dreamed about carrying Katherine over the threshold of one of the

69

Burridge Better Homes. She would love the kitchen. But Mr Burridge was right. There was no way he could afford the deposit, let alone the repayments. So they would take advantage of Grandma's offer and share her tiny cottage. Not quite the same as a home of their own, but the old lady was fiercely independent and active for her age. And she got on well with Katherine.

He always smiled when he thought of Katherine. Tall, strong-boned, with sun-streaked blonde hair and the bluest of blue eyes. Heads turned when she walked by his side, her long stride matching his. He knew what they were thinking — he often thought it himself. *How on earth did an ordinary-looking chap like him manage to attract such a beauty?* What they didn't know was that Katherine had made the decision on their first day at school. She'd eyed him up and down as she put her satchel on the desk next to his, then announced, 'I'm going to marry you. But you mustn't call me Kate — ever!'

From that moment on he'd loved her. Loved her strength of character. Her honesty. Her empathy with animals, although he didn't quite share her passion for horses. Every spare moment she was over at the stables, grooming, mucking out, cadging free rides. While she dreamed about owning a pony of her own, she compromised by offering her services to exercise other people's horses. And she was good. Over the years she covered a whole wall of her bedroom with rosettes from gymkhanas.

James tried to overcome his natural fear of large animals by taking riding lessons, but the beasts did little to help their cause, although they were like putty in Katherine's hands. The first bit his stomach as he attempted to buckle the harness, the second bolted with him clinging on the mane, and the third cantered nicely for a short stretch, then came to an abrupt halt. As James sailed over Brandy's head, he thought, 'Never again.'

In his early teens, he took up canoeing. The sea might be just as unpredictable, but it didn't have large, yellow teeth. And he loved it. Funnily enough, Katherine was as uneasy surrounded by water as he had been perched on the back of a horse. But there were plenty of other activities to share, like photography. They had never felt the need to join clubs or to dance, but were at their most comfortable when walking or cycling together. Perhaps because it allowed them to talk. And although she didn't play an instrument or sing, Katherine appreciated music, always sitting near him when he played.

The week he began his apprenticeship, Katherine had been taken on as a very junior assistant-cum-dogsbody by the local vet. The pay was appalling but she was in her element, never wanted to work anywhere else. She was still happily working for the same vet when James carried her over the threshold of Wisteria Cottage in nineteen-sixty-four. To his surprise, he'd enjoyed the wedding, and the reception at the Community Centre. The whole village seemed to have turned out to wish them well — after all, it was the amicable joining of two families whose roots had been founded in Bramblehurst generations ago.

They couldn't afford a honeymoon and Grandma

had announced, with a twinkle in her eye, that her sister had invited her to stay for a few days after the wedding. So she had been whisked away to Ringwood straight after the reception, and James and Katherine had the pretty little cottage on the outskirts of the village, all to themselves. As James stood in the doorway of the bedroom, watching his bride brushing confetti from her hair, he knew he would remember this day, this moment, this night, for ever. He wanted to tell her how much he loved her. He wanted to quote romantic poetry. But the words wouldn't come. Her reflection smiled back at him in the mirror, and he knew she was feeling exactly the same. No words could describe the way they felt. Still smiling that loving smile, slightly tinged with apprehension, Katherine turned and held out her hand. And as he moved towards her, a phrase ran through his mind. A perfect phrase for a sublime moment: *My cup runneth over.*

★　★　★

James took Katherine to the Sir John Barleycorn inn at Cadnam to celebrate their first anniversary. After they had ordered soup of the day and steak and kidney pie, he told her he had seriously considered pushing the boat out and booking a table at The Happy Cheese restaurant in Ashurst.

'What!' Mouth open, she stared at him. 'Have you any idea of their prices?'

'Well, yes. That's why I reconsidered the idea. But you should have seen the menu, Katherine. Out of this world.'

'I know. They even have kangaroo tail soup!' She laughed. 'Still — ' Her eyes softened with affection. 'It was a lovely thought.'

'One day — ' He smiled back into those incredibly blue eyes. 'One day, my dearest Katherine, we won't have to check the prices or the bank balance, I promise you. And I will buy you a horse of your own, not just a book about them.'

'I might just hold you to that. And when you are really stinking rich, I'll give you the best camera that money can buy, not just a little Kodak Brownie.'

At that moment, two bowls of steaming brown soup were placed in front of them. 'It smells delicious, what is it?' James asked the girl.

'Oxtail.'

Once Katherine began to laugh, James couldn't help but follow suit. 'I'm sorry,' he said to the bemused girl, who was offering them a basket of warm rolls. 'It's a private joke.'

'Oh.' Looking uncertain as to the sanity of her customers, the girl went back to the kitchen.

Still laughing, Katherine tasted the soup. 'It's good,' she said. 'Who wants kangaroos anyway?' She looked around the cosy bar with its array of gleaming horse-brasses. 'And I've always liked this place.'

For a while they chatted amicably about anything and everything, and agreed to go into Southampton on Saturday night to see the Julie Andrews film *The Sound of Music*. Then James mentioned a rumour that the piano shop was going to be amalgamated into a large chain of music shops.

Dessert spoon poised halfway to her mouth,

Katherine asked, 'And how will that affect you, James?'

'I'm not sure. Don't even know if it's true. But I do know that the Music Centre group are buying up shops in this area, and they specialise in guitars rather than pianos.'

'So that would be the end of the apprenticeship scheme for piano-tuners.'

He nodded. 'Mr Fielding has been looking decidedly worried of late, and hinting he might take early retirement, so I think it's possibly more than a rumour.'

'Would they offer you his job?'

'Maybe, unless they have someone of their own.' He pushed his empty plate away. 'But I'm not sure that I would want it, anyway. I'm a piano-tuner at heart, not a shop manager.'

Swirling the white wine around her glass, Katherine frowned silently until the girl had removed the dishes and brought their coffee. Then she looked up. 'I think the timing is right,' she said, decisively.

He knew what she meant, but he wasn't as positive. 'It's a big step,' he said, slowly. 'Supposing you become pregnant?'

Smiling, she reached across the table and took his hand. 'If we wait another year to start a baby, it will give you a chance to build up your round. And I'm due for a pay rise next month. Not much, but it will help, and I can earn some extra cash giving riding lessons.'

The following day James handed in his resignation and Mr Fielding confirmed that the shop would be under new ownership within three months. Fortunately, because of the change of policies, James would be able to keep a few of his existing clients, mainly those at the furthest distance from the shop, like Fivepenny Lanes.

It was more difficult than he had imagined to find new clients. Even some of his regulars were selling their pianos to make space for a television. They might not have survived without the support of their families. Loans to cover bills, baskets of groceries left on the kitchen table, Grandma prepared to wait for the rent.

Just when James was beginning to wonder whether he should look for a job, his brother, Raymond, a ship's steward, came to the rescue. Cruise pianos took such a hammering from professional pianists, passengers and stormy weather, they needed frequent and regular tuning and care. The chap who had been servicing the ships from Southampton had been offered a contract with a string of clubs in London, and a replacement hadn't yet been found. Thanks to Raymond having a quiet word with the relevant officer, James was able to repay his debts within six months and began to look for a second-hand motor-bike.

One evening, Katherine came home late from work and peered over his shoulder as he studied the classified ads.

'I know we'd decided to go for a Norton,' he said, raising his face for her kiss, 'but there's an Ariel here that might be worth looking at. What do you think?'

'Doesn't matter really, as long as it has a sidecar.'

Katherine's smile stretched from ear to ear. 'Dr Ewebank has just told me I'm pregnant!'

★   ★   ★

Across the Irish Sea, Mary Fitzgerald was fighting for her life, and that of her unborn child. She had been visiting her mother when she went into labour and the local midwife was on another call in the next village, so Mary's mother had gone round to ask Mrs Rafferty whether she should phone for an ambulance or wait. Mrs Rafferty was in her seventies and claimed she had delivered more babies than that young slip of a girl who called herself a midwife, and she had wet-nursed those whose mams hadn't enough milk. Hadn't she given birth to thirteen of her own, seven still living, thanks be to God? And didn't the whole village still come to her when they wanted someone to sit with the sick, or lay out the dead? From what Mrs Dolan had said, it was clear that a healthy young girl like Mary would not be needing to go into hospital. Such terrible places they are, to be sure, and what would the poor infant think when it opened its eyes and saw all those fearful instruments and people with masks on. Oh, no! Just keep rubbing the girl's back and walk her around the bedroom. Mrs Rafferty would come along as soon as she had finished the Monday wash.

Mrs Rafferty's Monday wash took most of the day and Mary was having pains every five minutes by the time the old biddy arrived. Nothing to worry about, Mrs Rafferty assured Mrs Dolan. It was early days yet. Try raspberry tea. Works wonders, does raspberry tea. When Mary begged her mother to get help, Mrs Dolan tried the midwife again. She was in the final stages of delivering twins, but would call in before she went on to Mrs Donovan, who was well away with her sixth. Nurse Driscoll looked thoughtful after she had examined Mary, then said she would come back as soon as possible — Mrs Donovan usually popped them out like peas from a pod. But if she was held up and Mary went into the second stage, call out the doctor.

Mrs Rafferty was convinced she could manage on her own. She didn't hold with all this first stage, second stage nonsense, she told Mary as she wiped the perspiration from the girl's brow. Just let nature take its course and soon she would be holding her darling child in her arms, God willing, and would have forgotten all about the pain. At that moment, Mary shrieked a terrible scream, arched her back and juddered from every part of her body.

'Holy mother, she's having a fit!' Mrs Dolan cried, and rushed to the telephone. After the emergency caesarean, Mary hovered between life and death, whispering a name from time to time, while her father searched the building sites around Limerick for his son-in-law. Eventually, it was Maeve's fiancé, Diarmid, who found Michael Fitzgerald. He was losing the remainder of his wage packet in a card game. Mr Dolan was all for giving him a hiding, but Michael promised it would be the last time. Now he was a family man, with a son, those days were behind him. They rushed him back to Dublin just in time for the baptism of little Brendan in the hospital. The doctors waffled with words and looked away when Michael asked them what were his wife and son's chances of survival, and Father O'Brien had never been so busy, leading the prayers at St Joseph's. A few days later, Brendan was lifted from his incubator and placed in his mother's arms for the first time. His cries were faint and her smile was weak, but they were winning the battle.

When the time came for Mary to leave the hospital, the doctors warned Michael that she should not become pregnant again too soon and, because their religion did not permit the use of birth control, it was up to him. He promised to heed their advice, but within four months she had miscarried and, by the end of the year, an ectopic pregnancy further diminished their chances of another child.

That was when Michael decided to go to Belfast, where he had been promised work at the dockyard. Mary was still unwell, and wanted their child to grow up in Dublin, so Michael found lodgings and crossed the border most weekends. At first, all was well, until she realised that their savings, which should have been increasing with the amount of overtime he said he was working, were actually dwindling, although neither of them could explain the reason. So they gave up the little house in Dublin and Mary moved back with her parents, it was only until their fortunes improved, she explained.

Surrounded by such a devoted family, the little boy thrived. He had his father's shock of dark hair and his mother's smiling eyes and gentle nature. Michael doted on him, bringing him extravagant presents, tossing him high in the air, and telling him what a fine young man he would grow up to be, worshipped by all his younger brothers and sisters. But when another pregnancy terminated early on, Mary began to fear for her chances. Michael was convinced that she was wrong, and decided that they needed pastures new. Somewhere he could be sure of regular work, not bits and pieces like he was getting now. With no money worries and a home of their own, they would be more relaxed, and she would carry a child full term. No, not Dublin. England! There was plenty of work in Liverpool, and once he had settled in he would send for her.

Mary was heartbroken at the thought of leaving her parents, especially now that Maeve had married Diarmid and moved to Dublin. But Michael was so excited about all the opportunities in England, and it was hardly fair to deprive him of his only son. So, with the little boy asleep on her shoulder and the soft Irish rain mingling with her tears, she faithfully set sail from Dublin to begin a new life, in a new country. If that was what she had to do to please her man, then so be it. But in her secret heart she was more than a little fearful of the future.

7

'A little girl? What joy she will bring you!' The Reverend Hugh Jenkins pumped James's hand enthusiastically, then called to his wife, 'Gwynneth. Come here a moment, my love. Mr Woodward has a daughter.'

'A baby girl. Why, that's wonderful news.' Mrs Jenkins shook her head as she wiped her hands on her apron. 'It seems like only yesterday you told us that your wife was expecting. But it must be six months, I suppose?'

James nodded. 'Last April, Mrs Jenkins.'

'My, how time flies. And have you decided on a name for the little one?'

'Julie. No second name, and she's not named after any relatives. Safer to choose a name we both liked, and keep both sides of the family happy at the same time.'

'Quite right.' Hugh Jenkins helped lift off the top of the Obermeier. 'Mr and Mrs Burridge had the same problem. I believe you know the builder who lives over on Chestnut Grove?'

'I do indeed. Mrs Burridge had just given birth to a son the last time I called.'

'A fine boy. Baptised him only two Sundays ago. Such a to-do with the grandparents over the name. Mr Burridge's father wanted him to be christened Percy, and Mrs Burridge's mother wanted Alfred, after her husband, who has recently passed away.

But young Susan Burridge would have none of it.'

'Ah, yes. She told me the little boy's name was Jonathan.'

'And Jonathan he was baptised. But I persuaded her that it was a poor start to the little boy's life if his parents and grandparents were to be estranged, and she agreed to talk to them with her husband, as a family, to see if they could arrive at a compromise.'

James opened his toolcase. 'And did they compromise?' he asked.

'Mrs Burridge was somewhat reluctant, but finally agreed to her husband's suggestion that the child be christened Jonathan Percy Alfred, and the grandparents also buried their hurt pride and came down for the baptism.'

Mrs Jenkins tut-tutted. 'Such a fuss over a name. It should be up to the parents to choose, not other people.'

James agreed.

'Mind you,' she went on. 'I would not have believed that Susan Burridge could be that forceful. She always seems so amenable at the Women's Institute meetings, but she told me she didn't care if she never spoke to her mother again, or her father-in-law!'

'Gwynneth, my love.' The Reverend Jenkins' voice was slightly reproachful. 'Young people say things without meaning them, especially when they have just had their first child. Remember how defensive you were when my mother discovered that Megan was to sleep in the little box room, not with us?'

'You are quite right, my dear. But even so, I never contemplated such a rift in the family.'

'No.' Hugh Jenkins smiled. 'And I am thankful that family unity means so much to you.' He crossed the room and sat near the fire, shaking out a copy of the *Hampshire Chronicle*. James was always quite happy to have the Reverend remain in the room with him, as he was with the Brigadier. They were not intrusive, but from time to time would make comments about music or general affairs.

Mrs Jenkins dropped a kiss on the top of her husband's head, then returned to the kitchen.

After a while, the Reverend looked across to James. 'I love all my children, dearly,' he said, 'but there is always a special feeling between a father and daughter.'

'I know exactly what you mean. Already I feel very protective towards Julie, thinking of the future.' He worked on the bass notes, then asked. 'How is Megan? Still winning medals for her singing?'

'Indeed, she is. Nominated as best student of her year as well.'

'Really? Please give her my congratulations.' James wondered what effect Megan was having on the students and tutors at the Guildhall in London. 'Is she planning to concentrate on concert work?' he asked, 'Or opera?'

'Her original plan was for the concert platform.' Hugh Jenkins hesitated. 'But I'm not sure she will ever reach that stage.'

'Oh?' James raised his head and was surprised to notice that the Reverend was frowning. 'She obviously has a fine voice, so why — ?'

'Glorious it is. But Megan has met a young man,

and I fear she will marry before her career even begins.'

'Oh, dear. That would be a shame.'

'It's not that I have anything against him, you understand. Indeed, you couldn't wish to meet a nicer young fellow. But Megan is such an impulsive girl, and always has to have what she wants *now*.'

'Is he also musical?'

'No. His degree course is in social philosophy, and he wants to take a post-graduate course afterwards and become a social worker.' Hugh Jenkins knocked his pipe out into the fireplace. 'But he told me he's often thought about being ordained. I really am quite concerned about it.'

James couldn't understand the problem, unless . . . 'Is he a Catholic?' he asked.

'Oh, no. It's not that. And I know I should be delighted that Megan is contemplating marriage to such a good young man.' The Reverend Jenkins laughed. 'If you had seen some of the young people she mixed with at first! Flower-power. Hippies. She thought they were all the bees' knees. At one point I was afraid she would leave the college and take off with a group of dropouts following some strange religious cult.'

That seemed more like the image of Megan that James remembered.

'Thank God she came to her senses,' the Reverend went on. 'My wife and I liked Nigel the moment we set eyes on him. It's just that — ' He paused. 'I know only too well how hard it is when you are a curate, often moving from church to church, sometimes from one end of the country to another. It was very difficult for my wife, with the children constantly changing schools, always a shortage of money, and no real home of your own.' He sighed. 'That's why we decided to stay in Fivepenny Lanes and not look further afield until I feel I have to retire, and that's not for a few years — ' Again his voice drifted and he stared into the fire.

'What would you like Megan to do, given a perfect world?' James asked, as he foraged in the toolbox.

'A perfect world?' The older man smiled. 'Something we constantly strive for, but never achieve. But as far as Megan is concerned, I would have liked her to realise some of her potential first, at least for a few years. She is only twenty, and it would be such a waste if that beautiful voice was not heard.' With a sigh, he turned the pages of his newspapers. 'But love does not listen to reason in this imperfect world any more than fathers stop wanting the best for their daughters. You will realise this more and more as your little one grows up.'

★ ★ ★

James was to be reminded of the rector's words on more than one occasion during the next few years, and they came back to him with particular meaning as he watched Julie pucker up her lips to blow out five candles. No matter how deeply he loved his sons, and he did love them deeply, there would always be something special about this little girl with her sun-streaked hair and intensely blue eyes, so like her mother in looks, but more akin to her father in personality. Despite Katherine's attempts to introduce her daughter to the world of pony clubs and gymkhanas, Julie could not be persuaded to do more than sit on the back of the most gentle pony down at the stables for about five minutes. Then she asked if she could get down. She didn't scream or make a fuss, just quietly said she would rather go home and listen to Daddy making music, thank you very much.

As a small baby, Julie could be easily soothed by music, anything in general and the piano in particular, her little fingers opening and closing until he finished and, for the past year, she had constantly pleaded to be allowed piano lessons. Now she slipped down from her chair, took the plate with the first slice of birthday cake from her mother, and placed it in front of James before standing on tiptoe and whispering in his ear, 'Don't forget, Daddy. You promised.'

Smiling, he hoisted her onto his lap. 'We'll go and see Mrs Grenville tomorrow, sweetheart, straight after school. But . . . ' he wagged a finger in front of her face, 'you know she doesn't usually take pupils until they are seven, so I can't promise that she will give you lessons yet awhile.'

'She will, Daddy,' Julie nodded solemnly, 'when she sees how much I want to play.'

James glanced over her head at Katherine, who grinned and passed a piece of cake to David, her own special child. David would celebrate his fourth birthday on Christmas Day and the only interest he showed in music was to stomp up and down to a military march, knees raised high, back straight, and a toasting fork, umbrella, or anything remotely acting as a rifle, sloped over his shoulder. Already he fulfilled his mother's hopes of another rider in the family, with a trio of rosettes for the 'egg and spoon', 'parent and child' and 'under five' pony races. He also showed remarkable dexterity and co-ordination in ball games and Mrs Varley, who ran the nursery school in the village, told Katherine that David organised his classmates during games more than she did. Certainly he bossed his older sister and younger brother and seemed destined to be the leader of the pack.

As for two-year-old Robert, sitting quietly in his high chair, oblivious of jelly and ice cream or birthday cake, his attention was focused on the toy pick-up truck he was putting back together after an altercation with one of Julie's more boisterous friends. What's more, he was doing it right. James glanced at his father, who raised his eyebrows and nodded, as if agreeing that it was remarkable for a child of his age.

When the last small guest had been collected and James had helped Katherine clear away the wreckage and persuade three reluctant children it was time for bed, he put a match to the fire.

'Evenings are getting a bit nippy now,' he observed, pouring a whisky for his father and father-in-law. 'What about you, Katherine, or are you having tea?'

'I need something stronger than tea to revive me.' Katherine collapsed onto the settee. 'Pour me a gin and tonic, there's a love. I've been thrown out of the kitchen.'

Through the open door, James glanced at the two grandmothers and one great-grandmother, chattering together as they washed up. He knew he was lucky to have such a close family, but he wondered how much longer these halcyon days would last. After seven years of marriage, he was no nearer to buying a house of his own.

Great-gran didn't seem to mind, said the children made her feel young. Certainly she was energetic and rarely ailed, but she would be eighty next summer. She deserved some peace and quiet in her remaining years, not a house full of lively youngsters. They had looked at a new development on the western edge of Totton, but Katherine feared they would eventually find themselves living in the middle of a vast estate and she wanted an older property that they could do up themselves. James wasn't a particularly good DIY man, but his father was a dab hand with a power drill, and Katherine and her father were eager to assist. However, old houses described as needing 'a little improvement', often needed complete rebuilding or demolishing, and prices soared ahead of their savings for those that seemed promising.

Last month they thought they had found their ideal home, a cottage near Fordingbridge with a decent-sized garden and planning permission for a new bathroom and kitchen. The owner accepted James's offer and wheels were put into motion until this morning, when he learned that they had been gazumped. All they had to show for their efforts were solicitor's and surveyor's bills. So, in a rare fit of frustration and extravagance, James had stopped off at the wine store on his way home.

As though following his line of thoughts, James's father studied his glass and murmured. 'Better luck next time, son.'

His father-in-law also raised his glass. 'I'll drink to that, James.' Then, thoughtfully, he observed. 'Time was when we only had Scotch in the house at Christmas.'

Katherine nodded. 'And time was when a man's word counted for something, Dad.'

'I know, love, and I think there should be a law against this gazumping lark. It's the second time it's happened to you.' He glanced at James. 'Can you manage the fees?'

'Just about.' Angrily James poked at the fire. 'But if it happens again, I don't know what we'd do. Yet we have to take the chance. Robert will soon be too big for the cot, and there's no room for three beds in that little room.'

The reflective silence was broken by the ladies coming through from the kitchen, Great-gran carrying a tray of tea. 'We were just saying how different the children are,' she said as she put the tray down on the table.

Katherine laughed. 'You'd never think they came out of the same stable, would you?' she said.

Her mother poured herself a cup of tea. 'And they're a credit to you, dear,' she said. 'Some of those other children were very rude, didn't you think so, Margaret?'

James's mother smiled. 'I expect they got a bit

over-excited, Jean. Children do at parties.'

'Spoiled, more like it. That girl in the pink ballet dress threw a right tantrum when she didn't win Pass the Parcel.'

Great-gran snorted. 'My fingers itched to slap her backside. Did you see her kick David in Musical Chairs? Mind you, she picked the wrong one there. I nearly cheered when he tipped her off the chair.'

Katherine laughed. 'And her mother had the nerve to tell me that she's a shy little thing who didn't mix easily, and would I please make sure she won some of the games, or she would cry!'

Great-gran's face was a picture. 'She'd have had something to cry for it I had my way. Can't abide spoiled children.'

James switched on the standard lamp. 'Then you certainly wouldn't like Jonathan Burridge over at Fivepenny Lanes, Great-gran. Whatever he wants, he gets, and he is becoming a most objectionable lad. Yet his parents are really very nice people.'

'Is that the builder's son?' Katherine asked.

James nodded. 'Perhaps the new brother or sister will sort him out for a bit. Thankfully, he'll be at school when I call tomorrow.'

'What time is your appointment?' asked Katherine. 'Only you promised Julie — '

'Two o'clock. I told Mrs Burridge I had to be finished by three as I was taking Julie to see a piano-teacher. She's my last appointment for the day, so I'll be back in plenty of time.'

★ ★ ★

Usually, once he had unlocked the piano, the caretaker went about his duties around the village hall, cleaning the toilets and windows, stacking chairs and so on. This morning he hovered around the piano. That meant he had something to tell, but James really didn't want to listen. The man was full of tittle-tattle and James made a point of not being involved in village gossip. Even politely nodding or shaking your head could be misinterpreted as agreeing or disagreeing. So, after the obligatory comments about the weather, James kept his head down and concentrated on trying to make the dreadful old piano a little more tuneful, ignoring the broom-head and feet which shuffled in and out of his vision. Eventually, the feet stopped and the caretaker cleared his throat.

'You've not been to the school yet?' It was a statement rather than a question.

'No.' James knew he was expected to ask, 'Why?' but he wasn't obliging.

After a pause, the man said, 'So you'll not have heard about the trouble?'

'No.' Do go away, James thought as he listened carefully for the top G. But the man was persistent.

'When did you phone about the appointment?'

James paused. 'Last Tuesday.'

'Oh . . . that would have been the day before it happened.' The unspoken question hung between them. James was curious, but he wasn't going to satisfy the man's eagerness to pass on a tasty morsel of gossip. Anyway, if it was really important, he would probably find out later from the headmistress.

Quickly slotting the front of the piano back into place, James handed the man an envelope. 'My invoice, for the treasurer,' he said. 'I'll phone the chairman in six months' time.' Before the man could say any more, James threw his tools back into the box and beat a hasty retreat. He didn't even wash his hands. Old Mrs Fairweather in Forge Lane wouldn't mind him cleaning up in her scullery before he started work on her piano. As usual, she had a kettle singing on the range and chattered non-stop while she made a pot of tea. The harvest supper had been a great success. Her dahlias were full of earwigs. Young Mr Seager next door had chopped a tidy pile of logs that should see her through to Christmas. No mention of the school. It couldn't have been that important, then.

He was wrong. Miss Harding looked pale and drawn, barely glancing at James as she handed him the key to the piano and asked him to leave the key and his invoice with her deputy when he had finished. She had to go into Winchester.

To James's surprise, the Reverend Jenkins almost burst into the office, his face deeply serious. 'Would you like me to come with you?' he said to Miss Harding. 'After all, I am chairman of the board of governors.'

'Oh, yes please, vicar.' Miss Harding looked close to tears as she took her handbag from a desk drawer. 'I am dreading it.'

As if noticing James for the first time, the vicar nodded a brief acknowledgement. 'I don't know when I'll be back,' he said. 'But Mrs Jenkins is at home.' With another curt nod, he ushered Miss

Harding through the door, and James heard him mutter, 'Nasty business, this,' as he followed them along the corridor, wondering what could have caused such distress.

As he worked on the piano in the assembly hall, James was aware of the strained atmosphere enveloping the school. Teachers talked in hushed voices as they walked along the corridor, and even the pupils looked subdued and confused, as though they didn't know what was going on, either. Usually the building was alive with chatter and cries of, 'Walk! Don't Run.'

Mrs Jenkins looked very concerned, but was equally unenlightening. She seemed to assume that James knew the reason for her husband accompanying Miss Harding to Winchester, murmuring, 'I don't believe a word of it,' as she closed the door of the sitting room and went back to the kitchen, leaving him alone with his thoughts. When she paid him, it was with a distracted air. Her thoughts were obviously elsewhere, and troubled.

The Brigadier was down by the river with his water bailiff, and James's following call was to a young woman on the Burridge estate. She couldn't wait for her firstborn to wake so she could show him off to James, who had forgotten how squidgy and wrinkled they looked. Only their parents really considered them to be beautiful.

His curiosity about the school still unsatisfied, James parked in Susan Burridge's drive at two o'clock. She would probably have heard something, he thought. Her son was in Miss Harding's class. His attention was drawn to a gleaming white

Triumph Herald Vitesse parked in the open garage. Another new car! Ruefully, he looked at his own little Ford Popular, not so much second-hand as fourth-hand, clean, but with the rust to prove it. Perhaps he was in the wrong business? But one day . . .

As the front door opened, his heart sank. 'Hullo, Jonathan,' he said.

The boy stared, his expression sullen.

'Will you let me past, please,' James asked through gritted teeth, easing the weight of his heavy box of tools. The boy did not budge. Even when James moved forward a little, Jonathan stood his ground, and tried to shut the door in his face.

At that moment, Susan came downstairs, smiling. 'There's nothing to be afraid of, Jonathan,' she said, ruffling his hair. 'It's only the piano-tuner. Let him come in, there's a good boy.'

As James stepped over the threshold, she held up her hand. 'Would you mind closing the garage door for me?' she asked. 'Percy doesn't want me to take any risks.' She patted her stomach, bulging almost to capacity.

When he returned to the house, James wasn't at all surprised to find the boy trying to open his toolcase. 'Please don't touch the tools, Jonathan,' he said. 'They cost a lot of money.'

'But I want to see.'

'Some of the things are sharp. They might hurt you.'

Jonathan looked at his mother, who eased herself on to the settee and picked up a glossy magazine. 'Look, but don't touch, darling.' She smiled indulgently at her son. 'We don't want you getting hurt, do we? Fetch your own little stool and sit by the side of the piano, pet, then you can see everything. He won't mind.'

James minded very much, but there wasn't much he could do about it. So, once again, he tried to ignore an unwelcome personage at his elbow. At first the boy sat quietly, although his head was usually in the way when James reached for another tool. But he soon became bored and wandered across to a huge toy box, where he noisily tossed toys out onto the carpet until he found what he wanted: a battery-operated keyboard. As the tinny sound filled the room, James was forced to stop work.

'Jonathan,' he said. 'I can't hear the notes if you play that.'

The unmusical din went on and on. Eventually, James was forced to appeal to Mrs Burridge.

'He's only trying to accompany you,' she said, her voice slightly irritated.

'I know, but it really is impossible for me to hear the pitch of the piano clearly.'

She sighed, then turned to her son. 'Why don't you watch the television in your room for a while?' she suggested. 'Your favourite cartoon is about to start.'

'I want to watch it here.' Jonathan ran across to the TV set and turned it on, the volume at full blast.

Susan Burridge covered her ears in mock protest. 'Not quite so loud, darling,' she laughed. 'You'll give Mummy a headache.'

James did the best he could under the difficult circumstances, but he wasn't satisfied that it was as good a job as usual. When Mrs Burridge went into the kitchen to make two mugs of tea, Jonathan turned the volume up again, staring at James as though defying him to protest.

'Here you are, Jonathan,' Susan Burridge handed her son a glass of orange juice. 'And I bought your favourite Jammy Dodgers.' She lowered the volume on the TV a little.

James wondered why the boy was home from school. He didn't appear to be ill. 'Is Jonathan off sick?' he asked, as he paused to drink his tea.

'No. I didn't want him there while all this business is going on. I expect you heard about the headmistress and her carryings-on?'

'Well, no.' His curiosity got the better of him. 'Miss Harding had to shoot off to Winchester, but she didn't say why.'

'Too ashamed, I reckon.' Susan Burridge glanced at her son then lowered her voice. 'You know that she's taken in a lodger?'

'Yes. Miss Harding mentioned last April that she had taken on a new teacher straight from training college. The young lady is a very good pianist, I believe.'

'Among other things.' Mrs Burridge sipped her tea before continuing. 'Apparently, they have become quite close and it has come to the notice of the education authorities.'

James was bewildered. 'Do you mean it caused jealousy among the other teachers? I wouldn't have thought they were that petty.'

'Oh, it was much worse than that.' Again she looked towards her son, who was by now engrossed in the cartoon. 'I've heard, on very good authority, that they have formed an unnatural relationship. You know — '

Aghast, James stared back. 'Miss Harding? Never! I can't believe that for a moment.'

'That's just what I said when I first heard. But there is quite a lot of evidence, I'm afraid.'

'What kind of evidence?' James was so shocked he forgot his usual cautionary rules.

'Well, they're practically inseparable — concerts, cinema, exhibitions — things like that. And Miss Tanner didn't go home for the summer holidays. Don't you think that's odd?'

'Perhaps she doesn't have a home to go to?'

'Everyone has a home, somewhere. And why hasn't Miss Harding ever married? She's not bad-looking, in an old-fashioned sort of way.'

James sprang to the headmistress's defence. 'She looked after her invalid mother for years, so perhaps there wasn't much opportunity for her to meet someone suitable.'

'Oh, yes, and I quite understand that some people prefer their independence. I'm the last person to think ill of someone because of a bit of gossip. But there's more to it than that, believe me.'

This time, James didn't rise to the bait. Silently, he turned back to work on the piano. But Susan Burridge told him anyway.

'One of the other mothers saw Miss Harding, in her garden, sitting on a bench with her arms around Miss Tanner. She said they looked very — cosy was the word she used. And they've booked a holiday together for half term, *and* Miss

Harding paid for the tickets!'

James made a very small grunting sound.

'You only visit here,' Susan Burridge went on. 'But when you live here you see things from a different viewpoint. That's why I'm signing the petition to have them removed from the school.'

'A petition?' James couldn't believe what he was hearing.

'I know, it does sound rather drastic, and I'm not the sort of person who would normally join in a witch hunt. They can't help the way they were born.' Her expression was sad as she looked across at James. 'But one of the other mothers felt our children might be at risk, and I have to admit I am rather concerned. Wouldn't you feel the same if you lived here?'

'It's true what you say, that I only come to the village twice a year, but I have been doing that for fourteen years, and I have always believed that Miss Harding is an excellent teacher, very popular with children and parents. Surely something would have been said before now if — ?'

'But this is the first time she has cohabited with one of them,' Susan Burridge interrupted. 'Would you want your children being taught by these people, while it was going on under their noses?'

James thought long and hard before he said, 'I don't know, is my honest answer. But even if the rumours are true, which I very much doubt, as long as the teachers keep their sexual preferences to themselves, surely the children would not be at risk?'

'Ah, but it's out in the open now, and young

children are very inquisitive when they hear people talking. Innocent little minds can be corrupted so easily. I really wouldn't feel Jonathan was safe at the school.'

At that moment, the cartoon ended and Jonathan looked at his mother. 'What are you saying about me?' he asked.

'I was only telling the piano-tuner why I'm keeping you home from school.'

'I hate school!' Jonathan cried. 'And I hate Miss Harding!' He looked at James. 'She made me stay in at playtime. And it was Nicky Stevens who threw the book, not me. But she called me a liar. And I'm not going back there, ever!'

'Ssh,' his mother soothed. 'You'll have to go back one day, darling, or Daddy will get into trouble. But you won't be in Miss Harding's class, I promise you.'

8

As James continued to work on the piano, he remembered a conversation he once had with Miss Harding, when she had told him she felt blessed to have taught two generations of village children, and how she would miss them when she retired. What would happen now? he wondered.

Susan Burridge interrupted his thoughts. 'I forgot to tell you,' she said. 'I've seen a piano for sale that I'm interested in. Don't ask me the name. It's Japanese, and they all sound the same to me.'

'Yamaha?'

'It might be. Whatever, it doesn't matter.'

'I thought you were happy with the Chappell?'

'Oh, I am.' She trailed a finger along the keys. 'But it's not white.'

'White?'

'Mm.' She waved an arm around the room. 'I saw such a lovely picture in *Homes and Gardens*. Everything was white. Walls, carpets, furnishings. And Percy agreed I can have it. The leather suite is being delivered next week.' She looked back at the piano. 'So I really have to have a white one, don't you agree?'

'Well, . . . I've seen one or two white grand pianos in clubs and they look very nice, but it does seem a shame —'

She carried on as though he hadn't spoken. 'You can imagine how excited I was when I saw one advertised in last night's *Echo*. It's less than a year old and only three hundred pounds. So I phoned and made an appointment for us to go there at half past three.'

'Us?'

'Of course. I don't know how to tell if it's any good, and you said I was your last appointment.'

'Because I'm taking my daughter to the local piano-teacher. I told you about it on the telephone.'

'I know, but surely your wife can take her? You can use my telephone to explain.'

'My wife knows nothing about music. I'm sorry, Mrs Burridge, but I promised Julie. It's an extra treat for her birthday.'

Susan Burridge stood still for a moment, her fingers drumming rapidly on the top of the piano. Then she said, 'I suppose I could phone the man and ask for another appointment tomorrow.'

James shook his head. 'I shall be down at the docks tomorrow. One of the cruise liners was badly damaged in a storm and the pianos need repairing. It will be a lengthy job, I'm afraid.' As her face became more troubled, he added, 'I could fit you in on Friday, if you like.'

'No good. I'll be too exhausted by the time the carpet fitters have finished, and Saturday's no good, either, my in-laws are coming down to look after Jonathan until the new baby arrives.'

'Oh. That will be nice for you.'

'Not really. My mother-in-law does nothing but moan the whole time she's here, and she will keep calling Jonathan 'little Percy'! But my mam suffers from agoraphobia, so I have no choice.' Her face began to crumple. 'I'd so set my heart on seeing it today. Can't you make another appointment with the piano-teacher? I'm sure your little girl would understand if you explained it was important to your business.' She dabbed at her nose with a tiny handkerchief. 'I'll make it worth your while, and buy her a nice new music-case as a birthday present. Please?' Pleadingly she gazed at him.

James had never before broken a promise to any of his children, and it grieved him to hear the hurt in Julie's voice as she quietly said, 'All right, Daddy. Do you want to speak to Mummy again?'

Katherine sounded as though she didn't understand, either, but agreed to phone Mrs Grenville.

Mrs Burridge was smiling again. 'I knew she'd understand,' she said. 'She sounds like a very sweet little girl. Such a pity you don't live closer. She could be a playmate for Jonathan.'

Over my dead body, thought James.

'Do you mind taking your car?' she went on. 'I find driving very uncomfortable now I'm so big. It was bad enough just going to the shops this morning, let alone all the way to Andover.'

He didn't mind taking his car. What he did mind was Jonathan bouncing around on the back seat, blocking the rearview mirror, butting in on their conversation and generally being a nuisance. Even his mother remonstrated a little by asking him not to make so much noise and promising to buy him crisps and sweets if he would be good. James hated seeing sweet wrappers and smelly crisp packets strewn around his car, but it was the lesser of two evils.

The piano was a good buy and on the way home, James asked Mrs Burridge if she had a buyer for the Chappell.

'Actually, I was wondering if you could ask at the shop where I bought it. It has been well looked after, as you know.'

'They mainly deal with keyboards these days, but I'll ask around. Your best bet is to put an ad in the local paper.'

She nodded. 'I'm giving the suite to a girl I met at antenatal. They live in a council house and haven't two pennies to rub together. She was ever so pleased.'

'I bet she was. That was extremely generous of you.'

'Well, I felt sorry for the poor little thing. And I've offered the carpet to the vicar's wife. I noticed theirs was rather threadbare around the French windows.' She sighed. 'I can't wait to see what my new one looks like once it's down.'

★   ★   ★

When James called a few weeks later to tune the new piano, Susan Burridge was in hospital, having just given birth to a baby girl. Her mother-in-law led the way into the pristine lounge, with its white walls and floor, snowy curtains, white leather suite with white woven cushions — and the white piano. The only touch of colour was a pale pastel print over the fireplace. It was like something out of an existentialist film.

'Daft idea, if you ask me,' said Mrs Burridge

102

senior, when she brought in the tea. 'But then Susan is full of daft ideas.' Her Yorkshire accent was even broader than her son's. 'Won't stay like this for long, I can tell you. Little Percy has already spilled his Ribena on one of they cushions. But he's just a normal, nice little lad with a bit of life in him, so what else can you expect.'

James almost choked on his tea. In his opinion, Jonathan wasn't at all nice, and James wasn't even sure that he was normal, compared to other children.

'What are they calling the new baby?' he asked, trying to get on to safer ground.

'Abigail!' Mrs Burridge's voice was scornful. 'Happen it's fashionable down here, but give me a good, solid name like Gladys, or Norah, every time. I said as much to our Percy, but he wouldn't listen, any more than he did when little Percy was born. Oh, no. Our family name wasn't good enough for her.' She sniffed. 'Still, I reckon our Percy is glad to have his mam in the kitchen again. You won't catch me cooking any of that fancy rubbish you eat down here, even if Susan does think it's posh to try out foreign recipes.'

As James busied himself with the piano, Mrs Burridge continued to complain about the south. The people were snooty; the neighbours could hardly bring themselves to pass the time of day; no chapel in the village; dreadful bus service; York was a much better place than Winchester. And as for the pubs — Father hadn't found one that sold a decent drop of ale. Watered-down muck, that's what he said it was. No wonder southerners all looked so pale and namby-pamby. What you people need is some good ale and proper food to build up your muscles, she declared. Percy had muscles a man could be proud of. But then he did a man's job, out all weathers. Did tha' know he'd bought more land other side of the village. Reckoned he could put up another fifty houses. Father was over with him now. She'd always reckoned he'd do well, although why he couldn't stay up north, where he belonged, she'd never know!

The more she prattled on, oblivious of any boundaries of good manners, the more sympathy James felt for Susan Burridge. She was stuck with the woman until a northbound coach whisked her out of sight. At least he would be going home to a family that smiled and supported, and children who behaved well.

He couldn't put his tools away quickly enough, but as he handed over the envelope containing his invoice, Mrs Burridge suddenly said, 'Hey up! Susan left something for you. Happen she'd give me a right mouthful if I forgot,' and delved into the cupboard under the stairs, reappearing with a large package, labelled, *For the piano-tuner's little girl.* 'Susan said you'd be knowing what it is.'

'I do indeed.' James smiled as he took the package. 'Please give her my thanks. Julie will be as pleased as punch.'

Julie was indeed as pleased as punch with her new music-case and, with James's help, sat down with her *Thank you* writing pad straight away. Then she climbed onto the piano stool to do her practice. James hoped her enthusiasm wouldn't wane.

By the following spring, when he set out once more for Fivepenny Lanes, Julie was showing signs of genuine talent and Mrs Grenville had ordered the music for the Grade I examination.

As he parked outside the school, James hoped Miss Harding would be there to greet him, but the new headmistress merely said her predecessor had taken early retirement. It wasn't until he arrived at the vicarage that he found out what had happened.

'Dreadful, it was.' The Reverend Jenkins shook his head sadly. 'I knew there wasn't a scrap of truth in the accusations, but by the time we managed to convince the officials, the damage was done. You know what village gossip is like.'

'Surely the villagers were on her side?'

'Most of them were. But there's always some who will say there's no smoke without fire.'

Mrs Jenkins removed a vase of daffodils from the piano. 'I just wish I knew who wrote that letter, so I could give them a piece of my mind!'

'Is that what started it? An anonymous letter?'

'Full of filthy innuendoes it was. Hugh saw it, didn't you, my love?'

The rector nodded. 'It pains me to think that one of my parishioners has such a sick mind.'

'Dirty mind, more like!' Mrs Jenkins scoffed. 'Accused Miss Harding of kissing and cuddling with the young woman, when all she was doing was comforting her after her grandmother died.' She began to remove the photographs. 'And all that fuss about the holidays. Her parents lived abroad. She had nowhere else to go.'

'And you have no idea who was behind it?'

'Not really.' Mrs Jenkins pursed her lips. 'The only person I could think of was a woman who was doing casual work on one of the farms. Her kiddie was caught stealing sweets from one of the other children and such a fuss she made when Miss Harding told her about it.'

'I don't think she was bright enough to write a letter like that, Gwynneth,' the rector said. 'And it was typed.'

'Well, she's gone now, so let's hope there's an end to it.'

James was still puzzled. 'But I can't understand why Miss Harding left. After all, her name was cleared.'

The Reverend Jenkins helped lift the heavy lid from the grand piano. 'She told me that if only one person felt she wasn't fit to teach their children, she would find it difficult to carry on. So, when she found out about the petition, Miss Harding asked for early retirement. Her heart wasn't in it any more.'

'Broken, that's what it was,' commented Mrs Jenkins. 'And our little school lost three lovely teachers. The deputy head resigned because she was disgusted at the way Miss Harding was treated, and Miss Tanner asked for a transfer.'

For a moment, they were all silent. Then Mrs Jenkins smiled. 'That's enough sadness for one day. Look — ' She held up a framed photograph. 'There's little Ruthie on her first birthday. Did I tell you that Megan and Nigel are living in Liverpool?'

106

'Really?' James opened his tool box. 'I don't suppose you see them so much, now?'

'No. And it's sorry I am that they're so far away.' Mrs Jenkins gently touched the face of the child in the photograph. 'But at least he has a steady job with the social services, and now they have Ruthie they've managed to get a council house. Megan misses the countryside, of course, so they come here for their holidays.' She smiled lovingly at her husband. 'It's a joy to see them, isn't it, my love?'

Hugh Jenkins nodded. 'Who would have thought our Megan would settle into domesticity so happily?'

'Well, it's glad I am that she has such a devoted husband.' Changing the subject completely, Mrs Jenkins looked at James. 'And how do you like my new carpet?' she asked.

Suddenly, he realised. The carpet had once been in Susan Burridge's lounge. But the modern squirls and squiggles design didn't quite fit in with the comfortable, if slightly worn, atmosphere of the vicarage.

'It's — very nice,' he said.

'Susan Burridge gave it to me. You know, the builder's wife.'

'Yes.'

'I'm not sure that I didn't prefer the old one, even though it was shabby.' Mrs Jenkins frowned as she stared at the carpet. 'But it was such a kind thought I didn't have the heart to say 'No'. Mrs Burridge is a very good-hearted young woman. Did you know that when she bought the new piano she gave the other one to the old folk's home on the Salisbury Road? There's goodness for you.' Mrs Jenkins placed the photograph of her granddaughter on the china cabinet. 'Now, I think it's time I made us all a nice cup of tea.'

9

As Mary Fitzgerald helped set out bowls of jelly and Angel Delight on the trestle tables stretching along the roadway, she realised that this was the nearest her son would get to a party for his twelfth birthday. Gaily coloured bunting, banners, shields and Union Jacks helped to disguise the dinginess of the little back street. Along with every village, town and city in Britain, Liverpool was celebrating the Silver Jubilee of Her Majesty Queen Elizabeth. Perhaps Brendan would make some friends he could invite to tea on his birthday next week, she thought. But he really wasn't very good at making friends. He'd told her there wasn't anyone in his class he knew well enough to invite home, even after one term. It wasn't the poor lad's fault, she mused, as she placed jugs of orange squash at intervals along the table.

'Hope the bloody rain holds off till the kids have done.' A strident voice interrupted her reverie. Mary vaguely recognised the woman who lived a few doors down from their rented rooms. As usual, she had her hair in rollers.

'It doesn't look very promising, does it?' Mary answered, glancing at the gathering clouds.

'You're the Irish family, aren't you?' the woman asked, staring rather rudely at Mary. 'Not been here long.'

'We moved in last January.'

The woman nodded. 'I've seen your old man once

or twice in the pub but you never come with him.'

'No. We have a son.' Mary nodded towards Brendan, who was quietly arranging chairs alongside the tables.

'Doesn't say much for himself, does he?' The woman's attention switched briefly to a group of boys who were charging around and bumping into people. Almost without pausing she cuffed one as he came within reach, shouted, 'Behave yourself, our Elvis, or there'll be no bloody party for you,' then turned back to Mary. 'So what do you do with yourself when he's at school? Go out to work or something?'

The last thing Mary wanted at the moment was to share her private life with the neighbours, but she felt obliged to say something. 'I work at home, making Christmas crackers.'

'Really?' The woman looked interested. 'How much do you earn at that, then? Only I might like to have a go if the money's any good.'

'I can give you the address if you're wanting to make enquiries.' Mary had no intention of discussing her paltry wages with anyone.

'Ta.' The woman repinned a stray roller. 'Though I'm not sure I'd like being stuck indoors all the time. If you get browned off, you can always come to bingo with Cassie and me. We go every Tuesday and Thursday.'

'Thanks. I'll remember that.' Although her mother enjoyed her weekly bingo club in the village, Mary had never found it to her liking, but she didn't want to sound too stand-offish. The woman was only trying to be friendly, after all, and that had happened precious few times. She smiled at her neighbour. 'Do you think it's time we should be calling the children to sit down? Everything seems to be ready.'

'Right, you lot!' The woman's bellow would have put a sergeant-major to shame. 'Get sat down and stuck in.'

Later that evening, when Michael had joined the men stoking the bonfire and drinking cans of beer, Mary stood outside the front door with Brendan, idly watching an impromptu concert, her mind on other things. By the time the last of the fireworks had exploded, the last knees-up danced, the last chorus of 'Anyone who had a heart' sung, and the last drunken neighbour staggered home, she had come to a decision. Listening to Michael snoring loudly at her side, she knew the decision would break her heart, but it had to be done.

During the past ten years, Michael had changed jobs eleven times and Brendan had sampled the education policies of five different counties, never staying at one school long enough to make friends. Small wonder his academic assessment was a year below normal. Patiently, Mary had packed their few belongings and followed Michael from Liverpool to Glasgow, Manchester, Barrow-in-Furness, Bradford, Aberdeen, Newcastle-upon-Tyne, and back to Liverpool. Now he wanted to move down south. London was where the work was, he said. It would be their last move, he promised. But this time Mary didn't believe him. Michael would never stop chasing rainbows and while she might be prepared to make excuses to the landlord about the outstanding rent, or lie through her teeth when the rough assortment of threatening debt collectors called, asking for Michael, there was no way she would ever involve Brendan. His father might think the boy's angelic face would protect him from the thugs, but enough was enough. She must send Brendan back to Ireland!

Her sister, Maeve, had offered time after time to care for the boy. Diarmid had remained with the firm of architects who had given him day-release for his studies, and they had rewarded his loyalty with a good salary, company car, and promotion, so it would be no hardship to have an extra child in the house. He would be able to attend the same school as one of his cousins, a good Catholic school, and Dublin was a fine place for a boy to live.

As Mary had expected, Michael raved and ranted. Brendan was his son. His only child. He would not have him being brought up by strangers, and far across the sea at that, where he would hardly ever see his parents. He might even forget them. What in God's name was she thinking of? It's off to the pub he'd be going now, for a pint of the black stuff, and when he came home, he wanted to hear no more of this nonsense.

Mary said nothing, and waited. She knew he would not be out for longer than an hour. He hadn't enough money for more than two pints of Guinness. She had sneaked the rest out of his pocket while he was in the toilet. Half an hour later, she sent young Brendan along to the chippy on the corner. Wing of skate and chips was his father's favourite supper. After Brendan was safely in bed, she changed into the blue dress that Michael liked, brushed her hair and found the remains of a bottle of Yardley Lavender Water that Michael had given her last Christmas. Holy Mother, she thought, it's as though I'm trying to seduce my own husband. But how else am I going to make the man see sense?

The Guinness had mellowed Michael enough for him to compliment Mary on her appearance, and when she brought in the two plates of fish and chips from the oven, he smiled. 'Now this is the way to a man's heart, me darlin' girl,' he said.

Smiling back, she waited until he had finished eating and had rolled a cigarette before she quietly asked, 'Have you work to go to in London, Michael?'

'The lads say there's jobs for the taking. They've not the unemployment we're plagued with up north. Young Andy McLeod is off as soon as we've finished this job on the docks. He's going to work his way down south.'

'And how will he be doing that?'

'They're building these new motorways all over the place, so there's always casual work to be had.'

'Is there now? Does it pay well?' The glimmer of an idea began to form in Mary's mind.

'Not bad, from what I hear. Mind you, he'll have to be prepared to muck in and live in caravans on site as he moves along. But it's a good way of getting to London.'

'Yes.' The idea grew. 'Would you be wanting to go with him, Michael?'

Surprised, he looked across at her. 'If I was single, like Andy, I'd be packing my bags. But there's no

113

way you can take a child on a job like that.'

'Supposing it was just you and me. Would you still go?'

'Now, Mary, let's not be starting on that again.' His voice showed signs of edginess.

'Just listen to me for a moment, Michael. Please. I have an idea that might work.' Mary poured another cup of tea and pushed it towards her husband, who looked downright suspicious. 'Brendan has been at this school for six months and Sister Theresa told me he's really struggling with his algebra and French. It won't be too long before he'll be taking his O-levels. He'll have to think about a career.'

'Brendan is a clever lad. He'll be fine.'

Mary drew a deep breath. 'Michael, darling, I will follow you to the ends of the earth if need be, but is it really fair on Brendan? He frets so if he can't keep up with the others.'

'I told you how I feel about him going to Ireland, Mary.' Michael picked up the evening paper in a dismissive way.

Mary knew he didn't like to think about his son being unhappy. Quickly, she went on, 'How would you feel about it if it was just for a wee while? While you're finding a steady job and getting settled?'

Michael looked up from the sports page. 'You mean, just for a few months?'

'Ye-es. Why don't we give it a try for a year? At least he'd have a chance of catching up with his schoolwork, and you wouldn't always be worrying if he was all right. I could take him over at the end of this term, while you start moving south with the

Scottish lad. Once you're in London, I'll come back and join you.'

For a while he quietly chewed over her words. Then he shook his head. 'It wouldn't seem right, splitting up the family.'

'But it's not for ever, and you could save much more money if you only had yourself to look to.'

'Well I'm not taking charity from Diarmid or your sister, and that's for sure.'

'It wouldn't be charity, Michael. You could pay them for our keep when you've got a proper job. And we can all be together in Dublin at Christmas.'

'I don't know, Mary. It all sounds a bit daft to me.'

'Not so daft as traipsing around one end of the country to another with a boy of Brendan's age. We have to think of what's best for him,' she pleaded.

Suddenly, Brendan came into the room, his face anxious. 'We're not leaving again, are we, Da'?' he asked.

'I have to go where the work is, son.' Michael held out his arms but the boy ran to his mother.

'They call me a gypsy at school,' he cried.

'That's because you're a fine-looking lad.' Mary smoothed back his dark curls. 'You mustn't mind them.'

'But I do mind, Mam. They say I'm backward because I can't do the maths.' Pleadingly he looked at her. 'Can't we stay somewhere just for a while longer?'

Mary glanced at Michael, then slowly answered, 'Your Da' and me were just talking about that very thing, and we were wondering whether you'd be

115

happier staying with Auntie Maeve and Uncle Diarmid for a while. Would you like that?'

'Oh, Mam! Da'! Would I go to school with Declan?'

'Yes. But only if your father agrees, mind.' Praying hard, she looked at Michael.

For a long, long moment, he puffed at his cigarette until it burned almost to his lips. Then he said, 'Is that what you'd be wanting, Brendan?'

Eagerly, the boy nodded his head. 'When can I go?' he asked.

★ ★ ★

At the end of July, Mary and Brendan boarded the steamer for Dublin, waving goodbye to Michael. He and Andy were going to join a gang of labourers in Stafford the following day. Despite her elation at the prospects of seeing her family again and of her son having the chance of a proper education, Mary was uneasy. Michael was right about families staying together. It had been dreadful when he had first left Ireland, but this time it would only be for a few months. She was determined to go back to England with him after Christmas, no matter what. He was the only man she had ever loved.

Mary hoped and prayed that Michael would hang on to any money he earned. If only he hadn't had that private bet with the crane driver, they wouldn't be in such a mess. He'd been so certain that Red Rum couldn't possibly win the Grand National three times, he'd lost them every penny they possessed, and some. One good thing about living on site: he wouldn't be popping off to the betting shop every five minutes. Then she remembered his other passion, apart from greyhounds and race-horses. The temptations of a card game amongst a group of workmates would be almost impossible for him to resist.

★　★　★

Would Norfolk be much colder than Oxford? Megan worried, as she sorted through the children's winter clothes. Ruthie had outgrown last year's jumpers and trousers, but they would fit Owen. Thankfully, three-year-olds weren't too fussy about hand-me-downs, which was just as well. But Ruthie's nighties and ribbed tights wouldn't be of any use, and she would need a different coloured uniform for the new infants' school. Sighing, Megan delegated more clothes to the pile for the Oxfam shop and made a mental note to ask her mother if she could help out with some knitting — again!

Her mind flitting from knitting to singing, she began to search for her music-case. She had put it away somewhere when she'd realised that she couldn't be the soloist in Bach's *Christmas Oratorio* at Christ Church Cathedral, but she'd forgotten to return the music. She wouldn't even be able to sing with her father's choir at Midnight Mass on Christmas Eve. Perhaps she would be allowed to join the choir at the new church? She was a good sight-reader and the carols would be familiar.

Still hunting for the elusive music-case, Megan smiled as she recalled how excited Nigel had been when he'd finished his theological training at College Hudston, back in the summer, and they had wondered where he would work for the next year. He would have been ordained as a curate and installed as a deacon by now if it hadn't been for that dreadful accident. The driver who had taken the corner too fast and knocked Nigel from his bicycle had sped away, not caring that Nigel was lying in agony in the road. Few people were about on that wet and miserable evening, so the car was never traced and no claim for damages could be made. They were both thankful that his injuries were not more serious than a broken leg, but sad that he couldn't take up any of the posts currently on offer. Now he had been offered an Advent ordination, and in a few days they would be unpacking their belongings in a small house in Norwich that she hadn't yet seen. But first they would stop overnight at Fivepenny Lanes.

Her mother had promised to cook a huge turkey for a pre-Christmas dinner, as this would be the first year since they were married that they hadn't celebrated Christmas all together. Nigel's parents ran a hotel near Newquay, which was always fully booked at Christmas and New Year, so their weekend get together was usually the last one before the guests arrived, then they would drive straight back to Fivepenny Lanes. Megan knew her mother would miss watching the children open their presents on Christmas morning. It was tough that the boys wouldn't be home, either. Thomas was touring in America with a rock and roll band and Geraint couldn't leave his sheep farm in Wales, so

Christmas dinner would be a lonely meal for Hugh and Gwynneth Jenkins — although, knowing her parents, Megan felt sure they would probably invite some of their elderly parishioners to share the day with them after morning service.

'Ah, there you are,' Megan cried, as she spotted the music-case at the back of her wardrobe, tucked behind two wrapped gifts for the parents: stockings for her mother and pipe tobacco for her father. They would understand their tight budget, but Megan hoped that the gifts might be a little less meagre next year. The last two years had been very difficult. Nigel only had a single person's diocese grant and they had been able to rent a college flat but, despite some assistance for the children from social security, it would have been almost impossible for Nigel to contemplate two years without a salary if his father hadn't supplemented their income with a small allowance. He was a good man, and knew how much his son wanted to work for God.

Sorting through the music, Megan wondered where they would be next year. They could be spending Christmas 1978 in London or Bath; Torquay or Coventry. Anywhere, in fact, that was large enough to warrant the appointment of a curate. Dorset or Wiltshire would be lovely, a Southampton parish even better. But, wherever their next move happened to be, there they would stay for three years so, please Lord, let it be somewhere pleasant, and let me be able to afford a piano again, she prayed.

★　★　★

Pencil scribbling furiously, James Woodward sat at the kitchen table, doing some rapid calculations before Katherine arrived home. Then he looked up. 'I think we can just about manage it,' he said.

Julie, an eleven-year-old fulfilling her earlier promise of becoming a beauty, jumped up and hugged her father, David cheered, and Robert grinned.

'Of course,' James went on, 'it will mean that you three won't have so much for your own Christmas presents this year, but I did explain that, didn't I?'

They all nodded agreement, then Julie asked, 'Will you give it to Mum on her birthday, or Christmas Day?'

'Oh, on her birthday I think. It's a special day, and only a couple of weeks before Christmas.' James paused for a moment. 'You know, I can't believe your mother is nearly forty.'

David laughed. 'That's what she said when it was your turn last April.'

'Mutual admiration society, that's what we are. She certainly organised a great surprise party. Hope she won't be disappointed that I haven't done the same.'

'Not when she sees the surprise you've got in store for her,' Julie said. 'Once the party is over, that's it, but this — '

'How will you give it to her?' Robert interrupted. 'You can't wrap it up with a ribbon bow.'

They all roared with laughter. 'I'll think of something,' James answered. 'But, in the meantime, not a word out of you three. Promise?'

'We promise,' the trio echoed.

After David had left to cycle to the Scouts meeting and Robert had gone up to his room to play with his Scalextric, James sat back and listened to Julie playing a Chopin nocturne. She had never needed reminding to practise, often playing for half an hour before she left for school in the morning, and that really was dedication. He enjoyed these quiet moments with his daughter, letting the music flow over him, and his thoughts drift around.

They now had the whole cottage to themselves. Grandma had caught an unaccustomed chill, which suddenly turned to pneumonia, the winter after Julie's fifth birth. Everyone said it was for the best. She'd always had a dreadful fear of being a burden, or becoming an invalid, like poor old Mrs Cooper next door, who depended on her daughter's daily visits, a home help and meals on wheels for survival. But James still missed Grandma's spunky humour and the clicking of her knitting needles as she sat by the fire.

He'd been surprised to find she had left him the cottage, thinking it would go to his mother, but the letter with Grandma's will had explained that her daughter already had a nice home and James's brother Raymond was always away at sea, so she was sure they would agree that James and Katherine needed it more.

James's reverie was broken by the sound of Katherine's little Mini. For the past three years, since Robert started school, she had been able to work part-time again, with the same vet. Normally, she only worked during school hours and term time, but this evening she'd been called back in to help with an emergency caesarean operation on a pedigree red setter. They needed all the hands they could muster when there was a large litter, and Katherine would be tired after hours of trying to rub life into the newborn pups.

As he made mugs of hot chocolate, James wished it were Katherine's birthday today. Even the children had saved their pocket money for weeks to go towards the special gift, and they were all so excited. He would blindfold her, he decided, and have his new camera at the ready when she opened her eyes. Only another ten days to wait.

★　★　★

It was not quite daylight when they led Katherine to the back door and along the garden path.

'It's freezing out here,' she protested, but with good humour. 'Have I got to plant a tree, or something?'

'Nearly there, love.' James shone the torch to guide the three giggling figures behind him, their breath clouding into the beam.

At the wicket gate into the paddock along the bottom of the garden, he paused, flashed the torch three times, and waited. As soon as he heard the sound he was listening for, he untied Katherine's blindfold.

'What on earth are you — ?' she began, then paused, as the beam picked up a shadowy figure cantering across the field towards them. 'But that's — ' Again she stopped in mid-sentence until the chestnut gelding had reached the gate and thrust his nose into Katherine's hand, snorting and tossing his head. 'Duke,' she murmured, 'What are you doing here?' She turned back towards her family. 'I don't understand, and I'm too scared to ask.'

James signalled the children. As with one voice, they burst into the opening bars of 'Happy Birthday to You'.

His heart full to exploding, James kissed his wife's cheek. 'Now do you understand?' he asked, softly.

'Yes — no — oh, goodness. You aren't telling me he's mine?'

David shouted, 'At last! The penny's dropped.'

'Did you know about this?' Katherine asked him, then turned to his brother and sister. 'And you? And you?'

Three heads nodded excitedly as Katherine looked at the horse, then James, with tears streaming down her face.

'He's from all of us,' he explained, loving every moment of her pleasure.

'Oh . . . ' Her joyful sigh drifted on the frosty air. 'I don't know who to hug first. You four or the horse.'

'Us first.' The children jumped up and down with delight.

When they had been well and truly hugged and kissed, Katherine turned to James. 'I love you,' she whispered, before she kissed him with a warmth that sent passionate shivers flooding through his body.

Unable to speak, he held her close, feeling her trembling with excitement, and knowing that he would never forget this moment, with the wisps of mist carpeting the field in the wintry dawn, the coldness of Katherine's nose against his cheek, the salty taste of her tears upon his lips as she kissed him again and again, one hand still fondling the horse's nose — and the love that enveloped them all, surrounding the family and enclosing the horse.

The spell was broken by a voice hailing them from half-way across the field. 'Looks like you're pleased with your birthday present.'

As the striding figure drew nearer, Katherine wiped the tears away with the back of her hand and yelled back, 'I might have known you had something to do with this.'

'Of course. Who do you think did all the negotiations?'

As he reached the little gate, Greg Sherringham nudged Duke to one side and planted a kiss on Katherine's cheek. 'Happy birthday, Kate,' he said, handing her a huge parcel. He was the only person who had ever been allowed to call her anything but Katherine, and that only because she had worked for him, on and off, since the day after she left school.

Katherine staggered back under the weight of the parcel and gasped as she tore a corner of the gift-wrap. 'It's a saddle!' she cried.

'I hope so,' Greg laughed. 'That's what they told me it was in the shop.'

'It's beautiful!' She grabbed the torch from James and explored the handsome gift. 'But you shouldn't have . . .'

'Ah, that's what all the girls say,' Greg jested, then was serious for a moment. 'It's not only for your birthday,' he said.

'Oh?' She raised her eyebrows.

'It's our anniversary as well, didn't you know?' He smiled at James. 'I suddenly realised that twenty-five years ago tomorrow, your good lady reported to me for her first day's work. Little did she realise that most of that day would be spent cleaning up and mucking out, but she was a great disappointment to all the vets.'

Katherine's jaw dropped. 'What do you mean by disappointment?' she spluttered indignantly. 'I did it properly, and I never complained.'

'I know. That was the trouble. We all thought you'd be crying with fatigue by the time you went home, but you actually seemed to enjoy it. Such a disappointment.'

'Oh, you . . . ' Words failed Katherine, so she hugged him, then opened the wicket gate. 'Can I ride him now?'

'Of course. I've warned the partners that you will definitely be late in, and I will probably be late — if James invites me in for coffee — when he's finished fiddling with his camera.'

Not bothering to saddle up, Katherine leaped up on to the blanket covering Duke's back, and walked him for a moment, then touched him lightly with her heels and asked him to 'trot on.' As James filled the kettle and watched from the kitchen window, he smiled at the sight of his wife urging the horse to a speed where he could canter, her hands loosely holding the mane, instructing him with her legs and voice. Oh, yes, he thought. Even though he'd taken out a sizeable bank loan, and they would have to put off updating the car, it had been the right decision.

Katherine and Duke were a team already.

After Katherine had warmed herself in the kitchen with coffee and hot buttered toast, the Cheshire cat grin never leaving her face, she pushed her chair back from the table and looked from James to Greg.

'Now then, you two,' she said. 'Tell me how you managed to do it without my finding out. And how did you guess he was the one for me?'

Some of the story she already knew. Duke was a two-year-old gelding who had been stabled at the local riding school while his owners went off to the south of France for a holiday that turned into a semi-permanent residency when they decided that winters in an apartment in Port Grimaud would be decidedly warmer than Hampshire, but a yacht would be a more useful method of transport than a New Forest pony, even one with Arab blood adding speed to his sturdiness. So Greg was asked if he could help find a new owner, and Katherine was sometimes asked to exercise Duke.

'Knowing you'd fallen in love was easy,' James answered. 'Every time you rode him you raved about how gorgeous he was and how tragic that he'd been dumped.'

'I still can't understand how anyone could do that. But in my wildest dreams I never imagined for a moment that we could buy him — not with that sort of money.'

'That was the tricky part. When Greg first told me how much they were asking, I didn't even consider it, but I did want to buy you something special for your birthday and I knew a horse would be perfect if the price was right.' James grinned as he remembered. 'I even went to the pony sales at Beaulieu Road in the hope I could pick up a bargain, but no such luck.'

'So how — ?' Katherine began.

'Ah,' Greg interrupted. 'That's where the luck turned. The Simpsons found their dream boat but they needed cash quickly so they drastically reduced the price, rather than continue to pay livery and vet fees indefinitely. I managed to persuade them to throw in the tack as well, but the saddle had been pinched from the stable, so that solved my own problem of what to buy you.'

'You're both wonderful, but it still seems too much.' Katherine looked at James. 'Are you sure we can afford it?'

'I'm sure.' Later he would tell her about the bank loan and that he'd sold his canoe. But not today. 'You enjoy your birthday.'

'Oh, I will. Believe me, I will.' Katherine stopped suddenly. 'Will Mrs Cooper let me keep him in her paddock?'

James nodded. 'She's agreed to rent it to us, just for grazing, and your dad is going to build a shelter against the hedge. That's part of their birthday present to you.'

'Part of? That's a great present on its own.'

'Well, generous souls that they are, they are also paying Mrs Cooper for a year's rental on the paddock. And my folks have ordered enough bales of hay to see you through the winter.'

'That's wonderful.' Katherine looked perilously close to tears again.

Pulling on his shoes, David asked, 'Haven't we got grazing rights with the cottage, Dad?'

'You know, I do believe you're right. Grandad used to say he was a New Forest Commoner, and his father had a pony.'

Indignantly, Katherine said, 'I'm not running Duke loose on the forest to be mown down by some crazy motorist.'

'No, you're right. He's far too good a horse.' Looking at the clock, James gulped down the remainder of his coffee. 'I'd better take the kids to school while you give Greg a hand getting Duke into the horse-box.'

'Where's he going?' She looked startled.

'Back with me to the hospital,' Greg answered. 'It's too cold for him out there without a shelter. We've got an empty stable he can use for the time being.'

David picked up his sports bag. 'And I've written out a rota so we can help you groom him. Julie's not too keen on such close contact, so she's in charge of checking the feed and water.'

Grinning again, Katherine put her mug in the sink. 'Looks like you've all got everything worked out between you, so who am I to argue?'

As they all tumbled out of the back door, she yelled at the top of her voice, 'I'm forty today! And it's the bestest birthday I shall ever have!'

10

In April 1982 news bulletins on radio and television were not to be missed, newspapers carried front page stories with maps of a group of islands that many people had never heard of or had to grab their atlases to discover exactly where they were, and prayers were said with great feeling. Argentina had invaded the Falkland Islands and, for the first time in more than thirty-five years, Great Britain was at war.

Driving towards Fivepenny Lanes, James Woodward turned the volume up on his car radio, listened, and was thankful that David, at fourteen, was too young to do anything more dangerous than attend meetings with the cadets, although, if he had his way, he would be down at Southampton Docks, waiting to embark with the other troops who were being mustered to sail out to the South Atlantic to protect one of the few Crown Colonies still owned by Great Britain. David was determined to go into the services when he left school, had never considered anything else as a career.

James expected that the caretaker of the village hall would be full of talk about what the government should and should not do, being something of an armchair politician, but he was very down in the mouth, with good reason. His son served on the *Sir Galahad*, which had just sailed from Devonport. The headmistress of the school was equally concerned. Her brother was one of the Harrier jump-jet pilots preparing to go into battle aboard HMS Invincible. There was a general air of quiet anxiety around the school, even the little ones seemed aware that something unpleasant was happening. It reminded James of the time when Miss Harding was unfairly hounded from the village. They'd never found out who was responsible and there had been no further malicious letters; or so he thought.

After Mrs Jenkins had informed James that her husband was comforting the landlady of the Blacksmith's Arms, whose son had just been recalled to his unit, and they had discussed the general pros and cons of the situation, she busied herself in the kitchen, returning later with two cups of coffee and the latest village gossip.

'Dreadful it is, to find it happening all over again in Fivepenny Lanes. I haven't seen the anonymous letter, of course, but poor Mrs Faversham was quite distraught.'

James sipped his coffee and waited for Mrs Jenkins to continue.

'For a God-fearing lady like her to be accused of cheating the tax people . . . well, you can imagine how humiliating it was.'

'Do you think it was written by the same person as before?'

'No way of knowing, Mr Woodward. We all knew that she'd had a couple of caravans on the farm for years, but I can't think of anyone who would care whether she used them for her casual workers or let them out to holiday-makers.'

'Maybe it wasn't the same person. After all, the allegation wasn't so damning as the one about Miss Harding.'

'It was to Mrs Faversham, I'm afraid. We haven't seen her since all the officials came to the farm and the rumours started about investigations by the Inland Revenue, not to mention the planning people.'

'She's not leaving the village, is she?'

'No, she won't do that. There have been Favershams at River Farm for over two hundred years. That was what the row was all about at the Women's Institute. Quite ferocious it was. And now she has resigned.'

James grinned. 'And I thought the WI was a sedate affair.'

'Oh, I know, everyone thinks we're just 'Jam and Jerusalem', but when we believe strongly in something, we say so in no uncertain terms.' Mrs Jenkins paused, a worried expression on her face, then slowly went on, 'Surely one of the members wouldn't have — ? Mind you, Mrs Faversham was quite scathing about the new villagers, as she calls them, and quite adamant that they shouldn't be nominated for president, so I could understand them feeling aggrieved, but I can't think of anyone who would go so far as to write to the authorities.'

As James finished his coffee, Mrs Jenkins held out her hand for his cup and saucer. 'It was all such a silly storm in a teacup, anyway,' she said, smiling. 'Nobody objected when I was president last year, and we've only been in Fivepenny Lanes for twenty-one years, so that makes us newcomers, as far as the villagers are concerned.'

'Ah, but you play a different role in community life. I would imagine that having the lady of the vicarage serve on a committee adds quite an air of respectability to their image.'

'You know, I never thought of it like that, but you are probably right, Mr Woodward. I am frequently asked to head up all sorts of groups as well as those associated with the church, like the Mothers' Union. There's the theatre club, needle-workers, writers' circle, the art group — oh, many more than I can commit to. But I always make time for the church fête committee. It's such fun and quite challenging to think up new ideas each year.' She laughed. 'I don't even mind being asked to judge the Junior flower arrangements.'

'It must be difficult, when every mother thinks her child should have been the winner.'

'Oh, indeed, and sometimes there are tears. But I usually give them all a little prize so they are not too disappointed.' At the door, she turned back. 'Are you going on to my Megan's next?'

James looked at his watch. 'Not for a couple of hours. I have to go to Cranleigh Manor and Mrs Burridge first.'

'Oh, yes. Well, I wonder if you would mind very much taking a parcel up to Megan for me, only I have a list of ladies to telephone about spring-cleaning the church and I promised I'd call in to see old Mrs Fairweather this afternoon. You know she's moving to Bournemouth, to live with her daughter?'

'Yes. She told me when I phoned last week about her appointment.'

'Did she tell you she has sold her piano to Megan?'

'No.' He looked up in surprise. 'I've been tuning that piano for years. It's old, but has a lovely tone. I shall look forward to continuing to work on it, and to seeing Megan again after such a long time.' James searched in his box for another tool. 'You must be delighted to have your daughter living so near.'

'Over the moon I am. When poor old Mr Rutherford died and Hugh suggested that our son-in-law would make an ideal replacement, with his background in social work, I couldn't sleep until he'd been accepted. You see, they had to approach the Church Housing Association about buying him a house, and I was so afraid they would turn him down, but the good Lord answered my prayers.'

'Where did Mr Rutherford live?'

'Oh, he had a tiny cottage up the lane, no room to swing a cat. But he'd never married, and he was quite content just being the warden of the almshouses.'

'And is that what Megan's husband will be doing?'

Mrs Jenkins nodded. 'And much more. Hugh managed to persuade the Bishop that his parish has grown so with the new estates that he really needs a younger man as curate. Mr Rutherford had been too frail to be of much assistance, bless him.'

'Will your son-in-law have to move on in three or four years?'

'Not unless he wants to have a parish of his own. Because it is a combined post, linked to the almshouses, Nigel can stay as long as he wishes. He

133

knows how much it means to Megan to be back in the village, and he does seem to enjoy working with Hugh.'

'Well, I'm very pleased that it has worked out so well for you all.' James played part of Litholff's *Scherzo* to test his handiwork, nodded with satisfaction, and put the Obermeier back together again.

When Mrs Jenkins came back into the room with her cheque book, she said, 'Brecon has had her pups. Would you like to see them?'

Five tiny bundles of black and white fur sucked greedily from their mother in a cosy corner of the huge kitchen, squealing and pushing each other as though their lunch box was going to be removed at any moment. Brecon raised her head as Mrs Jenkins smiled down at her, wagged her tail a couple of times, then got on with the business of being a good mother.

'You've always had Welsh border collies, haven't you?' James commented, smiling at the antics of the pups.

'Oh, yes. Wouldn't have anything else. They're lively, mind you, but marvellous with the children.' She glanced at James. 'I'm looking for good homes for them. Would you be interested?'

Thoughtfully, James studied the puppies. Katherine had always wanted a dog, but Grandma's evil-tempered black cat would not tolerate any canine within spitting or clawing distance. They had promised Grandma that they would continue to care for him if anything happened to her, and he had outlived his mistress by four years. Now that

Satan had finally decided that twenty-one years, something like the equivalent of more than a hundred in human terms, was quite enough and had relinquished his ninth life, they had talked of acquiring a dog.

'I admit I'm tempted,' he said, 'but Katherine had rather set her heart on a labrador. Yet I feel that if she sees these gorgeous little creatures — '

'They won't be weaned for a few weeks yet,' Mrs Jenkins said. 'Why don't you bring the family later and let them decide? I'd like to meet your wife.'

'Thank you, that is a good idea. They've never been to Fivepenny Lanes.' James felt in his pocket for his car keys. 'And don't forget to give me the parcel for Megan.'

★　★　★

As James had expected, the Brigadier had definite views on the situation in the South Atlantic.

'The islands belong to us,' he proclaimed. 'Have done since 1690. They were even named after Viscount Falkland and the population is almost entirely British.'

He had obviously read up well on the history, James thought, as he prepared the Broadwood.

'The Argentinians are always trying to raise their flag, but they have no right to the land. No right at all!' The Brigadier bristled with indignation. 'And we had no choice but to send military support, whatever the pacifists say.' He pointed to the account he was reading in *The Times*. 'Not many nations can convert a cruise liner the size of the

Canberra into a trooper carrier in two days.'

'As quickly as that?'

'Jolly good show in my book. We'll show the world that the British Army is still a force to be reckoned with.'

'Is your nephew in the services, sir?'

'No. When I'm laid to rest in the churchyard, that will be the end of the Beresford-Lawson contribution to the defence of the realm.' Sadly, the elderly squire shook his head. 'Ralph is in banking. Different breed altogether. Divorced. Now he prefers to keep his fillies dangling on a string.' He sighed. 'I was engaged once. In India, you know. The colonel's daughter. Fine-looking girl.'

James worked silently on while the Brigadier remained immersed in his thoughts.

Suddenly, the silence was broken. 'Caught one of those blasted tropical diseases. Died on her twenty-fourth birthday.'

James thought of Katherine. 'What a dreadful thing to happen,' he said.

Still deep in thought, the Brigadier slowly nodded. 'Then Hitler and his henchmen tried to steal land that wasn't his. Just like the Argentinians.' Another silence, until, 'I was posted overseas for the duration. No so much chance of meeting English girls in the North African desert. And when hostilities ceased, I found that the young women were being — liberated is the word, I believe. None of them could match Harriet.' He produced a wallet from his pocket and handed a photograph to James. A rather faded photograph of a vivacious young brunette, tennis racquet over her shoulder. James felt a pang as he gazed at the smiling face that had been carried close to the Brigadier's heart for so many years. He must have loved her very much.

'A very beautiful young lady,' James murmured, as he handed back the photograph.

'Harriet wasn't like Hedy Lamarr or the other glamorous film stars. But you're quite right. She was beautiful.' After a few moments, the Brigadier asked, 'Are you married, Woodson?' It was the first time he had ever asked anything about James's private life.

'Yes.'

'Children?'

'A girl and two boys.'

The old soldier nodded. 'At least you have an heir. My one regret is that I didn't produce a son.' He stood up, as erect and impressive as he must have looked when he put fear into his inspection lines forty years earlier. 'Have to brief my estate manager,' he said. 'Mrs Henshaw will give you my cheque.' For a moment, he paused, then said, reflectively, 'By the time you call again in the autumn, we'll have taught those marauding devils a thing or two, you mark my words.'

'I hope so, sir.'

With a brief nod and a sharp whistle, the Brigadier was gone, the two gun dogs close to his heels.

★ ★ ★

James's next encounter with a dog almost landed him in hospital. Susan Burridge had left her front door open and called out, 'Come in,' as soon as he rang the bell. Before he had both feet on the doormat, a heavyweight Staffordshire bull terrier jumped from the stairs and hurled him backwards. Growling with a ferocity that would have terrified Genghis Kahn, the wretched animal locked its jaws on to James's shoulder, and proceeded to wrench the sleeve from his jacket. Only the shoulder padding stopped those determined teeth from separating his arm from his body.

Unable to shift the bulk from his chest, James's cries for help were feeble but, eventually, Susan Burridge appeared in the doorway.

'Boris! Bad dog! Let go at once!' she ordered, grabbing the dog's thickly studded collar.

As he painfully hauled himself to a sitting position, James saw, over her shoulder, Jonathan watching from the stairs, twisting and turning Rubik's cube. The expression on his face could only be described as evilly triumphant.

Following James's gaze, Mrs Burridge mildly reproved her son. 'I particularly asked you to keep Boris out of the way, darling,' she said, trying to make herself heard above the pounding beat of *Fame*, coming from upstairs.

'Can't hear you Mother.' His grin was sadistic, and James was certain he had let the dog loose on purpose, probably instructing it to 'Kill!'

'Then please turn the volume down, you naughty boy.' She was half-laughing. 'You know the piano-tuner needs a quiet atmosphere. Do put something else on, there's a good boy.' She turned back to James. 'Oh, dear, I'm sorry about your jacket. You must send us the bill for the repairs.

You're not hurt, are you?'

James had a feeling he would have some very nasty bruises later, and that the jacket might be beyond repair, but he shook his head.

Mrs Burridge turned back into the house. 'Jonathan doesn't mean any harm, but you know what teenagers are like.'

'Yes. I have two of my own.' But they wouldn't behave so badly, James thought. And if they did, they would be disciplined in no uncertain terms.

'Percy feels I need a good guard dog. He has Boris's brother at the site. But Jonathan has taken on the responsibility of training them, which I think is very good of him, don't you?'

James was sure that Jonathan was relishing every moment in training an animal to hurt and maim, but he muttered something noncommittal and followed Mrs Burridge into the lounge. As usual, there had been changes. Now there was a green Dralon suit, matching velvet curtains, and a sage-green plain carpet.

'Green is so restful, don't you think?' Mrs Burridge waved an arm around the room.

'Yes.' Certainly he preferred it to the glare of the white room. 'Very nice.'

The piano was new, too. Mrs Burridge had complained that the white one didn't go with the new furnishings, so now a pine-coloured Schreiber tucked into an alcove by the fire. Last October, James had warned that it wasn't the best place for a piano, but it was still there.

Just as he reached a critical point in the tuning, a cacophony of sound thundered through the room.

Jonathan was playing *The Eye of the Tiger* at full blast. Even Mrs Burridge thought it was too much.

'Jonathan, dear,' she called from the foot of the stairs. 'Please turn it down. I can't hear myself think. Why don't you play quietly with that cube thing for a bit? And ask Maria to bring tea and biscuits into the lounge, there's a dear. She's cleaning the bathroom.'

When the dark-haired girl carried the tray in from the kitchen, there was only one cup.

'I am very sorry, Madam,' the girl began. 'Jonathan said — ' She bit her lip, then scuttled nervously back into the kitchen to fetch another cup and saucer.

'Maria is a good worker,' Mrs Burridge explained, 'but her English leaves much to be desired.'

'Your last au pair spoke very good English.' Glancing round at Susan Burridge, James was surprised to see her face close and become tight-lipped.

'Yes.' Her voice was abrupt, almost angry. 'The Scandinavians are keener linguists than the Spaniards. But Ingrid had other failings. We had to ask her to leave.' She poured two cups of tea and pushed the tray towards James.

'Thank you.' Trying to change the subject, and the mood, he asked after Mr Burridge.

Immediately, Susan Burridge snapped out of her irritation and smiled, her small, even teeth gleaming white. 'He's doing really well, is Percy. Did I tell you he's diversifying into industrial building?'

'No. In this area?'

'Just a few miles along the Andover road. Bought

ten acres of marshland beyond the river.' She laughed. 'There were a few moans and groans when people realised it was going to become an industrial estate and not housing, but Percy had an answer for all their objections at the meeting.'

James sipped his tea, and waited, knowing she would explain.

'Heavy traffic will travel on the new by-pass, well clear of the village. And he plans to screen the area with trees. Even when somebody asked what about disturbing the ducks and natural habitat, he was able to convince them that the wildlife would soon settle down elsewhere. Percy was magnificent. Really magnificent.' She glowed with pride.

'Well, I hope all this business in the Falklands doesn't interfere with his plans.'

'I don't think so. One of his steel fixers is in the Territorials so he might be needed for the engineering side, building bridges and things, but that's about all.'

James finished his tea and carried on working.

After a while, Mrs Burridge said, 'Thank God Jonathan is too young to be called up or anything like that. I'd die if he had to go away, just die!'

A spot of army discipline wouldn't do that young man any harm, he thought, listening to the music still thumping overhead. 'My eldest son is a Venture Scout and he's very cut up that he's not old enough,' James commented. 'Must admit I'm relieved, although I know he'll be straight in the services when he's eighteen, so I hope we don't get any more incidents like the Falklands.'

'I didn't even know where they are.' Mrs Burridge

shivered. 'And I'm glad Jonathan has never shown the slightest inclination to join the cadets — ' She broke off as Jonathan came into the room, still challenging Rubik's cube. 'Hullo, darling,' she cooed. 'I was just telling the piano-tuner how glad I am that you've never wanted to play any of those silly war games.'

'Not likely.' Jonathan scoffed. 'And as for those stupid Scouts. Right load of wallies they look with their dib-dib-dib.' He pulled a face, blinking like Benny Hill in one of his sketches, and made a mock salute.

'You mustn't make fun of them, darling. The piano-tuner's son is a Scout.'

'I know. Heard you talking.'

Listening outside the door, more like, James thought, lifting his head from the piano to stare straight back into the arrogant little sod's face. The boy was quite good-looking really, had his father's stocky build and his mother's good head of hair and perfect white teeth. It was the expression that was his undoing. Grandma used to say that the eyes were the mirrors of the soul. If so, this one had a soul to rival Damien in *The Omen*.

At that moment, Maria came into the room to collect the tray and, as Jonathan turned towards her, she stopped, as though frozen to the spot. Something in her expression reminded James of an occasion when he had shone his torch on a rabbit. It had just stared at the glaring light, too terrified to move.

'*Por favor*,' the Spanish girl murmured, before she dropped the tray and fled to the kitchen.

Susan's mouth dropped open. 'Maria!' she called. 'Come back here. At once.'

There was no movement from the kitchen, just the sound of a tiny muffled sob.

'Leave it, Mother,' Jonathan said. 'I'll make her come back.'

He closed the door behind him, and all that James could hear was the boy's low voice, punctuated by a louder cry from the girl. Then the door opened and Jonathan ushered the girl into the room.

'Now apologise to my mother,' he ordered, in a toneless voice.

'I am very sorry, Madam.' The girl's voice was tearful.

'So you should be. Disgraceful behaviour. Now, please clear up here and start on the supper. Abigail will be in soon and she'll need a bath run after messing about with that pony of hers.' Mrs Burridge picked up a magazine from the coffee table and flicked angrily through the pages.

James was pretty sure she hadn't noticed the red mark on Maria's wrist. But would she have questioned it if she had noticed? Probably not. So far as Susan Burridge was concerned, the sun shone from every orifice of her sixteen-year-old son. But something was very, very wrong, and James was glad his work was almost finished.

'There!' he said, putting the lid back on. 'Back in tune for another six months. Do you play regularly?'

'Not as much as I used to.' Mrs Burridge crossed to the bureau and took a cheque book from a pigeon-hole. 'And I'll have even less time now that

143

I've been nominated to be president of the Women's Institute.'

An unkind thought flashed through James's mind, but was quickly dismissed.

'By the way,' she handed him the cheque, 'I believe you're doing Megan Taylor's piano next?'

'That's right. Do you know her?'

'Oh, yes. I had to do all the paperwork when the church people bought their house. We're great friends.'

'That's nice.' James wondered if she also had a parcel for him to take to Megan. But it was a message.

'I'm taking her daughter to watch Abigail ride in the gymkhana tomorrow. They bore me to tears, but Abigail adores them, bless her. Anyway, will you tell her I'll pick Ruthie up at eight, and drop off Maria so she can help Megan with her spring-cleaning. Oh, and tell her I'm thinking of buying Abigail a new bedroom suite, one of those white Regency ones with the gold trimming. So she's very welcome to the old one. Actually, we only bought it when Abigail started school, so it's not that old. You won't forget, will you?'

'No, I won't forget.' As James drove the short distance to Susan Close, he muttered, 'Eight; Maria; bedroom suite,' trying to fix it in his mind.

Number nineteen was at the far end of the Close, next to the footpath that led across to the churchyard.

Still muttering the words like a mantra, and clutching Mrs Jenkins's parcel, he rang the bell. It must be nearly twenty years since he had seen

Megan, he thought, remembering the voluptuous teenager, so she would be about thirty-five now.

Change he expected, but the young woman peering at him through thick lenses, her hair untidily drawn back into a knot, was unrecognisable. And she was very, very fat.

'It's twins this time, see.' Only her lilting voice was the same. 'Mother tells me that you are a family man, too. Come in, come in.' A tot of about four hovered in the hall, thumb in mouth, huge dark eyes fixed on James. 'It's only the piano-tuner, silly,' Megan soothed. 'Go and play with Owen and Ruthie, there's a good girl, while I make a cup of tea for Mr — I'm so sorry, I've forgotten your name.'

'Woodward.' But Megan wasn't listening. A familiar sound of squabbling siblings reached James's ears.

'Now then, you two,' Megan called upstairs. 'I told you the piano-tuner was coming, so let's be having a bit of peace and quiet, if you don't mind.'

Two subdued voices called back. 'Sorry, Mum.'

'And if you behave yourselves, I'll play Monopoly with you afterwards.'

That's more like Katherine, James thought. Discipline and affection.

Smiling, she murmured to James. 'Board games are much more fun than housework, don't you think?'

'That reminds me.' He passed on Susan's message.

'Isn't that kind of her? I like Maria, and she's such a willing worker. But the poor little thing is so nervous, she doesn't like being on her own in the house when Susan and Percy are out, not even when Jonathan is there.'

Unsurprised, James handed over the parcel.

'Thank you. Mum said you were bringing them over. She has been knitting frantically ever since I had the scan. Don't know what I'd do without her, I really don't. And Susan has given me loads of things that her children have grown out of. Such lovely things, too. She's a good friend.'

Megan led the way into the lounge, closely followed by her youngest child. 'Don't you want to go upstairs?' Megan asked. 'No? OK, then, but you mustn't get in the way. Do you understand?'

Silently, the child nodded.

'It's not a bad idea to have a quiet child in the family,' Megan laughed, side-stepping a huge teddy bear.

'She's very much like you,' James commented, as he picked his way through a minefield of toys and found the piano, buried under a heap of clothes.

'I like to watch television while I'm ironing,' Megan said, sweeping the laundry, letters and newspapers on to the floor with one movement. 'There, now you can see what you're doing.' She picked the child up and sat her on the piano stool, studying her face. 'Yes, everyone says she looks like me, but she has her daddy's sweet nature.' Stroking the little girl's raven-black hair, Megan smiled at James. 'Sometimes I think Nigel is too nice for his own good. People do tend to take advantage of him. But everyone loves him, especially me. Now, I'll go and put that kettle on.'

'Not for me, thank you. I've just had a cup with Mrs Burridge.'

'Are you sure? Then I'll get on with the ironing. Will it bother you if I put the television on without the sound? There's a children's programme on that Dilys likes.'

'Not at all.'

The piano hadn't taken kindly to the house move, and needed twice the normal amount of attention before the tone was to his liking.

'That's better, isn't it?' Megan murmured, as he played a Schubert waltz. 'We didn't have room for a piano in Macclesfield, so I've really missed it.' She ferreted amongst a pile of music on the floor, pulled out a piece of music and propped it up in front of him. 'It's not often that I sing with a pianist now. Would you mind? Please?'

Although he was running late, as he listened to her glorious top C at the end of Puccini's 'One Fine Day', James was glad he hadn't refused. Megan still sang like an angel, and he told her so.

'I was booked to do some concert work before we moved,' she sighed, 'but I got big so quickly I had to turn it down.' Megan tapped her stomach. 'It's all your fault,' she murmured. 'And we could have done with the money. Still, I'm sure you'll be worth it. Now, where's my cheque book?'

It was in a toy box. James knew he should have charged extra for the refelting but, looking at the threadbare rugs and shabby furnishings, he hadn't the heart.

'It has been lovely seeing you again.' She smiled.

'And you really haven't changed at all. I suppose it's the hair.'

'Pardon?'

'If men lose their hair it makes them look — different. Yours is still as thick as ever, and you're not at all grey.'

Slightly embarrassed, James held out his hand. 'Nice to see you again, too. And to hear you sing. I'll phone you in October for the next appointment.'

'Please God I'll have two new little Taylors to show you.' Sounds of hilarious laughter drifted down the stairs. 'Who knows, I might even be able to introduce you to Ruthie and Owen.'

'How old are they now?'

'Ruthie's ten and Owen is seven.'

'You're going to have your hands full when the twins arrive.'

'I know, and it's thankful I am to be back in Fivepenny Lanes. Mum is so excited that she has children around the place again. Especially now that Geraint is divorced and Thomas doesn't stay in one place long enough to find a girlfriend. And we're going to have one of Brecon's puppies, aren't we, poppet?'

Dilys smiled happily.

'Snap! I'm hoping to persuade Katherine to forget about labradors and go for a Welsh sheepdog instead. Your mother has kindly suggested that we all come over to make a choice when the pups are old enough.'

'Really? That's wonderful. I'll ask Mum to let me know when you're coming, so we can come round and meet your family, help you choose. That will be something to look forward to.'

As he drove home, he wondered what Katherine would think of the young woman he had always described as being a *femme fatale*. Then he smiled. Katherine would recognise that Megan might not still be a slender teenage beauty, but she had mellowed into a loving young woman with a warm heart, just like her mother — and just like Katherine.

11

'Here she comes.' David pointed into the distance.

Screwing up her eyes, Julie shook her head. 'Where? I can't see anything.'

Robert jumped up and down. 'I can see it! I can see it!'

His big brother playfully pushed him. '*Her*, silly. Ships are always *her*. Never *it*.'

'Why?'

'Because — '

David's explanation, if he had one, was interrupted by his sister grabbing his arm. 'Yes!' she cried. 'I can see her now. Oh yes — ' Julie's voice trailed, and there was a moment's hush from the thousands lining the beach as the ethereal hulk pushed its way through the July morning mist and came into view. Then a voice broke the silence.

'It's the Great White Whale!' A ray of sunshine searched for the liner, with its escort of hundreds of little ships of every description, fireboats sending jets of water high into the air, speedboats recklessly nipping in and out, ferries sounding hooters. And then an enormous cheer rippled along the shore, like a vast wave heading out to sea. The *Canberra* was home from the war, her cargo of battle-weary commandos lining the decks. Soon they would have a truly royal welcome from the heir to the throne, who was to join the ship for the last leg of her journey. James wondered whether the Prince would be thinking of his brother, who had flown alongside the other naval pilots, shared their dangers and, thankfully, survived the war.

'Wow!' Julie gasped. 'She's so close, I feel I could paddle out and touch her.'

'I know,' Katherine said, her eyes moist. 'Isn't it the most marvellous sight?'

As the ship made her way carefully through the Solent, with the Isle of Wight appearing as a backdrop now that the mist was clearing, people began to run along the beach, waving Union Jacks of all sizes and holding high above their heads enormous banners printed with the name of the man they were longing to hug.

James captured the historic moment on his Olympus, photographing the *Canberra* from every angle, then his family frantically waving, and the crowds keeping pace with the flotilla until they could go no further and huddled together in an attempt to catch a last glimpse of the spectacle. Finally, as the liner rounded the point to enter Southampton Water, James used his wide lens to frame the modern ship sailing close to the ancient Calshot Castle, built by King Henry VIII to protect the shores from invading Spaniards. Now it was under siege again from advancing Britons, pushing their way towards those already surrounding the circular fortress, some brave enough to climb high to get a better view.

'You'll be taking a cold bath if you're not careful,' Katherine warned, as James leaned over the sea wall at an impossible angle, still snapping away.

'That's the lot.' He hauled himself back. 'I've run

out of film. Should be some good ones there for the family album, I hope.' He turned to his children, squashed in behind their mother. 'Glad you came?' he asked.

Their response left no doubt as to their pleasure. This would be a moment they would remember all their lives, he knew. Watching it on television would show the overall picture, but nothing could ever be the same as feeling the emotions, the tears and cheers all around them, the good-humoured banter as people made their way back past the old aircraft hangars, many greeting friends and arranging to meet later for a Sunday lunchtime drink. It was like this on VE Day, James reflected. He had only been eight years old, but the memories were crystal clear.

Glancing at a stack of canoes piled outside the Calshot Activity Centre, Katherine said, 'I still feel horribly guilty about you selling your canoe.'

'Don't. I had my own canoe for years — you had never had your own horse.'

'I know, but — '

'No buts. It was four years ago and I haven't really missed it, honestly.'

'But I thought you were looking forward to canoeing with David.'

'I was, but he's as happy as a sandboy crewing on Greg's Westerly. Anyway, I love watching you with Duke. You two were just made for each other.'

Katherine smiled her agreement, then commented, 'It's funny that I'm scared of the water and you're wary of horses, but David takes it all in his stride.'

'I know. There's nothing that lad won't attempt. If

we had mountains in the New Forest, he'd be climbing them.'

'He told me he wants to become a commando so he can climb mountains.'

'Well, let's thank God that he wasn't old enough to climb Mount Tumbledown, like some of those boys.'

Quietly, Katherine said, 'It's the ones still there that I'm thinking of.'

For a while they walked silently, until Julie interrupted their painful thoughts by asking, 'Where are we going now?'

'First we have to find the car.' He glanced at his watch. 'That's going to take another half hour at least, but it's still too early for a pub lunch.'

'I'm hungry,' Robert complained.

'You're never anything else,' David tweaked his brother's ear. 'Did you bring any sandwiches, Mum?'

Katherine shook her head. 'It was all too much of a rush.'

'Tell you what,' James decided. 'Let's find a café and have a late breakfast instead of an early lunch.'

'Yes!' the children chorused, quickening their steps and side-stepping the dawdlers.

Katherine linked her arm with James's, letting their offspring hurry ahead. 'I'm so glad you suggested coming here first. What time are they expecting us?'

'Mrs Jenkins said they usually have lunch about one o'clock, which fits in with the two morning services and evensong, so any time after two will be OK. Fortunately, they haven't any baptisms this afternoon, so we should be able to see all their family.'

'I'm glad you don't have to work on my days off. Vicars have a funny old time-table, don't they? Especially in the summer, with all the weddings.'

'Not to mention funerals. You can't plan those in advance.' James squeezed her arm. 'I do hope you like the dogs. They really are lovely.'

'Well, whether I do or not, I'm sure I'll like the people, from what you say.'

'I've become very fond of them over the years. Genuine people, who practise what they preach.'

Ahead of them, their children sat on a farm gate, beckoning.

'Come on, you two,' Robert bellowed. 'We're starving!'

'Why don't you shout a bit louder?' Katherine teased. 'There might be a few people on the Isle of Wight who haven't heard how hungry you are.'

As Robert opened his mouth, Julie promptly clasped her hand over it.

James saw the possibility of some more photographs. 'See if you can keep them up there while I reload the camera,' he asked Katherine. 'The light's good.'

As he brought the zoom lens into focus, James felt a familiar sense of pride at the framed picture of Julie, with her straw-coloured hair and incredibly blue eyes, David on one side of her, with his wide grin, and Robert on the other side, pulling a face and rubbing his stomach. No wonder people were glancing in their direction and smiling.

'And what would you be staring at?' Mary asked her husband as they moved slowly along with the crowd.

'Those grand-looking children having their photos taken.'

'Where? You're taller than I am.'

'Further up, by the gate. I couldn't help noticing them back at the castle.'

'What's special about them?'

'They're the sort of good-looking family you see on the ads. You know, all smiling at each other over the breakfast table because they're eating the right cereal and Mam's using the best soap powder. But this lot's for real. It makes you wish — '

Mary wondered if Michael knew that his words cut through her like a twisting knife. She'd never forgiven herself for not being able to provide him with the string of sons and daughters he'd wanted, and expected. And sometimes she felt he hadn't been able to forgive her, either. But if she'd had a large family, how would he have fed and clothed them? They hadn't been able to keep one child with them, and that was an issue that still caused many problems. What Michael would say when she showed him Brendan's latest letter, she dreaded to think. She would have to tell him today, that was for sure, but not now. First, she must put him in a good mood before she presented him with the bombshell.

Thrusting the dark thought to the back of her mind, Mary strained her eyes to follow Michael's gaze. 'Ah, yes. Now I see them, sitting on the gate.

And aren't they the loveliest children you ever set eyes upon?'

'What else would you expect with a mother like that? Now there's a fine-looking woman, and no mistake.'

Mary glanced sharply sideways at her husband. She didn't mind Michael having an eye for a pretty face, but sometimes his expression showed more than a passing interest, and she wondered.

'I can't see her,' she murmured.

'The tall, blonde woman with good legs. She's certainly managed to keep her figure, and she's had three kids.'

Ignoring his hurtful remark, Mary craned her neck to see the woman ushering the children into the back of a car. She couldn't see her face, but it was true, the woman did have good legs. As the father handed a packet of sweets to the youngest boy, he smiled at a remark made by his wife. Mary felt a pang as she realised it was a long time since Michael had looked at her like that, with such pride and devotion.

By now, they were almost level with the car, and Mary couldn't resist sneaking a look at the woman, wondering what it was about her that had caught Michael's attention. She was fastening her seat belt and, immediately, Mary was struck by the woman's stunning beauty, which did not come merely from her heart-shaped face with the windswept honey-coloured hair springing back from the widow's peak, nor from her smooth skin and perfect profile. This woman had something else which made men look twice and women wonder why they bothered. Mary understood why Michael had that look in his eye, but she couldn't have put into words what it was.

Suddenly, the woman looked up, through the open window, directly into Mary's face. The brilliantly blue eyes stared for a moment, then smiled, and Mary smiled back. It was a very strange experience, as though the two women were recognising something, or sharing a secret thought. Then Mary was pushed forward by the crowd, and the moment was over.

Michael took her arm and pulled her along. 'We'll never get away from here if you're going to dawdle like that,' he said.

'What's the rush, darling? We've got all day.'

'I just don't like being pushed and shoved. If I'd known that thousands of others would have the same idea as you, I might have said 'no'.'

'But it was a grand sight, wasn't it? And thank you for bringing me.'

'It's time you learned to drive. Then I wouldn't be a taxi-driver.'

Oh, dear, he was grumpy this morning, Mary thought. And as for learning to drive! They couldn't afford proper lessons, and the few times Michael had tried to teach her she had finished up in tears. If he hadn't shouted so much, she might have listened to what he said.

'What would you like to do for the rest of the day, Michael dear?' She tried to get the conversation back on to a happier note.

'Well, now that we're out, we might as well look around. Then, as soon as they're open, we'll be having a pub lunch somewhere.'

157

Mary said, 'Mrs Whitcher — you know, the woman who looks after the caravan site — well, she was telling me there are some smashing little pubs in the New Forest.'

'We don't want anything too posh, mind.' Michael paused to light a cigarette, then went on, 'And afterwards, I thought I'd take a look at one of those pony races the lads at work were talking about.'

'Horse racing? I didn't think it was allowed on a Sunday.'

'It's not like Goodwood, not at all. Just a bunch of farmers getting together and racing their ponies in a field. A harmless bit of fun.'

'Would you know where to go?'

Casually, almost too casually, Michael said, 'It's — er — somewhere near Brockenhurst, or so they tell me.'

'Brockenhurst? Now that's a name I remember. Mrs Whitcher said there's a very nice pub right in the village that has a skittle alley and a garden. And they do all sorts of food, she said.'

'As long as it doesn't cost the earth.'

'Well, if it looks expensive, we'll find somewhere else.' Determined to say nothing to spoil the day, she took his arm. 'Isn't this the very nicest place we've lived since we left Ireland, Michael? We've got the New Forest, the seaside — Bournemouth is only a few miles away, and Mrs Whitcher says Salisbury and Winchester are well worth a visit. And they're all on our doorstep.'

'You can hardly call a step into a tatty caravan a doorstep.'

Oh, he was being difficult. But Mary persisted.

158

'I'll soon have the caravan put to rights, don't you worry. We only moved in last week. But at least you have a secure job for a while. Let's count our blessings,' she pleaded.

For a moment, she thought he wasn't going to respond. Then he smiled down at her. 'And the sun is getting warmer.'

Mary felt more hopeful than she had for many years. When she had left Ireland with Michael that New Year's Day in 1978, she thought her husband had learned his lesson, and would start saving money to replace the huge amount lost in an all-night poker game on the last stretch of motorway. But London streets had not been paved with gold, as Michael had expected, and he became more expert at studying the current form of sleek racehorses and greyhounds than profiting from his knowledge. As for the steady job, he drifted in and out of low-paid casual work, none lasting more than a few weeks. Mary had also worked at anything she could find; in a factory that made electrical goods, serving in a shoe-shop, as a waitress in a restaurant, even as an attendant in a ladies' lavatory. But they always had to move on to another area when they owed too much rent. The one blessing was that Brendan had a happy home with Maeve and Diarmid and their lively brood, and he was doing really well at school.

Eventually, Michael realised that he needed to put more distance between himself and the bookies, had the sense to invest his last fifty pounds into an old Morris Minor instead of another hot tip, and headed for Southampton. For once, he'd struck lucky, and been taken on straight away, and Mary was to start tomorrow as an assistant cook in a canteen. It really seemed as though their luck was turning at last, apart from Brendan's news.

But for now, Michael's smile and the warmth of the sun on her back were enough. 'It's going to be a grand day,' she said, and thought — I'll tell him later.

★　★　★

Percy Burridge halted so abruptly that Abigail nearly collided with him and Susan looked back to see what had happened. Regardless of the crowds dividing each side of him, he stood still, a thoughtful expression on his face.

Susan retraced her steps, peered closely at him, then slowly moved her hand across his face. 'Anyone at home?' she asked.

'Sorry, love.' He grinned back at her but didn't move. 'But I just had an idea.'

Behind him, Jonathan smirked. 'Will wonders never cease?'

Percy turned and frowned slightly at his son, but went back to his train of thought. 'Why don't we have one of these?' He jerked his head towards the beach.

'One of what, dear?' Susan looked along the row of wooden beach huts, expecting to find a SAAB or BMW parked outside one of them.

'A beach hut.'

'A beach hut?' Susan and Abigail echoed, as Jonathan's mouth dropped open.

'You must be joking!' He glared at his father.

Percy still seemed to be thinking out loud. 'The foreman was telling me how he's got one and he and the wife come here most Sundays for a quiet day by the sea. Sets him up for the week ahead, he reckons.'

Amazed, Susan looked at him. 'But you play golf on Sunday mornings.'

'Aye, and I'm getting fed up to the teeth with doing business on what is supposed to be my day off. I can't even relax in the garden without the phone ringing.' He looked appealingly at his wife. 'Think on it, lass.'

Susan thought on it. 'What about the time-share villa?' she enquired mildly.

'It won't make any difference. We can still go to the Costa Brava once or twice a year, and you can top up your tan on fine days at Costa del Calshot. It's nowt but an hour's drive from Fivepenny Lanes.'

'That's true, Percy, love. I suppose it would be quite nice for the children.' She looked at Jonathan and Abigail. 'What do you think?'

Abigail nodded eagerly. 'I'd like to bring Ruthie, please. Who would you bring, Jonathan?'

Her brother exploded. 'I wouldn't come here myself, let alone invite the chaps. Can you imagine it?' His voice rose to falsetto. 'Would you like to join us for a day at our beach hut?' As his tone dropped, he sneered at his father. 'Just who do you think I am?'

Percy spun on his heel and grabbed Jonathan by the lapels of his blazer. 'You're my son, that's who you are,' he said. 'And you'll go where I say and do what I say while you live under my roof. Do you understand me?'

Sullen-faced, Jonathan remained silent.

His father raised his voice. 'Do you understand me?' he repeated, shaking him slightly, 'because if you don't, I'll be on to the headmaster of that fancy school of yours tomorrow and tell him he'll get no more brass out of me.'

Jonathan looked shocked. 'You can't do that,' he spluttered. 'I need my A-levels if I'm to go on to university.'

'Then tha'll have to take your chance at comprehensive with rest of them, won't thee?' He flung the boy away from him.

Susan recognised the warning signs even if Jonathan didn't. When Percy was really wild, his Yorkshire roots came to the fore. She put a hand on her husband's arm in an effort to calm him. 'Shush, love,' she said. 'People are looking.' It was the wrong thing to say.

'I don't care if whole bloody world is looking,' Percy said, his voice still angry. 'I'll not have him talking to me like that.'

'I'm sure he didn't mean it, love. Perhaps he just thought the idea of having a beach hut was a bit — well, you know.'

'Common? Is that what you're trying to say, Susan?'

'Perhaps — just a little?'

'Common?' He waved an arm in the direction of the beach huts. 'Look at the people sitting outside. They're just decent folks enjoying a quiet Sunday morning on the beach with their families and friends, watching ships sailing by, and minding their own business. That's not common.'

'No, of course not, Percy. It was the wrong word.' Susan tried to placate him. 'Some of them have very nice cars. Boats even.'

'Aye.' Percy gazed at his wife for a moment or two, then turned back to his son. 'I bet you'd soon change your tune about inviting your high and mighty mates if we had a boat parked outside, like that one.'

Jonathan's expression turned to one of excitement as he noticed the gleaming red speedboat coming into shore. 'Do you mean it? A speedboat? Aw, Dad, why didn't you tell us that was what you had in mind, instead of letting us go on thinking it was just a rotten old beach hut?'

Slowly, Percy looked from one to the other of his family. Then he said, 'Now, listen to me. All of you.' He waved a stubby finger in front of their faces. 'My father had nowt but a few days at Scarborough and an outing to Blackpool all his life. He'd have thought this was paradise.' Pointing to the beach huts, he went on. 'And if I'd turned my nose up at one of those, he'd have given me a good tanning just to let me know he was still gaffer.'

Jonathan's lip curled. 'Not now, he wouldn't. The law would be on him like a ton of bricks.'

'When did your grandfather, or me, ever let anything stand in the way of doing what we know is right?' Percy studied his son's face as though seeing him for the first time. 'Just because I've never laid a finger on thee doesn't mean I never will, so don't give me cause.' Jonathan's eyes dropped before his father's stern gaze. 'Any road,' Percy went on, 'there's more ways than a clout to bring cheeky young nippers to order.'

Jonathan looked concerned, then foolishly tried a little bravado. 'There's nothing you can threaten me with that will make me lose any sleep.'

'You reckon?' Percy smiled, but Susan knew, by the whiteness around his mouth, that it was not with good humour.

'Yes, I reckon. What exactly did you have in mind, Father?'

Without taking his eyes from his son's face, Percy said, 'Happen you'll remember I bought thee a brand new moped for your birthday just gone, and promised a car and driving lessons when tha's seventeen?'

Now Jonathan looked more concerned than brave. 'You wouldn't go back on your word. Would you?' As Percy raised his eyebrows, the supercilious smile left the boy's face. 'But you can't — I've told everyone — '

'I can, and will, if need be. And I'll not think twice about taking that Yamaha thing straight back to the shop.' Percy shook his head, as though bemused. 'You've had everything you ever asked for, all of you.' His gaze went on Susan. 'New furniture, clothes, cars, the villa, a pony for Abigail.' He turned back to Jonathan. 'It's not the brass I mind, it's the fact that you look on me as someone who just provides the brass, but doesn't really matter in the long run.'

'Please, Dad. Not the bike. I'm the only guy in the year with an FS1E.'

'Then it's up to you, lad. There's to be no more

164

answering back to me, or anyone else.' Again that thoughtful gaze. 'And I'll have no more of the goings-on I've put up with this last twelve month.'

'What do you mean, Dad? I've not done anything wrong.'

'No? Have you forgotten why you had to change schools in a hurry?' Jonathan didn't answer. 'Because the headmaster asked me to move you, that's why. And what about the time our maid left because she said that you crept into her room when she was asleep? Then there was the neighbour who complained that you swore at him.'

'They were lying, Dad. I told you, they just had it in for me.'

Percy nodded. 'I gave you the benefit of the doubt, but I've still got a few doubts of my own tucked away. So don't chance your luck any more, lad, it just might run out.'

Looking considerably subdued, Jonathan nodded.

Breathing deeply, Percy looked out to sea. 'Now that's settled, let's get on with having a day out.' As he began to walk ahead, he called back over his shoulder, 'And if I want to buy a bloody beach hut, I'll buy a bloody beach hut! Come on, there's an ice cream van up the road.' He grinned at his daughter. 'You don't think it's common to eat a cornet in public, do you?'

Abigail grinned back. ''Course not, Daddy. Can I have a 99?'

Behind them, Susan and Jonathan trailed a little. Then Jonathan said, 'I've never seen Dad like that before. Have you?'

'No. He's quite even-tempered as a rule, but I've

165

heard tell from men on the site that he can be a demon if he's roused. You'll have to learn to back off if you feel he's getting steamed up.'

'It's not fair to put the onus on me. Abigail gets away with everything.'

Gently, Susan said, 'Abigail has learned how to please and displease her father. Perhaps you should take a leaf out of her book?'

'But it wasn't my fault. I only said — '

'Shush.' Susan put a finger to her lips. 'It's over now, let it be. And I believe you, despite what those people said, or your father thinks.'

'Well, I'm glad someone's on my side. Sometimes I think the whole world's against me.'

'No, love.' Susan ran a sympathetic hand across Jonathan's hair. 'I'm always on your side, you know that. Just try and be extra nice to Dad, and he'll soon get over it.'

Jonathan sulked for a little while longer, then said, 'Do you think he will buy a boat?'

'I don't know.' Susan mused on the idea for a moment, then smiled. 'Mind you, it would be one in the eye for Mrs Faversham, wouldn't it? She's always on about her son racing his yacht during Cowes week.'

'Is that the old girl you had drummed out of the Women's Institute?'

Shocked, Susan stopped. 'That's a terrible thing to say, Jonathan.'

'Oh, come on, Mum. I knew all along you had a hand in it. Nobody else in Fivepenny Lanes would be clever enough. You'd made up your mind to be president, and nobody was going to stop you. I thought it was brilliant.'

'I really don't know what you're talking about.' Flustered, Susan tried to change the subject. 'We seem to have been walking for ages. Can you see the Rover?'

Jonathan stretched his neck to look ahead. 'No — but I can see a smashing bit of talent.'

'Oh, darling, please don't be coarse. You know I hate it.'

He laughed. 'Can you see her? The blonde with the gorgeous legs in the pink shorts. Her old woman's not bad, either.'

'Jonathan!'

'Sorry. But you've got to admit they've both got what it takes. Look at all the guys drooling over them.'

Half-irritated, half-curious, Susan followed his gaze. Then she frowned, 'I think I know that car — yes, it is him.'

'Wonderful! Can you introduce me to the bimbo?'

'Certainly not. Don't you recognise the father?'

'I wasn't looking at him. Anyway, he's in the car now, so I can't see him.'

'I hope Percy doesn't spot him. I'm not in the mood for polite conversation and introductions to his family, not after your father going on at you like that.'

'Who is he, anyway?'

'Nobody. Only the piano-tuner.'

12

James sensed that all was not well with Mrs Jenkins as soon as she opened the door. She greeted Katherine and the children with genuine warmth, leading them through into the garden, where the pups were frolicking, but her thoughts appeared to be elsewhere as she went back into the kitchen to put the kettle on. There was no sign of Megan, or anyone else, until a very dark little head peeped around the door into the garden. The child looked as though she had been crying.

'Hullo, Dilys,' James said. 'Do you remember me?'

A shy nod, and a little more of the tot's body edged around the door.

'Is your mummy here?'

A shake of the head, and a whispered, 'Owen fell off his bike.'

'Oh, dear. Did he hurt his knee?'

This time the whole of Dilys appeared in the open doorway. Thumb in mouth, she murmured, 'Mummy's taken him to the hospital.'

Julie moved nearer to the child and crouched down. Gently, she asked, 'Would you like to tell me the names of your puppies?'

For a moment, Dilys gazed back, then she seemed to recognise a friend, nodded, and led Julie to the far side of the lawn, where the litter were tormenting their mother, who was sprawled in the sunshine,

168

trying unsuccessfully to have a quiet snooze.

By the time Mrs Jenkins reappeared, Dilys had got over her shyness and all four youngsters were having a fine time with Brecon and her brood. Placing the tray on the garden table, Mrs Jenkins glanced across at her granddaughter and smiled. 'It will help keep her mind off things,' she said. 'I heard her telling you about Owen's accident.'

'Only that he'd fallen off his bike and has been taken to hospital. I do hope he's not too badly hurt.'

'His arm looked a most peculiar shape. He tried to be brave, poor little mite, but he couldn't help crying, and Dilys was very upset.' She began to pour tea. 'I offered to look after them all, but Megan had to take the twins. She's feeding them herself, you see, and you know how long you can sit around waiting for X-rays and so on.' She handed a cup to Katherine. 'Ruthie insisted on going with her mother. Says she wants to be a nurse when she grows up — but she'll be a help with the babies, anyway. I did manage to persuade Dilys to stay with me, although she was a bit clingy when Megan left.'

'Has your son-in-law taken them?'

'No. Unfortunately, an old gentleman who lives in the almshouses is very ill, and Nigel promised to stay with him.' Mrs Jenkins lowered her voice. 'The poor old soul is afraid he might die if he's left alone.' She pushed a plate of biscuits towards Katherine. 'They are home-made, my love. Do try one.' Still talking while she poured her own tea, she went on, 'So Hugh said he would drive Megan to the hospital so that she could cuddle Owen in the back. She can drive, of course. Nowadays young people have to, don't they, with all the fetching and carrying they have to do for the children. Guides, cubs, dancing classes, swimming lessons, birthday parties. There's always something.' She sipped her tea. 'We never had to do so much when ours were small, so I never bothered. Sometimes I wish I had plucked up a little more courage. The buses are very few and far between, and I have to ask Hugh to take me everywhere.'

'These are delicious. May I?' Katherine helped herself to another biscuit. 'I know what you mean. The older they get, the more the children want to do. We always had to cycle, or walk, but it's not safe to let them do that on their own now.'

'When Hugh was a curate, we lived all over the place, but didn't need neighbourhood watches or burglar alarms. Now they're a necessity.' Mrs Jenkins sighed. 'And what kind of a person would want to slash horses with a knife?'

'A pervert, Mrs Jenkins. I'm terrified that Duke might be attacked. He's in the paddock behind our cottage, and it's easy to get into it from the lane on the other side. I'm hoping that a dog will give him some protection, and us.'

'Indeed it will. A border collie has a good loud bark, and our Brecon has been known to send a new insurance man running, with his trouser leg between her teeth! Come and see what you think of her pups.'

As James had hoped, Katherine was entranced, and the choice of which one to take home was incredibly difficult.

'Megan is taking Dylan,' Mrs Jenkins pointed to

the one Julie was holding, 'and the landlady of the Blacksmith's Arms wants that pretty little bitch, so that leaves another bitch and the two little dogs.'

They were all adorable but, eventually, it was decided that the bitch was the spunkiest, coming back again and again to David for a tug-of-war with an old piece of blanket, her little tail thumping joyfully. Mrs Jenkins would not let them pay for the dog.

'You're an old friend, Mr Woodward. I'm just happy she's going to such a good home.'

'Will you let me make a donation to church funds then, please.'

She hesitated, then said, 'Thank you. As a matter of fact, the profits from the church fête next week are going towards hymn books — the old ones are in a terrible state — and new music for the choir. If you really want to, that would be very kind.'

'And close to my heart.' As James finished writing out the cheque, he handed his car keys to David. 'Will you get the collar and lead from the boot of the car, please.'

Katherine stared at him in amazement. 'Were you so sure I would change my mind?'

'Of course.' He grinned at her. 'Don't forget, I'd already seen them.' Putting his pen away, he asked his children, 'Well, have you chosen a name yet?'

Robert answered for the three nodding heads. 'I wanted to call her Canberra, David wanted Falkland, and Julie said Georgia would be appropriate — you know, after South Georgia, the first bit the commandos recaptured.'

Thinking of shortened versions of Canberra and

171

Falkland, James mentally crossed his fingers and hoped they had chosen Georgia as the least of three evils for calling a dog to heel.

Screwing his eyes up in concentration, Robert went on, 'But we couldn't agree on any of those.'

Fervently, James said a short prayer of thanks.

'So we're calling her Bess.'

'Bess.' James thought it over. 'Sounds OK to me. How about you, Katherine?'

Katherine grinned at Mrs Jenkins. 'Good name for a collie, don't you think?'

The corners of Mrs Jenkins's mouth tweaked, but she managed to keep a straight face. 'Oh, yes.' She said. 'A very good choice. Reminds me of a lovely old sheepdog we had when I was a child.'

'Talking of names,' Katherine said, 'What are Megan's twins called? I notice her other children have lovely Welsh names.'

'That's why Megan said it was only fair that Nigel should choose this time. He's decided upon Matthew and Sarah.'

'Good biblical names. It's nice that they have one of each, but Megan is certainly going to have her hands full.'

'Oh, yes. I go over each morning to help out at bathtime — it's no distance along the footpath. They are such sweet babies. A pity you couldn't see them.' Mrs Jenkins picked up the puppy and buried her face in its fur. 'Goodbye, Bess. You guard them well, mind.'

Katherine held out her hand to Mrs Jenkins. 'She'll be greatly loved, I promise you. And thank you for the tea.'

'Oh, goodness me, what am I thinking of?' Mrs Jenkins gasped. 'I forgot to make the jug of lemonade for the children. It has been such a topsy-turvy day. But it won't take me a minute.'

James shook his head. 'We must be on our way, thanks just the same. I promised the family I'd take them for a walk around the village, and we've had a very long day. We went to Calshot to see the *Canberra* return home.'

'Wasn't that a glorious sight? I watched it on television — and I am not ashamed to say I cried like a baby.'

Katherine smiled. 'I think everyone on the beach was either in tears or close to.'

'I'm not surprised. Now, before you go, let me show you the puppy food that Bess likes. And she's not quite house-trained yet, so you'll need to use a litter tray to start with. Take that old piece of blanket with you. She's taken a fancy to it and it will help her to settle down.'

Ten minutes later, armed with bags of puppy meal, litter grit, and home-made biscuits for the children, they had said their goodbyes and driven down to the village. James parked in the bus lay-by near the village green, having discovered that the next bus wasn't due until the following morning. For a short while, they watched the cricket match, but only James and David were really interested, so they walked back to the pond. The children argued over whose turn it was to hold the lead, and Bess barked so at the ducks that James thought a diversion was in order.

'There's a tea-shop across the road,' he said to

Katherine. 'How about a cream tea before we go home?' He knew how she loved cream teas.

'Wonderful!' she said, then stopped. 'What about Bess? We can't leave her in the car.'

'I believe there's a garden. She'd be all right there.'

'Have you been in there before?' Katherine asked, picking up the puppy before she crossed the road.

'No. They don't do lunches, only coffees and teas. That's why I bring sandwiches and a flask. And any stale bread I can find, to feed the ducks.'

'Mind your head, James!' Katherine ducked under the beams and led the way through to the tiny garden at the rear of the tea-shop.

The waitress was quite elderly and asked them, in no uncertain terms, to make sure that 'the animal' was kept on the lead and not allowed to run loose. James remembered hearing that the tea-shop was owned by two spinster sisters, both sadly lacking in humour. This must be one of them, he thought. But the cream tea was delicious.

After Bess had been fed a few nibbles of scone by the children, she decided that all the fuss and attention was rather tiring, yawned widely, then made herself comfortable on Katherine's lap.

'No regrets?' James asked.

'Over Bess? No. She's gorgeous.' Katherine scooped up a dollop of cream from her plate and licked it from her fingers. 'I just hope she and Duke get on together.'

'Don't see why not. Duke's a good-tempered beast, and dogs usually enjoy the company of other animals, even cats.'

'Funny you should mention that. I was wondering — '

'Hold on a minute!' James cut her short. 'I've only just got used to being without that monstrous moggie of Grandma's. Let's just stick to dogs and horses, shall we?'

Katherine sighed. 'They're not all as hostile as Satan. But perhaps you're right.'

James knew he hadn't heard the last of it, but for now was content to watch his wife lift her face up to the sun, and his children chatting happily around the table.

'It's been a perfect day,' she murmured, her eyes half-closed. 'One of those days you tuck away in your memory bank and bring out from time to time when you need to smile.'

'Couldn't have put it better — oh! Katherine!'

'And to finish up with a cream tea.'

'Katherine!'

'So very English, a cream tea on a Sunday afternoon, don't you — oh, no! Why didn't you tell me?'

Eyes now wide open, she dumped the pup on the grass under the table and gazed in dismay at the damp patch on her skirt. 'It's not funny,' she told her giggling children, then rounded on James. 'And you can wipe that smile from your face. She's peeing on your shoe now.'

★ ★ ★

A convoy of four coaches were queuing at the exit from the Lyndhurst car park, waiting to take their passengers home to Swansea, Bristol, Birmingham and Portsmouth. Most of the Sunday drivers had already left, so Michael had a choice of parking spaces.

'You'll be lucky to find anywhere open here,' he said, as he locked the door.

Mary was finding it difficult to talk to him, so she didn't. But she longed for a cup of tea. The restaurant on the corner of the car park was open, but it was full. Probably another coach party. The one with the bow windows on the opposite side of the road looked attractive, but was probably too expensive. She looked down the High Street.

'There's a café further down. The boards are still out.'

'Do you have any money?' Michael asked.

Furious, Mary opened her purse and counted. She knew she had a five-pound note tucked away in the zip pocket of her handbag, but that was needed to get them through the week, until they were paid.

'Eighty-five pence,' she told him, clicking her bag shut. 'Just about enough for two teas.'

Open mouthed, he stared at her. 'And how am I supposed to manage until Friday?'

'If you'd thought about it earlier, you wouldn't be asking me that now.'

'Don't start on that again, Mary. I've had nothing else since we left Brockenhurst and I'll hear no more about it. Anyone would think I lost the money on purpose.'

'What else am I to think? You arranged to meet that man at the pony races, *knowing* there was to be illegal betting, and *knowing* that was our last ten pounds.'

'You wouldn't be going on so if the horse had won, would you now?'

'Of course I would. You promised me you'd stop the gambling and start saving for a proper home of our own. We've only been here a week and you're off again already. You've done nothing but lie to me since we arrived. How could you, Michael?'

'Never mind that. What are we going to live on next week? I haven't even got enough for a packet of cigarette papers, and here you are, spending the last of our money in a café, when we have a perfectly good teapot back in the caravan. Now that doesn't make sense.'

'I'm thirsty *now* Michael. That's sense enough for me.' Mary pushed open the door of the café, which was nearly empty. 'And don't worry. You'll have your sandwiches to take with you and a hot meal at night and it won't hurt you to smoke a little less.'

'Oh, really. And I suppose it won't hurt me to go without my pint at the end of a hard day's work, either.'

Mary gave him such a look over her shoulder, words were not necessary. While Michael sulkily sat at a table at the back of the café, Mary ordered and paid for two teas, and decided that as soon as the remaining people had left, she would tell him about Brendan. No point in waiting any longer for Michael to be in a good mood. Might as well get it over and done with. The day had been well and truly ruined already, it couldn't get much worse. Or could it?

177

A few minutes later, they had the café to themselves. The owner was busy counting the takings. Now was the time.

She pushed the letter across the table to her husband. 'This came yesterday,' she said. 'It's from Brendan.'

His face brightened, as it always did when there was a letter from his son. 'Why didn't you show it to me before?' he asked, as he pulled the letter from the envelope.

'Because Mrs Whitcher forgot to give it to me until late, and you were down at the pub with your new friends. And I hoped that our day out today would put you in a good mood before you read it.'

'And why would I need to be in a good mood? Is he wanting to stay in Ireland when he leaves college? Because he can forget about that. I've been five years without a son, and I'll not be without him a day longer than — '

'Just read the letter, Michael,' Mary quietly said.

It was page two that caused the explosion.

'He wants to do *what?*' Michael shouted so loudly, the proprietor looked up, then re-counted the same pile of coins.

'He wants to become a priest. And there's more. Read on.'

This time Michael finished the letter. His face white, he pushed it back towards Mary. 'I need a drink,' he said.

'It's too early and we have no money,' she reminded him. 'But we both need to discuss it.'

'There's nothing to discuss. It's out of the question.'

'Michael, listen to me. Next summer Brendan will be eighteen. He will then have the legal right to do as he wishes. And if he wishes to become a priest, that's what he will become.'

Michael stared at her, as though not believing her words. 'You're a hard woman, Mary Fitzgerald, to be sure. Is that what you want? To have our only child living thousands of miles away in some God-forsaken country?'

'No. That's not what I want.' She fought back the tears as she went on. 'I would dearly love to have Brendan living close to us again. I would dearly love to see him married, to hold grandchildren in my arms. But it's not what *I* want that counts. Nor what *you* want. It's what *Brendan* wants that's important.'

For a while Michael just stared into his cup of tea. Then he reached across for the letter, read it again, and looked appealingly into Mary's face.

'It could be just a whim — couldn't it?'

Slowly, she shook her head. 'I don't think so. Maeve has been trying to warn me for some time that his inclinations were leaning towards the priesthood, and when we visited him last Christmas he told me how much he admired the missionaries.'

'Why didn't you tell me?'

'I suppose that, like you, I thought it was just a whim. I hoped it was just a whim.' All Mary's anger at the loss of their money evaporated as she gazed into Michael's anguished face. Her voice was gentle as she added, 'I don't want to alienate him from us.'

'Neither do I. But I don't know what to do, Mary. I don't know what to say.'

'We only have two choices, Michael, dear. Either we argue with him and put up a barrier that we may never be able to take down, or — '

'Or?'

'Or we give him our blessing and accept that it is God's will.'

'Couldn't we compromise? Allow him to become a priest, but in Ireland or England, so that we can at least visit.'

'Not if he goes into a missionary order. Then it will be expected that he goes abroad. But it will be several years before he is ordained, so we will be able to visit him.'

'But why in heaven's name does he want to go into some jungle thousands of miles away, to live with savages?'

'He may not have to. Sometimes the missionaries go to a different type of jungle.'

'What do you mean?'

'Concrete jungles.' Mary managed a tiny smile. 'Some of the big cities have savages who need help.'

Michael looked tired, defeated. 'Do you know what he will have to do? You're closer to the Church than I am.'

She nodded. 'I spoke to Father Dogherty after confession last night. He said Brendan will probably become a novitiate of the Franciscan Order in Dublin when he is eighteen.'

'I've heard of them. Would he be there for long?'

'About a year. Then he will have to study philosophy for two years and theology for four years.'

Michael looked very slightly happier. 'And if he

changes his mind during that time, he can leave, can't he?'

'I suppose so. But, to be honest, I don't really think he will. Brendan has never been an impulsive boy. He thinks things out very carefully before he makes up his mind about anything. You can see from the letter that his heart is set upon becoming a missionary. And once his mind is made up, he rarely changes it.'

Michael's head drooped with unhappiness. 'What shall we do, Mary? Without him, I mean.'

'We'll do what we've been doing for the past five years without him. We'll work hard and we'll make a home.' She stretched out her hand and covered his. 'And we'll have each other.'

'I know.' He looked up into her face, with tears in his eyes. 'You've been a good wife, Mary. I couldn't have asked for better.' His voice cracked a little. 'But I'm not at all sure that I can go on without my son.'

13

The brother of the headmistress and the son of the landlady of the Blacksmith's Arms both came back safe and sound from the Falklands, but the caretaker's son was not so lucky. Even three years later, his father could not control his grief.

'If only he was buried in the village churchyard, so we could put flowers on his grave, but to think of him all those thousands of miles away at the bottom of the sea — ' He turned away to wipe his eyes with his handkerchief, then recovered a little and went on, 'At least they should have brought the bodies back so we could mourn our boys properly, not just scuttle the ship and call it a war grave.'

James had never particularly liked the caretaker, but he felt an overwhelming sympathy for the man, who was struggling to come to terms with his loss and needed a grave to weep over before he could accept what had happened.

'I suppose it would have risked other lives to attempt it — the *Sir Galahad* was very badly damaged.' He didn't add that there wouldn't have been whole bodies to recover, just charred remains.

'That's what the wife said. She keeps telling me to pull myself together.'

Tightening and testing the strings of the piano, which had deteriorated each time he tuned it, James said, 'Do you have any other family?'

'I've got a married son out in Saudi; he only

comes back once in a blue moon; and a daughter who works for a television company in London. Production secretary or something like that, she calls herself.'

James detected a note of bitterness. 'That's a very good job,' he commented. 'At least she's near enough to visit.'

The caretaker looked away. 'She's living with some coloured bloke and she knows I don't like him, so she keeps her distance.'

'Oh.'

'But Dave was different. He thought the world of Freda and me.'

'Dave?' James's head jerked up. 'Your son was called David?'

The caretaker nodded. 'He was a smashing-looking lad. Did I ever show you his picture?'

'No.' James's heart turned over as he studied the snapshot of the young man in uniform. The name, and the uniform, brought the tragedy too close to home. 'A handsome boy,' he agreed, handing back the photograph. 'I have a son called David,' he went on. 'He went along to the Naval Recruitment office in Southampton yesterday.'

'Fancies a life at sea, does he?'

'Marines.'

'Talk him out of it. They always cop it when there's trouble.'

'I know. That's why I was so relieved he was too young for the Falklands.' James began to pack away his tools. 'They've told him he can apply to go to Lympston next year.'

'Where's that?'

'Somewhere in Devon. It's a training place for young officers.'

'Will you let him go?'

'He'll be eighteen on Christmas Day. I couldn't stop him even if I wanted to.'

'Don't you want to?'

James pondered for a moment. 'From the risk point of view — yes, of course. But he's never wanted to do anything else. Joined the Scouts and Cadets as soon as he was old enough. In fact his whole life has revolved around a service career, and sport.' James clipped the toolcase shut. 'I think David will make a good officer and I can only wish him well and pray that we won't have another Falklands.'

★ ★ ★

The Brigadier knew where Lympston was, and he was most interested in David's plans.

'Fine bunch of men, the Marines. Can't do better than to encourage your sons to join the services. Is your other boy just as keen?'

'No. Robert is the mechanical one. Actually, he's struck lucky. The local garage has agreed to take him on as an apprentice when he leaves school in July.'

The Brigadier nodded. 'Good training for a young fellow who's useful with his hands. And the girl?'

'Julie's the only one following in my footsteps.'

'A female piano-tuner, eh?'

'Not quite.' James laughed aloud at the thought, then wondered briefly why there shouldn't be female piano-tuners. 'I meant the interest in music. She's a gifted pianist. Could probably have been good enough for concert work, but decided she would rather teach. She's in her second year at music college.'

The Brigadier looked impressed. 'You must be a proud man.'

'Indeed I am, sir. I couldn't have wished for them to turn out differently.'

James was surprised at the way the conversation was turning. The Brigadier had rarely shown any interest in his private life. Perhaps it had something to do with growing older? Reflecting on what he might have missed by not having a family.

As if thinking aloud, the old gentleman quietly murmured, 'I had hoped Ralph would continue the family tradition. But he prefers to play around with the money markets.' He stood up and walked across to the open window, with its impressive view of landscaped gardens, sloping lawns, and acres of woodlands beyond the river. 'All this will be his one day,' he mused.

'Does he have sons who might be interested?'

'No. Married once. American heiress. Didn't last.' After a pause, he quietly said, 'I suppose Ralph will find a way of profiting from his inheritance. More than likely he'll open it up to the public, like Beaulieu and Broadlands. Or sell it to the National Trust.'

James eased his back muscles and glanced out of the window. 'We have a family membership for the National Trust,' he commented. 'And I must say I'm very impressed with the way they care for beautiful places like this.'

The Brigadier nodded. 'Better than letting them go to seed. But not quite what I had in mind for Cranleigh Manor.' Suddenly, he turned. 'I've been wondering whether you can assist me in a plan of campaign.'

His mind half on the conversation and half on a fractious G sharp, James looked up, wondering what the Brigadier had in mind. 'If I can sir, of course.'

'I've invited the people from the village to help me celebrate my birthday. I'm told that eighty years is worth celebrating, so felt I should do something. Last time I had a garden party was for the Silver Jubilee of Her Majesty.'

'From what I heard, it was most enjoyable. Something for all ages, I believe.'

'Exactly. Games and tea for the children. It seems those big castle things they bounce on are very popular. The catering people have promised a splendid buffet for the adults. With champagne, of course. And it has been suggested that a dance of some sort might be a nice way to round off the day. I believe they call it a disco.'

'I'm sure it will be a great success.' James still couldn't fathom out his own involvement.

'It was also suggested that we have some kind of musical entertainment,' the Brigadier continued. 'Chappie from the golf club offered to organise taped music. But I'd prefer proper music, you know. Wondered if you could oblige?'

'You'd like me to recommend a string quartet, or something like that?'

'Hadn't thought of that. Good idea, Woodson, but

what I really have in mind is a pianist.'

'Oh, I see. Background cabaret music.'

'That sort of thing, yes. With the windows open, we should be able to use the Broadwood, don't you think?'

'It may need a little amplification, but yes, the sound should carry quite well.'

'And I'm wondering whether the young curate's wife would agree to sing for us. Haven't heard her myself, but understand that she has a trained voice. Do you think she might be persuaded?'

'I don't see why not, and she does have a wonderful voice.' So that's what he's trying to say, James thought. 'Would you like me to ask her? I shall be tuning her piano this afternoon.'

'Very good of you, young man. Thank you.' The Brigadier tidied his moustache. 'And would you be able to accompany her, and provide some pleasing music during the afternoon?'

'Me?' This wasn't quite what James had expected.

The Brigadier looked searchingly at James. 'You've been tuning this piano for — how long?'

James searched his mind. 'Twenty years or more, I suppose.'

'And I have heard you play some damned good music during that time.' The old gentleman ran his hand lovingly across the polished surface of the piano. 'You care about this piano. Others might not. So I'd be much obliged if you would . . . '

Now James knew what the Brigadier had in mind. He wanted to make sure that no one stood a glass of wine on the piano or allowed it to become damaged in any way. It wasn't just a pianist he needed, but a

187

minder. And James felt honoured that he was so trusted. Only too often had he seen what could happen to pianos that were neglected, like the one in the village hall. That had been a good piano until too many pints of beer had slopped inside. But this one was a treasure. It would be sacrilege to allow any harm to come to such a beautiful instrument.

'What date is your birthday, sir?' he asked.

'Seventh of June. A Friday. Saturday would be more convenient for the villagers. So the garden party will be on the eighth. You're not on holiday?'

James flicked through his diary. 'Not this year. We've just bought the adjoining cottage so all our resources will be heading in that direction.'

Mrs Cooper had finally been persuaded by her daughter to go into a retirement home and James and Katherine had jumped at the opportunity to buy the property cheaply. It was rather dilapidated and would need months of work to put right years of neglect. They planned to knock down the communicating wall and extend the lounge and kitchen right across and create a downstairs cloakroom, enlarge their bedroom to include a shower unit and so end the morning queue for the bathroom. James knew he ought to keep every weekend free for the project until it was finished, but he really was quite fond of the old gentleman — and his piano.

He looked up. 'I'd be happy to oblige, and thank you for asking.'

'Splendid.' The Brigadier smiled. 'I trust your good lady won't object? She is, of course, welcome to accompany you.'

'It's very kind of you to suggest it, Brigadier, but my wife is a weekend riding instructor and the summer months are particularly busy for her.'

'Of course. Now, about the fee. Does forty pounds sound adequate?'

'Forty pounds? Why yes — thank you — that's fine.'

Forty pounds would pay for the hire of the cement mixer. Oh, yes, thought James. That was adequate. More than adequate.

14

Cranleigh Manor was buzzing with activity when James set out his music. Caterers were polishing wine glasses in a huge marquee under the watchful eye of the butler, while Mrs Jenkins' team of flower arrangers placed posies on the tables. Electricians were running cables from the house to provide lighting for the evening, and Nigel Taylor was hurrying backwards and forwards to an open site down near the river, carrying huge boxes marked **HANDLE WITH CARE!** and covering them with what looked like sandbags.

'He's terrified the children might arrive early and pre-empt the fireworks display,' Megan explained, coming into the drawing room and handing her music to James.

'Ah, I wondered what he was up to.' James slotted her music into place and turned to look at her. 'You look very nice,' he said, and meant it. Although she had lost little weight since the birth of her twins, the straight style of the black and white outfit with the loose tunic made her appear slimmer, and her hair had been swept up into a more flattering style than usual. And she was wearing make-up.

'Thank you.' She looked pleased. 'I didn't have anything that was quite right for today until Susan took me shopping. She insisted on buying it for me as an advance birthday present. And she did my hair and make-up.'

'It suits you. In fact, you look quite elegant.'

Again that pleased, slightly shy, smile. 'Susan is incredibly generous. Sometimes I think too much so. I can't give anything back, you see.'

'You give her your friendship. Money can't buy that.'

'That's true. I'd never thought of it like that. And she seems to get such pleasure in giving things to people. When we were collecting prizes for the Christmas raffle, she gave her complete Swarovski collection — and you know how expensive they are! But she said she was now collecting Capodimonte and wanted someone else to enjoy looking at the crystal. Isn't that a wonderful kindness?'

'Very much so. Megan, have you seen the Brigadier? I need to check one or two things with him.'

'No, I'm afraid I haven't.' Megan glanced nervously at her reflection in a mirror, and added, 'I do hope he will think this is suitable for the occasion.'

'I'm sure he — ' Before James could complete the sentence, the gentleman in question came into the room, accompanied as usual by his dogs.

'Ah, there you are, Woodson. And Mrs — '

'Taylor,' Megan finished for him. 'Megan Taylor.'

'Forgive me. I'm so accustomed to referring to your husband as 'the young curate'. Bad habit, I'm afraid.' He held out his hand. 'And if I may say so, my dear, you look charming. Quite charming.'

'Thank you, Brigadier.' Megan blushed very slightly as he brushed her hand with his lips.

'I understand from Woodson here that you are

including the ballad 'Songs My Mother Taught Me,' in your repertoire?'

Megan looked a little anxious as she nodded.

'Dvořák wrote some memorable pieces. Splendid choice.'

James was delighted. He had also chosen one of Dvořák's preludes as part of the 'background' music.

'Before I forget,' the Brigadier continued. 'Message from your husband. Your son has tripped over near the river. No real damage done. 'Boys will be boys' were his exact words.' There was a twinkle in the Brigadier's eye.

'It'll be that little demon, Matthew,' Megan sighed. 'It's my fault for leaving him while Nigel was so busy.' Then she chuckled. 'Sounds as though a complete change of clothing is called for. Excuse me.'

The Brigadier watched Megan cross the lawn in search of her wayward son. 'The young curate has got himself a fine wife there,' he mused. 'As for the rector — my housekeeper tells me she doesn't know how she would have managed without him and his good lady.'

'An event on this scale would take quite a lot of organising,' James commented.

'Needs the preparation of a military operation. But you can't commandeer your men for a private celebration. Not that I needed to, of course.'

'I'm sure you weren't short of willing volunteers.'

'Got it in one, Woodson. The manager of the golf club has taken on all the catering arrangements, together with Johnson and Mrs Henshaw, of course.

And Bridges, the builder chappie, organised the marquee and labour.'

'They've made a very good job of it.'

'Quite so. And Mrs Bridges offered her services as hostess. Damned good of her to take over that duty from the housekeeper.'

James wondered how Mrs Henshaw felt about the arrangement, remembering that she had mentioned how much she had enjoyed hostessing the last garden party.

The Brigadier was still speaking. 'And much of the entertainment has been arranged by the village people. They refuse to tell me what to expect.' He chuckled. 'The only item we couldn't order in advance was the weather.'

'Ah, that's always a wild card.'

'Indeed. Listened to the forecast this morning. Fair — winds five to six — chance of odd showers. But we can take shelter in the marquee if necessary.'

After they had checked his programme of music, James took a gift-wrapped package and card from his case. 'I'd just like to wish you many happy returns of yesterday, sir.'

The Brigadier looked surprised as he unwrapped the package. Two years ago, James had been persuaded to join the Bramblehurst Woodcarvers' Group. He was sure he would never be able to reach the excellence of those who could carve breathtaking pieces in great detail, but discovered he had a talent for simple designs, allowing the shape and grain of the wood to dictate the finished work. Recently, he had been given a partly used block of beech and immediately he felt that the hollowed

193

area suggested the features of an owl. He knew the Brigadier liked owls, and decided to carve it as a gift. As he worked on the wood, the curves became more suggestion than precise copy of a barn owl, perched on a tree stump, head half turned in a watchful manner. Katherine loved it, and had polished it to a satin finish. But James awaited the Brigadier's reaction with apprehension.

The old gentleman took the carving over to the light, turning it this way and that. Then he turned back to James.

'Whoever carved this has captured the spirit of the barn owl. I have often watched them on the estate and admired their grace in flight.'

As pleased as Punch, James nodded. 'Actually, I carved it myself,' he said. 'I'm very much an amateur, but I hoped you might like it.'

The Brigadier's head turned sharply. 'You astonish me, Woodson,' he declared, then studied the carving again. 'Nothing amateurish about it. Obviously a man of many talents.' Holding out his hand, he came back to the piano. 'Greatly appreciated. It will have pride of place in my study, we can keep an eye on each other.' He laughed a little gruffly at his own humour, then pointed to a carriage clock on the mantelpiece. 'The staff presented me with that handsome timepiece yesterday. Everyone so kind.' He glanced out of the window. 'Guests arriving. Must ask Mrs Bridges to remind me of their names.' At the door into the garden, he paused for a moment to say, 'Thank you, young man. Very good of you.' Then he was off, his long stride and straight back belying his years.

It amused James to be called a young man, especially now he was in his late forties. But he supposed that everyone under sixty must appear young to an octogenarian. For a short while he watched the Brigadier greeting his guests with old-world courtesy, while Johnson proffered champagne, his white gloves ensuring that no smudge spoiled the gleam on the silver salver. He must be getting on a bit, James thought. Probably about seventy. But, like his employer, he showed no signs of the stiffness that often comes with ageing. Mrs Henshaw, wearing a navy dress that looked like the 'Sunday best' version of her normal uniform, circulated with a tray of canapés. James wondered how old she was. Apart from her hair being completely grey and a slight limp from a knee operation, she was another who had changed little over the years, but she must be nudging sixty. As she directed a group of children towards the bouncy castle, Mrs Henshaw glanced across at Susan Burridge — with 'one of her looks'. No, she was obviously not happy with the arrangement.

His attention turned to Susan. Her daffodil-yellow silk dress and matching, wide-brimmed hat would not have looked out of place at a Buckingham Palace Garden Party, but he had to admit she looked extremely attractive, the bright colour of the outfit enhanced by her honey-coloured tan.

Time to provide the background music. The amplification was just right, and James enjoyed playing a selection of light music, ranging from Noël Coward and Cole Porter, to the more modern tunes of the Beatles and Michel Legrand. After the visitors had satisfied their appetites from tables groaning with goodies, Mrs Henshaw popped her head around the door.

'The Brigadier asked me to let you know that the children are about to entertain him, so perhaps you would like to have a break. I've set aside a plate of food for you in the marquee, Mr Woodward. Must dash — Johnson needs clean gloves.'

James found a vacant chair outside the marquee and watched as two boys approached the Brigadier, carrying a standard rose tree, swathed in gold satin ribbons.

'We all collected for this, sir, and Leanne — ' the spokesboy beckoned fiercely to a small girl carrying a huge card. 'Leanne has your birthday card. All the children in the school have signed it . . . and — and — ' Frantically he looked at the headmistress, who quietly prompted him, 'And,' he continued with a rush of words, 'we all hope you have many more happy birthdays, Brigadier Beresford-Lawson and — ' Another quick glance at the headmistress, 'and thank you very much sir, for inviting us to your lovely party.' With a stiff bow from the waist, both boys thrust the tree towards the startled Brigadier, who stood up and bent over the boys to formally shake each hand.

'Thank you, young sirs,' he said, then turned towards the girl. 'And is this splendid card for me?' Speechless, she nodded, gave him the card, uncertainly held out her hand, then leaned forward and quickly kissed him on the cheek, before running back to the security of the headmistress.

The Brigadier said, 'It is many years since I have

been kissed by a pretty girl. And it is still a rewarding experience.' He looked at the headmistress. 'Thank you for your thoughtfulness. It means a great deal.'

Smiling, Mrs Warren said, 'We have another surprise for you, sir. I heard recently that a lady who lived and worked in this village for many years will shortly be moving to live with her niece in Kent, and I took the liberty of asking Johnson and Mrs Henshaw whether she could be invited to your celebration. They felt you would be pleased to see her before she moves away.' Mrs Warren stood to one side as a frail figure moved slowly towards the Brigadier, leaning heavily upon her stick, her other arm supported by a companion. It was Miss Harding, the headmistress who had left under such painful circumstances almost fifteen years earlier.

Now *she* really has changed, James thought. Snowy-haired and with stooped shoulders, Miss Harding had aged beyond belief.

The Brigadier held out his hands. 'My dear lady, I am delighted to see you.' Then, to James's surprise, he kissed her on both cheeks.

Suddenly, James noticed Susan Burridge, standing behind the Brigadier, one hand protecting her hat from the breeze. The expression upon her face was so full of anger, he drew a sharp breath. Then it was gone, so suddenly that he wondered whether he had imagined it. Smiling graciously, she beckoned to Johnson.

'Would you please find a chair for Miss Harding, and her companion,' she asked. 'Perhaps they would be more comfortable over there, in the shade?'

But the Brigadier preferred to have his old friend sit by his side, and Johnson was well prepared. Before Mrs Burridge could protest further, the headmistress was being helped into a cushioned chair and a car rug tucked snugly around her knees. The other lady sat near Mrs Warren.

Next it was the turn of the school choir to sing, 'Nymphs and Shepherds'. They sang rather well, James thought. While the maypole was being made secure, supervised by the head gardener, obviously concerned about his precious lawn, the Brigadier and Miss Harding remained deep in conversation until the children from the playgroup took the brightly coloured ribbons and positioned themselves ready for the first dance. All went well until three-year-old Matthew Taylor decided that it would be much more fun if he did a reverse turn and skipped in the opposite direction. His twin sister thought the best solution was to shove him back into place, he tripped over for the second time that day, and the children tumbled over him until their ribbons were hopelessly tangled. And while Megan and Mrs Warren extricated children from the scrum and sorted out ribbons, Matthew giggled, quite unconcerned as to the chaos he had caused. Oh, yes, James thought. He was certainly a little demon. But such a handsome little demon. Unlike his siblings, Matthew favoured his father's colouring, his fair hair and huge blue eyes giving him an angelic choirboy appearance, which probably got him out of as many scrapes as he managed to get into. The onlookers thought the whole scenario was hilarious and Matthew played to the crowd, bowing and laughing, until a few quiet words from his mother wiped the smile from his face.

Eventually, the dance was recommenced, and the errant youngster behaved himself, casting a nervous glance at his mother from time to time, but rewarded with a hug after the dance had ended. The infants performed a more intricate pattern, and the juniors donned their bells and hobby-horses and gave a demonstration of local Morris Dances, followed by the Hampshire Garland Ladies, who had been booked as a surprise.

The Reverend Jenkins, who had been appointed MC, then announced that the children could play on the bouncy castle until their tea was ready and, in the meantime, it was his pleasure to introduce his daughter, Megan, who would be accompanied by James Woodward, 'who has visited Fivepenny Lanes twice a year for as long as I have lived in the Vicarage, and left our pianos sounding much more harmonious.'

When Megan came to the piano to check her music, James couldn't resist asking her how she had managed to tame Matthew.

'Oh, I just said, 'no more bouncy castle — unless . . . ' He knew I meant it.' With a smile as mischievous as her son's, she took her place just outside the French doors, where a microphone was waiting.

Her voice was so rich, it barely needed amplification, and James noticed the Brigadier smile as she followed the Dvořák piece with Gershwin's haunting 'Summertime'. He also noticed his host glance once or twice towards the driveway at the

199

side of the house, then at his watch, as though expecting someone. It wasn't until half-way through the final song, Romberg's 'One Kiss', that the missing guest arrived, with as much noise as though heralded by a fanfare of trumpets, but not so tuneful. All heads turned as the turbo engine of a very fast car blasted their eardrums, churned gravel on the drive, and revved fiercely for too long, until blessed peace was restored, punctuated by the slam of a car door. As the driver came into view near the French windows and halted, obviously realising just in time that he was about to cross in front of the singer, James glanced at the tall figure carrying a flat gift-wrapped package. Apart from the receding hairline, there was a strong likeness to the Brigadier. Ralph Beresford-Lawson, heir to Cranleigh Manor, had finally deigned to put in an appearance at his uncle's birthday party.

After the enthusiastic applause had died away, the new arrival crossed to his uncle, shook his hand, and apologised.

'Traffic was bloody awful. About time they widened that bottleneck near Marwell.'

'I was becoming anxious, knowing your preference for speed.' The Brigadier's smile was a little wry. 'Was that your new toy we heard?'

'The Lotus? Yes. I really opened her up once I was clear of London.' Ralph interpreted his uncle's expression correctly. 'Kept an eye out for the police, of course. Don't want to lose my licence again.' He motioned to Johnson. 'I've left my bags in the car. Take them up to my room, will you, old boy?' As the butler nodded and walked towards the house, Ralph commented, 'Isn't it about time you put Johnson out to grass, uncle? He must be past his sell-by date.'

The Brigadier's expression was thunderous, his voice tight. 'When Johnson wishes to retire, we will discuss it. Until then, I would be obliged if you would refer to him with more respect.'

'Sorry.' Ralph's tone was flippant. 'No wish to offend the old retainer. Now . . . ' He offered the parcel. 'I expect you can guess what this is by the shape. Happy birthday, Uncle Edwin.'

As the Brigadier removed the final wrapping, there was a gasp from the onlookers and someone murmured, 'It's a David Hockney — must have cost the earth!' It looked as though it was one of his theatrical designs, with masks and flames. But James wasn't sure that it would be quite to the old gentleman's taste. It would be more at home in an art gallery.

After quite a long pause, the Brigadier murmured, 'It's certainly colourful. Will brighten up the dining room. Thank you, my boy.'

'A friend sold it to me, privately. He was terribly cash-strapped and needed money quickly, so I was able to knock him down somewhat. Otherwise it would have gone to auction.' Ralph rubbed his hands together. 'Knew I couldn't go wrong with it. Anything by Hockney is a good investment.' He glanced towards the marquee. 'Ah, Mrs Henshaw. Just the person I want to see. Rustle me up a plate of something while I help myself to some champers, will you?'

Megan glanced sideways at James. 'If that's our

'squire apparent', I can only hope and pray that the Brigadier lives for ever,' she murmured.

'A few other people might say 'Amen' to that,' he answered. 'Not quite a chip off the old block, is he?' Then, feeling he might have said too much, James quickly changed the subject. 'You sang beautifully, Megan. It was a pleasure to play for you.'

'Thank you. I really enjoyed it. Perhaps when my scallywags are a little older I can do some concert work again.'

'Good — and if you need an accompanist . . . '

'I'll know where to come.'

James looked out at the little groups of chattering guests. 'I suppose I ought to play again, while there's not much going on.'

'Hang on a moment, will you? Daddy has a presentation in a moment. I'll just go and remove my offspring from under Mother's wing while she still has her sanity.'

The Brigadier and Susan Burridge had followed his nephew into the marquee, so James decided to have a word with Miss Harding.

'I so enjoyed your playing, Mr Woodward,' she said. 'And such a delight to hear Megan sing again.' She returned a wave to someone. 'Do you know, I taught most of these young mothers. And here they are with their own children.' For a moment she was thoughtful, then said. 'I wasn't sure that I could ever show my face in the village again, but everyone has been so welcoming.'

'They've missed you.'

'Well, I have certainly missed them. Mrs Jenkins has kept in touch, and my good friend, Miss

Partridge, gave me the confidence to come today. She ordered a taxi and just would not take no for an answer. Do you know Miss Partridge? She lives out at Deepdene Farm.'

Following her gaze towards a lady engrossed in intimate conversation with another, James shook his head.

'Miss Partridge is the librarian in Winchester,' Miss Harding went on, 'and she told me that another of those dreadful letters was sent about Mrs Faversham when she was president of the WI. As you can imagine, I understood perfectly how the poor lady must have felt.' She shook her head. 'I still cannot believe that anyone I know could be quite so unpleasant.'

'Neither can I. And you didn't have to leave the village, you know. Nobody believed the rumours.'

'It was the petition. It stated that I wasn't fit to teach children. A few believed the rumours enough to sign it, Mr Woodward.' The pain was evident on her face.

'I was told that they were all newcomers who didn't know you. They were very much in the minority. Just following like sheep.'

'Perhaps. But I was so aware of the whispering and speculation. And each time, I wondered whether it was this person who had written the letter, or that one.'

'Did the police not find any clues at all from the letter?'

'Not really.' Miss Harding smiled a tiny smile. 'The envelope was manila and the paper of the kind anyone can buy from W H Smith's or Woolworth's.

They examined it carefully, of course, to see if there was anything significant about the typewriter. It reminded me of an Agatha Christie investigation.'

'And did they come up with anything?'

'Only that it was a manual typewriter. I felt it had been hurriedly typed, or perhaps the person was inexperienced.'

It was James's turn to smile. 'Now you are beginning to sound like Miss Marples. What made you think that?'

'Oh, merely that the double letters jammed. For instance, in the sentence, 'Innocent little lives can be corrupted so easily', the double n's, t's and r's were all overtyped, as one letter. Not very much of a clue, was it?' Miss Harding sighed and shook her head. 'But it happened a long time ago, and I am so pleased to see all my good friends again before I leave. Now, do tell me about your family. Miss Partridge informs me that your daughter is at music college and your son is an officer in the Marines. And has the Border collie settled in happily?'

How on earth did she know all that? James wondered, looking again at the librarian. He had never met her before today and the only people who knew anything about his family were the Brigadier — highly unlikely; the caretaker — quite unlikely; and Mrs Jenkins. Ah! The mobile library. What a wonderful grapevine it must be.

After a few moments' pleasant conversation, another lady hovered near Miss Harding's chair. James stood up and offered his own chair.

'Oh, that's all right, thanks. I won't be a moment. Just want to thank you for writing when our Dave was killed, Miss Harding. It was very good of you.'

'Not at all, Mrs Mason. I was so very sad when I read about it in the newspaper. All your children were a credit to you, and David was one of my favourite pupils.'

'I should have written back, but there were so many letters, and George was in such a state — still is.'

'So I understand, and I am truly sorry. It must make life doubly difficult for you. How long is it now, two years?'

'Actually, it's three years today. That's why George didn't come. Said he couldn't face it.'

This must be 'Mrs Caretaker', James realised, as Miss Harding nodded in sympathy.

'That's understandable,' she said. 'It's very courageous of you to come.'

'Dave wouldn't want us to grieve for ever. He believed that you should care more about the living than the dead. Perhaps that's the way soldiers have to think.'

Before the headmistress could answer, Percy Burridge approached James.

'Sorry for barging in, but I've got a bit of a problem. Happen you might be able to help out.'

'If I can. What's the problem?'

'The DJ has just arrived to set up for the disco, and daft so-and-so has left speakers at home. He noticed you had one linked into the piano, and wondered if he could borrow it — and have you got another?'

'Actually, it's not mine. I borrowed it from a friend and promised to return it this evening.' James glanced at Mrs Mason. 'But there are a couple in the village hall. Do you think your husband would lend them?'

Mrs Mason nodded and turned to Mr Burridge. 'Tell George I said you could borrow them. He should be earthing up the potatoes. Holly Cottage. Bottom end of Forge Lane. If he's not there, he'll be up at the village hall, fiddling about with something or other.'

As Mr Burridge hurried away, the Brigadier reappeared, together with his nephew and Mrs Burridge. Immediately, the Reverend Jenkins grabbed the microphone.

'As you all know — all, that is, apart from Brigadier Beresford-Lawson — we have been having secret-service type meetings with the estate manager over a suitable gift to mark a special birthday, and this comes with the very best wishes of every person in Fivepenny Lanes.'

Speechless, the Brigadier unwrapped a handsome, handmade twelve-bore. As he examined the engraving on the stock, ran his hand along the smoothly polished barrel, and lifted the gun to his eye, James could have sworn that he saw the glistening of a tear. And no wonder. The gun must have cost a couple of thousand at least. It said much for the respect and affection felt for the squire.

The estate manager stepped forward. 'The sighting pin can be adjusted, sir, if necessary.'

'It looks spot on.' The Brigadier shook the man's hand. 'Thank you, Goddard. This is the one I would have chosen.' His gaze embraced everyone. 'I thank you all — from the heart. Not sure it is deserved.

But greatly appreciated.'

At that moment, the two sisters who ran the tea-shop appeared, carrying between them an enormous square birthday cake, which they placed on a small table and waited — without a word, without a smile.

Mrs Henshaw quickly came to the rescue. 'A birthday party is not complete without a cake, sir, and when Miss Felicity and Miss Patience offered to make one, we knew it would be perfect.'

'It is perfection indeed.' The old gentleman smiled as he examined the beautifully executed figure eighty and the iced plaques depicting his love of hunting, shooting and fishing placed in the circles of the figures. 'I am quite overwhelmed.' He beamed at the two ladies. 'Such skill. Thank you so much, Miss . . . and . . . ' Mrs Henshaw prompted him as he shook hands with the sisters. Photographs were taken of the Brigadier, presentation knife poised for the first cut, while everyone sang the traditional birthday song. Then the two po-faced ladies promptly lifted the cake and silently toddled into the marquee.

'I'll help them,' the housekeeper murmured, obviously trying to stifle a twitch from her lips. 'And while the children are having their tea, would you mind playing some more of your lovely music, please, Mr Woodward.'

This time, James had chosen a selection of songs from the shows, and he was quietly playing 'Sunrise, Sunset' from *Fiddler on the Roof*, when he became aware of voices in low conversation. With the French windows open, they were just near enough for him to recognise Susan Burridge and Ralph Beresford-Lawson.

'Do you live in London?' Mrs Burridge was asking.

'When I was a naughty boy and drove a bit fast, it became awkward to commute from Gloucestershire. So I bought one of the Canary Wharf apartments. More convenient for the office.' His voice sounded a little woolly, as though the champagne was beginning to take effect.

'What sort of work do you do?'

'The sort that makes megabucks for investors.'

'Oh, that sounds like the sort of thing my son will be looking for when he graduates. He's taking — reading — accountancy.'

'Really. And is your husband an accountant, Mrs Burridge?' He emphasised the *Mrs*.

'Heavens, no.' James recognised that Mrs Burridge was putting on her 'posh' voice. 'My husband is a builder of some note in this area. He is responsible for all the better quality developments, as well as the industrial estate on the Andover Road. You must have seen the signs, *Better Burridge Homes*?'

'Afraid I was whizzing along a bit.' There was a slight pause, then Ralph's voice became more seductive. 'Busy man is he, Percy Burridge, builder of better homes? Travels around a bit?'

'Sometimes. When he travels to London, I try to accompany him. It keeps me in touch with the real world.'

'I see.' Another pause. 'Perhaps we could have lunch one day, if your husband is busy at a meeting.'

This time Mrs Burridge paused, for quite a while, before she said, 'That would be nice. Shall I give you one of our cards?'

'No. I'll give you one of mine.'

'Thank you.' Susan sighed. 'I'd better go over to your uncle while he's circulating. After all, I am his hostess for the day.'

'If you must. Tally-ho.'

Well, well, thought James, as he went into his own arrangement of 'Baubles, Bangles and Beads'. Susan Burridge is playing with fire if she gets involved with the Brigadier's nephew. She'd always seemed such a devoted wife — but perhaps she has her husband's interests at heart? Or Jonathan's? Still, if Percy Burridge found out . . .

It was time for Megan to join him again. But just as she was half-way through Andrew Lloyd Webber's 'Memory', there was a disturbance, which halted the entertainment, and the party. Percy Burridge almost fell through the open doors and collapsed on to a chair.

'Where's Susan?' he gasped.

James could see her hurrying towards the house. She must have seen her husband. 'She's coming,' he said.

'What's happened?' Susan asked, looking frightened as she knelt beside her husband. 'Have you had an accident?'

'No. Not me. The caretaker.' His eyes were wide with horror as he stared back at her. 'The daft bugger's gone and hanged himself!'

★ ★ ★

The shocked silence was broken by Susan's whispered, 'Where?'

'In the village hall.' Her husband rubbed a hand across his eyes, as though trying to obliterate the image. 'I'll have to get someone to come back with me and help cut the poor blighter down. Can't let his missus see him like that.' He breathed deeply. 'He's not a pretty sight.'

'Do you want me to come?' James asked, hoping he would say no.

'Thanks, but I suppose it ought to be the new village copper — and we'll need Dr Morrissey for the death certificate.'

'They're both over near the marquee, talking to Daddy,' Megan said. 'I'd better get Mum as well, and Mrs Mason.'

Susan Burridge placed a comforting hand on her husband's shoulder. 'What can I do to help, love?' she asked.

He patted her hand. 'The Brigadier will have to know. Can you find him, lass?'

She didn't have to. The Brigadier had realised something was amiss and come to investigate. After Mr Burridge had told the grim story, the old gentleman looked shocked, but quickly took charge, as befitted a man of his rank.

'Take your parents and the man's wife into my study, my dear,' he told Megan. 'I'll deal with the others.' He turned to Susan Burridge. 'If you would be so kind as to ask the doctor and the police officer to join us here?' Next, he crossed to a silver tray with a decanter and glasses and poured a generous measure of brandy and handed it to Percy Burridge.

'I can't — I'm driving.'

'The doctor can drive — ' The Brigadier paused and glanced at James. 'Have to make an announcement, of course — later.'

'Do you want me to wait in the garden?' James asked.

'No need. You already know about the unfortunate incident.' The Brigadier beckoned to his estate manager from the window. 'And some might be tempted to question you.'

By the time everything had been explained, the brandy had restored some of the colour to Mr Burridge's face. 'Better get it over and done with,' he said, returning the empty brandy balloon to the tray.

As the young policeman closed his notebook, he said, 'First thing I must do is to look for any evidence that might assist the coroner. Did you find a letter, or a note, Mr Burridge?'

'Not as such. I looked for one in his office, and the bookings diary was open at today's date. He'd just written, 'Sorry Freda' across the page.'

'Ah. Anything else?'

'A half-empty whisky bottle was on the — Oh, I see what you mean. Only a few more words, but couldn't make out the scrawl. And I started to feel a bit funny, like, so had to get out.'

'Are you sure you're up to going back, sir?'

Before Mr Burridge could answer, the door opened and Mrs Mason came into the room, with Mr and Mrs Jenkins. The Brigadier stepped forward and took both her hands.

'My dear lady,' he said, his voice full of

compassion. 'Can't tell you how sorry I am — we all are.'

'Thank you, Brigadier.' Mrs Mason was pale but composed. She glanced at the men waiting by the French door, as though realising unpleasant tasks were ahead. 'Can someone tell me what I have to do now?' she asked.

The Brigadier led her to a chair. 'Just rest there, my dear. These gentlemen will take care of everything.' He motioned for them to leave, then turned back to Mrs Mason. 'A small brandy? Good for shock.'

Mrs Mason shook her head. 'I'm perfectly all right, thank you. Perhaps a glass of water?'

After she had taken a few sips, the Reverend Jenkins said, 'Would you like us to take you back to the Vicarage, Mrs Mason? You can phone your daughter from there if you wish.'

'Thank you, Vicar, but you are needed here. You have to announce the prizes for the children's games — and the dance — and the fireworks.'

They all looked at each other in astonishment. Then the Brigadier gently said, 'But we must cancel them, I'm afraid — in respect for your husband.'

'Respect!' Her voice was so fierce, James blinked. 'My husband showed no respect to anyone. Not to me. Or my other children. All he could think about was himself and his own grief.'

Mrs Jenkins patted her shoulder. 'Some people take longer than others to recover from grief, dear.'

Mrs Mason sighed. 'There's not a day goes by that I don't think about our Dave,' she said. 'But I have to think about Keith and Sandra as well. Did you know George wouldn't let me see my own daughter because he didn't approve of her boyfriend?' She smiled a wry little smile. 'At least I won't have to meet them in secret any more.'

So much unhappiness, James thought. And so unnecessary.

'And it would really upset me if I felt my husband had managed to ruin something the whole village is enjoying,' Mrs Mason continued. 'Please — they don't need to know about George until tomorrow.'

The Brigadier looked towards the rector, who slowly said, 'There will be some who will ask what has happened, but I suppose we could fob them off, if you're sure that's what you want, Mrs Mason?'

'It's what I want, Vicar.' Her voice was firm. 'And it's what Dave would have wanted. Cancelling the party won't bring either of them back, will it?'

'That's true,' Megan said, 'and the children have been looking forward to the fireworks. But you should have somebody with you. Can we contact your daughter?'

'Sandra's filming somewhere in Wiltshire, I believe, but I've got her mobile number at home. She'll get hold of Keith for me — he's in Dubai.' Mrs Mason sighed. 'I'd arranged to go over to my sister's at Romsey tonight, anyway. Had a bit of an argument with George this morning because he wouldn't come to the party with me. So I told him I'd stay the night at Dorothy's.' She took another sip of the water. 'I expect you think I'm hard. But it was just that — I couldn't bear to hear him keep on talking about Dave and what had happened when

213

the ship caught fire. I had to take my mind off it somehow.'

Quietly, Megan said, 'I'll run you over to Romsey, when you're ready.'

'That's all right, dear. I've got to go home for my bag, I can easily phone for a taxi. We've caused quite enough trouble as it is.'

The Brigadier held up his hand. 'My estate manager will drive you. Wherever you wish. I insist.'

'Well, if you're sure? Thank you. You've been very kind.'

'Not at all. Least I can do.'

'Can I wait here till they come back? Just in case there's something ... ' Mrs Mason suddenly stopped, as though a thought had occurred to her. 'If Mr Burridge hadn't gone up to the hall, who would have found him?'

Megan's face was horrified. 'It would have been me,' she whispered. 'With the children for Sunday School.'

'And George knew that.' Mrs Mason's voice was also low. 'He knew I wouldn't go up there tonight. How could he do that?'

Nobody answered. There wasn't an answer.

Eventually, the men returned. The policeman only wanted one piece of information from Mrs Mason. Could she decipher the scribble on the page of the diary? After a moment, she raised her eyes.

'It just says, 'Sorry Freda. I miss him too much.' Nothing else.'

Hours later, after James had packed away his music and commenced his homeward journey, he knew he would never forget the sight of the widow who had politely thanked him for playing some of her favourite music before she had been taken home to memories of a bitter quarrel with her husband only hours before he ended his life. If only she had cried. It would have been more natural.

Then, despite all his efforts, the thought that James had pushed to the back of his mind all afternoon insisted on being acknowledged. Supposing one of his own children died. How would he be able to cope with it? Would Katherine be able to cope with it? The mere thought made him feel physically sick, and he had to take several deep breaths before the nausea cleared.

Then he put his foot down on the accelerator. He couldn't wait to get back to Wisteria Cottage and hold them close.

15

Four years later, building work ceased before the new Town Quay development in Southampton was completed. The builders had gone into liquidation. Michael Fitzgerald thought it was a good opportunity to up sticks and move on. His wife had other ideas.

'It's only a temporary stoppage, Michael,' she protested.

'And what do we live on during this *temporary* stoppage?'

'Sign on at the Job Centre and see what they have to offer. There's that big site up near the civic centre — Marlands. They must need an army of building workers.'

'They've already got an army of building workers. I've asked. And before you come up with any more useless ideas, I've also asked at the Ocean Village site and the office blocks. None of the big builders have any jobs going — take my word for it.'

'Then why not try the small builders? See if there are any housing developments needing someone for a few weeks.'

'There's a recession on, Mary, and it's hitting the housing market — or hadn't you noticed?'

'Of course I noticed. But you've been saying that for years, yet you always managed to find something. When you finished working on the Bargate Centre, you went straight on to that big

216

toyshop, then there was the enormous cinema complex, and the Gateway supermarket. There's always something around the corner.'

'I'm thinking you and me are turning different corners, Mary. The building trade is slipping downhill faster and faster. Look at the way house prices have dropped. People are having to practically give their homes away.'

'I know. And isn't this exactly the right time to start looking for a little house of our own. We wouldn't be wanting anything big. A two-bedroomed terraced house would be within our range.'

He looked at her in astonishment. 'The repayments on the mortgage might be within our range — *Just*. As long as we both have a job.'

'And haven't I just been made chief cook in the canteen? With a rise?'

'So what do we use for a deposit? You tell me.'

Tempted, Mary bit her lip. For some time she had been putting part of her wages into a building society account, letting Michael think she earned less. And after she had made a 'Thomas the Tank Engine' birthday cake for Mrs Whitcher's grandson, orders came in quite regularly. She enjoyed making novelty cakes for children and creating hobby-themed cakes for grown-ups. Most of all, she enjoyed putting a few more pounds in the secret account each week. Michael thought she just did it for the fun of the thing and the cost of the materials. There wasn't much profit and she never lied to Michael — she just didn't enlighten him. Even now, she wasn't sure that it was wise to tell him they almost had enough money for a deposit. He was sure to decide he could turn it into a fortune down at Ladbroke's. So she hedged.

'Well, there's no harm in making a few enquiries, surely? And before you know it, you'll be back working on the Town Quay.'

'I can be working in London.'

'London! Don't they have a recession in London?'

Angrily, Michael waved his arm. 'It's time we moved on, anyway. We've been here too long already.'

'We've tried London once and had to leave because we couldn't afford the terrible high rents. Remember?'

'Maybe we'll have better luck this time.'

'No, Michael. We've had better luck here than anywhere else we've lived. I like my job, and for the first time since we left Ireland, more than twenty years ago, I've been able to make friends. Real friends.'

'You can make new friends in London.'

'I didn't before. How could I, when we were always on the run?'

He didn't answer.

Suddenly, Mary had a brainwave. 'Why don't we go over to Ireland for a few days? Before the winter sets in. Maeve's dying to give us a belated silver wedding party. And it will be the last chance to see Brendan before he's ordained as a deacon. You'd love to see Brendan, now, wouldn't you, darling?'

Mary knew, by Michael's expression, that she'd touched a vulnerable spot.

'Surely we can't afford it?' he said.

Careful now, she thought. Don't give the game away. 'I've some back pay owing to me,' she replied. It was only a little white lie. 'Overtime. And a week's holiday. Let's do it. By the time we come back, someone else will have taken over and you'll be up and down those ladders again.'

'If there's no work, we'll go to London?'

'We'll — talk about it.'

London? Over my dead body, Mary thought. I'll take some of the savings and learn to drive properly, that I will. If I have to call on every builder in Hampshire, touting for work for you, it will be worth it. I won't be dependent on you if I can drive. So if you want to go to London that much, Michael Fitzgerald, you can leave me here. And I'll save harder than ever towards the deposit. One day soon, God willing, we will have that little home of our own.

★　★　★

Percy Burridge gazed out of the drawing room window and watched one of the gardeners sweeping crisp russet leaves from the lawn nearest to the house. His eyes went beyond the man and towards the river, where the water bailiff checked a stretch of bank, thigh-length waders only just protecting him from the swirling waters. If only he could convince the Brigadier that it was the best thing to do in the circumstances.

His dream was interrupted by the door opening. It was the piano-tuner.

219

'Oh, sorry, Mr Burridge. I didn't realise you were in here.'

'Housekeeper asked me to wait in here. Said the nurse insists on the old boy resting in the afternoon. But he won't let anyone see them carrying him downstairs. And he won't have one of those stair-lift things.'

'Rotten thing to happen to someone like him. He's always been so fit for his age.'

'Aye. Thankfully it's only a slight stroke. I thought I might have to see that nephew of his, but the Brigadier is still very much in charge.'

'Good for him.'

Percy nodded. 'Any road, don't let me stop you from getting on.'

His gaze went back to the garden. Must be a good few acres other side of river, he thought. Some of the trees had already been uprooted in the hurricane, exposing a wide area. Enough for two rows of houses, with a wide, tree-lined road between. Not much market at the moment for small family houses. Too many blokes being made redundant. Too many unpaid mortgages. But those at the top of the tree were still buying something grand with good-sized plots. Landscaped gardens, of course. 'Aye, I can see it all now,' he muttered.

'I beg your pardon?'

Percy swung around. He'd forgotten the piano-tuner. 'What? Oh, sorry, Woodward. Thinking out loud. They say it's first signs.' He laughed, then turned back to the window. 'Houses fit for senior management. Five bedrooms, two ensuite. Luxury bathroom with Jacuzzi. Double glazing, of course.

And — to cap it all — your own stretch of river frontage, with fishing rights. What do you reckon?'

Looking surprised, Mr Woodward followed his gaze. 'Not here, surely?' he said.

'Why not? Once those damaged trees are out of the way, there's land enough for a dozen or so houses along river — more at back. Nothing under two hundred grand, so should make a nice bit of brass. Always promised Susan I'd be a millionaire one day.' He smiled. 'Happen it's a bit later than I reckoned, but I'm not queuing up at Post Office for pension yet. Better late than never, I say.'

'Has the Brigadier agreed?'

'That's what I'm here for. Have a chat, like.' Percy Burridge turned back towards the piano-tuner. 'He's no fool. He knows young Ralph won't keep the estate in the family. Why should he? He's got his own place in Gloucestershire.'

'What do you think he'll do with it, Mr Burridge?'

'He won't care, as long as it makes brass.' Percy laughed. 'Said as much to our Susan only the other day. Did she tell you our lad's a neighbour of his at Canary Wharf?'

'No. Your wife is my next call. I expect she'll tell me about it then.'

'Landed himself a right good job, has our Jonathan. Foreign investments and the like. Brigadier's nephew put in a word for him with one of those merchant banks in the city. And when he heard about a flat going along by him, he helped lad move in.'

'That was — very kind of him.'

'Aye. Any road, Ralph happened to bump into our Susan and told her he didn't want the bother of running two estates. He also said he thought his uncle was going a bit ga-ga. So Susan and me put our heads together and decided to make a bid before Ralph steps in and it all gets a bit complicated with one of those legal notices.'

'Power of Attorney?'

'Aye, that's it. I'm right sorry that the old boy is like this, but you can't blame me for having a go, can you?'

The piano-tuner made a grunting noise from the depths of the piano.

Before Percy could say any more, the butler arrived to usher him into his lord and master's presence.

At first glance, there didn't seem to be much wrong with the Brigadier at all, except that he didn't rise, as was his custom, to greet his visitor. His handshake was firm enough, but his left arm remained by his side throughout their conversation, his hand lying limply in his lap. It was only when he spoke, after motioning Percy to a chair, that the tell-tale signs of a slight speech impairment became noticeable.

'And what do you wish to discuss with me, Bridges? Understand it's a business proposition?'

Percy restrained a smile. The old boy never remembered his name properly, and he never bothered to correct him. Then the businessman in the builder came to the fore and he outlined his plan to build a small row of luxury houses beyond the river, more or less out of sight of the manor house, and asked if he would consider selling off a few acres.

It was such a long time before the Brigadier answered that Percy began to worry that perhaps the old boy was ga-ga after all, and wondered if he should call for the butler. But eventually the blue eyes, only slightly faded, stared straight at him across the desk and Percy realised that there was nothing even remotely wrong with the Brigadier's powers of reasoning. He also realised that he wasn't going to realise his dream of *Cranleigh Manor Riverside Residences*. However, the squire had an alternative proposition, something Percy hadn't thought of, but well worth considering.

'As I've explained, Bridges, my nephew expects to inherit the entire estate. Must have fair play. But the Dower House belonged to my mother's family. They owned Cranleigh Lodge, adjoining my estate.'

'Wasn't there a fire, some years ago?'

'Started in a chimney. Whole house gone by the time the fire brigade arrived.'

'And it wasn't rebuilt?'

'No. They sold the land to neighbouring farmers. Retained the Dower House.' The Brigadier frowned at his thoughts. 'Everything in dust covers now. Should have sold it after Mother died.' Again he looked up at Percy. 'No more than a couple of acres. And I wouldn't want the house bulldozed down. Not quite what you had in mind, I suppose.'

Percy's thoughts rattled around in his head. The Dower House. Right next door to the gates of Cranleigh Manor's drive. He could turn it into a fine house and office, a showroom for his luxury kitchen and bathroom suites. It would stretch him a bit, of course, until he could get a return on his investment. He liked the old boy and was pretty sure he still had a few years in him. But he was eighty-four, after all, and not quite in the pink. Once Ralph had inherited, who knew . . . ?

And — by heck — it would make a grand silver wedding present for Susan. To tell her she was going to live in the Dower House of Cranleigh Manor! Oh, aye. He had to have it.

By the time Percy stood up, they had outlined some figures and agreed to contact their solicitors. As he reached across the desk, his hand brushed against a wooden carving, which toppled over.

'Sorry, sir. Clumsy of me.' He righted the carving. 'That's a handsome piece of work, if you don't mind my saying so.'

'Notice how he watches you, whichever way you turn it.' The Brigadier smiled. 'Woodson carved it. Has he arrived yet?'

'The piano-tuner? He's working in the drawing room right now.' Impressed, Percy examined the carving. 'Magnificent, and no mistake. I'll tell him so on the way out.'

'Would you be good enough to also ask him to come in here when he's finished? Have to ask him to write out the cheque. Never can remember the fellow's name.'

16

The first month of 1990 began with a whimper and ended with a bang. After two weeks of mild, fairly sunny weather, the winds gathered strength until they battered the south of England with an unbelievable ferocity. Gusts of a hundred mph took down the trees weakened by the 1987 hurricane, and more besides. Many roads in Hampshire were impassable and those who were determined or foolhardy enough to try to walk to work kept a wary eye out for branches and other debris flying around like Dorothy's house in *The Wizard of Oz*.

In Fivepenny Lanes, loose thatch was ripped from the roof of the tea-shop, a bench outside the George and Dragon was blown right across the road and through the window of the cricket pavilion, and the few children who had braved the journey to school were immediately sent home: a poplar tree had demolished the cycle shed and ended up jammed across the main entrance. Not only that, there was no power. The lucky ones were those with open fires. At least they kept warm. Fortunately, the telephone wires were still operating and busily buzzing as the safety of friends and relatives was checked, and emergency messages by the dozen sent to the fire brigade, police, and other rescue services, not to mention insurance companies, tree surgeons and suppliers of fences. Even the RSPCA were called to check on the ducks, who quacked their distress at being marooned by a sixty-foot conifer creating a dam across the pond.

The Brigadier's estate had really suffered and Susan was anxious. Her housekeeper, Mrs Graham, had just telephoned to say she was waiting for the man to come and replace the tiles on her roof and would Mrs Burridge please be sure not to open the freezer until the electrics were back on, because there had been a large delivery from Homer Farms only yesterday and she didn't want all those packs of meat thawing out if it could be helped.

To make matters worse, Percy was in Yorkshire. His father was in the last stages of lung cancer. Everyone had tried to warn him for years of the dangers of smoking twenty a day, but he wouldn't listen. Susan didn't mind the old man so much, but Mrs Burridge senior gloried at every possibility to humiliate her daughter-in-law. The older she got, and she was nearly eighty-five, the worse she got, and Susan knew there would have been a blazing row before Percy's father breathed his last. So she excused herself, reminding Percy that they had only moved in just before Christmas and she had masses of jobs that absolutely had to be done. But would he please give her fondest love to the parents? She would be thinking of them all the time and prayed that Mr Burridge would have a speedy recovery. Percy muttered that the best thing she could pray for would be a speedy end, knowing the state of his father, but he'd pass on her good wishes.

Restless, Susan tried the light switch. Nothing. She couldn't use the hi-fi, or the radio, or the TV — damn! If the power wasn't back by evening, she'd miss two of her favourite programmes: *The Bill* and *Brass*! And nobody to talk to. They really must get another dog. After Jonathan had moved to London, Boris had become difficult to handle. Jonathan was the only one who could really control the powerful beast, and he had trained him to guard the house. So it wasn't the dog's fault that the milkman had rushed up the path and startled him, and the bite had barely broken the skin. But the stupid magistrate had decided that the dog was dangerous and wouldn't accept that the previous incident was the fault of the child, who had been rattling a stick along the wrought-iron gates, enough to make any dog jump over the wall. Despite her pleas, a court order was issued for Boris to be put down. She had thought Jonathan would be devastated, but he was busy settling in to his new flat and job and didn't seem too fussed. If truth were told, she wasn't that upset herself. The dog had been quite a handful, but it was the principle of the thing. She hadn't been able to find out anything about the magistrate, but had made sure the honesty of the milkman was no longer beyond reproach. All it took was an unsigned letter to the dairy asking them to check his records carefully as people on his round had been complaining that they were being overcharged. The seeds of suspicion were easily sown around Chestnut Grove and, by the time the manager called to investigate, one or two women recalled thinking the milk bill was a bit more than it should be, but they hadn't written it down, so couldn't prove it. When he spoke to Susan, she sighed and said she had wondered if the milkman had taken her to court because she had queried her bill the previous week. No, she hadn't reported the discrepancy to the dairy. After all, she didn't want the poor man to lose his job — but — could the manager ask him to be sure to check her order? Her orange juice had been forgotten two weeks running, but she'd still been charged for it. The following week a new driver was assigned to the round. She didn't ask what had happened to the old one.

Now, Susan decided she definitely had to have a dog. Not another Staffordshire bull terrier, for certain. What about a poodle? No. That was more in keeping with an address in Mayfair or one of the new marinas. Cranleigh Manor Dower House needed a dog that looked completely at home in the country. A retriever, perhaps, like the Brigadier's? She picked up the current issue of *Country Life* from the coffee table and flicked through the pages. Then she found it. The very thing. A beautiful little King Charles Spaniel sitting at the feet of a duchess. Oh, yes. She turned to the classified pages, looking for any advertisements from breeders. As soon as the wretched weather improved, she would . . .

Her thoughts were interrupted by the horrendous sound of splintering wood and she rushed to the window. The tallest conifer alongside the drive had split through the centre, as though a giant axe had cleaved down into the top branches, leaving half of them swaying dangerously towards the house. Oh, God! What should she do?

No point in phoning Percy. He couldn't get here in time. Neither could Jonathan or Abigail. The police? Mrs Graham had already told her that the village bobby was helping to clear a way through the lane for the fire brigade, who needed to extricate someone trapped in their car. She rang a couple of local handymen, but the numbers were engaged, and the nearest she got to the tree surgeons in Yellow Pages was to leave a message on their answering machines. But she desperately needed someone here now, someone to talk to, someone to reassure her that the tree wouldn't come through the bedroom window. Frantically, she dialled Megan's number.

She knew she was hysterical, and she knew she was babbling, but she couldn't help herself. And either the line was damaged, or Megan was losing her voice. Finally, Susan managed to calm down and begin again.

'Is Nigel there? Only this huge tree is dangling over the roof and I'm terrified.'

'He's needed down at the almshouses,' Megan croaked, 'and he's just pumping up his bicycle tyres. No use taking the car, not with the roads like this.'

'Oh, please ask him to come here first. Just to tell me what to do. I can't get hold of anyone at all, and I'm on my own.'

There was a long pause, then Megan said, 'All right, then. I'll ask him. But don't keep him long, mind, he has a lot to see to at the almshouses. And Susan — '

'Yes?'

'Go to the other end of the house, where it's safer. Just in case.'

Ten minutes later an agonised groaning and creaking sent her rushing to the dining room window, but she couldn't see the tree clearly from this end of the house. If she went outside and watched, she would be able to run in the opposite direction if the tree came down. Safer than being trapped in the house, surely? Grabbing a coat from a hook in the lobby, she opened the back door. The wind had eased for the moment, so she made her way carefully around the corner of the house, prepared to sprint away down the garden if necessary. But she had reckoned without the next gust of wind, fiercer than ever, which plucked her from the path as though she were a feather and slammed her against the side wall of the house. She tried to scream, but it was as though the breath had been sucked from her body. All she could do was to cling there and wait to die.

'Susan!' Nigel's shout just about reached her through the howling wind.

She turned her head and watched him fling down his bicycle and inch his way towards her. The next lull was sufficient for him to pull her away from the wall and thrust her back around the corner and through the open back door, to safety, where she collapsed onto the floor, sobbing.

'For God's sake, what were you doing out there?' Nigel asked, lifting her to her feet and half carrying her into the kitchen.

'I don't know . . . I thought I could run away . . . it was stupid.' She clung to him. 'Oh, Nigel. I've never been so frightened in my life.'

For a while, he allowed her to cry. Then he gently disentangled her arms and studied her face. 'That's a nasty graze you have there, Susan. Any other injuries? Legs? Arms?'

Still weeping, she shook her head.

After he had bathed her face and applied a soothing cream, Nigel said. 'Now something for the shock. A cup of tea is called for, I think.' He reached for the kettle, gently steaming on the Aga.

'I could do with a brandy,' she sniffed.

The hot, sweet tea laced with cognac was reviving, but Susan didn't want to be alone.

'I'm sorry, Susan, but I really have to go. Miss Kemish was tossed around just like you, but she thinks she has broken her hip. I must go to her until the ambulance arrives. And I don't want to leave Megan for too long. You know the twins have chickenpox, and now she's going down with the flu.'

'But I need you, too,' Susan wailed. 'What about the tree?'

'Leave it to me. As soon as I've settled Miss Kemish and checked on the others, I'll phone around until I find someone who can come out and make it secure.'

'But supposing it comes down before then?'

'I had a good look at it on the way in. If the top does fall, it won't reach the house.' He poured her another cup of tea. 'Why don't you lie down for a bit?'

'How can I rest, with this racket going on? Anyway, it's cold upstairs. The heating's off.'

'Then stay here. This is the safest and warmest room in the house. Wrap yourself in a blanket and cuddle a hot water bottle.' He zipped up his anorak.

'Please, Nigel, don't leave me alone. I don't feel well.'

'Of course you don't,' he soothed. 'You've had a nasty experience. But I really must go, Susan.' At the door, he turned back. 'Phone Percy,' he suggested. 'You'll feel all the better for hearing his voice.'

For some moments she sat there, shivering, but with anger, not cold. How could Nigel desert her like this? He was supposed to be their friend. Their best friend. In a few weeks' time he and Megan would be skiing down the slopes at St Moritz and living it up in a posh hotel, thanks to her and Percy. And he couldn't even be bothered to help her out when she needed him. He thought more of those stupid old people who demanded his attention all the time and gave him nothing in return. Wait until she told Percy about the snub.

But the telephone at Percy Senior's house was engaged. Again and again she redialled without luck. Probably that bloody woman yakking away to someone. Tearfully, Susan looked out of the window. Another tree down in the paddock next door. There must be someone else she could phone. Mrs Graham should have been here by now. How long does it take to fix a couple of tiles, for goodness sake?

Mrs Graham was sorry. The man still hadn't come and the roof was exposed to the elements. She had to keep an eye on the buckets, and she really wasn't happy about driving from the other side of the village in these conditions. Could Mrs Burridge manage to get across to her friend, the curate's wife? It wasn't too far, and the lane up to the main road didn't have many trees to worry about.

Just as Susan irritably tried to explain about the chickenpox and flu, and Nigel dashing in and out again, the telephone began to crackle and she had to repeat everything.

'I thought we were friends. It really upset me.' Crackle.

'Sorry, Mrs Burridge. Did you say the curate upset you?'

'Yes. The best he could do was to suggest I cuddle up with a hot water bottle!' Crackle. Fizz.

'I can hardly hear you, Mrs Burridge. What did the curate say?' Her voice grew fainter.

Susan heard a sound like someone dialling. 'Mrs Graham?' She shouted into the receiver, 'Are you still there?' Faintly, she heard her housekeeper, then a man's voice. He had obviously crossed into their line. 'Oh, you wretched man,' she angrily told him. 'Will you please hang up.'

'Pardon?'

'For goodness sake, go away!' Click.

'Mrs Graham?' Nothing. Susan dialled the number again, but there was no sound. The line was dead. She poured herself another brandy and stoked up the Aga. Mustn't let that go out. Then she dragged the Windsor rocking chair close to the range, filled the hot water bottle, and wrapped herself in a blanket.

When she awoke, it was dark and there was still no sound from the telephone, although the relentless wind was as noisy as ever. The electric wall clock had stopped so she had no idea how long she had slept. They always kept a torch and candles handy, so soon she had a little light and was able to place candles at strategic points in the hall, on the landing and in the bedroom. Her digital watch told her it was a little after four o'clock, and her stomach told her she was hungry. Thank God for the Aga. At least she wouldn't die of starvation. But she might die from boredom.

An hour later, Nigel rang the doorbell. He had managed to track down a tree surgeon who would come early next morning to secure the tree. How was she off for lighting?

'I've only got candles — can't see to read, and I'm going to miss what's happening in *Brass* so I'm really miffed off. And I can't even talk to Percy. The phone's gone dead.'

'I know. I tried to phone you just now. Tell you what, I'll cycle up to the Manor and see if I can borrow a couple of oil lamps or something. They're bound to be better equipped.'

'Can you stay with me for a bit when you come back?'

'I'm sorry, Susan, but I must get back to Megan. She's got her hands full with the children and really she should be in bed.'

'I know I shan't sleep a wink tonight, worrying about that tree.'

'You can come back to our place if you're willing to chance the bugs.'

Susan hesitated for a moment, but she'd never had chickenpox and had heard it could be quite unpleasant for an adult. 'I don't think I'll risk it, thanks just the same.'

About twenty minutes later Nigel was back, with the estate manager. 'Mr Goddard brought me back

234

in the Range Rover. The big hurricane lamps should give you a better light, and he's loaning you a Calor gas heater for the bedroom.' Nigel stood back to let the estate manager through.

'I've managed to get the old generator going, so we've got power up at the Manor,' Mr Goddard explained, as he filled the lamps. 'Just as well. The Brigadier is confined to bed with this flu bug that's going around. Not good for a gentleman of his age.' The gloom lifted as he put a match to the lamps. 'Mrs Henshaw doesn't look too bright, either, but she said you're welcome to go up there and stay the night if you wish.'

The thought of light and warmth was tempting, but Susan didn't fancy a cosy evening with Mrs Henshaw. 'It's very kind of the housekeeper, but I think I'll stay here. My family will be anxious about me and if the telephone lines are repaired, they will be trying to get through.'

He nodded. 'I saw the BT van just now and the foreman told me they've located the problem, so it shouldn't be too long.' He looked at Nigel. 'Could you give me a lift upstairs with this, please? Then I must be on my way.'

Percy phoned at half past six. He's been trying to get through for ages to see if she was all right. The pictures of the storm on television were right worrying.

Susan fought hard to control her tears as she explained the situation. Percy hated tears. The line still wasn't very clear, so she didn't say too much about Nigel, just that he had called in. Better to tell Percy all about it when he came home. He had enough to worry about just at the moment. His father wasn't expected to last the night.

'So when will you be back, dear? I do miss you.'

'I miss you too, love. Pity you didn't come with me. You'd have been safer up here. Oh, heck. I must go. Mother's calling me. Why don't you go up to the Manor, Susan? At least there'll be folks to talk to. Mrs Henshaw's a kindly soul when you get to know her.'

Susan sniffed. Kindly was hardly a description that she would hang on Mrs Henshaw, and she had no desire to get to know the housekeeper. But Percy hadn't seen the looks, or heard the barbed remarks. 'She's got enough to do with the Brigadier ill. I'll be all right,' she said, trying to sound stoic. She knew one of the things Percy admired about her was her ability to cope with problems.

'You're a brave lass, Susan.'

'Give my love to your mother.' She had to force the words out.

'Aye. And I'll phone thee first thing.'

It was dawn before Susan dropped into a deeper sleep, filled with dreams of falling trees, howling winds lifting her over the rooftops, loud bicycle bells, her mother-in-law screaming her name — but she wasn't calling her Susan, she screamed 'Mrs Burridge!' over and over — and the wretched bells kept ringing and ringing.

'Mrs Burridge! Wake up Mrs Burridge.'

'What? Why aren't you in Yorkshire.' Confused, Susan tried to open her eyes. 'Was it you ringing those bells?'

As the curtains swished along the track, Susan

blinked at the daylight, then recognised the person standing by the bed. It wasn't her mother-in-law. It was Mrs Graham.

'The telephone was ringing when I let myself in, Mrs Burridge. It's your husband. And the men have arrived to see about the tree. They were ringing the doorbell.' The housekeeper helped Susan slip into her housecoat. 'How is your head? It looks quite bruised.'

'It feels bruised. Is the heating back on?'

'Yes. And the wind has died down — for now.' Mrs Graham lifted the telephone receiver. 'While you talk to Mrs Burridge, I'll make a pot of coffee.'

'Thank you.' Susan sat on the edge of the bed. 'Hullo, Percy.'

'Susan! Where were you? I've been holding on for ages.'

'Sorry, love. I'd only just got off to sleep, and I couldn't wake up.' Then she remembered. 'How's Dad?' she asked.

'He passed away half an hour ago.'

'Oh, I'm sorry.'

'Don't be. It was a merciful release.'

She felt obliged to ask, 'How is your mother taking it?'

'Quite calmly, actually. I suppose because she's been expecting it for so long.'

'Are your brother and sister with her?'

'They've been coming here every day.'

'That's nice. What time do you think you might be home?'

'I'm not sure, Susan. There's the registrar to see and the funeral arrangements and so on. Have to get everything sorted out today. Some of them don't work on Saturdays.'

'Can't Alfie see to it? You've got your business to run, dear. And the men are here about the storm damage. They will probably prefer to deal with you — as the master of the house.'

There was a long pause, then Percy said, 'It's my duty, Susan, as the eldest. But I tell you what, I'll do as much as I can this morning, and leave Alfie to do the things like notices in the paper and so on. I'll ask Brenda to book a caterer for the wake. There's bound to be a lot of his friends and neighbours turn up. With luck I'll get away early afternoon. It'll be late, mind, before I get home.'

'Oh, Percy. That's good of you. I'll tell the men to make sure the trees are secure, and contact you tomorrow.'

'That's right, lass. I know I can leave everything to you. And Susan — '

'Yes, dear?'

'Don't forget you'll need some black for the funeral.'

Oh, God. She'd have to go up for the funeral. Everyone would be in mourning. It was the custom. And they'd all be weeping copiously and saying what a lovely man old Percy was. Nobody would dare mention his drunken Saturday nights and bad temper, nor his bigoted attitude. Because he had departed this life, he would suddenly become a saint. Susan had seen it all before, when her grandparents died, and things hadn't changed at her father's funeral. But she would have to go and smile graciously and be just as hypocritical as the others. It was expected.

'Of course. I'll look through my wardrobe and if there isn't anything suitable, perhaps I can go into Southampton on Monday? If the roads are clear by then.'

'You do whatever is necessary, Susan. I know I can trust you to look just right. You always do.'

Susan knew she would look more than just right at her father-in-law's funeral. She wouldn't check her wardrobe, either. Her new outfit would be the envy of every woman there, even the lady mayoress. And it would be expensive. Once Percy saw her injured head, he wouldn't even ask the price.

Downstairs, she had a quick word with the tree surgeon, then returned to the kitchen and the pot of coffee.

Mrs Graham replaced the pot on the Aga. 'What was that you were saying about the curate, Mrs Burridge?' she asked. 'It was a dreadful line.'

'Oh, nothing.' Susan didn't want to go into it again, not with her housekeeper. And she decided that she wouldn't say anything about it to Percy, after all. He had enough on his plate, just now, and he had been looking forward to the holiday in Switzerland. It would be a pity if there was an uncomfortable atmosphere.

But, as she warmed her feet on the shiny bottom rail of the Aga, Susan knew she wouldn't forget how Nigel had let her down.

17

As they turned the last bend, the village opened up before them, looking just as grand as the view from the top of the hill had promised. Yes, there was the pond and the row of thatched cottages, and yes, there was the village green and cricket pitch. Mary sighed with pleasure and changed down to second gear.

'Isn't it the most darling place you ever saw?' she asked her companion. 'And look, it has a tea-shop just waiting for us. Where shall I park?'

Mrs Whitcher smiled. 'Just pull in to the lay-by there. Don't forget to indicate. Good. You're doing very well, Mary. Have you told Michael yet?'

'No.' Mary pulled the handbrake up another notch, checked the mirror, and opened her door. 'I'm going to surprise him when I pass my test — God willing.'

'Just a little more practice, and you can apply.' Mrs Whitcher looked around. 'I thought I knew every village in Hampshire, but I've not been here before.'

'Well, then, wasn't it lucky that I took that wrong turning coming out of Southampton? We might never have found it otherwise. What's it called?'

The only people in sight were two men rethatching part of the roof above the tea-shop. 'Can you tell us the name of this village, please?' Mrs Whitcher asked.

'Fivepenny Lanes,' one of them called down.

'Thank you.' Mrs Whitcher turned to Mary. 'Never heard of it,' she said. 'Probably not even on the map.'

'It's an enchanted village, that's what it is. Placed here by the little people, so no one can find it.'

'Oh, you and your Irish folklore!'

Mary laughed, then said, 'Come on, I'll buy you a cup of tea. Then we can explore this magical place.'

They ducked under the scaffolding around the door, and ducked again under the beams. No other customers, so they were able to sit by one of the tiny windows and watch the ducks hovering around the perimeter of the pond, begging for a crust.

A rather prim lady, in black skirt and white blouse, took their order wordlessly, only her nod telling them that she had understood. Mary and Mrs Whitcher exchanged amused glances, then turned their attention to the view outside the window.

There had been a frost earlier, but now the sun sparkled on the water across the road. 'I hope it keeps like this for Easter,' Mary mused.

'So do I, but April's so unpredictable. Anything can happen in a week, with English weather.'

'So I'm going to enjoy every minute of today.' Mary looked affectionately at her companion. 'You are a good soul, Elsie Whitcher, to give me so much time, not to mention the free driving lessons.'

'Not really. Any excuse to skive off from chores I should be doing around the site. And you're a good pupil.'

'Well, I want you to know I appreciate it.' Mary

paused while the silent waitress placed a pot of tea and two toasted teacakes on the table. 'And thanks be to the boss for reminding me I still had a day of my holiday due,' she went on. 'If I hadn't taken it before the end of the month I would have lost it.'

'At least it's given you a good long drive. You can't learn much in the odd half hour you grab before Michael gets home from work.'

'I know. And I'm still not happy with my three-point turn.'

'We'll have another go at that before we go home.'

They sat in companionable silence for a few minutes, then Elsie Whitcher asked, 'Is Michael more settled now he's working at Ocean Village?'

'I think so. I hope so. But you know Michael. He's never settled for long.'

'But surely he realises how lucky he is to have a more or less guaranteed job for a few years to come.'

'And isn't that just what I told him? If he hadn't been offered the job by his old foreman, he would have gone back to Town Quay when he came back from Ireland. And that's all finished now, so he would have been unemployed again.' Mary sighed. 'But Michael has never been one to count his blessings, I'm afraid.'

Curiosity halted the conversation as two young women came in to the tea-shop and sat at the table by the other window. Then Elsie Whitcher said, 'Did you and Michael look at those new houses at Hedge End?'

'We did and all.' Mary pulled a face. 'Michael didn't like the houses being grouped around a communal play area. He said the kids would smash the windows playing ball, and he didn't want to have to walk round to the next road to get at his car, which wasn't at all true, of course. The garages were only at the bottom of the garden.'

'There's always something, isn't there? Did you like the house?'

'It was a nice enough little house, but — '

'What?'

'This will be the first house we have ever bought, and will probably be the last. I want it to feel just right, and I didn't get that feeling.' Mary licked her buttery fingers. 'Perhaps I'm expecting too much, Elsie, but I have it in my mind to live in a village again, like the one where I grew up, in Ireland.'

'But with house prices the way they are, a tiny box on an estate is all you're likely to be offered. Even run-down cottages are snapped up at dreadful prices for weekend homes.'

'I know, but that's the sort of home I dream about.'

'With roses round the door and chickens at the bottom of the garden?'

'Except that in Ireland the chickens were usually in the house.' They both laughed, then Mary became thoughtful again as she added more hot water to the teapot. 'I'm happy in the caravan, and you've been a good friend to me for these past eight years. But every time Michael comes through the door I'm afraid that he'll start talking about going to London, or Manchester, or Timbuktu. If I can find the right house, he'll have to stay put.'

Sipping her tea, Elsie said. 'I don't know how you've put up with so many moves, I really don't.'

'The hardest part was having to let Brendan go. It seemed the best thing for him at the time, but sometimes I wonder whether Michael might have stayed in London for the boy's sake.'

'I doubt it. And you wouldn't have been happy living in a big city, would you?'

'That's why I want to create a home where we can both be happy. One he won't want to leave.'

Across the road, a Volvo estate car parked behind Elsie Whitcher's little Ford Escort. Idly, Mary watched the driver take a paper bag to the edge of the pond. 'Will you look at the ducks fighting over those crusts?' she commented.

The two young women at the other table were also curious about the man, now chatting to a pleasant-faced young woman who helped him feed the ducks. 'Who's that with the curate's wife?' asked one. 'They seem very pally.'

'It's only the piano-tuner,' her companion said. 'He'll be calling at number twelve in a minute, then the Taylors'. Twice a year, regular as clockwork.'

'I've never noticed him.'

'Well, I'm nosier than you are.' They both roared with laughter. 'Come on, playgroup's out.'

Mary looked at her watch. 'I suppose we'd better make a move as well,' she said to Elsie, 'although, to be honest, I could sit here all day. It's so peaceful.'

They crossed the road and stood at the side of the bench, taking in the ducks, the general store the other side of the pond, flanked by a small gift shop, an even smaller art gallery and a traditional country pub, with a traditional name.

'Michael would like it here,' Mary observed.

'How do you know?'

'Would you believe how many pubs there are?' She counted on her fingers. 'We passed the Cup and Stirrup just now, there's the George and Dragon by the signpost, the Blacksmith's Arms around that corner, and the Dog and Duck across the pond. That's four pubs within spitting distance.'

'Six.'

They both turned and looked at the man sitting on the bench.

He smiled. 'I'm sorry, I shouldn't have spoken out of turn, but I couldn't help overhearing.'

'Not at all.' Mary smiled back. 'So where would the other two pubs be hiding?'

He pointed. 'The Red Lion is along the road to the Burridge Estate, just by the recreation ground.' He turned and pointed in the opposite direction. 'And the Royal Oak is on the far side of the village green, see the huge oak tree?'

'Oh, yes.' Elsie Whitcher turned back to Mary. 'You're right, dear. Michael would be as happy as Larry living here.'

The piano-tuner screwed the lid firmly back onto his vacuum flask and shook out the crumbs from his lunch box, to the delight of a hovering robin.

Mary hesitated, then said, 'Excuse me — you mentioned an estate. Is it far?'

'About a mile along the Salisbury Road. The locals call it the Burridge Estate. That's the name of the builder. But its proper name is Chestnut Grove.'

'Oh, what a lovely name,' Mary breathed. 'Sounds expensive, though?'

'I don't know what the current prices are.

Somewhere in the region of a hundred thousand pounds, I would imagine.'

'Holy Mother of God!' Mary exclaimed. 'That's way out of my reach.'

'And mine.' He smiled again as Mary pulled a quizzical face.

'Would there be anything not quite so — frightening — in the area?' she asked.

Thoughtfully he frowned, then shook his head. 'Not that I know of. There was a little cottage in Forge Lane, but I see it now has a *Sold* notice outside. It might be worth trying the estate agents in Winchester.'

The two friends exchanged glances, then nodded. 'We'll do that,' Elsie said.

'And thanks for your help,' Mary added, as he unlocked his car.

'My pleasure.' As he reversed away from their car, he leaned across and wound down the passenger window. 'Good luck with your house-hunting,' he called, then drove away, turning on to the road leading to Salisbury.

'What a nice man,' Mary murmured.

Elsie nodded agreement, studying the signpost. 'It's only seven miles to Winchester,' she observed. 'Why don't we have a little stroll around the village, then go off and find some estate agents.' She glanced at her watch. 'And if you like, we can have a snack lunch in the Cathedral Tea Rooms.'

They wandered along the road on the other side of the pond, browsed in the gift shop and admired the paintings in the art gallery, then turned back and followed the route the piano-tuner had taken, past the cricket pitch, football pitch, and recreation ground, stopping outside the Red Lion.

'Do you want to look around the housing estate?' Elsie asked.

'Better not, or I might start dreaming way beyond my means. I can see them from here, and aren't they just beautiful?' She sighed. 'Let's go back towards the church. Then I suppose we should be on our way.' Mary was reluctant to leave her dream village, and had several things on her mind. As they retraced their steps, her companion asked why she was so quiet.

'Are you worried about driving in Winchester, Mary?'

'Oh, no. The more practice the better, although I am wondering whether I shall ever be good enough to pass the test. No, I was just thinking about those houses, and I suddenly remembered our evenings around the piano back home. I wonder why I should do that?'

'Meeting a piano-tuner, I suppose. Did you play?'

'We all did. Not brilliantly, but I enjoyed it. It would be grand to have a piano again.'

'Not in a caravan, it wouldn't.'

Mary laughed. 'Too true. But perhaps — later on — I might be able to look around . . . ' Outside the church, she stopped and looked up at the spire, a puzzled frown on her face. 'And I keep wondering about that man.'

'The piano-tuner?'

The image of a man in his fifties, with a shy smile and a fine head of hair, came into Mary's mind. 'I can't help thinking that I've seen him before,' she said, 'but for the life of me I can't remember where!'

★ ★ ★

By the time James rang the bell at 19 Susan Close, he had a splitting headache. Young Mrs Green at number twelve had talked non-stop, about the price of children's shoes, the fact that she hadn't had a decent holiday for three years, and several instances of her husband's selfishness. And the new baby hadn't stopped wailing once during the hour it had taken him to tune the piano. Mrs Green said it was too early to feed him, so he would just have to cry.

Megan's smile was welcoming as she opened the door. 'Here we are again, then. Cup of tea?'

'Please. Could I have a drink of water first? I want to take a paracetamol.'

'Of course.' She brought it through from the kitchen. 'Caroline Green been bending your ear about her trials and tribulations, has she?'

Nodding, James popped a tablet into his mouth.

'Thought so. It's becoming her mission in life.' Megan went back into the kitchen, still talking. 'I think she's lonely, with Steve being away so much, but she does go on a bit once she has a captive audience. Nigel has the patience of a saint, and will listen to Caroline for hours. I wish I was more like him.' She brought two mugs into the living room. 'Now then, before you start work, tell me about your family. Has your son been posted yet?'

'He came back from another training stint in Norway last month. They're helping clear up some of the storm damage along the south coast now.'

'That's going to take quite a while. Did you see the destruction in the churchyard?'

He nodded. 'I hate seeing beautiful trees brought down like that.'

'It must have been even worse for you. More trees in the New Forest than round here.'

'It was pretty bad.' He helped himself to a biscuit. 'But no injuries in our village, thank God. People are more important than trees and fences.'

'Indeed they are.' Megan raised an inquisitive eyebrow. 'And are there likely to be any wedding bells ringing in your village church?'

'Sorry?'

Wide-eyed, she looked at him. 'Surely one of your children must be courting by now, at least.'

'Oh, I see what you mean. Well — ' James reflected for a moment. 'David did dance a lot with the captain's daughter at the Christmas party, but I wouldn't exactly call that courting.'

'Pretty, is she?'

'Very.'

'And does your other son also have a pretty girlfriend?'

'Actually, yes. You know, I always thought Robert would only go steady with four wheels and an engine, but he seems to have found a kindred spirit.'

'You mean a girl who is fanatical about cars?'

He nodded. 'Lucy is taking a degree in mechanical engineering. At Southampton University.'

Megan spluttered into her coffee. 'Sorry, I shouldn't laugh. But I can't even change a sparking plug. What's she like?'

'Nice girl. Bright. But, as you say, a bit fanatical about cars, especially the old classics. They're thinking of joining the TR Register.'

'Not musical then, like your daughter.'

'Oh, no. But Julie is just as dedicated to her music as Robert is to his cars. And ambitious. She's short-listed to be head of department next term.'

'No time for boyfriends, then?'

'Not seriously, although she has occasional dates. Mainly concerts and so on. As a matter of fact, she's off to see the Bournemouth Symphony Orchestra perform tonight.' He sighed. 'I offered to take her, but she'd already made arrangements to go with some Australian sheep farmer she met at a party.'

Megan smiled sympathetically. 'You look just like Daddy the first time I told him I had another escort.'

'Do I?'

'It's hard to realise they're growing up and you have to let go, isn't it? And you'll never think the fellow is good enough, whether he's an Australian sheep farmer or the Prince of Wales.'

'Oh, I don't think there's any danger of a romance with this guy. He's only over here for six months, and part of that is touring Europe.' Silent for a moment, James stared into the dregs of his coffee. Of course no one would be good enough. But the day would come when he would have to stand at his daughter's side in church and place her hand into the care of another man. And Julie would leave Wisteria Cottage for ever. The thought struck through him like cold steel.

Shaking off the dark thought, he replaced his mug on the tray. 'And how about your young ones?' he asked. 'Is Ruthie enjoying her nursing?'

'Oh, indeed, yes. She loves it. It's hard work, mind, but Ruthie was never one to dodge work. Not like Owen. He used to bribe Dilys with sweets to do his share of the washing up.'

'He'll be leaving school soon, won't he?'

Megan nodded. 'To tell you the truth, I'd like him to go straight out to work. He needs more sense of responsibility. But he wants to go on to university. Doesn't know what he wants to study, mind, but he reckons it's easier than looking for a job the way things are.' She picked up the tray. 'At least Dilys knows what she wants to do. Only twelve, but she has decided on a secretarial course.'

James unlocked his toolcase. 'Do you have any budding singers among your little brood?'

'Matthew sings in the choir and he shows promise, but his voice will break eventually, of course.' Megan laughed. 'His teachers adore him — but he is always up to something. Complete opposite of Sarah, who is a very solemn bossy-boots.' At the door, she paused, then said, 'It's strange, you know.'

'What is?'

'Well, you've been coming to Fivepenny Lanes for — how long?'

James thought for a moment. 'Since 1957. I was a mere 'improver' then. Barely out of my teens.'

'That was before we came here. I remember the first time you tuned our piano. You'd just finished your National Service, and I thought you were the bees' knees.'

A little embarrassed, he carried on dismantling the piano.

'That was before I met my lovely husband, of course. Once I'd set eyes on Nigel, that was it.' Megan's voice was dreamy. 'What is it about a person that makes the chemistry work? Nigel doesn't look like Harrison Ford, except that he wears glasses. He's too tall, and too thin, and he lets people walk all over him. Yet to me, he's Mister Wonderful.'

'Much better than the bees' knees.'

'Yes.' She came back into the room. 'I mean, what attracted you to your wife in the first place?'

Thoughtfully, James looked up. 'She was five years old, very determined, and absolutely gorgeous. And she hasn't changed.'

'Ah . . . that's so romantic.' Megan smiled. 'I was really sorry I didn't meet her that time when Owen broke his arm. Mam said she was a lovely person. Do you know, all these years, you've seen my children grow up, but I've never seen your family. Not once.'

A familiar furry shape sniffed at James's shoes, black and white tale wagging a greeting.

'Hullo, Dylan.' James reached down and rubbed behind the dog's ears. 'Can you smell your sister on me?'

'You see,' Megan said. 'You even have one of our dogs. We're practically family.' She went back into the kitchen to wash up, leaving James to finish tuning the piano.

As usual, she sang a song before he left, to test the notes. Her voice was as beautiful as ever, James thought, as he tucked her cheque into his wallet.

'Are you going to the Dower House next?' Megan asked.

'Yes.'

'I promised Susan I'd get her a set of the photos Ruthie took at a party recently. Would you do me a favour? I can't get over there today.' She handed him an envelope. 'There's some good ones of Abigail. Look . . . ' Megan took the packet back and pulled out a snapshot of the two girls, arms around each other, wine glasses in hand and pulling silly faces at whoever was taking the photograph.

Laughing, James shook his head. 'They're obviously having a lot of fun. Nice that they're training at the same hospital.'

'They've been inseparable since we moved here, even though Abigail went to a private school. Susan was very disappointed that she didn't go to university, like her brother.' A slight frown crossed Megan's face. 'I hope it won't cause problems when one of them gets a boyfriend. It's bound to happen sooner or later.'

'They'll sort themselves out. Oh, by the way, forgot to ask. Did you enjoy your holiday in the snow?'

'It was really lovely. Mind you, I made a right spectacle of myself. I mean, can you imagine me trying to keep my balance on skis? Landlocked whale, more likely. But Nigel was remarkably good. He and Susan went on to the next piste.'

'Glad you enjoyed it.' James picked up his toolcase. 'And if the weather keeps like this, you'll soon be able to go to the beach hut again, won't you.'

'Oh, they got rid of that just after the storm. Susan said it wasn't worth keeping it now that Jonathan and Abigail were in London. Not that Jonathan ever used it, but Abigail loved it.'

'You'll miss it too, I expect.'

'The twins were rather upset, but I told them it's lucky we've been able to have the use of it all these years. And Susan said they can use the swimming pool any time they like.'

'A swimming pool? At the Dower House?'

'So many trees blew down, they've decided to build a pool in the back garden. Susan showed me the picture in a magazine. Lovely it is. And she's ordering new patio furniture to go with it. From that French firm.'

'Alibert?'

'That's the one. She's given us her old set already. See?'

James followed her gaze through to where a white iron table and chairs awaited the summer. 'I remember them,' he said. 'They're very swish.'

'And she won't take a penny for them. So I'm going to buy her a terracotta planter with some fuchsias, just as a thank you. I just hope it will go with her ideas.'

'I'm sure it will. 'Bye for now, Megan. See you in October.'

As he took the lane towards Cranleigh Manor, James reflected on their conversation. It was true, he did have a strange sort of one-sided relationship with his customers, seeing their homes and families, hearing their stories. Very few were interested in what happened to him once he had left Fivepenny Lanes, apart from the Taylors and the Jenkinses. He also thought about another relationship which could also be called one-sided in a way. Was Susan really as generous to her friends as it appeared? Or would it, like one of Grandma's little sayings, 'all end in tears?'

18

It was just as well that James had brought his umbrella. There had been quite a crowd waiting outside the church when he arrived, and he had to park his car way down the road, almost as far as the almshouses. The first spots of rain sent everyone scurrying into the church and he quickly slipped inside the door, intending to sit at the back, but Mrs Jenkins beckoned him and motioned her grandchildren to move along a bit so that James could sit in their pew.

'He asked that Megan should sing a solo,' she whispered, 'so she's sitting in the choir stalls, where she can keep an eye on Matthew. It's bad enough when he has a fit of giggles at a wedding, but at a funeral . . . '

Today would have been the Brigadier's eighty-fifth birthday. Instead . . . James glanced around the church. Many familiar faces. Practically the whole village had turned out to pay their respects. Susan Burridge wore no make-up, but her plain black dress relieved by a diamanté brooch, and little black hat decorated only by a short veil, gave her the appearance of a chief mourner. She looked surprised when she noticed James, but smiled graciously, then whispered something to her husband, who turned and smiled a broader greeting before returning his attention to the service sheet.

Following his example, James noted the hymns.

'Abide with me' and 'Jerusalem'. Good choices for an old soldier. The third was rather surprising. 'All things bright and beautiful', to be sung by the school choir. Mrs Jenkins explained that the Brigadier had left precise instructions as to his own funeral service, and he had so enjoyed listening to the Sunday School children singing at Easter, he had requested it should be included. She also brought James's attention to a brass plaque on the wall, bearing the name of Miss Amelia Harding, who had died the previous year.

A murmur rippled through the church and the congregation stood as the coffin, covered with a Union Jack, was brought down the aisle. Among the pallbearers, James recognised the nephew, estate manager, river bailiff, chauffeur, and Johnson, the butler. The other man was in uniform, an officer from the Brigadier's regiment.

The Reverend Hugh Jenkins conducted the service with a perfect balance of respect and affection. He spoke warmly of the Brigadier as being much more than the squire of Fivepenny Lanes, continuing a family tradition. Brigadier Beresford-Lawson made a point of knowing what was going on and he never lost touch with the villagers. If he heard that someone was in need, he discreetly sent along a member of his staff to see what was needed. There wasn't a person in the village who would not miss his friendly greeting: even though the Brigadier could never remember their names, he always knew who they were. James was not the only member of the congregation to hide a smile behind the service sheet.

When the Reverend Jenkins introduced Edward Smith to continue the celebration of the Brigadier's life, James was surprised when an elderly man tapped his white stick towards the pulpit, leaving his golden labrador seated by his pew.

Mr Smith wore ribbons from the North African campaign on his jacket, and when he spoke, it was obvious that he was from London. He announced that he had been the Brigadier's batman for some years before and during the Second World War, and had been quite overwhelmed when the Reverend Jenkins had asked if he would speak of an area of the Brigadier's life that was little known to anyone outside Cranleigh Manor or the army.

'I owe my life to Brigadier Beresford-Lawson,' he said, simply. 'When we suddenly came under fire, approaching Tobruk, he called to me to take cover only seconds before a shell exploded near me. The last time I was able to see him was when he ran towards me. If he hadn't shouted, I wouldn't have moved quickly enough, and if he hadn't dragged me across open ground to the safety of his armoured vehicle, I wouldn't be standing here today. And it didn't end there.'

Edward Smith took a deep breath before continuing. 'I was only a private, but I'd been a regular soldier for twenty years, and didn't know what I was going to do in civvy street. Because my wife had to be my eyes, she had to give up her job, but the Brigadier contacted all sorts of associations and, before too long, I was a telephone operator and being trained to use my first guide dog. Bonnie, there, is the latest.' He nodded in the direction of his pew. 'The Brigadier visited us regular in Bermond-sey, bought me books in Braille, and talking books when they became available. Then one day he phoned and told me that the Forces Help Society could arrange a holiday for Flo and me, and every year we went somewhere nice, until Flo passed away seven years ago.'

Ah, thought James. So that was why the Brigadier had requested donations to the Forces Help Society instead of flowers.

For a few moments, Private Smith stared sightlessly down at the pulpit. Then he went on. 'I tried to manage on my own, but the Brigadier knew it was getting harder as I got older, and the street was being pulled down for redevelopment, so I had to move. Anyhow, he got in touch with the Forces Help Society again — and they found me this lovely little place on the Isle of Wight. We're all disabled in some way, but we watch out for each other.' He smiled. 'In the summer, he would come over with his chauffeur and take some of us out in his car. And every Christmas, he'd bring a big hamper and sing along with all of us at the concert. We'll miss him.' After another pause, he concluded, 'I don't reckon there's many of you knew what he was really like, and I'm glad to have had the chance to tell you. Brigadier Beresford-Lawson was an officer and a gentleman in every sense of the word, and I'm proud to have served under him.'

As Private Edward Smith tapped his way down the steps from the pulpit, there was a spontaneous round of applause. When Reverend Jenkins invited the congregation to have a moment's silence with their own particular memory of the Brigadier, James recalled the day when the Brigadier had talked of his fiancée, and he hoped her photograph had remained next to the old gentleman's heart — in death as it had been in life.

Nigel led the prayers and introduced Megan, who wore the attractive black and white suit Susan had bought five years' earlier. James had from time to time accompanied Megan for concert work, but now the church's perfect acoustics and fine organ combined with her superb voice to give the most exquisite rendering of Gounod's 'Ave Maria' he was ever likely to hear. Then it was the turn of the children to sing their delightful hymn while the coffin was slowly carried out of the church. Many hands, including James's, sought a handkerchief from a pocket or handbag, and even young Matthew's high spirits were subdued by the atmosphere.

James held his umbrella over Mrs Jenkins throughout the interment, then escorted her back to her husband, who waited at the door of the church. Megan was standing with Nigel and the children. Under normal circumstances, he would have said goodbye and driven home, but Johnson had phoned him during the week, informing him that the Brigadier had unfortunately had another, this time fatal, stroke, and particularly requesting that James go back to the Manor after the service. James couldn't understand why. He was not a relative, nor staff or villager. But the butler had been quite insistent. Katherine had also been invited and had intended to come, but yesterday a vicious horse-fly had taken a fancy to the back of her knee, and by the time she sought help, it was too late for the gentian violet to have much effect on the swelling and inflammation.

Back at the house, James found himself standing next to Susan Burridge.

'Nice of you to come,' she murmured.

'He was a good man. I felt it was the least I could do. But I admit I was surprised to be asked to come back to the house.'

'You were invited? I wonder why?' Mrs Burridge looked equally puzzled, then turned her attention to Mrs Henshaw, who was quietly talking to a waitress carrying a salver of wine glasses. 'Are you sure you are able to manage?' Mrs Burridge asked the housekeeper.

'Yes, thank you, Madam. The Brigadier had left instructions that outside caterers were to deal with the refreshments, so I wouldn't have to worry about it.'

'He was always so considerate, even to staff.'

'Yes, Madam. But the Brigadier never treated us like servants.'

Thoughtfully, James watched Mrs Henshaw walk away. What would happen to her, and Johnson, he wondered? Would the new squire keep them on, or would he sell the Manor? After all, he had two homes of his own.

Ralph was standing on the other side of the drawing room, listening intently to the solicitor. Suddenly, he looked up and stared straight at Susan Burridge, with a rather strange, quizzical expression. A half-smile hovered around his lips, and James could have sworn he winked, although it might have been a trick of the light. Whatever the meaning of the expression, it seemed to unnerve Mrs Burridge, whose hand shook just enough to splash wine on to her black gloves before she lowered her gaze and turned to her husband to ask if he knew whether any of the antique furniture in the house might be going to auction.

Soon, the room began to empty, and James was about to say goodbye to Ralph when Johnson approached. 'Excuse me, sir. Would you please go into the library. The solicitor will be reading the Will shortly and has requested that you be present.'

Amazed and confused, James stared at him. 'Are you sure it was my name he mentioned?'

'Yes, sir.' He consulted a list. 'Mr James Woodward, the piano-tuner,' he read out. 'There is no mistake.'

The estate manager, chauffeur, and river bailiff nodded to James as he found a seat in a far corner of the library. Soon they were joined by other members of staff, the headmistress, Hugh and Gwynneth Jenkins, the manager of the golf club, the solicitor, and the new owner of Cranleigh Manor. Edward Smith and Bonnie were the last to arrive, escorted by Johnson, who closed the door before sitting down next to Mrs Henshaw.

The solicitor carefully moved James's carving further back on the desk before he opened his briefcase and took out a sheaf of papers. First he apologised for the slightly melodramatic way he had requested that they all be present for the reading of the Will.

'It is merely for convenience, as you all attended the funeral,' he explained. 'The Will itself is simple and straightforward, with one main beneficiary and several minor bequests. If any of you are not clear about the terms, this will give you an opportunity to speak to me personally. Everything will, of course, be confirmed in writing.'

Taking a pair of spectacles from his pocket, the solicitor went on to inform them that the original Will had been drawn up many years ago, but there had been codicils since then and, more recently, a letter elaborating upon the Brigadier's wishes. First to be mentioned were Johnson and Mrs Henshaw, who received fifty thousand pounds each and the grateful thanks of their employer for their loyal service. In addition, Johnson was given the presentation carriage clock and Mrs Henshaw the Wedgwood tea service. He trusted that his heir would ensure that, when they retired, they were comfortably housed and cared for.

Next came the estate manager and river bailiff with smaller bequests and similar thanks, plus the gun presented on behalf of the villagers at his eightieth birthday and his fly-fishing tackle, respectively. To the chauffeur, in addition to twenty thousand pounds, he bequeathed the Daimler, and it would be at Mr Manning's discretion whether he wished to auction the vehicle. A wry little footnote was that the petrol consumption would probably be too prohibitive for a retired chauffeur to consider keeping the car for his personal use.

The daily staff were equally well respected and rewarded, and a sum of money was donated to the golf club for the provision of an annual award to encourage promising new players. Edward Smith became quite emotional when his name was mentioned. In addition to a personal legacy to the batman, there had been a monetary benefaction to the Forces Help Society and the Guide Dogs for the Blind Association.

All Saints Church would benefit by a kitchen and inside toilet facility. The Brigadier had noted how inconvenient it was for worshippers to have to ask for the key to the rather primitive toilet down by the gate, and he expressed his thanks to the team who had provided coffee after services by bringing their own water supplies. James noticed that Mrs Jenkins breathed a little sigh, probably of gratitude.

The needs of the school were not forgotten, either. Their gift was a minibus to take the children to festivals and events. In addition, the Brigadier requested that a rose garden be planted in memory of Miss Amelia Harding, who had been such a splendid headmistress.

Now it was James's turn; the last codicil. In appreciation of his years of caring for the Broadwood piano, and for their many pleasant conversations, the Brigadier had bequeathed to him the sum of one thousand pounds and, as a memento of those years, he wished Mr Woodward to have his woodcarving, which had been a treasured companion in his study.

The solicitor glanced at the owl and commented, 'I have often admired this beautiful piece of work when I visited, privately thinking it was not unlike the Brigadier — wise and watchful.'

James found he had a lump in his throat which was increasingly difficult to swallow, and he was thankful he had chosen to sit in a dark corner.

The only beneficiary remaining was the nephew, Ralph Richard Beresford-Lawson, who would inherit Cranleigh Manor and the remainder of his uncle's estate.

Then it was over. Deep in thought, they said goodbye and thank you to the new squire of Cranleigh Manor and his solicitor, who told James that the carving and cheque would be sent to him after probate had been granted.

Johnson and Mrs Henshaw had taken up stations by the front door, dispensing coats and umbrellas and courteous goodbyes. James asked Johnson if he had plans for the future.

'I feel that the time is provident for me to retire, sir,' he answered, 'although I have not yet decided where I shall live. However, I have agreed with Mr Ralph that I shall remain until the end of the year.' He nodded to the manager of the golf club as he went through the door, then went on. 'There is much to be done before Mr Ralph can take up residence.'

'So is he going to live here then?' James said. 'Not in Gloucester?'

'I believe that, for the time being, Mr Ralph intends to divide his weekends between Grantham Hall and the Manor. He will, of course, use his London residence during the week.'

James nodded. 'There will, no doubt, be many changes.' He smiled at Mrs Henshaw. 'Once things have settled, perhaps your role will be a little less strenuous if Mr Beresford-Lawson is not to be in permanent residence?'

She returned his smile. 'After the end of the year, my role will be very much less strenuous,' she said. 'My sister was widowed last year, and has often asked me to share her home. I wouldn't, of course, while the Brigadier was still alive, but now . . . ' She spread her hands expressively.

'Will you be moving far away?'

'Sussex. My sister runs a cattery near Haywards Heath and is finding it difficult to look after her home as well as the business.' Mrs Henshaw looked up at the vaulted ceiling. 'So a small bungalow will definitely be much easier to care for. And, thanks to the Brigadier's generosity, I shall be more than comfortable.'

'Well, you earned it, both of you,' James said. 'Although I admit I was more than surprised to receive a legacy myself.'

Johnson allowed himself a rare smile. 'The Brigadier held you in high esteem, sir. He mentioned to me on more than one occasion that he was looking forward to your next visit.'

Thoughtfully, James gazed around the huge entrance hall with the family portraits looking down on every step of the magnificent curving staircase. 'I have been coming here for nearly thirty years,' he mused, 'and it will not be the same without him — or you.' His glance embraced both of them. 'But you deserve your retirement.' He held out his hand. 'I wish you both well.'

'Thank you, sir.' The butler handed James his umbrella. 'I shall pack your carving personally and have it ready for your next visit, Mr Woodward. Safer than sending it via the postal services, don't you agree?' He glanced down the drive. 'Ah, here is the taxi to take Mr Smith to the ferry terminal.'

As James unlocked his car, he glanced back at the two old retainers standing by the open front door, doing their duty to the end. Soon they would be leaving the only home they had known for virtually the whole of their working life. He remembered the first day he had arrived, nervous and inexperienced, and absolutely awestruck by the imposing building — and the gleaming Daimler. Twenty-eight years ago, he could only afford a second-hand Vespa. Now, he had a Volvo. Not quite in the same class as the Daimler, but gleaming nevertheless. Then, he had been terrified of the dignified butler and not at all sure about the housekeeper. But, over the years, they had developed a mutual respect, and he knew he would miss them.

As he put the car into gear and eased away, along the curving drive, he looked in the rear-view mirror at the handsome building. No. It would never be the same again.

On the drive home, he thought about his inheritance, and wondered. The bedroom suite was more than a little shabby and the fridge freezer would soon need replacing, but . . . No, it didn't seem quite right. He would, of course, consult with Katherine, but felt the Brigadier would have liked him to spend the money on something a little more special.

Suddenly, he knew. A holiday. A proper holiday. Usually, they only managed a few days in the West

Country or a long weekend on Guernsey, because of the animals. But if he could arrange for Julie to be around for two weeks during the school holidays, instead of touring Europe for six weeks with her friends, as usual, he and Katherine could take off. Fly to Vienna to see the Lipizzaner horses she had long admired or — better still — take the car on the ferry to Le Havre and drive south. Katherine loved the sun. It could be a second honeymoon. Come to think of it, they'd never really had a first one. And they had cancelled their silver wedding party last year because his father had died. Yes: a thousand pounds should give them a holiday to remember.

★   ★   ★

There was an air of expectancy about Wisteria Cottage. James sensed it before he'd gone through the kitchen, calling Katherine's name, and into the living room, where his wife was sprawled on the settee, a cushion under her knee, a tremulous smile on her lips, and a tear upon her cheek. Julie was sitting on the floor, holding her mother's hand, and the Australian sheep farmer stood by the fireplace.

'What's wrong?' James asked, looking from one to the other.

'Nothing's wrong, Dad.' Julie jumped to her feet and hugged him. 'Come and sit down while I pour you a whisky. The champagne can come later.'

James bent over his wife and kissed her. 'Why the tear?' he asked, stroking it away with his finger. 'And why champagne?'

Suddenly, he knew. Closing his eyes and taking a

deep breath, he knew what they were about to tell him. And Katherine recognised that he knew.

'It had to happen sometime,' she said, reaching for a tissue. 'I haven't quite got used to the idea myself.'

He opened his eyes and stared at Julie as she handed him his drink, happiness radiating from her face.

'Neither have I,' she said. 'Paul only asked me an hour ago.'

James's head swivelled sharply towards the Australian sheep farmer. 'But you've only just met!' he said. 'You hardly know each other.'

'I knew I wanted to marry Julie the moment I saw her,' Paul said. 'It took her a few weeks longer.' He looked down into his glass, then straight at James. 'I know all prospective sons-in-law are supposed to say this, Mr Woodward, but I really do love her and I'll take care of her for the rest of my life — that's a promise.'

'But — but you're going back to Australia in October,' James stammered.

Softly, Julie corrected him. 'We're going to Australia in October.' She guided James to his armchair and sat on the arm, the way she had often done as a child. 'I know it's short notice, but I don't want Paul to go back alone. I want to go with him, as his wife.'

'Does it have to be so soon?' He looked appealingly at Paul. 'You've hardly met any of the family and there's not much time to arrange everything. Couldn't you stay over here for a bit longer?' James knew he was clutching at straws.

'Afraid not, Mr Woodward. Got to get back for the lambing, and I won't be able to get away again for a bit. Julie tells me your other son's going to be in London soon so I'm looking forward to meeting him, and I'll try to see as many of your folks as I can before we leave.' Paul looked slightly uncomfortable. 'I can understand your reservations, but Julie particularly wants to get married over here, so we haven't really got a lot of choice.'

Julie laid her cheek against her father's head. 'I've never felt this way about anyone else, Dad, and I know I never will again. Please give us your blessing. Please.'

What else could he do, but hug her and extend his hand to the man who was going to take his precious daughter away from him? Not just a few miles down the road, either. Oh, Julie, he thought. There must have been nice boys from Southampton at that party. If you were going to fall in love with a handsome sheep farmer, couldn't it have been one from Dorset? Why pick on one who was going to whisk you away to the other side of the world?

As he downed his second whisky, James listened, with a fixed smile on his face, to the popping of champagne corks and excited chatter about bridesmaids and flowers and where should they have the reception? Rhinefield House perhaps, or Parkhill Hotel?

Then, out of the alcoholic haze, a thought flashed through his mind. Bang goes my inheritance — and some!

★　★　★

270

On a warm, sunny day in October, James gave his daughter's hand in marriage to Paul and stepped back. The feeling of emptiness was as dreadful as he had imagined. No longer would he be the only man in her life. No longer would she run to him for comfort or help. Another man would share her fears and joys. But this other man was almost a stranger and soon he would be taking her away — far away. They knew very little about him except that he had inherited a vast spread of land and a considerable amount of money when his parents were killed in a plane crash; he was five years older than Julie and had the rugged good looks and physique of a man who has spent most of his life on the back of a horse. Did he know that Julie had an inherent distrust of horses? It was true that Paul had promised to buy her a piano as a wedding present, but would he be able to listen to her playing and know where she was brilliant and where she needed extra practice? Could he discuss the merits of a Chopin étude or a Rachmaninoff concerto for hours on end? Where were the nearest concert halls? Hundreds or thousands of miles away? What sort of social life would they have in the outback? Like most girls of her age, Julie loved shopping and dancing and parties. Now all that was finished. Oh, God, Julie, he thought. Do you really know what you have let yourself in for?

As he turned to sit beside Katherine, James caught the eye of her father, sitting in the pew behind. His expression was full of compassion and understanding. Of course, James thought, he was reliving the day, twenty-six years earlier, when he had been in the same position, having handed over the responsibility for his only daughter to James. He must have had similar thoughts and fears. At that time, James was a fledgeling piano-tuner on a low income and the only home he could offer was a bedroom in his grandmother's cottage. They didn't share hobbies, and neither of them had ever gone out with anyone else. Father-in-law must have wondered whether things might change for Katherine and James. But love had bonded them together so they were able to cope with life as it happened. James glanced at Julie, gazing up into Paul's eyes as they repeated their vows, and he turned and smiled at her grandfather, sharing the moment and understanding that Paul and Julie would also be able to cope with life as it happened.

Bartley Lodge had finally been decided upon for the reception and Paul had insisted on paying for everything: champagne, flowers, photographer, vintage Rolls-Royce, evening disco and buffet, an exquisite crinoline dress for Julie and similar styles for her bridesmaids but in different jewel colours. She had chosen two friends from the school where she worked, one from college — and Lucy. James had watched with amusement the reaction of guests when Robert told them that the stunning redhead in emerald green taffeta was studying to become a designer — of cars. What did she do for relaxation? Oh, her favourite hobby was tinkering about underneath the engine of a classic car.

When the DJ finally announced the last waltz, the guests packed the dance floor, then gathered their belongings together and waved goodbye, leaving

Paul and Julie standing on the steps of the hotel. The newly-weds were staying overnight and driving to Cumbria the next day, to tour the lakes and visit a great-aunt of Paul's who hadn't been able to travel to the wedding.

Wisteria Cottage was unnaturally quiet after the hubbub of the previous weeks. Even Bess couldn't manage more than a sleepy 'Woof', before she settled down comfortably again in her basket. Jaffa was nowhere to be seen. Probably hunting mice or voles in the paddock.

Katherine filled the kettle. 'Cup of tea?' she called over her shoulder.

'Please.' James walked through to the lounge, cluttered with crates and boxes of every description. He hadn't thought there would be enough containers to hold his daughter's collection of cuddly toys, music and books, as well as her clothes, but eventually the souvenirs of twenty-four years were packed and awaiting collection.

'Your mum's a bit upset,' James commented, as he moved a packing case away from the settee.

'I know. She actually admitted she's beginning to feel her age. The pain in her hip is getting her down and I think she's afraid she won't see Julie again.'

'She said as much to me, but I told her that Paul had promised he'd put her on the next plane if any of us were ill.' James frowned thoughtfully. 'Your mum really ought to go to the doctor. They do marvels with replacement hips these days.'

Katherine sighed. 'That's what I've been telling her since last Christmas. I knew something was wrong when she didn't argue about us going to

Devon. But she's never had an operation in her life and I think she's scared stiff of the idea. Robert said he'd have a word with her when he takes them home. She usually listens to him — certainly more than me, or Dad!'

'I suppose that's the next thing you'll be planning, Christmas.'

'Oh, don't! Let me get over this lot first. I just wish — '

'That she wasn't going so far away?'

'No — yes. Of course I wish that. But I was thinking about David and wishing he had been able to get away.'

'He was desperately sorry when I spoke to him on the telephone.'

'You don't think he'll have to go out there, do you? Honestly.'

James would have loved to reassure her, but he knew she wanted him to be truthful. 'I hope not, love, but if Hussein doesn't respond to the United Nations, then they'll probably have to go out on standby at least.'

'Oh, that bloody man! How dare he just march into Kuwait as though the world belongs to him?'

'Trouble is, his people believe everything he says, just as the Germans believed Hitler.'

'Then let's hope he comes to the same sticky end before it blows up into another war.' Tears were not far away from her eyes. 'Why did David have to choose a career in the forces?'

'Because that's what he wanted to do. He never considered another option.'

'But he was so good at sport. Show-jumping;

cricket; rugby. He could have been a professional at any one of them.'

'Probably,' James agreed, remembering how splendid David had looked on horseback at the Royal Tournament. 'And don't forget, he could have come a cropper just as easily in sport.'

'It's not quite the same as having snipers taking pot shots at you.'

'I know, and I'm not particularly happy about the prospect, either, but it goes with the job I'm afraid.'

Katherine shuddered. 'I can't bear to think about it.'

'Then don't. Think about our holiday instead. This time next week we'll be on the Autoroute du Soleil, heading for the Mediterranean beaches.' He didn't add, 'and Julie will be on a Boeing Jumbo Jet, heading for Australia.'

'Yes. I mustn't spoil the lovely day.' Katherine smiled. 'It was a lovely day, wasn't it?'

'A beautiful day,' James agreed. 'And I've got to admit I quite fancied the mother of the bride.' He leaned across to kiss her lips.

'You two aren't at it again?' Robert stood just inside the door, grinning hugely.

'Don't sneak up on us like that!' James protested.

'Sorry. Still, at least I know that I won't be too old for it when I'm your age. Some of my mates are convinced their parents had lost interest as soon as they found out it wasn't quite like the birds and the bees.'

'That's enough of that kind of talk,' Katherine said, trying unsuccessfully to look stern. 'Where's Lucy?'

'Lifting yards of frock out of the back of the car.'

'Ah. Did Grandma and Grandad get home OK?'

'No. We dumped them at Bramshaw. They're still walking. Where did you dump Gran and Uncle Raymond?' Robert ducked the cushion thrown by his mother and carried Lucy's overnight bag up to the spare room, still laughing.

James picked up the mugs and took them through to the kitchen. 'Thank God we still have Robert to keep us in order,' he observed.

'True.' Katherine called back 'Goodnight' to Lucy and looked around the living room, her mind obviously on other things. 'What did I do with those little cake boxes? We'll have to collect the wedding cake from the hotel, and I mustn't forget to pack up the top tier for shipping out to Australia — it will need lots of protection, and — '

'Tomorrow, dear.'

'And I forgot to ask Robert if he talked to my mother.'

'Tomorrow,' James repeated firmly, taking her hand and leading her towards the staircase. 'You've done quite enough for one day.'

★   ★   ★

It took James a few weeks to catch up on his appointments, and the trees were quite bare the next time he drove into Fivepenny Lanes. The weather had changed dramatically from a late Indian summer to cold, damp and fog, and it didn't help that the heating wasn't on at the village hall. Mrs Mason had taken over her late husband's duties as

276

caretaker and she was a more pleasant companion, but James was glad to go on to the warmth of the school, and even more pleased to see the blazing log fire at the Vicarage.

'What a change in the weather!' Mrs Jenkins remarked as she ushered him indoors. 'Who would think that yesterday I worked in the garden all afternoon, tidying up leaves and so on. Lovely it was.' She pulled a chair closer to the fire. 'Sit down for a moment and warm your hands while I make the coffee. Kettle has just boiled.' As she bustled away into the kitchen, she called back, 'I hope you brought the wedding pictures.'

'They're in the car. You did ask.'

'Oh, do bring them in, please. I can look at them while we have our coffee.'

Mrs Jenkins oohed and aahed over the dresses, and how beautiful Julie was, and hadn't Robert grown tall since she saw him last?

'That was eight years ago,' James reflected. 'When we came to choose Bess.' He leaned forward to stroke Brecon's silky head, noticing the grey hairs around her muzzle as she looked up at him. 'And you weren't much more than a pup yourself, eh, Brecon?'

'She's eleven now. Quite an old lady — like me.'

'You?' James laughed. 'You don't seem to have changed much at all since I first met you.'

'Mr Woodward! You'll have me blushing in a moment.' Chuckling, Mrs Jenkins returned her attention to the photo album. 'And was the best man Australian as well?'

'No. He's a distant cousin of Paul's. The one he

came to visit in Southampton. His wife is a teacher friend of Julie's.'

'And that's how they met?' Mrs Jenkins studied the family group. 'Such a pity your older boy couldn't be there,' she commented.

He nodded. 'And to make matters worse, we were in France when his unit had their orders. They flew out the day before we arrived home.'

'Oh, you poor dears. Is he out in Kuwait now?'

'Somewhere in the vicinity. Every time you switch on the television there's something different to worry about. And it doesn't help that Julie is so far away.'

'It must be very strange for her, getting used to married life *and* a new country.'

'She seems to be settling in happily enough. Apparently, Paul has a wonderful music room with stacks of records and CDs. And he has his own little plane, so they can get to Melbourne quite easily.'

'His own aeroplane! My goodness, it's a different world out there.'

James laughed. 'Too right, as Paul would say. Julie's worried about David, of course, and phones us two or three times a week to see if there is any news.'

Mrs Jenkins stood up. 'I will remember him in my prayers.' She handed back the photograph album. 'These are lovely. Don't forget to show them to Megan, now, will you?'

★ ★ ★

Megan also thought the photographs were lovely, and was as concerned as her mother about David being out in the firing line — and about the Gulf War. 'Thank God Owen isn't old enough yet. He's been in the Air Force cadets for a couple of years and is quite keen to become a pilot.'

'I remember saying something similar to Mr Mason about David, when the trouble started in the Falklands.'

'And we all thought it would never happen again.' Megan laughed a short little laugh. 'I wonder what the Brigadier would have had to say about Saddam Hussein.'

'He's probably turning in his grave.' James carefully laid out his tools. 'I shall miss seeing him up at Cranleigh Manor. Expect I shall find a few changes.'

★　★　★

The changes were apparent as soon as Mrs Henshaw took James through to the drawing room. Most of the furniture was covered with dust sheets, including the piano. Mr Ralph had only visited the Manor twice since the funeral, Mrs Henshaw told James, and planned to spend Christmas in New Jersey, so they now had only a skeleton staff. It had been agreed that Mrs Henshaw would spend Christmas with her sister, but come back for a few days in the New Year to help the new housekeeper settle in and introduce her to the daily cleaning staff.

When James had replaced the dust sheet on the

piano, Johnson the butler asked James if he would like to join him for a moment in his own living quarters. It was the first time that James had been inside the tiny flat, once called the 'butler's pantry', and it was surprisingly well furnished and cosy. Mrs Henshaw sat at the table, inviting James to sample her home-made shortbread and seed cake. Both were delicious and, to James's surprise, Johnson poured them all a glass of very good sherry and toasted their respective futures. For a pleasant half hour they chatted, enquired after James's family, and talked of their own plans. Johnson told James that an acquaintance of his, also a retired butler, had informed him of a vacant flat where he now resided in Boscombe. It was most pleasant, on the ground floor, with a view towards the sea, and Johnson had no hesitation in purchasing the lease. Therefore he would be leaving Cranleigh Manor in mid-December, earlier than planned, as Mr Beresford-Lawson would not be in residence over Christmas, and his friend had very kindly invited him to dinner on Christmas Day. No, Mr Beresford-Lawson would not be employing another butler, as he preferred to hire temporary staff if he was entertaining.

The estate manager, river bailiff and head gardener would continue to live in their cottages, but the chauffeur had already left. Manning had long dreamed of setting up a business specialising in restoring vintage cars, and had found the ideal premises on the outskirts of Eastleigh. The magnificent Daimler would be the showpiece. James made a mental note to tell Robert, who would probably be interested.

When the time came to say goodbye, James knew that this was the end of an era, rather like the day he had left school, and when he had left the piano shop to set up on his own. Nothing would be quite the same again. Cranleigh Manor would have its memories and its ghosts, but no longer would Johnson and Mrs Henshaw be there to greet him.

19

James whistled as he drove into Fivepenny Lanes the following April. He had two good reasons to be cheerful apart from the sunshine and the fringe of bright daffodils alongside the pond. The Gulf War was over and they had heard from David at the weekend. He was doing what he called 'mopping up and monitoring' operations along the border between Kuwait and Iraq, making sure communications were functioning. Choking black smoke from the burning oil wells still blotted the horizon following Hussein's final act of unbelievable vandalism, and David's unit would probably be there for some time. But at least he was safe — and he had just been promoted to lieutenant. Already Katherine was planning a celebration party for his return.

The second reason for his tuneful whistle was a phone call that had roused them from their bed at ten past one in the morning.

'Dad? Didn't wake you, did I? Sorry, but I just had to phone straight away.'

Julie's voice was so excited, he guessed the news before she told him what the doctor had just confirmed. Needless to say, he and Katherine had little sleep for the rest of the night, and at breakfast, Katherine had asked him to pick up some flight details. He still couldn't believe that he was about to become a grandfather. But then, he couldn't quite believe that his little girl was old enough to be expecting a baby on her first wedding anniversary.

The Reverend and Mrs Jenkins were as pleased as he had expected them to be, pumping his hand with as much enthusiasm as when James had told them Katherine had given birth to Julie, twenty-four years earlier. While he was working on the piano, Megan called in to the Vicarage, and she hugged him and kissed his cheek when she heard the news.

'I am so happy for you all,' she beamed, then went on, 'and I'm glad I caught you, Mr Woodward. I have to take Matthew to Casualty.' She caught sight of her mother's face and hastily added, 'It's nothing serious, Mam, honestly. Just a knock on his knee playing football, but it is rather swollen, so the doctor said I should take him for an X-ray, to be on the safe side, see. You know Matthew. He has a season ticket to the place.'

Mrs Jenkins didn't look too reassured as she hurried out to the car to have a word with her youngest grandson.

James waited, expecting that Megan would cancel her appointment, but she only wanted a change of time. 'Susan has said she doesn't mind swapping, and if I'm your last appointment of the day, that should give me plenty of time to be home. Well, I hope so, but you know what these places are like. Hope it's not awkward for you?'

'Not at all.' It would mean doubling back because of Mrs Green and Cranleigh Manor, but Megan rarely changed her appointment, unlike some, who made other arrangements without phoning him, then calmly suggested he call back another day when it was more convenient. 'Anyway,' he grinned, 'I'm afraid I'm going to be the one to change appointments again next time. Katherine and I will be in Australia for the whole of October, so it's going to be November before I can come to the village again.'

'And I shall want to hear all about Australia, and your grandchild.' Megan glanced at her watch. 'Goodness, I must be on my way, or we'll be there all night.'

Mrs Jenkins didn't close the front door until Megan's car was out of sight. 'Really swollen, it is,' she told James as she came back into the room. 'Like a balloon. Poor little mite. If it isn't one thing it's another.'

'It's amazing, the number of accidents and illnesses that children manage to get through before they become adults.'

'Indeed, yes. And with each one, there's another crop of grey hairs for the poor mother, not to mention the grandmother. Anyway, I've told Megan I'll keep Dilys and Sarah after school, so she won't have to worry about them.'

'Megan must be pleased that you're always on hand to help out.'

'Oh, yes. One or the other of them is in here almost every day. And I wouldn't have it any other way.'

As he continued to work on the Obermeier, James reflected that he and Katherine would be lucky if they saw their grandchild once a year.

★ ★ ★

Susan didn't give James a chance to tell her his news. As soon as he arrived, she led him out through the French windows to see the swimming pool.

'Percy was that busy last year he didn't have a chance to organise it, but he promised me I should have it all finished by this summer, and Percy never breaks a promise. What do you think?'

Whistling at the spectacle, James surveyed the azure, kidney-shaped pool and Jacuzzi, with its tiled terrace surround, backed by an expensive-looking pergola and gazebo, and built-in barbecue area.

'I'm very impressed,' he said, truthfully. 'This is not your average garden pool — more like something film stars have in Hollywood.'

Susan laughed. 'That's exactly what I thought when I saw the picture in the magazine. Look.' She pointed to the underwater lights. 'Can you imagine what that will look like in the evening? And the gardener is going to train roses all over the pergola, with hidden fairy lights, and lanterns dotted amongst the plants in the raised flower beds. I'll bet you've not seen anything quite as grand in any of the big houses you go to?'

'That's true. The closest I've seen is one in the garden of a hotel I service near Bournemouth. It's like a huge conservatory, with a sliding roof, so they can swim whatever the weather.'

'Really?' Susan's eyes were like saucers. 'I suppose you don't know how much it cost?'

'Sorry.'

'I'll get some brochures.' They went back into the house. 'Although Percy has promised me a pedigree

285

King Charles Spaniel, if his new plans come off, so I mustn't be greedy. Did I tell you about them when you phoned?'

'No.' James began to clear the top of the piano.

'Well, another builder has asked Percy to help him out with a big building project. A huge out-of-town superstore. He has a secretary now who handles his business affairs. I really didn't have time to learn the new word-processing machines. Anyway, I can't remember if he said it's Sainsbury's or Asda. Might be Tesco. Whatever, it should bring in a lot of money.'

'Whereabouts is this one going to be?'

'Somewhere around Southampton, I believe.'

'Oh.' As if Southampton didn't already have enough superstores, James thought, but said, 'I'm glad he has plenty of work. It must be quite a worry, the way the recession is affecting building.'

'That's why he's holding back on houses after he's finished the luxury development near Chandlers Ford. He's no fool is my Percy. Always manages to keep one step ahead of the market. Jonathan is just like him. Real clever.'

As James laid out a sheet to protect the polished woodblock floor, he wondered if Jonathan was still as obnoxious as ever, or whether he had become more humane, like his father. Probably not. The cut and thrust of city life was hardly the environment to mellow a ruthless young man.

The work on the piano was almost completed when James's mobile phone rang. It was Greg Sherringham, the vet. He said Katherine hadn't returned from lunch and when he phoned he only got the answerphone. He didn't want to worry James, but did he have any idea where she might be? She'd been so excited about Julie's baby and David's promotion — could she have gone to Mothercare, or a travel agent, or something?

James was pretty sure none of those things had happened, but he tried to quell the nerves in his stomach. 'It might be something like that, Greg. Tell you what, I'll phone Robert at the garage. He can be home in five minutes. I'll let you know as soon as I hear from him.'

As he quickly finished tuning Susan's piano and waited for Robert's call, the knot in James's stomach tightened. Supposing Katherine had fallen down the stairs and was lying there, unable to call for help. Or — worse — she might have taken Duke for a quick gallop and taken a tumble. Then they wouldn't know where she was. Of course, it could be a car accident, but the police would surely have notified him by now. She always had some sort of identification on her. Unless the car had caught fire. Oh, God! Phone back, Robert. Quickly.

He was just packing away his tools when his mobile rang again.

'You'd better come home, Dad . . . don't ask why . . . ' Robert's voice broke as he whispered, 'Just come home.'

Susan said she would post his cheque and James managed to drive beyond speed limits without attracting attention from the law, finally screeching to a halt outside Wisteria Cottage. Another car was parked by the gate. Dr Pritchard? Robert knelt by his mother's chair, his face buried in her shoulder.

He didn't look up. Katherine sat so terribly still, she resembled a statue. Her face was expressionless and drained of colour, and an untouched glass of water was on the table by her side. Then James saw the two men, and as soon as he recognised the uniform, he knew.

His lips were so dry, no sound came at first, then a hoarse whisper. 'It's David, isn't it?'

'I'm terribly sorry, sir.' The padre's words echoed round and round in James's head. David was dead.

★　★　★

The next few weeks were a blurred nightmare to James. People coming and going. The doctor; his mother, Katherine's parents; friends; neighbours, the vicar. And a representative from the Marines. They had met Captain Chegwin at the Royal Tournament. He was very kind, told them what had happened, made arrangements for their son's body — what was left of it — to be brought home; asked if they wanted a military funeral. They didn't. He suggested counselling. They didn't want that either. All they wanted was to wake up from the nightmare.

The whole village seemed to be weeping for David. All except Katherine and James, both too numb to weep, Katherine too shocked to speak. Drifting in and out of sedation, she ate little of the food placed in front of her, just sat staring blankly into the distance, until she lay down and closed her eyes again.

Then there was Julie. James phoned her and tried to explain, as gently as possible, that her brother's vehicle had hit a mine while he was touring border posts. Just a routine patrol, they had said, but David had been killed instantly and his driver was fighting for his life in hospital. After an agonising silence, she quietly said, 'I'll be with you tomorrow, Dad.' But she didn't arrive. While she was making the flight reservations, she began to bleed, heavily. Paul radioed the flying doctor, who advised complete bed rest, but eventually Julie had to be flown to the hospital in Melbourne. When James told Katherine that Julie wouldn't be coming to the funeral, she nodded, but he wasn't sure she understood that Julie had lost the baby.

During the funeral, James concentrated his efforts on supporting Katherine, with Robert on her other side. He didn't listen to any of the words of the service, or the hymns, and couldn't bear to look at the coffin. All he could think of was the proud expression on a thirteen-year-old boy's face when he wore his cadet uniform for the first time at a St George's Day parade.

After the coffin was lowered into the grave, people shook his hand, patted his shoulder, or hugged, murmuring words of comfort. He supposed he must have responded in some way, and for one crazy moment he thought he was at the Brigadier's funeral, when Captain Chegwin spoke to him. It wasn't until the captain's tearful daughter told James that she and David had planned to announce their engagement when he returned from the Middle East that the full realisation struck James. The mine buried in sand hadn't only taken away their son's life, it had taken away future promises of marriage and grandchildren. Even their first grandchild in Australia had been denied to them. And all they had left of David was the past. There could be no future that included their eldest son; not for James, nor Katherine, nor David's pretty girlfriend. A scream built up inside him, and he longed to cry out loud and beat his fists against a wall. For the first time he understood why other cultures and religions felt the need to wail their grief for all to hear. But he belonged to the 'stiff upper lip' British culture that forced him to clench his teeth and fight back the emotion. For years afterwards, whenever he thought of that moment, he remembered acutely the overpowering scent of lilac, and the desperate fear that his knees would buckle before he could help Katherine into the car.

Robert was a tower of strength, and as for Lucy, as soon as she heard the news, she had driven to Bramblehurst to support Robert, and became the main support of the whole family. James didn't know what they would have done without her. The mothers did what they could, but both were in their seventies, and brother Robert had not long retired from a lifetime of being at sea and couldn't even drive. But Lucy took on all the housekeeping duties, phoned James's clients, arranged for Duke to be exercised and quietly read the many letters of sympathy with James. There was no point in reading them out to Katherine, she was in a dark world of her own. So Lucy slipped a rubber band around them and tucked them into the bureau drawer for later.

Came the day, though, when people stopped

calling. James had to look at his appointment diary again, and Lucy had to return to university. Life had to go on and gradually he was able to pick up the pieces of normality, a few at a time. But for Katherine, life had stopped the moment she heard the grim news. She hadn't even spoken to Julie on the telephone, or looked out of the window at her beloved horse. It was as though they didn't exist.

The doctor told James that she was suffering from clinical depression and there was no way of telling how long it would take before she recovered, or even if she would recover. The anti-depressant tablets had little or no effect upon her, and there was no point in suggesting counselling until she could at least listen and respond. All they could do was wait.

Each morning before he left home, James tackled the necessary chores, and left Katherine sitting in her armchair, knowing his mother would come in later. On the rare occasions when he didn't have time to dress Katherine, his mother found her still sitting in her dressing gown, unwashed. She spoke only in answer to direct questions, and then only in monosyllables. As the weeks dragged into months, James began to wonder how much longer this would go on. It was the desolation that awaited him when he came home that gradually wore him down. No conversation, no music, no affection. Nothing. It was as though they had been buried in the churchyard with their son.

When Dr Pritchard told James, for the umpteenth time, that he must be patient, James came pretty close to thumping him. The only other suggestion was that Katherine be admitted to a psychiatric unit. James almost said, 'Over my dead body'. The thoughts of his wife having to undergo electrical shock treatment filled him with horror. But even as he vehemently shook his head, he knew it might have to come to that in the end. He began to think of ways he might stimulate her interest. Perhaps if they went to Australia in October, as planned before the tragedies? Air travel, a new country, Julie and Paul. He used every persuasion he could think of, but Katherine just said, 'No'. Nothing else, just 'No'.

When Paul suggested that he bring Julie over to England instead, James jumped at the idea. He decided not to tell Katherine, in the hope that the surprise of seeing Julie would shock her into some kind of reaction. At Heathrow, he was saddened to see the dark circles under Julie's eyes, and she'd lost quite a bit of weight.

'She's still not well,' Paul murmured quietly to James. 'But she's really trying to pull herself together and I'm proud of her.'

'Let's hope some of it will rub off on Katherine,' James said. 'If this doesn't work, I really don't know what else can bring her back.'

It was the first time there had been any expression on Katherine's face for six months. Just a flicker in the eyes, but it gave James hope. Julie wept as she hugged her mother, but Katherine still didn't cry, she just said, 'Julie — what are you doing here?' in a puzzled sort of voice. At least that was an improvement on 'Yes'. 'No'. 'Please'. and 'Thank you.' But she didn't mention the baby, and she didn't mention David. Even when Julie visited the grave the next day, and gently talked to her mother about the flowers she had taken, Katherine merely nodded, then asked, 'Is it raining? Your coat is wet.'

By the time their visit was over, Katherine was talking in sentences of slightly more than five words, but only on trivial matters. When anyone asked, 'How are you?' she murmured, 'All right,' and left the room. The evening before they left, Julie begged her mother to come to Australia for Christmas.

'It will be so warm and sunny. I'm dying to show you over the farm,' she pleaded. 'And you'll just love the horses.'

'Not for Christmas!' Katherine's voice showed signs of panic, then lowered to a plaintive childlike whisper as she said, 'I don't want Christmas.'

As Julie turned into Paul's arms, her eyes filled with tears and James knew they all shared the same thought. It would have been David's twenty-fourth birthday on Christmas Day.

20

'So, when we go to Ireland for Christmas, I'll be able to take turns driving to Fishguard, and you'll be able to admire the scenery, or snooze. Don't you think that's grand?' Mary pushed the certificate across the table towards Michael, then went on, 'And I'm going to do something I've been wanting to do for a very long time.' She took a large pair of scissors from her needlework box and, with a great flourish, cut one of the L-plates in half. Then she handed the scissors to Mrs Whitcher, who stood at her side. 'And you can have the other one. I'd never have made it without you.'

With equal theatricals, Elsie Whitcher cut the L-plate into pieces. 'You should have passed last time, I reckon,' she commented. 'That examiner was a right old misery-guts.'

'To be fair, Elsie, I did bump the kerb on my three-point. But he made me so nervous, sighing and tut-tutting.' They both laughed as she imitated the man. 'Still, I did it this time, and that's all that matters.' She looked at her husband. 'Aren't you pleased for me, Michael, dear?' she asked.

Michael silently read the certificate of his wife's ability to drive a motor car, picked up the pieces of L-plates then, frowning, looked from one to the other of the two women. 'When has all this been going on?' he asked.

'Oh, whenever Elsie could find the time to teach

me,' Mary said. 'She's been a real brick, putting up with my kangaroo hops and not complaining when I jangled the gears on her car.'

'You never said a word.'

'I wanted to surprise you. And, judging by your face — I have.'

'Surprised? I'm gobsmacked.'

Elsie laughed. 'You should be very proud of her, Michael. I am. And, like she says, she can share some of the driving, so that should make life easier for you.'

'I suppose.' His brows still met in a frown. 'Although I don't want her to start gadding about all over the place, not with petrol the price it is and all.'

'As if I would,' Mary protested. 'But I will be able to go to the new Sainsbury's on my own. Now you know how you hate taking me to the shops, so that should please you. Go on, tell me you're pleased.'

The frown was replaced by a smile. 'Yes, it's pleased I am. But . . . ' he wagged a finger at her. 'I'll be wanting to come with you a few times before I let you loose on my car. Understood?'

'Of course.' Mary turned and winked at Elsie.

Grinning back, Elsie picked up her keys. 'I'd better be on my way and get cooking, or I'll never get out again tonight. Are you two coming up to the pub later on?'

Michael shrugged. 'Maybe, or I might go over to Woolston and meet the lads.'

'Don't forget, Mary will be able to drive you home now, so there'll be no problems looking out for the coppers.'

A light dawned on Michael's face, then a slow smile, as he murmured, 'So she will and all. Perhaps we will come along when I've had me dinner. It'll give me a chance to see whether that examiner knew what he was — ' Suddenly, he looked anxious as he turned to Mary. 'For heaven's sake, Mary, what are we eating tonight? It's turned six o'clock and there's not a sign of a potato peeled, nor a smell from the oven!'

'I thought I'd splash out on fish and chips tonight, to celebrate me passing my driving test.'

'Oh — ' Michael pondered. 'What would we have eaten if you'd failed?'

Mary grinned. 'Fish and chips. As a commiseration. Now don't be looking so sour. You know it's your favourite.' She dropped a kiss on the top of his head, then grabbed her coat and followed Elsie. 'I'll be off up the road now. What's it to be? Skate wings or rock eel?'

As she queued at the fish shop, Mary carefully planned the evening ahead. She had to be careful. You could never tell with Michael which way the wind might blow. But if she waited until he'd eaten his fill and downed a couple of cans of Murphys, he might be in the right frame of mind to listen before they went out again. She would show him the article first. Unlike Mary, Michael never read much beyond the headlines and the sports pages, so she would have to point it out.

The penny hadn't dropped the first time she'd read it. The man in the photograph looked pleasant enough and she almost turned the page until she read his name in the caption. Percy Burridge.

Something rang a bell so she read on. 'Percy Burridge already had an enviable reputation before he moved south, and soon the logo, *Burridge Better Homes* became as well known in Hampshire as it had been in Yorkshire. During the past thirty years, his name has been established as a builder of high quality housing, although he has at times diversified into commercial and industrial development. Two years ago he purchased the Dower House of Cranleigh Manor at Fivepenny Lanes, still preferring to work from his home office rather than a suite of offices in a modern building. 'Can't beat the personal touch,' he is often quoted as saying, and clients and staff alike know the door is always open for them.

'Now, Mr Burridge finds himself at the centre of controversy, since joining forces with Frank Griffiths for a planned out-of-town shopping centre between Fareham and Southampton. Mr Griffiths is no stranger to protests, having already built two similar complexes, and Mr Burridge said that he had overcome similar contention when he first presented plans for an industrial development near Fivepenny Lanes. 'There will always be those who are worried about progress,' he commented, 'and I try to see their point and put their fears at rest. As far as out-of-town shopping centres are concerned, there's nowt wrong with making life easier for the wife, now, is there?' Mr Burridge's wife, Susan, agrees wholeheartedly with her husband's views. 'I adore the village,' she said, 'and wouldn't wish to live anywhere else. But I am an extremely busy person, very much involved with the community, and often away visiting my son and daughter in London. Jonathan is what you would call a 'high flyer' in the city, and Abigail has chosen a nursing career. So it is vital to me that I can shop easily and quickly. There is no reason at all why my husband's plans should upset any of the local residents.'

After she had finished reading the article, Mary had thought deeply. Then she browsed through the tattered remains of a telephone directory in the kiosk near the campsite. Elsie wouldn't have minded if Mary had asked to use her telephone, but Mary wanted to keep this one to herself. Yes, there it was: Percy Burridge, Builder of Better Homes, The Dower House, Cranleigh Manor, Fivepenny Lanes.

Before she had time for second thoughts, she dialled. As luck had it, Mr Burridge answered the telephone, and listened politely while she explained that she had read the article and was phoning on behalf of her husband.

'Aye, I will be taking on more men,' he said, in answer to her question. 'once plans are approved — and I'm not too bothered about that. There's more in favour than against, by my reckoning.'

'What sort of labour will you be looking for, Mr Burridge?'

'Everything and anything. Carpenters, electricians, steel fixers, painters and decorators and brickies of course. Always need plenty of them. What skills does your husband have?'

Mary thought deeply but briefly before she answered. Michael had never wanted to bother with an apprenticeship when he was younger, but he claimed he'd learned more trades by working with the men than he ever would have by formal training. She plumped for bricklaying — Mr Burridge had said he needed plenty of those.

'And, of course, he's worked on some of the multi-shopping complexes in Southampton, and Ocean Village and Town Quay.'

'Has he, now? Sounds like a useful chap to have around. When did you say he'll be available?'

'The job he's working on should be finished before Christmas.'

'And I'm hoping to get this one off ground in January, so that's about right. If he drops me a line, I'll keep him in mind. What did you say his name was?'

'Michael Fitzgerald.' Mary said a swift prayer. 'Mr Burridge, I know it's a terrible liberty, but I'd like Michael to see Fivepenny Lanes.' She explained how she had fallen in love with the place the previous year. 'And I was wondering — would it be in order if he called in on you tomorrow? Then you could see for yourself what kind of a man he is, and ask any questions you want, and — oh, no, I'm really asking too much, with it being a Saturday and all. I'm sorry.'

There was a slight pause, then Mr Burridge asked, 'Do you have a particular reason for asking, Mrs Fitzgerald?'

The only answer was the truth. Mary told him that Michael was talking again of moving to London, and why she wanted to stay in Southampton and would do anything to help her husband find work in the area. 'He's a good man and a hard worker,' she concluded, 'but I'm sore afraid that if he doesn't find another job before Christmas, he'll be dragging me off to London.'

'And we can't have that if it can be helped, can we?' There was a smile in Mr Burridge's voice. 'Tell your husband I'll be here in the office till noon tomorrow and he's welcome to have a word. If he's as good a worker as you say, and if jobs keep coming in, there's no reason why we shouldn't have work enough for a few years yet.'

'Oh, thank you, Mr Burridge,' Mary breathed. 'May you always have good luck.'

This time he chuckled out loud as he said, 'Thank *you*, Mrs Fitzgerald. I hope your husband appreciates he's right lucky to have a lass like you on his side.'

Trouble was, Mary thought, as she gave her order for two skate wings with chips — would Michael think he was lucky, or would he rave and rant at her for interfering?

★   ★   ★

When it came to it, he didn't rave and rant, neither did he give the impression that he thought he was lucky. In some ways he seemed a little deflated. Perhaps he'd had too many surprises for one day. Still, at least he agreed to go and see Mr Burridge. And he also agreed she could drive him home from the pub that night. Thankfully, he was too drunk to notice how many manoeuvres she made to reverse the car out of the car park, but then it was partly his fault for parking in such a tight corner.

So the next morning found them driving to

Fivepenny Lanes or, rather, Michael driving and Mary navigating, praying that she would remember the way. It would be too awful if she misdirected him and became lost, but they arrived at the village just before ten o'clock. The weather couldn't have been kinder. One of those crisp November days with a little bite to the wind, but clear blue sky and sunshine accentuating the skeletal outlines of the elm trees standing like sentinels along one side of the village green. It was even more beautiful than Mary remembered.

'Will you pull in to that lay-by, Michael?' she asked, as they approached the pond. 'I'll just have a little wander around the village.' She remembered the gift shop on the corner of the road to Romsey. 'Might find something suitable for Maeve's Christmas present.'

He nodded. 'Don't be spending too much, now,' he warned. 'It's not positive that I'll get this job. And we've already bought that expensive pair of candlesticks for their silver wedding.'

'I'll be careful,' she agreed, although she had enough confidence for the two of them. 'And what do you think of the village?' she asked.

His glance took in the pond, the green, thatched cottages — and the three pubs within view, and not even he could deny it was a pretty enough place — for England. 'Now, which road do I take out of this little lot?' he asked, staring at the sign-post.

Mary had already explained it clearly, but she hid her exasperation. 'Mr Burridge said to take the Salisbury road, that's the one over there past the George and Dragon.' Michael always found it easier to remember pub names than other landmarks, so she continued, 'Then on past the Red Lion, you'll see the Chestnut — '

'Is that another pub?' he asked.

'No, it's the Chestnut Grove housing development, the first one Mr Burridge built in Hampshire. He used to live in the show house, he told me.'

'So where's this Dower House?'

'I'm trying to explain, dear. The next lane on your left past Chestnut Grove leads to Cranleigh Manor, and the Dower House is right by the gate. He said you can't miss it, and if you walk around to the back of the house, you'll see the sign on the door where he has his office.'

'Right. And where do I find you afterwards? It's too cold to hang around for long.'

Mary had it all planned beforehand, but she glanced around, as though looking for inspiration, before she said, 'What about that little tea shop? You can tell me all about your interview while we have a nice hot drink. Shall we say an hour?'

'Right, but don't keep me waiting, now. I know you when you start wandering around the shops.'

'There's only three shops, so I should be able to wander round them all in far less than an hour.' Smiling, Mary kissed his cheek before she closed the car door, 'Away with you, now, and good luck!'

She watched until the rather ancient car wheezed its way up the hill, then turned up her coat collar against the wind, and smiled as she surveyed the scene. Even on a cold winter's day, Fivepenny Lanes could have come straight off the lid of a box of chocolates or jigsaw puzzle.

First she ferreted in her handbag for the crusts she had brought for the ducks. That reminded her of the piano-tuner, and she wondered if she would see him again. Unlikely, as it was a Saturday. Then she walked along the Romsey Road to the tiny art gallery, admired the three paintings in the window, bought some sausages for that evening's supper in the small supermarket next door, and turned into the gift shop. Since she and Elsie Whitcher had last looked in there, a corner of the crowded space had been devoted to crafts, and that was where Mary found the perfect gift for her sister. Maeve was never without a piece of embroidery in her hands, and the shop had quite a selection. Eventually, Mary settled for a cross-stitch kit showing a vase of sunflowers. Oh, yes, Maeve would really love those bright yellows. And it wasn't too expensive, so Michael wouldn't moan — she hoped. But she removed the price sticker, to be on the safe side.

There were only two couples in the tea-shop, and the hot chocolate was much more welcoming than the frosty look on the face of the waitress, who seemed to be having problems with her feet. As she sat warming her hands around the mug, Mary's thoughts turned to Ireland. What a Christmas it would be, to be sure. Brendan had almost completed the diaconate, and had written to say how wonderful it had felt to be able to be a greater part of the sacrament. Even though he couldn't take confessions or offer the Eucharist, he had officiated at baptisms and weddings, such joyous occasions, he said. Next month, on the afternoon of Saturday, 21 December, to be exact, he would be ordained as a priest, and on Christmas Eve he would celebrate his first Mass. He had chosen that day particularly as it was also the twenty-fifth wedding anniversary of Maeve and Diarmid, and it was to be his very special way of saying 'thank you' to them for taking him into their home fourteen years before and treating him like their own son. Oh, yes, it would be a grand Christmas indeed. Mary tried not to think too hard about the following month. For in January, once Father Brendan had received his obedience, he would be flying off to a new life on the other side of the world. He said he felt privileged to be allowed to serve the Lord in the outback of Victoria, and Mary was proud that he had made such a choice. But you couldn't afford to pop across to Australia for Christmas and summer holidays, and it might be years before she saw her only child again. And she knew Michael still blamed her for the fact that he hadn't been able to influence Brendan's growth to manhood. He felt that Diarmid had taken his place and when he read that Brendan was dedicating his first Mass to Diarmid and Maeve, the look on his face had filled Mary's heart with anguish. Oh, she so hoped he got this job with Mr Burridge. He desperately needed something good to come back to after Christmas.

Wondering how he was getting on, her attention was distracted by the waitress rattling cups as she served the couple at the next table. After the old woman had shuffled back to the kitchen, Mary couldn't help overhearing part of the conversation between the man and woman, even though their voices were low.

'I'm surprised they've stayed on so long,' the woman said.

The man agreed. 'Can't be any profit in winter, with no coach parties.'

'If they cheered up a bit, more of us would pop in. I'm told their home-made soup is very good, and this fruit cake is delicious, so it's not the food.'

The man watched while the other waitress cleared a table, then said, 'They look like two of the witches from Macbeth.'

His companion giggled. 'Now you're making me wonder what they put in the soup pot.'

'Rats' tails and lizards, I expect.' Then, seriously, he asked, 'Are you sure they're selling up? You know what the village is like for rumours.'

'When Tina came to do my hair last week, she said that they've been fed up ever since the storm. And now they're getting on a bit they're thinking seriously about retiring. That's what one of them told Tina when she was giving her a perm, anyway.'

'Do they own the freehold?'

'No. And I shouldn't think there's many years left on the lease, so it should be quite cheap. The goodwill can't amount to much, especially as the coach drivers are looking elsewhere for next season.'

'How do you know that?'

'Tina's brother works at the garage along the road, and he said the drivers are fed up with the moans and groans from this place. Apparently one of them is scouting around King's Somborne to see if there's anywhere a bit more cheery.'

'Well, if they lose the coach trade, they'll have no

305

choice but to sell. It's only the tourists that keep the place going.'

'But who would want to take on a dying business out here?' The woman pulled on her woollen gloves and picked up her shopping bag. 'Ready for the trek home?'

As Mary watched the couple turn on to the Andover lane, their heads together in conversation, once again a tiny seed began to germinate in her mind.

★ ★ ★

Mary and Michael moved into the Fivepenny Lanes Tea Shoppe on one of those days when the drizzle got under your skin and chilled you to the marrow. The village was deserted and even the ducks looked sad and bedraggled. Michael had packed their belongings into the self-drive van. It was the cheapest one they could hire, and that's just what it looked — and sounded — like. Mary had bought a bed of pre-war vintage from Elsie Whitcher, and a deal table and two chairs from a junk shop. She hoped and prayed they didn't have woodworm, and decided she would get rid of them at the first opportunity. Any other furniture would have to wait until she had paid some money back into the bank and could scan the small ads for bargains. The bank manager in Winchester had been reluctant to make a loan without collateral, apart from a lovely pearl choker left to Mary by her grandmother, which she had, with great difficulty, managed to keep out of the clutches of her husband's bookie. However, after

Mr Winslow had read her excellent references from the canteen manager and heard that her husband was on the payroll of Mr Percy Burridge, the builder, who had an account at the same bank, he understood that their future prospects were reasonably healthy. Something of her enthusiasm and determination must have communicated itself to the young bank manager, who finally agreed to a loan to cover the short-fall on the purchase price of the remainder of the lease, legal fees, and enough stock to get her off the ground. The overdraft was to be reviewed in six months.

Mary was over the moon. At last they would have a home of their own. Well, not so much a home, it was only three rooms and a bathroom over the shop, with bare boards and a damp patch on the living room wall, but it was hers — theirs — and she would turn it into a home in no time, for sure. If only Michael had such faith. He'd done nothing but moan from the moment he set foot out of the pull-down bed in the caravan this morning.

'Look at that weather,' he'd complained. 'It's cats and dogs out there. And what else can you expect if you choose to move house on April the first?'

She'd said nothing, just finished packing the bed linen with one hand while she cooked him a hearty breakfast with the other. Anything to pacify that scowling face. To be honest, she was amazed they were going at all. At first, Michael had refused to consider the idea, and had hit the roof when he discovered that she had dared to open a secret savings account without his permission. If he had known that there was so much money available, they could have won five thousand pounds last September, instead of a measly fifty. Mary, equally heated, reminded him of three things. One: that it was the only win he'd had in six months; two: that the ten-to-one outsider actually came in second and only won because the favourite was disqualified; and three: the fifty pounds had been reclaimed by the bookmakers before the month was out. Then he had another go at her because she had gone behind his back to arrange the loan, but Mary justified her action by telling him there was no point in asking him about buying the lease if she couldn't borrow the extra money in the first place. When Elsie, right on cue, bless her heart, called in, she was able to lend a little weight to Mary's argument by announcing that she was seriously considering selling the caravan site and moving to the Isle of Wight to be near her daughter. She'd had a good offer from a company who planned to get rid of the older vans, like theirs, and if they brought in more modern vans, the rents would be bound to increase, quite a bit. Finally, after several days of sulks, punctuated by bursts of temper, Michael gave in to the inevitable.

Mary's farewell to Elsie was tearful, as had been the surprise party in the canteen last night, when she had been presented with a beautiful bouquet and, to her amazement, a set of good quality cake tins and baking trays, the result of a whip-round amongst the workers and staff.

'If those two ladies have lived there since Coronation year, you can bet your boots the equipment will be well past its sell-by date,' the canteen manager said, in his farewell speech.

It was true. Mary's heart had sunk when she had checked the inventory of kitchen equipment. Anything decent was going with the two sisters, and there was much she would have to replace. Her heart filled with gratitude, and her eyes with tears, as the manager made her a personal presentation.

'For ten years you've fed us well, listened to our problems, and your lovely smile has cheered us up when we've been down. We're going to miss you, Mary, and I felt you should have something for yourself, not just for the kitchen, as a reward.'

When Mary had carefully opened the beautifully gift-wrapped little package, she gasped, 'Oh! And aren't they simply gorgeous?'

And a male voice from the back of the canteen called out, 'So are you, Mary Macushla.'

The drop ear-rings shimmered with the colours of the abalone shell they were made from. Emerald, turquoise, Mediterranean blue; all the colours of the sea were there. 'What can I say?' She was quite overcome.

'Just thank you, will do.' The manager grinned. 'And a hug.'

The cheers and applause of her colleagues still rang in Mary's ears as she parked their car in front of the tea-shop. It had no garage and no access to the garden at the back, so she would have to leave it in the lay-by opposite until she could find something more permanent. Michael was already in the shop, grumbling as he carried two bags up the narrow staircase.

'We'll never get the bed and table up this lot,

309

Mary. You didn't think of that, now, did you?'

'The sisters had furniture, Michael. There must be a way.' She went through to the garden and pointed to the upstairs windows. One of them was large enough. 'If you can take that frame out, it will go through right enough. I'll look for a ladder.'

'In the name of God, what are you talking about, woman? I can't carry that bed up a ladder on my back. And the sisters would have hired a removal firm to do everything for them. They would have had the money, the price they charged for a few years on a lease!'

'Oh, Michael, please don't go on so. I'll ask at the garage along the road, see if someone will give you a hand.'

'More money down the drain, I suppose. But don't be long about it. I've only got the morning off, not all day.'

Mary turned back into the café. What had happened to the happy-go-lucky Irishman she'd married? Perhaps it was her fault that, most of the time, he was so ill-tempered? Brushing away the tears from her eyes, she almost collided with a stocky man coming through the front door. She recognised the voice as soon as he spoke.

'Steady on, lass! You nearly had me over.'

'I'm sorry, Mr Burridge, I had something in my eye — it is Mr Burridge, isn't it?'

'Aye, and you must be Mrs Fitzgerald, Michael's wife.' Her hand was gripped in the firmest handshake she had known. 'Michael mentioned he was doing everything himself, so I brought a couple of the lads down with me to see if we can help.

Reckon you'll not get bedroom furniture up that daft little staircase.'

'There's not much, we lived in a caravan. But you're right about the staircase. It's very good of you to come, and Michael will be dead pleased. He's through the back.' She stood aside to let Mr Burridge and his companions walk past, then peered through the front door. Parked outside was a lorry, with hoisting equipment, ladders, everything they needed. Percy Burridge was a saint indeed.

While they hoisted the few pieces of furniture up through the window, and restored the frame to its rightful place, Mary staggered up the stairs with load after load of personal belongings. Then she went back down to the kitchen, tried the water, electricity and gas supplies — all working, thank God — and put the kettle on.

'Ah, tea, just what the doctor ordered.' Mr Burridge beamed as he came over to the sink and rinsed his hands. Mary had packed a small bag with emergency supplies, and she handed him a towel.

'Thanks, love.' His eyes strayed to the flowers on the draining board. 'From Michael?'

'No, from my friends in the canteen. They are grand, aren't they? Look, there's freesias as well. My favourites.'

'I can smell them from here. Hope you've got a vase large enough.'

Slowly, she shook her head. 'I'll have to look around to see if there's a jug or something.'

'Shouldn't bank on it.'

For the first time, Mary looked closely at Mr Burridge. He was shorter than she'd imagined, and quite well built. Probably in his early sixties. But there was a look about him, the smile, the piercing blue eyes, that was very attractive. Like Michael, he was a man's man, but very attractive to women.

He picked up the bouquet and smelled the freesias. 'Aye, they're grand, right enough. Tell you what, Mrs Fitzgerald — can I call you Mary?'

'Of course, most people do.'

He smiled. 'Then, tell you what, Mary, I'll ring the wife and ask her to bring down a couple of vases. She's got cupboards full of them.'

'Oh, I couldn't, it's so much bother.'

'Susan won't mind, and you can let her have them back when the flowers are done.' Without any more ado, he'd dialled on his mobile phone, made the request, and pushed down the aerial. 'Susan will be down in about half an hour. If there's anything else you want, just ask. She's a good lass, is my Susan.' He took the mug of tea from Mary and brushed aside her thanks. 'Least we can do. We were newcomers here once. Happen we still are, even after nigh on thirty years.' He sipped his tea. 'A word of advice, Mary. Just remember, the real villagers tend to be a bit distant with newcomers. But they're a grand lot, once you get to know them, and they get to know you.' At that moment, the other men came downstairs. 'Ah, Michael. As soon as I've drunk tea, I'll have a word with Terry, at garage along the road. Happen he'll let you keep car down there. It gets a bit cluttered up here at times with coaches and that lay-by is not over large. Now, if you want rest of day off, it's all right by me. Reckon your missus will need some help.' He nodded towards the boxes cluttering up the kitchen.

'Oh, that's not necessary, thanks just the same, sir. Mary will soon have this place ship-shape.'

'Well, if you're sure.' Mr Burridge raised an eyebrow in Mary's direction, and she nodded, with a false smile. It would have been nice to have Michael's help. She needed to do a batch of baking today if the shop was going to reopen tomorrow. But that was Michael for you.

True to her word, Susan Burridge called in with half a dozen vases. 'Use which ones you like, and there's no rush to have them back,' she said.

Mary was surprised that she was the wife of Percy Burridge. She must be at least fifteen years younger, with a trim figure that Mary envied. She looked attractive in her stone-coloured slacks and black sweatshirt, and her smile was bright, but there was something about her — Mary couldn't put her finger on it, but she felt slightly uneasy. Michael, on the other hand, had no such reservations. His scowl turned to a broad smile when Mrs Burridge introduced herself.

'It's a good woman that you are, to come all the way down here on a day like this, just to bring vases. I hope my wife has thanked you properly.'

'Yes, of course, and I've told her to phone me if there's any thing at all I can do to help. Naturally, that goes for you as well, Michael.'

After their visitors had left, Michael whistled as he fixed up a rail to hang their clothes on, and Mary decided she had been churlish. If Mrs Burridge had helped put Michael into a good mood, then she should be thankful.

For the first two weeks, business was slow, mainly locals curious to see who the new owner was, and she managed perfectly well on her own, baking scones and cakes in between serving customers. She was, however, a little concerned about Easter, wondering whether there would be many tourists in the village. On days when the weather improved, a few people had driven or walked to the village, calling in for morning coffee, lunchtime soup, or afternoon tea. She had decided to keep the menu virtually as it was for a while, until she had the feel of the trade.

It was the Monday before the holy weekend when Mary saw him again. The piano-tuner was feeding the ducks. Dashing into the kitchen to collect the crusts cut off when she'd made a bread pudding, she crossed the road.

'Would you like to give them these, as well?'

His expression was surprised when he looked round. 'Hullo, there! Are you still house-hunting?'

Mary pointed to the tea-shop. 'Moved in on April Fool's day, would you believe?'

'So it's you? The caretaker of the village hall told me that it had been sold to an Irish lady, but I didn't realise it was you.'

'I've been wanting to live in Fivepenny Lanes from the moment I first saw the darling place. And God has granted me my wish.' She glanced over her shoulder. 'I must be getting back, there's baking in the oven. Why don't you come over for a bowl of home-made vegetable soup to warm you up? The wind's got an edge to it and that's for sure.'

'Well, my coffee has gone rather cold.' The piano-tuner looked at his watch. 'I've just time before my next appointment.'

The other customers had left by the time Mary took her bread pudding from the oven, and she was able to chat briefly to the piano-tuner.

'I suppose you wouldn't be knowing someone looking for a part-time job? A student working on Saturdays and in the holidays would do.'

He thought for a moment, then said, 'I can't think of anyone offhand, but it would be worth having a word with Mrs Jenkins, the vicar's wife. She knows most of the youngsters in the village.'

'But I'm of a different faith.'

'She doesn't worry about things like that. Gwynneth Jenkins is a lovely lady, like her daughter, Megan. She's married to the curate and they run the Sunday School and youth club, so they may know of a youngster who would be suitable. And have you thought about putting a card in the window?'

'No, but I will. Thanks, you've been very helpful.'

'Not at all.' He stopped, and sniffed. 'Is that bread pudding I smell?'

'Yes, fresh out of the oven. Would you be wanting a piece?'

Again he looked at his watch. 'I haven't time now, I'm afraid, but I'll call in on my way home. Do you do take-away?'

'I haven't so far, because I wasn't sure whether it would be popular. Do you think I should?'

'Why not give it a try? And will you save three

pieces for me to take home tonight, please. My grandmother used to make wonderful bread puddings, and we haven't had any since the poor old soul died.'

By the time the piano-tuner returned, Mary had placed a card in the window, but it wasn't advertising for an assistant. She had already telephoned Mrs Jenkins, who knew of a girl who was looking for a Saturday job. Sharon Corbin lived in a cottage just beyond the almshouses — her father was a farm labourer so there wasn't much money to go around. She was a very modern and lively girl, Mrs Jenkins said, but a good worker, turn her hand to anything to earn a few shillings, baby-sitting, potato and strawberry picking, cleaning. The family weren't on the telephone, but she was sure they wouldn't mind if Mrs Fitzgerald called round later on, when Sharon was home from school. And Mrs Jenkins was also pretty sure that Sharon would be only too glad to help out over the Easter holiday — she'd asked Megan if she knew of any work going.

When the piano-tuner came back for his bread pudding he lingered long enough to have a cup of tea. He had noticed the card in the window, and said he was sure that hot cross buns, simnel cakes, and Easter biscuits would be popular with the villagers as well as the tourists. That was when she mentioned her other idea. Did he think she should advertise her novelty cakes?

'Oh, yes. Without a doubt. To the best of my knowledge, there's no one around here that makes anything other than the traditional wedding or birthday cakes. Come to think of it, there's nobody in my area, either, so my wife might be interested. She's a good cook, but when it comes to Christmas, she tends to ruffle up the top like snow and stick a piece of holly on top.'

'Most people do, I think. And my ideas were quite popular where I used to live. But I wouldn't be knowing how to do it in a professional manner.'

'Your best plan is to have a photograph album to show people.'

'But I haven't any photographs.'

'Then start with a list of suggestions, and prices. Don't undercharge.'

'It's true that I'm told I don't charge enough, considering how long they take me. But if the prices are too high, then people won't order, surely?'

'People will always pay for something that's a little special. Just keep tabs on the cost of the materials and add on a fair hourly rate for your labour. And when you have a few photographs, perhaps I can borrow them to show to Katherine.'

'Your wife?'

'Yes.' Mary noticed how affectionate his smile was when he mentioned his wife's name, but there was a sadness behind the smile that disturbed her. 'We live out in the Forest,' he went on, 'but perhaps she'll visit Fivepenny Lanes again now that she's feeling better.'

'Oh, I'm sorry she's not been well — ' Mary paused, uncertain whether to ask what was wrong.

The piano-tuner hesitated for a moment, then said, 'Our son was killed last year and . . . Katherine had a breakdown.'

'Holy mother of God, that's a terrible thing to happen. Was he your only child?'

'No. We have another son, and a daughter. But David was particularly close to his mother.'

'How old was he?'

'Twenty-three.'

A pang shot through Mary's heart as she thought of Brendan. 'My son is not much older,' she murmured. 'I don't know how I would cope if anything happened to him. It's bad enough that he's in Australia — ' She had to stop speaking, the tears were too close.

'My daughter lives in Australia now. We're hoping to go out there before too long.'

She told him about Brendan being a priest, and he told her about his daughter losing the baby, and his son who was a mechanic. He also talked about David's death. When he broke off suddenly, Mary realised that he was also feeling very emotional.

'I remember reading about it in the paper,' she said, softly. 'Such a terrible waste. No wonder your poor wife was so devastated.' She covered his hand with her own. 'It must have been a terrible time for you, not being able to talk to her about your own grief.'

He looked up into her eyes for a moment, then nodded. Slowly, he said, 'That was the worst part. I needed to share the grieving with Katherine, but she was so far away, I couldn't reach her.'

Mary sensed that he needed to talk, so she nodded sympathetically, and listened.

'I felt so helpless,' he went on. 'It didn't matter what we did, we couldn't break through the wall she had built around herself. Then — on Christmas Day — I reached breaking-point.'

After a moment, Mary asked, 'What happened?'

'It would have been David's birthday, so I'd been dreading it. I tried very hard to rescue something, for everybody's sake, and I could understand that she didn't want decorations or anything like that. But she wouldn't open her presents, or come to Midnight Mass with me. We always went to Midnight Mass together, even the night before David was born. Then I became angry. Very angry.'

'Because she wouldn't respond?'

'No — yes, of course that made me unhappy — but not angry. The anger came when I found out that Katherine knew there was no one available to look after her horse over the holiday period. She used to idolise that horse. Sometimes . . . ' He managed a wry smile. 'Sometimes I complained that she spent more time with Duke than with me. But she hadn't been near him since David died. It was as though she just couldn't care less what happened to him.' Deep in thought, he paused.

'And how did she react when you became angry?'

'At first, she just sat there while I shouted. Then I told her that if she didn't care about the horse, I might as well get rid of him.'

'And that did the trick?'

'Not at first. I was so angry I had to do something. So, after I'd cleaned out Duke's stable I decided that I would ride him.'

'Sounds like a good way to let off steam.'

'If you like riding yes. But I've been scared stiff of

horses all my life, even of Duke, and he's a right softie.'

'Oh.' A little smile forced its way onto Mary's face. 'And I suppose you fell off?'

'Actually, no. Although I did fear for my life when Katherine came into the paddock and he broke into a trot.'

'And did she ride him?'

He nodded. 'She galloped him round a few times, then collapsed, sobbing. The most dreadful sobs I've ever heard.'

Mary covered her mouth with her hands, but said nothing.

'It was the best thing that could have happened,' he went on. 'She hadn't cried at all, and there was no other way she could release the agony and begin to live again.'

Eventually, Mary asked, 'And were you able to talk together after that?'

'Oh, yes. For hours. She didn't recover overnight, but that was the turning-point.' He stared into his cup. 'Life will never be quite the same as it was when David was alive, but Katherine realises now that her other children need her.'

'And you.'

'Of course. I thought I had lost Katherine for ever, but thankfully I was wrong.'

For some moments they sat in silence, sipping their tea. Then Mary gently said, 'Christmas Day is the time for miracles.'

After the piano-tuner had left, clutching two bags, one containing the three pieces of bread pudding and half a dozen scones in the other, Mary thought over their long conversation. It was as though they had been friends for years, and she didn't even know his name.

Her reverie was broken by the bell over the door. Michael was home.

'Did you see my card in the window?' she asked. 'I'm going to try doing some take-aways. What do you think?' She wondered if he would mutter something about being cold and hungry and go straight upstairs, but he went back outside to study the card. When he came inside again, he was smiling.

'It's worth a go,' he said. 'And while you're about it, why don't you advertise those funny cakes you make?'

Smiling inwardly, Mary asked, 'Do you think I might get some orders?'

'You'll never know if you don't try, will you?'

'You're right, Michael. And aren't you the clever one, thinking up such good ideas.' She kissed his lips. 'And what sort of a day have you had?'

'Not bad. Mr Burridge has offered us a bonus if we work part of the Easter weekend. Help to get the job moving along after all the rain we've had. You don't mind, do you, dear?'

It was a long time since he'd smiled so lovingly and called her 'dear'. No, Mary didn't mind at all. She hoped she'd be very busy over Easter. If it went as well as she hoped, with the take-away trade and all, she would soon have that nice young bank manager smiling at her.

21

Usually James kept to the same schedule when he visited Fivepenny Lanes: the village hall, school and Vicarage before he ate his sandwiches and fed the ducks, then up to the Chestnut Grove and Cranleigh Manor. But it was a flexible arrangement and he would change the order around to suit his clients' convenience. Sometimes the clients would change it around, whether it was convenient for him or not. Like today, when he had already swapped the Vicarage appointment with 12 Susan Close because Mrs Green had to go out in the afternoon. But when he drew up outside number 12, she was unlocking her car.

'Sorry,' she said, rather abruptly. 'I've got an appointment with my solicitor. Forgot you were coming. I'm not even sure whether I want it done at all — phone me tomorrow.' Then she was gone.

Thanks very much, he thought, as he checked his appointment book. Not much point in going to the Dower House. Mrs Burridge had particularly asked him to leave it until after lunch.

'It's the housekeeper's day off and I shall be in and out all morning, either baking masses of plaited loaves, or taking them up to the village hall for the Harvest Supper.'

He looked at his watch. Just turned eleven. Too early for lunch, although he was tempted to fill the time by having a cup of coffee and a piece of Mary

Fitzgerald's delicious bread pudding. But the recollection of their last meeting held him back. He had so opened up his heart to her, talked about his innermost feelings in a way he hadn't been able to do with anyone else — not Katherine, not even Julie when she phoned. It's true what they say about it being easier to talk to strangers, but the new owner of the tea-shop had not seemed like a stranger, more like a trusted friend. What bothered him was that she might have been embarrassed by his outpourings. Perhaps it would be better if he didn't call in today.

He checked his schedule again. Might as well go up to the Manor as he was so close. Then, with luck, he could be home early. Maybe take Katherine out for a meal. Her recovery had been helped famously by having recently been told that Julie had become pregnant again. What could be nicer than to discuss a trip to Australia over a satisfactory meal and a glass of wine? They could go to the Happy Cheese at Ashurst. He could afford it now, although after the dreadful fire, it had been rebuilt into a pub with a restaurant; not quite so upper crust as the old place, but he'd heard the food was very good.

Two cars were parked outside Cranleigh Manor. A Lotus — obviously the owner was home — and another brand new car, a Civic Honda. Ralph Beresford-Lawson had visitors. James hoped it wouldn't mean he had to come back later, but the new housekeeper ushered him in through the hall, as usual.

'Mr Ralph said not to disturb him before lunch, but I'm sure it will be quite in order for you to tune the piano now.' She threw open the double doors to the drawing room, adding, 'He usually pays your account at the end of the month, anyway, doesn't he?'

More usually at the end of the following month, after one or two reminders, James thought, wryly.

The dust sheets had been removed from the furniture and huge arrangements of flowers were everywhere. The squire must be entertaining on a grand scale. James removed the silver-framed photographs and vase of chrysanthemums, wishing that people would take his advice and not put flowers or drinks on top of a piano. One untimely nudge and there would be irreparable damage, and the Broadwood was too valuable and rare to risk. He must have another word with the housekeeper before he left.

As he carefully lifted off the top, he heard running footsteps upstairs, a light laugh, a man's voice, low, then a breathless squeal. Two people seemed to be playing tag in and out of the bedrooms. He wondered if it was Mr Ralph — or perhaps he was having a house party? More likely to be Mr Ralph, if he'd given instructions not to be disturbed before lunch. James smiled as his imagination followed the sounds. Then, to his horror, the lid of the keyboard slipped down from where he had rested it against the wall, with a resounding crash. Upstairs, the skylarking was interrupted by a sudden 'Sssh!' Feeling intrusive, James decided to close the doors.

An enormous gilt-framed mirror in the hall reflected the lower part of a slight figure tiptoeing down the staircase, swamped in a large towelling robe. Judging by the bare feet, a feminine figure.

Another step down and a face came into the frame. Good Lord! It was Susan Burridge. He tried to duck behind one of the doors, but it was too late. Their startled expressions met in the mirror. Then, with a strangled sound, she scuttled back upstairs.

Thoughtfully, he began to tune the piano. He didn't care that his clients had been caught in *flagrante delicto*, and it didn't really surprise him, having read between the lines of meaningful glances between the two people concerned. What did concern him was whether he should keep his afternoon appointment at the Dower House.

The decision was made for him, in the brief note presented by the housekeeper. Mrs Burridge would be grateful if he could bring his appointment forward to twelve-thirty. She had telephoned Megan Taylor to explain she had changed the times around and that was fine by her. Obviously, she was afraid he might say something to her best friend, although she should have known better.

When he'd finished his work, James quickly left, forgetting to remind the housekeeper about flowers on the piano. There wasn't time to drive down to the village, eat his sandwiches, and be back again by twelve-thirty, so he parked his car a little way along the lane and had a short break. After a few moments, the Honda came out of the gates to the Manor and turned into the drive of the Dower House.

Dressed casually in a navy track suit, Mrs Burridge seemed to have recovered her composure as she showed him into the sitting room. When she reappeared with a tray of coffee and biscuits, he began to wonder whether he had imagined the whole thing. Curled up in the huge armchair, both hands cupped around her mug and the little King Charles spaniel begging for a biscuit, she looked vulnerable. Perhaps it was the navy suit reminding him of school uniforms, or her freshly washed and brushed hair, worn as always in a well-cut bob with a fringe, but there was a childlike quality about her.

As though reading his thoughts, she said, 'I'm not really a scarlet woman, Mr Woodward.'

He tried to stop her. 'Really, it's none of my business.'

'But I want to explain.' She leaned forward. 'As you know, my husband has been wanting to buy Cranleigh Manor land for some time. We became chummy with Ralph, hoping he'd sell to Percy eventually. It was one of the reasons we bought the Dower House.' She lifted the dog on to her lap, then went on. 'Percy told me to do everything I could.'

James wondered if her husband had realised how literally his words would be taken.

'Being unmarried, Ralph often needed a hostess when he was staying here. We went riding together, played tennis, entertained — things like that. He seemed to enjoy my company. Then he — ' She groped in her pocket for a tissue. 'He made it quite clear that he was prepared to consider my husband's offer, if I — ' Hurriedly, she went on, 'I didn't want to. You must understand that. I love my husband and have never been unfaithful to him before. But I knew how much he wanted that land. And Ralph had been very good to Jonathan, with his career and the apartment, and everything. I felt under an obligation.' She refilled her mug from the elegant bone china coffee pot. 'So I thought it wouldn't hurt, just the once. As long as Percy didn't know. He thinks the world of me.' She clenched the tissue. 'If he found out, through idle gossip, I don't know what he'd do.' Her voice dropped to a tearful whisper. 'I'm so ashamed.'

Acutely embarrassed, James cleared his throat. 'As I said, Mrs Burridge, it's none of my business. And I'm not in the habit of gossiping to my clients.' He refrained from adding, 'as you should know after all these years,' but the silent reproof obviously reached her.

'I know,' she said, 'but I needed to hear you say it. Thank you.' She stood up. 'Would you like another coffee? Or something stronger?'

'No, thank you. I'd best be getting on with the piano or I'll be late for my next appointment.'

The only person he told was Katherine, while they were having a pre-dinner drink at the Happy Cheese.

'Watch out for that one,' she commented. 'She's trouble.'

'Oh, I don't know. More likely led astray by the Lord of the Manor, with promises of this and that. Susan Burridge is ambitious, but she's quite a simple woman, really. No match for the wiles of someone like Ralph Beresford-Lawson. And I think she genuinely loves her husband.'

'Hmm. It's the sweet and innocent types I'm most suspicious of. And I bet his nibs will forget all about his promise, now he's had his wicked way. Although it doesn't sound as though it was the first time, from what you've said.'

'No. I think some of her trips to London to see the children included some extra-marital activities with our Mr Ralph.'

'More than likely.' Katherine reached into her handbag for a blue airmail letter and her spectacle case. Since she'd been prescribed reading glasses for eyestrain, she'd been wearing a pair of half-moon 'granny' glasses. James loved them, especially when she peered at him over the top, like now. 'Letter from Julie,' she said. 'They're not too sure of the date when the baby is due, and Paul is going to fly her to Melbourne a month beforehand and stay with her so that medical help is to hand if she needs it.'

'Let's hope she doesn't.'

'Exactly, but they're taking no chances, after what happened last time, and he is insisting she rests more than she wants to.' Again that look over the top of the half-spectacles, then Katherine went back to the letter. 'What she's suggesting is that we go over afterwards, for the christening.'

'That sounds like a much better idea.' James had been dreading the thought of hanging around indefinitely, worrying about Julie and unable to do anything to help.

'I've told her I'll take over the christening robe — you know, the one Grandma made when I was born.'

'Supposing it's a boy?'

'Oh, that won't matter.' Katherine waved her hand airily. 'He'll be too young to worry about things like that.' She tapped the letter against her teeth. 'I'd like to take the cake over as well. Julie said the Aborigine girl who cooks for them is quite good, but I don't suppose she'd be up to an iced cake. Do you think it would travel?'

'Don't see why not, if it's not too elaborate and carefully packed for the flight.' James suddenly had a brilliant idea. This would give him the perfect excuse to break the ice without just going in for a coffee. 'Why don't I ask the woman who's bought the tea-shop in Fivepenny Lanes. She makes cakes to order.'

Katherine thought for a moment, then nodded. 'I don't see why not. Ask her if she has any good ideas for something a little unusual, but not too fragile.'

Mary Fitzgerald had a very good idea, and Katherine loved it when they talked on the telephone.

'She's going to design one that's quite simple, with just the child's name, and a little kangaroo in moulded icing, carrying the baby in its pouch. Now that's a bit different to a cradle and bootees, isn't it? She sounds like a nice person, James. I'm looking forward to meeting her.'

Unfortunately, Katherine didn't get over to Fivepenny Lanes. And she didn't get to Australia when Benjie was born the following spring.

★ ★ ★

It was the silliest thing. Katherine had jumped much higher jumps without a problem, but afterwards she told James she knew as she approached the jump

329

that Duke was wrong-footed and tried, too late, to correct him. Even so she wasn't concerned — it certainly wasn't the first time she'd fallen off a horse. But it was the first time she had fallen on to the point of her knee. Several months later, they were still no nearer to holding their first grandchild, and Julie fretted and fumed because she'd had a caesarean, with complications, and couldn't get to England to see her mum. But they weren't the only ones fuming and fretting.

22

Susan slammed the receiver down and sat staring at the telephone for some minutes. Even when he didn't return her earlier calls, she hadn't anticipated this, and at first she couldn't believe what he was saying. But Ralph finally made it quite clear. He was dumping her!

The arrogance of the man. He wouldn't even give her a reason. Just said she would find out soon enough and it was better for both of them that they didn't continue their little 'arrangement'. It might be better for him, but not for her. After all she had done for him, playing the perfect hostess, entertaining his 'Hooray Henry' friends, keeping an eye on the Manor while he was away, giving herself to him whenever he'd fancied. And what about the promises he'd made? Percy so wanted that piece of land across the river, and Ralph had assured her that he would have first refusal if it was decided to sell. He couldn't welsh on it, not after all this time.

The worst part was not being able to talk about it. She wanted everyone to know what a bastard he was. But who could she tell? Not Percy, nor her children; not that she saw much of them nowadays. Her closest friend was Megan, and she certainly couldn't tell the curate's wife. If only there was some way she could discredit him. How dare he toss her aside like a piece of garbage!

Going through into the sitting room she poured

herself a large whisky and flopped into a chair, racking her brain. After her second large whisky, she came to the conclusion that one of her letters would not work this time. Who would she send it to, and what would she say? All his co-directors were tarred with the same brush. One or two had even made suggestions that she might share their beds from time to time if old Ralph didn't come up to scratch. No, Mr Ralph bloody Beresford-Lawson was too rich and influential to be touched by anything she might say. He would only retaliate by reminding her that Percy didn't know *why* his son had been introduced to the merchant bankers and *who* had helped Jonathan to furnish the apartment.

The third whisky unleashed tears of self-pity. She felt used. And, she had to admit, she would miss the lifestyle; the boxes at the theatre in London, the plush restaurants, the night-clubs where they mixed with the famous and infamous. Percy was generous to a fault, but he didn't move in quite the same circles. And his libido hadn't been quite so virulent of late. Ralph wasn't as thoughtful a lover as Percy, but he was powerful and knew how to awaken her passion, never far below the surface. Susan sighed. She would miss the sex.

The doorbell interrupted her miserable thoughts. Who could it be at this time of the morning? Percy was in Southampton and Mrs Graham had a key. Probably cowboys anxious to resurface the drive, or Jehovah's Witnesses. They would go away eventually. But this visitor was persistent. In fact, he called through the letterbox.

'Susan. Are you all right? Susan!'

It was Nigel. Damn. She'd have to open the door, or he would be phoning Percy at work to make sure everything was OK.

Rapidly drying her tears, she tied the belt of her housecoat as she called back, 'Just a minute, Nigel. I was on the phone.' As she opened the front door, the gardener cycled along the drive. She ignored him.

Nigel took one look at her and his mouth gaped, 'Susan! What on earth has happened?'

The compassion on his face was the law straw. Bursting once more into tears, she flung her arms around him. 'Oh, Nigel, I'm so unhappy. Do come in.'

Still clinging to him, she was led into the sitting room. Nigel looked as though he was about to pour her a brandy, then his eyes noted the whisky glass, and he sat on a footstool at her feet and took her hand.

'Do you want to tell me about it?' he gently asked.

For a moment she was tempted. He was a man of the cloth. Not quite in the same league as a Catholic priest taking confession, but an Anglican curate would respect confidentialty. But he was also the husband of her best friend. Too dodgy, even for a cleric, she thought. So she lied.

'It's bad news about a friend, in Yorkshire.' Susan improvised as she went along. 'Rather personal, I'm afraid.'

Nigel patted her hand. 'If you want to tell me about it, the information won't go beyond these walls, I promise you.'

'Well . . .' Perhaps she could offload some of the

anger and hurt. 'You promise you won't say anything to anyone? Not Megan? Not even Percy?'

'Of course not. I expect you'll want to tell Percy about it yourself later.'

'No! My friend made me vow that I wouldn't tell him. She feels so humiliated, she said I was the only person she could confide in.'

'Right. Now, take your time, Susan. I'll just listen.'

So Susan found herself telling the whole wretched story in the third person, adapting the story line and changing the places to those north of the Watford Gap, and being careful not to mention any names. It might trip her up later. 'My friend' and 'that dreadful man' would suffice.

' . . . and my poor friend feels so alone, and really doesn't know who to turn to,' she concluded.

Patting her hand in an almost absent-minded way, Nigel handed Susan the box of tissues. 'All I can say, my dear, is that your friend is lucky to have someone like you to talk to. You are obviously feeling her pain and suffering.'

'Oh, indeed I am,' she breathed. 'But what do you think she should do?'

He reflected upon her words for quite a while, then said, 'There isn't very much she can do. She has been a very foolish lady, and — '

'Foolish!' Susan felt quite indignant.

'Perhaps that was too strong a word. But she did trust the scoundrel when he promised that he could help her poor mother to have the operation she needed. It's rather like something out of *East Lynne*, but I suppose there are women who would accept his word. Gullible is perhaps a better description of your friend than foolish.'

'Yes — oh, yes. My poor friend was so gullible. So, Nigel, do you think there is any way that she can extract justice from this dreadful man?'

'Justice? I would think it highly unlikely. And I'm sure you would not want your friend to consider — revenge?'

'No, no, of course not.' Revenge had been uppermost in her mind, but perhaps it wouldn't be prudent to pursue that path. 'So what do you think she should do?' she asked.

Again his gaze went into middle distance. Then he slowly said, 'I don't truly believe that your friend can do anything. But you could remind her that the Lord has a way of exacting his own revenge on those who have ill-treated others. Continue to be a listening ear and a good friend. That in itself must be helpful. But she must forget the dreadful man and continue to support her mother. And we will pray for them.'

Susan didn't find very much solace in his words, but she nodded, and closed her eyes sanctimoniously. Then, reaching for the whisky glass, she had another thought.

'Why did you come, Nigel?'

'Ah.' His eyes opened. 'Megan asked me to let you have this back.' He handed her the catalogue of an auction sale. 'She can't go with you this afternoon, I'm afraid, as Matthew has spots. Looks like measles this time, so she's keeping him home from school. Sorry.'

'Oh, dear.' Another tear crept down Susan's cheek as she looked at the catalogue. She had been particularly looking forward to bidding for a secretaire bookcase. 'I did so want to go to this sale.'

'Then go, Susan, dear. It will do you good.'

'I know it will. But I really don't want to go on my own. I don't feel up to driving.' She hesitated. 'Nigel, would you — could you — come with me?'

He looked flustered. 'Oh, I'm not sure that I can. I should be writing my sermon. I'm helping Megan's father to take the parish service on Sunday.'

'It will only be for a couple of hours. And I will be so grateful. Please. I do need cheering up.'

A few more moments' hesitation, then Nigel nodded. 'I'll pick you up at — ' He glanced at the catalogue. 'Will one o'clock be OK?'

'Oh, yes.' For the second time she flung her arms around him, crying, 'Thank you, Nigel. I owe you.'

'Not at all. Isn't that what friends are for?'

As he kissed her cheek, Susan noticed Mrs Graham standing in the doorway, and felt embarrassed. Pushing him away, she murmured, 'Really, Nigel, this won't do. What will Mrs Graham think?'

Turning, he blushed scarlet, and stammered, 'G-good morning, Mrs Graham. How are you?'

'I am very well, thank you, Mr Taylor.' Mrs Graham's eyebrows rose a fraction as she looked at Susan, who shook her head and turned away, biting her lower lip. Then the housekeeper asked, 'Will you be needing coffee, Mrs Burridge?'

Quickly, Susan replied, 'No, thank you. You have to be going, don't you, Nigel?'

'Yes, of course.' Nigel looked decidedly uncomfortable as he foraged in his pocket for his car keys. 'We have some problems with the roof of the almshouses.'

Susan nodded, then said, 'If you'll excuse me, I have to run my bath. Mrs Graham will show you out.' Then she hurried from the room.

When Nigel returned after lunch, Mrs Graham was cleaning the back bedrooms. Susan had merely said that she was going to an auction in Salisbury, she didn't mention that Nigel was taking her. After asking if she felt better, he was silent for some miles. Then he blurted out, 'I hope we didn't embarrass Mrs Graham.'

Glancing sideways at him, she said, 'Of course not.'

'Good.' His voice was full of relief. 'I'm sure she understood your explanation.'

Susan didn't reply, just looked out of the window.

The auction room was crowded and Nigel asked if she minded him wandering off on his own for a while. When Megan had given him the catalogue he'd flicked through it and noticed some silver pieces and antique jewellery in the list. Their silver wedding was only a few months away and it wouldn't hurt to find out if anything might be suitable — and affordable. They agreed to meet in half an hour.

Susan was studying the secretaire and wondering what ceiling she should set on her bidding, when she became aware that she was being watched. At first she tried to ignore the feeling that she was under scrutiny, but curiosity got the better of her and she slowly walked around to the back of the piece of furniture, pretending to examine every detail, then casually looked up.

The man lounged against a wall a few feet away, staring straight at her, and he made no attempt to look away. Instead, he raised his catalogue, almost in a bidding gesture, and smiled. His teeth were incredibly white against the dark colour of his skin, which looked as though he spent much of his time out of doors, and his black curly hair was worn loose and slightly longer than fashionable. He reminded her of someone — yes — Michael Fitzgerald, the Irishman who lived above the tea-shop with his fat wife. But whereas Michael's eyes were very blue, this man's eyes were gypsy-black, and twinkling. A devilish face, but very attractive.

Feeling her face might be expressing her thoughts, Susan turned away and pulled down the writing table, minutely examining the joints of the drawers. Next moment, the stranger was at her side.

'Nice piece that. Are you a collector, or trade?' His voice had a strong Hampshire accent.

Licking her lips, she tried to sound offhand as she answered, 'Neither, really, although I do appreciate fine things.'

'Know much about antique furniture?'

Susan was about to resort to her usual ploy of pretending she knew more about a subject than she really did, then she hesitated. Just as it had paid off to be honest about her lack of horse-racing knowledge when she first met Percy, so it might be more interesting to be truthful now.

'Actually, no. Just that I love the look and feel of

things like this.' Her hand stroked the polished surface and when she looked up at him again, a mischievous little smile played around his mouth.

Slowly, he said, 'So do I.' His hand was only an inch or so away from hers as he touched the secretaire, copying her movement. 'It's almost as good as touching a woman.'

He was testing her. She knew he was testing her, and she also knew she should walk away. But she felt as helpless as a fly drawn towards a web. An inner voice warned her to be careful as she said, 'Are you an expert?'

'You'd have to ask the women.'

'I meant — '

'I know what you meant. Sorry, I was teasing.' He turned back to the piece of furniture. 'You could say I was a bit of a Lovejoy, I suppose. I can usually spot something worth having at a hundred paces, and I'm known for negotiating a good price. If there's anything you particularly want, I can always try to provide it — if you're interested.'

He'd put the ball squarely back into her court and Susan wasn't quite sure whether she should return it or not. Just at that moment, Nigel appeared.

'Susan! I've seen a beautiful silver pendant. Will you come and tell me what you think?' Then he noticed the stranger. 'Oh, I'm sorry, I didn't mean to interrupt.'

'That's all right, Nigel. This gentleman is an antique dealer; that is right, isn't it?'

'You could say that, Vicar.' The stranger had noted Nigel's collar. 'And I was just telling your wife that I might be able to help her if she's looking for a bargain.'

'Oh! We're not married. We're just — '

Susan laughed at the expression on Nigel's face as the implication of his words sank in. 'What Nigel means is that he's the husband of my closest friend and very kindly brought me over.'

They all laughed, in a slightly self-conscious way, then Nigel looked at his watch. 'The auction starts in five minutes, Susan. If I could just tear you away for a moment?'

'Of course. Let me have another look at the secretaire and I'll be right over.'

Nigel left them, and Susan made a hurried decision. Reaching into her handbag, she took out one of Percy's business cards and a pen. 'If you do find something that you think might interest me, phone this number, not the office number.'

He read the card and raised his eyebrows. 'I've heard of Percy Burridge. Isn't he the old boy who's been building the big shopping complexes?' She nodded. 'Is he your dad, then?'

'My husband. He *is* considerably older than me.' The words hung meaningfully between them, before he spoke again.

'And you are — ?'

'Susan. Susan Burridge.'

'Right, Susan Burridge. I'll give you a bell some time.' Turning away, he called over his shoulder, 'By the way, the name's Josh. Josh Smith. Easy enough to remember.' Then he was gone, pushing his way through the crowd.

The secretaire bookcase was within Susan's price

range — just. And Nigel bought the silver pendant for Megan. He'd asked Susan if she would pay for it with one of her cheques, so that he could refund it with cash, and Megan wouldn't notice the name of the auction house on the cheque stub. On the way home, he enthused about his purchase, and asked her whether she thought Megan would be pleased. Secretly, Susan thought it was too heavy and ornate, but Megan would probably like it. She wasn't really paying a great deal of attention to Nigel's prattling. Her thoughts drifted back to a man with a devastating smile and a wicked line in innuendoes.

She hadn't seen him again, but already she knew how easy he was to remember.

23

It would be Percy's birthday in a few weeks. His sixty-fifth. Susan loved her husband, but she hated the thoughts of being married to a pensioner. It made her feel old. He was the one who had the 'headache' nowadays, and it was the wrong way round. She desperately needed someone like Ralph, or Josh — particularly Josh — to make her feel young again. But Josh was in Harrogate. She'd wanted to go with him, but he was travelling with fellow antique dealers, and he said it would be difficult, but not to worry, he'd phone her as soon as he was back. So here she was, trying to plan her husband's birthday party, and wondering what to give him.

What on earth could she buy for a sixty-five-year-old man who already had everything? He'd given up smoking when his father took ill, so a gold cigar case was no good, and she wanted to buy him a Rolex watch for their pearl anniversary next year. His only sport was golf, and he already had state of the art gear. Actually, he didn't play quite so much nowadays, said he hadn't the time, and he had put on a bit of weight. Perhaps membership to an exclusive health club would be a good idea? But if he didn't have time for golf, he wouldn't have time to go to a health club.

Eventually, she decided upon one of those home exercise machines. More flexible with his timetable.

And if he couldn't find the time to use it, she would. Her figure was still trim, but you couldn't take chances when you were almost fifty, especially as she'd told Josh she was only forty-three. He wasn't quite forty yet, and if he knew her real age he might feel like a toyboy and back off. She'd almost let the cat out of the bag when he asked how old her children were, and only just stopped in time from telling him that Jonathan was twenty-seven and Abigail twenty-two. So a few years had to be knocked off their ages as well. But all in a good cause.

How she missed him. He was such an exciting lover, much more so than Ralph. And, just as Ralph had introduced her to a world inhabited by the rich and famous, so Josh was teaching her to appreciate another world, one she hadn't realised existed — the world of antiques. And she had fallen hopelessly in love with these beautiful objects that could be displayed and admired, especially the furniture. There wasn't much Josh didn't know about antiques; porcelain was his speciality, and he would examine each piece minutely. She never ceased to marvel that his brown, roughened hands could be so careful and loving when he handled a delicate Spode dish. He held it with as much — no, more — tenderness than he would a woman, and went on to explain to her how the design, shape and style, together with the colour of the marks on the back of the piece, told him whether it was made by the first, second or third Josiah Spode. She had bought small pieces of furniture to add to the items already in the Dower House, and was learning fast, but buying books and browsing in antique shops wasn't the same as having Josh by her side to teach her. Not the same at all. The hardest thing for her to accept was that he had gypsy blood from his father's side, and gypsies like freedom. Susan was terrified of being dumped again. Even now, the memory of Ralph's cold voice on the telephone made her feel sick in the pit of her stomach.

Her thoughts went back to Percy. He was a good husband, there was no doubt about it, and she was pretty sure he'd never been unfaithful. But she didn't feel she was being unfaithful. After all, she'd only ever loved him, only ever *could* love him. Ralph and Josh satisfied a deep sexual need, that was all. When Percy was younger and virile, she had never needed to look further, but now he was older and tired from all the travelling to meetings with architects and business consortiums in London, there were times when the loneliness was almost unbearable. But she had to be careful. If Percy found out, he wouldn't understand that it was only boredom that had driven her to look elsewhere for companionship, and the one thing she was not prepared to do was to risk her marriage and security.

The birthday party was fairly simple, by Susan's standards of entertaining. But Percy had said he didn't want a fuss made just because he was eligible for a bus pass. Then he'd said he'd like to ask Alfie and Brenda down for that weekend. They were the only relatives he had now, apart from a distant cousin, and they had never been to Hampshire. Although she'd written warm letters of invitation,

Susan had been sure they wouldn't come. Alfie had just taken early retirement from the railways because of his dodgy back, and always said he'd had enough of travel to last him for the rest of his life, and his sister, still running the corner shop with her husband, had never been further than Scarborough. To her surprise, Brenda phoned and said her husband's niece would look after the shop for a couple of days and she'd like to see Percy's new house. It would make a nice change — but it wouldn't be a posh do, would it? She didn't have an evening dress.

Secretly livid, Susan purred down the telephone that of course she wouldn't need an evening dress. It would just be an informal little gathering, and they would feel quite at home. Then Alfie's wife Vera wrote — she didn't like the telephone — and said that as Alfie still had free rail travel, they might as well come. After all, none of them were getting any younger, and so they ought to get together once more, or it would be too late.

At first, Susan was tempted to arrange such a lavish evening in the grandest hotel that they would all wish they'd never come. But then she realised it wouldn't be fair to Percy, and it was his party, after all. So she smiled sweetly, agreed with Percy that it would be lovely to see his brother and sister again, and set about organising the buffet with Mrs Graham.

'Nothing too complicated, mind. My husband's relatives have simpler taste than ours.'

'I could bake a whole gammon, Mrs Burridge, to slice at the table, with bowls of salad. And what do you think for a second joint — turkey or beef?'

'Beef, my husband's favourite.' Sometimes, Susan thought, she would like to have something different on a Sunday, but Percy was a stickler for his roast beef and Yorkshire pudding, and it had to be from the butcher, not from a supermarket.

'Right.' Mrs Graham wrote rapidly. 'And I expect you'll be wanting sausage rolls and vol-au-vents, a sherry trifle, selection of cheeses — and we mustn't forget the cake!'

Susan nodded. 'Only thing is, I wasn't too happy with the one we had made for our silver wedding. The icing was rockhard and the cake was like sawdust. I suppose you don't — ?'

'Cakes are the one thing I'm not particularly good with, I'm afraid, but last Christmas we had a beauty from Mary at the village tea-shop. Nice soft fondant icing over a lovely moist fruit cake. Everybody said it was the best they'd ever had, and she'll do any design you ask for.'

Susan was thoughtful for a moment. She didn't particularly like the Irishwoman, although she'd never said anything out of place. But if her cakes were that good, and it was only up the road . . . 'OK,' she said, 'I'll have a word with her.'

After Susan had browsed through the photo album, Mary Fitzgerald roughed out one or two designs, and finally Susan decided upon one that had a grinning figure in a hard hat lounging in a garden hammock, reading a newspaper, with a tankard of beer in his hand and a set of golf clubs lying by his side.

'Not that Percy has any intention of retiring,'

Susan commented, 'But perhaps it will be a reminder that he should take it a bit easier.'

'I could put, 'Every day is Sunday now'?' Mary suggested, but Susan preferred her own idea of, 'Think on it, Percy, now you're sixty-five!' She had to admit that Mary's designs were good, and they were both chuckling over the photographs of other cakes when Michael came through from the back of the shop. It was a Saturday and he looked quite smart, as though he was going out.

'Well, now,' he said, a broad smile on his face, 'and isn't that the grandest sound for a man to hear? Two lovely ladies enjoying a chat. Good evening, Susan.'

'Good evening, Michael.' The man must have kissed the Blarney Stone at some time or other, she thought, but you couldn't help enjoying his charm when it was delivered with such a delightful accent. 'And how are you?'

'Grand, Susan. Really grand.' He turned to Mary. 'Charlie has just phoned and asked me over to watch the big fight live on his satellite. Don't bother with dinner for me, dear, we'll probably have a take-away.'

'But Michael, I thought we were going to Ocean Village tonight, to see that picture.'

'Oh, so we were. I'm that forgetful. Never mind, darling — we can always go another time.' He kissed her cheek. 'I might be a bit late back, so don't wait up for me.' Once again he turned his blue eyes on Susan. 'A very good night to you, Susan.' Then he was gone.

For a moment there was silence, then Mary

sighed and shook her head. 'Men!' she said, closing the photograph album. 'What can we do with them?'

Slowly, Susan said, 'And what can we do without them?'

★ ★ ★

Percy's relatives arrived quite late on the afternoon of his birthday. Brenda was suitably impressed with the house and the pool but Vera, as usual, found much to worry about.

'You're rather remote out here. Aren't you afraid of burglars? There was that terrible case a few years back when they were all murdered and the house set on fire. That was in Hampshire, too. And mind that dear little dog doesn't fall into the pool. She might drown, Susan.'

Percy had been quite chuffed with his home gymnasium, showing it off with a jest. 'I think Susan's trying to tell me something. Happen she's right.' He laughed and patted his expanding waistline.

But Vera was more worried about his back than his waistline. 'Just you be careful on that contraption, Percy, or you'll finish up with a slipped disc, like Alfie.'

Jonathan and Abigail had arrived the previous evening. Abigail was a great help with the preparations during the morning, but Jonathan seemed a little withdrawn and had stayed in his room until lunchtime. When Susan asked him if everything was all right, he said everything was fine, just some business to see to. He wasn't the only one with things on his mind, but at least Abigail was willing to talk about her thoughts and plans. Over lunch, she had told them that she would be going to Rwanda in the New Year, with a party of like-minded nurses and doctors. Open-mouthed, Susan looked at Percy, then back at Abigail.

'But why Rwanda?' she asked.

Abigail smiled. 'Because that's where we're needed.'

'But it's dangerous out there. All the fighting and terrible things happening.'

'And sickness.' Abigail laid her hand on her mother's arm. 'I have to go,' she said, simply. 'It's something I've wanted to do for some time. Not just because I'm a trained nurse and have something to offer, but because I think God wants me to go.'

Jonathan laughed. 'Been having visions, have you?' he said.

'No.' Abigail's expression was almost sad as she looked at him. 'But I do think that if I hadn't become a nurse, I might have become a missionary.'

Jonathan spluttered into his wine. 'Oh, Lordy Lordy. My sister's gone all religious.'

'Jonathan!' Percy's voice was sharp. Then he turned to Abigail. 'If you feel that strongly about it, you have to follow your instincts, lass. But what about the house?'

'I've spoken to Ruthie, and she's going to take in some student nurses after I've left. That will help out with my share of the mortgage and keep the option open if I come back.'

Susan was shocked. '*If* you come back? Surely you

mean *when* you come back?'

Abigail toyed with the roll on her plate. 'It could be either. I might go on to other areas. Africa has always fascinated me.' Her smile had been very sweet and patient as she said, 'Don't worry, Mummy. Whatever I decide, I'll come back and visit.'

Jonathan poured himself another glass of wine. 'Like the prodigal daughter, expecting the fatted calf, eh?'

Abigail smiled, but didn't comment. While Percy questioned his daughter about the practicalities of such a step, Susan worried about both her children. Something must be bothering Jonathan for him to make such sarcastic remarks to his sister. Although there was a five-year gap in their ages, so they'd never been particularly close, they'd always got on reasonably well, and she'd assumed they saw each other fairly regularly in London. But today he seemed almost antagonistic towards her.

After lunch Jonathan had gone straight out into the garden and wandered over to the pool, covered up for the winter, constantly using his mobile phone. Susan would have liked to talk to Percy about him, but there was too much to do, and in no time at all, the Yorkshire guests had to be collected from the station. It would have to wait until tomorrow.

Apart from the family, only a few other guests had been invited. Megan and Nigel, of course, and Megan's parents; Frank Griffiths, Malcolm Groves, the golf club manager, and Dr Morrissey, all with their wives. Percy had suggested asking Michael and

Mary Fitzgerald, but Susan had managed to convince him that it wasn't a very good idea. After all, Michael was only one of his labourers, and they'd never mixed socially. It well might embarrass them if they couldn't return the invitation. Better not set a precedent.

Everything was going swimmingly, all the presents had been opened, the buffet table depleted, the cake admired, laughed over and cut, Vera was telling Mrs Morrissey about Alfie's bad back, Brenda was chatting happily to Gwynneth Jenkins about the shop, and Alfie was talking to Frank Griffiths about the changes to the railways, when it happened.

It was one of those moments when the hubbub has died a little, so one voice carries to the whole room, and Percy had a loud voice. He was opening another bottle of champagne at the time. 'Nearly forgot to tell you, Susan,' he said. 'While I was parking car at station, I bumped into Goddard — estate manager up at Manor. You'll never guess what he told me. Our squire's getting wed again. To a Lady Deborah somebody or other. The announcement's going in *The Times* on Monday.' The cork popped explosively. 'What do you make of that, then, love?'

★　★　★

It wasn't that Megan didn't trust her husband, it was just — he'd been behaving so strangely of late. Ever since last summer, when Matthew had the measles, he'd got into the habit of suddenly disappearing without a word and, if she asked him

351

where he'd been, he made so many different excuses, she didn't know what to believe. He'd always told her where he was going, in case of emergencies. He'd never lied to her before, but once or twice she had accidentally found out that he hadn't been with her father, or at the school, or wherever. And sometimes she found him deep in thought, as though worried about something. But whatever if was, he wouldn't tell her, however much she tried to wheedle it out of him — and she was quite good at wheedling out information. With five children, you had to be.

Then there was the strange incident at Percy's birthday party. Everything lovely until people started talking about Mr Ralph's engagement when, all of a sudden, Susan ran out of the room. Megan had wanted to go after her, but Percy shook his head. 'She'll be all right, lass. Just a bit of news this morning that's upset her, and what with the party and all. Leave her be for now. She hates a fuss, does Susan.'

But to Megan's surprise, Nigel said, 'I think I might be able to help,' and left her. After a few minutes, her anxiety and curiosity got the better of her, and she followed the sound of weeping into the kitchen. Susan was sobbing in Nigel's arms. Neither saw Megan at first.

'Oh, Nigel,' Susan cried, 'What would I do without you. You're the only one who understands what I'm going through. I can't talk to Percy the way I can with you.' And she clung closer, weeping into his handkerchief.

It wasn't so much the fact that Susan was being

comforted so closely by Nigel that had disturbed Megan. It was their reaction when they noticed her. Nigel jumped back like a scalded cat, and Susan had guilt written all over her face.

Susan was the first to recover. 'I'm sorry for running out like that,' she said, blowing her nose in the handkerchief. 'But Abigail told us today that she's going out to Rwanda, and I'm so worried.'

This time it was Nigel's reaction that made Megan wonder. At first, he looked surprised, as though he knew nothing about it. Then he said quickly, almost too quickly, 'That's right, Megan. That's why Susan is so upset.'

Ever since then, he'd tried to avoid social occasions that included Susan, and never asked after her when Megan visited. That in itself was unusual, he'd often made little quips, such as, 'And what has our good friend given you this time?'

But soon, it would be their silver wedding anniversary, and Megan had to decide whether they should have a small party at home, or go out for a meal. Nigel said he didn't mind. In the event, her parents made the decision for her, and suggested a meal at the Vicarage for the family and the Burridges, who were their closest friends. Nigel's parents were in poor health and couldn't travel up from Cornwall, but Ruthie managed to get down from London, and Owen was on his Easter vacation from university. Dilys wouldn't leave school until July, but was eager to start her business studies course at the Southampton Institute.

The day had started so well, with Nigel giving her the loveliest of gifts. 'Oh, Nigel,' she'd gasped, as he

353

fastened the clasp at the back of her neck. 'I've never seen a locket quite like it. Where did you manage to get such a beauty?'

'Do you remember the day when you couldn't go to the auction because Matthew had measles? Well, I went instead, and Susan helped me to buy it. Even loaned me the money so you wouldn't see the cheque stub. And I didn't know where I could hide it from your prying eyes, so she kept it for me.'

'So that's the reason for all the secrecy? And I thought — '

'What did you think, Megan?' he quietly asked.

'Oh, nothing. Nothing at all, my love.' She smiled at her reflection in the mirror. 'I can't wait to show it to Ruthie.'

And there the matter should have ended, his suspicious behaviour having been explained. Gwynneth Jenkins managed to seat everyone at the huge refectory table and the roast turkey was delicious. It was like Christmas all over again, with presents and toasts and singing around the piano. Even Matthew behaved himself, singing with his mother the lovely duet, 'Pie Jesu', by Andrew Lloyd Webber.

It wasn't until later in the evening, when she'd gone into the kitchen for a drink of water, that she heard the voices in her father's study. Quiet voices, but unmistakably Nigel's and Susan's voices.

'Don't you think it would be better to tell her?' he said.

'Please, Nigel,' she pleaded. 'I couldn't bear it if Megan found out. It's over, anyway.'

'I know, but I still feel — '

'No.' Susan's voice was more decisive now. 'Let's

just keep it between ourselves. Our little secret. Now, we'd better get back to the party or people will start getting suspicious.'

Megan stood for some time in the dark, empty glass in her hand. It's too late, she thought, the suspicions have already started — again. Oh, Nigel, what is this secret you are keeping from me?

24

At last — she had her piano! There it was, coming through the frameless window and being carefully wheeled into position on the little trolley. Mary still couldn't believe her luck. When James Woodward had phoned to tell her that a lady in Susan Close was selling it for the give-away price of forty pounds, and it was worth much more, she had begged and begged until Michael had given in. The poor thing had been hanging around in mid-air on that hoist contraption for the past half-hour, helped on its journey by Michael, Percy Burridge, and Mr Woodward, who would soon restore it to good health and a lovely sound, so he said. What a grand present to celebrate thirty years of marriage. There couldn't be better, except perhaps two air tickets to Australia, but that was way beyond their means just now.

As soon as they had drunk their tea, Michael and Percy were off back to the building site, and Mr Woodward started work on the piano. Sharon was now working at the tea-shop full time, and business was quiet this morning, although Mary had two coaches booked in for the afternoon.

After watching quietly for a while, Mary said, 'It's a pity Mrs Green couldn't take her piano with her, although her loss is my gain.' She shook her head. 'It's always a sad thing when a marriage breaks down, especially when there are little ones.'

Mr Woodward looked up. 'True. But her mother has a piano, so the girls will be able to have piano lessons.'

'Oh, that's good.' Mary was reluctant to move away from her precious piano, but Sharon was calling up the stairs. The timer was pinging in the kitchen. After she'd taken the trays of scones from the oven, and put in the cherry genoas, she made another pot of tea and put it on a tray with two cups and saucers. 'Will you be able to manage for a while longer, Sharon?' she asked.

'Of course I will.' The girl grinned. 'Up you go and play with your new toy.'

The piano sounded wonderful the way James Woodward played it.

'I'd give anything to play like that,' she said.

'It's mainly practice, Mrs Fitzgerald. My daughter is the gifted one.'

'Mary, please. Everybody calls me Mary.' She handed him a cup of tea and pointed to the bread pudding on the plate, then asked, 'And how is your daughter? I know what it's like when you only hear a voice on the telephone, and long to see them.'

He nodded. 'Julie is recovering, thank you, but the doctors think it would be unwise for her to fly just yet.'

'Oh, that's a shame. You were hoping she'd be coming over when I last spoke to you. You must be longing to see the little one.'

He nodded. 'And my wife has to have an operation on her knee, so we still can't get over there.' He stood back from the piano. 'See what you think of it now,' he said.

Tentatively, Mary tried a few notes. 'I'm going to enjoy this, that's for sure. With Michael out so much with his friends, it will be lovely to practise again in the evenings. There's not much I'm really wanting to see on the television.'

'I agree. Most evenings I prefer to listen to music.' Gently he closed the top lid. 'Does your husband play?'

'No, although he used to play the flute in Ireland. Perhaps I can encourage him to take it up again.' Mary sighed with pure pleasure. 'But wasn't it good of him to buy it for my anniversary present?'

'Very good indeed. How long?'

'Thirty years.'

'Really? We must have got married the same year.'

'Are you planning a celebration?'

'It's a bit difficult just now. What I'd really like is to have the celebration in Australia. That would be the best present we could give to each other.'

'I'll pray for you both.' Mary quickly wrote out a cheque and handed it to him.

'Thank you, for the cheque, and the prayer.' He picked up his case. 'And, Mary — '

'Yes?'

'You won't put your anniversary flowers on top of the piano, will you?'

As she led the way down the stairs, Mary knew there was little danger of that. Michael had never bought her flowers in his life.

★ ★ ★

Salisbury had always been one of James's favourite cities. If he was in the area, he liked nothing better than to browse around the narrow streets, perhaps sit in the cathedral for a while and, if he was lucky, listen to the organist practising. There were new shops and malls now, but they didn't seem to tarnish the pleasant image of the city. The twice-weekly market days were lively. No longer any cattle in the square, but a bustling populace of stalls and market traders selling their wares, and people searching for a bargain. Today was a Tuesday, so James had brought his camera, hoping to get some unusual shots of the market-place in between his hotel appointments. He walked around for a while, snapping whenever there was an opportunity, until the heat got the better of him. The summer showed no signs of giving way to autumn, and he felt the need for a long, cool drink. Might as well have an early lunch, before the pubs became too crowded.

The old inn overlooked the square, and James was fortunate enough to find a small table by an open window. Not only was his thirst quenched by the ice-cold bitter-shandy, but his flagging spirits revived, and soon he realised that he had a wonderful view from the window. Testing out his new zoom lens, he took several quick shots. The one focused on the flower stall should be bright and colourful.

He was replacing the camera in its case when the girl behind the bar called his number. As he was taking the ploughman's back to his table, he noticed the smooth golden tan of a woman who had just come in and was reaching for the menu on her table. Even with her back to him, she looked a picture of glowing health with her short, glossy hair, the white shorts and sleeveless top complementing a neat figure, and her unvarnished, capable hands expressing a point as she talked. Her attentive companion had the dark looks of a slightly gypsyish trader.

It wasn't until he was level with the couple that James realised who the woman was. Should he sneak past to his own table and pretend he hadn't seen her? Or should he . . . ? Too late. Susan Burridge had already looked up at him. For a brief moment, her expression was that of a child caught at the jam-pot, then she quickly recovered her composure.

'Hullo,' she said brightly. 'Fancy meeting you here. We've just been to a sale.' She smiled towards her companion. 'Josh is my adviser on antiques. Don't know what I'd do without him.'

She showed no signs of introducing James, so he nodded and moved on, hearing her reply to her companion's question. 'Oh, it's only the piano-tuner.' James smiled to himself. He should be used to it by now.

While he was eating his ploughman's, he wondered whether Susan Burridge's companion was just her adviser, or whether there was more to it. There had been that incident with Ralph Beresford-Lawson, but Megan had told him the squire was engaged to be married to a wealthy socialite, so he would be out of the picture now. Still, it was none of his business.

★　★　★

360

As often happens in mid-December, a sudden cold snap arrived with the Christmas cards, and the countryside was blanketed with frost. When James looked out of the bedroom window, the panoramic vision was too tempting, and he had the camera balanced on the window sill while Katherine was in the shower. Snapping away, he dreamed — but not of a white Christmas. At last, Katherine had discarded her crutches, the doctors had given her the thumbs up sign, and James had dashed straight out to buy the air tickets. This time next week they would be soaking up the sun in Australia, watching Benjie improve his skills at walking, and preparing for a fabulous Christmas-cum-belated Pearl Anniversary party. Robert and Lucy would be joining them on Christmas Eve — and it was all thanks to the generosity of Paul, who had insisted on paying for all the air fares as an anniversary gift. James almost whooped aloud with excitement at the thought of it all.

Robert and Lucy were just as excited at their prospects for the New Year. Out of curiosity, they had visited the Brigadier's chauffeur in Eastleigh. His order book was quite healthy and he had been considering advertising for an assistant when they arrived. Impressed with their expertise, and Lucy's honours degree, he contacted them later with a suggestion. How would they feel about coming into the business with him? As junior partners, of course, but with management of a specialist unit dealing with restoring classic cars, leaving him free to continue with the vintage car section of the business. It didn't take them very long to sign the contract, once the financial side was completed, and Reg Manning even offered them a couple of rooms 'over the shop', so they had already moved in together. Katherine wasn't too happy that they weren't planning to get married and, to tell the truth, neither was James, but he had to accept that couples nowadays were more likely to become an 'item', or a 'relationship' than to be husband and wife.

The camera clicked impotently and James decided to reload ready for their holiday, but a cry from the shower cubicle stopped him.

'James! There's a terrible draught. Has the heating gone off?'

'Sorry, love.' He quickly shut the window. 'I was just taking some pictures.'

Her head appeared around the shower curtain. 'Never mind the pictures. Spare a thought for your freezing wife, if you don't mind.'

'Ah, the beautiful ice maiden . . . ' He moved towards her, but he was out of luck.

'You can stop right there, James Woodward. I'm far too busy this morning.'

'Oh. Is that a variation on a headache?' His voice showed his disappointment, then he brightened. 'Never mind. You'll soon thaw out once we're in Australia.'

Rubbing herself briskly with the towel, Katherine laughed gleefully. 'Oh, James, just think. In a few days I'll see our lovely girl again. And I can't wait to cuddle that baby.'

'That baby is getting on for two years old, don't forget. He may be a macho little Aussie and not want to be cuddled.'

Katherine looked alarmed. 'You don't think he'll be frightened of us, do you? After all, they don't see many strangers.'

'He might be a little shy, but I don't think he'll be frightened. Anyway, you'll soon win him round.' James slipped out of his dressing gown. 'Better get on with the day, I suppose.' Then he noticed that Katherine was pulling on her jodhpurs.

'You're not going riding?' Duke had been taken down to the stables a few days ago, to be housed and cared for while they were away. 'I thought the doctors said to leave it a bit longer?'

'Duke's been cooped up for days because of the weather. I just want to give him a little bit of exercise, that's all. And say goodbye to him. I'll be careful.'

'But that black ice is treacherous. At least leave it till later, when it's thawed out a bit.'

Shrugging into a thick, polo-necked sweater, Katherine said, 'I've invited Robert and Lucy over for lunch, and I'm going to do a roast, so now is the only time.'

'Then for God's sake, take it easy. Duke's not getting any younger, and neither are you.'

'Thanks very much,' she retorted jovially. 'I love you, too.' Then she smiled gently at his anxious expression. 'Don't worry, love. I'll only be half an hour or so. Too cold and too much to do.' The smile broadened to a grin. 'Fancy a big plate of cholesterol — a real Sunday breakfast?'

'You're on. I'll get everything ready. Don't you dare be late!'

Picking up her hard hat, she blew him a kiss. 'I do

love you, you know, even though you are an old worry-guts.'

As he stepped into the shower cubicle, Katherine called back from the door, 'By the way, there's a big feature about your Mr Ralph's wedding in *Hello!* magazine. It's on the coffee table.'

It really was a big feature. Three pages in fact. The Lady Deborah was a typical socialite beauty. Blonde hair swept back to reveal the tiara, long slim dress flattering a long slim body with curves in all the right places. And a bevy of bored-looking bridesmaids wearing velvet gowns and huge hats trimmed with feathers. James wondered what Susan would think, now that the die had been finally cast. He also wondered whether Ralph had played ball and agreed to Percy buying some of his land, or whether he would welsh on the deal. Probably the latter. Why any woman worth her salt would look twice at the balding, chinless wonder, was beyond him.

He looked at the clock. Time to start on the breakfast. Katherine should be home soon. Half an hour later, with the table laid, frying pan at the ready, bacon rinds trimmed off, and eggs, sausages, mushrooms and tomatoes standing by, his uneasiness was so strong he decided to go looking for her. No point in phoning the stables, they wouldn't hear it ringing from the yard, and he doubted whether they had mobiles — they were only young girls.

He eased the car down the slight incline from the garage, and took it steadily along the lanes. There was still quite a bit of ice shining, although the edges were slowly melting.

As he turned into the lane leading to the stables, an ambulance was pulling into the yard, and his heart began to pound uncontrollably. When he drew up behind it, he still couldn't see anything, except for a small group of girls staring at something the other side of the ambulance. The expression on their faces was enough to turn the fear into a monster clutching at his stomach. Then he heard the noise, and knew it was Duke. For a moment he hoped and prayed that it was only the horse that was in trouble, but his worst fears were realised as he pushed past the girls.

Katherine was trapped underneath the horse, which threshed around pathetically. Dropping to his knees, James cradled his wife's head in his arms, while one of the young girls sobbed out the story.

'Duke didn't really want to go out. It was too cold. So Mrs Woodward said she'd just walk him around the yard for a bit, then give him a good rub down.' The youngster wiped her cuff across her face. 'Just as she was dismounting, he stepped on a bit of ice near the water trough. She had one foot in the stirrup, but her other leg sort of gave way.' The sobs almost muffled the girl's voice. 'Next thing, she'd slid under Duke, and he was on top of her. I think his leg is broken. And we couldn't pull Mrs Woodward out.'

A paramedic knelt by Katherine. 'What's her name?' he asked, as he checked her pulse.

'Katherine. Katherine Woodward. How serious is it?'

'Difficult to say. You her husband?' James nodded. 'Right.' The man spoke slowly and distinctly.

'Katherine. Can you hear me? Open your eyes, Katherine.' There was no response. The man looked around, summing up the situation. 'We need to get this animal off the patient. Who's in charge here?'

One of the girls answered, 'Mrs Hampton. She's been trying to get hold of the vet.'

At that moment, a Range Rover trailing a horse-box drove into the yard. It was Greg, and it didn't take him long to realise there wasn't much he could do for Duke.

'Sorry, James,' he said. 'I've no choice.'

'It's Katherine I'm worried about. Just get him off her — quickly.'

Although she was unconscious, James tried to shield Katherine's face as her beloved Duke was freed from his agony. One final jerk, and he was silent.

Katherine opened her eyes and looked at James with an anguished expression. Then those beautiful blue eyes clouded over and he felt the life drain from her. For a long moment he stared at her, willing her to blink. Behind him, the paramedic was talking to Greg.

'Careful how you lift the horse,' he warned. 'She may have internal injuries.'

Even now, James could not believe, would not accept.

'No!' His scream of denial echoed around the yard. 'Dear God, no!' He held her close, rocking backwards and forwards as he called her name.

The paramedic knelt at the other side of Katherine and put his fingers to her throat. Then he gently closed her eyes.

25

James drove slowly along the winding lane, more slowly than was necessary. It was going to be tough, his first visit to Fivepenny Lanes since . . . He'd been dreading it more than his other appointments. When he'd first been allowed out on his own, as an improver, his very first call had been to the village hall and, for some reason, he had been closer to his clients in this little village with the funny name than anywhere else. He'd watched their children grow up, felt anger when the headmistress was hounded from the school, and mourned with them at their squire's funeral. Even old Bess had come from a litter at the vicarage. A thought occurred to him. Only the vicar's wife had ever met Katherine.

Gwynneth Jenkins had written such a lovely letter after she had read the little piece in the *Echo*, and her daughter and Mary Fitzgerald had telephoned, with tears in their voices. Now he would have to talk about it, and it was the last thing he wanted to do, but it couldn't be avoided any longer.

Julie had flown over alone for the funeral, which was crystal-clear in his memory, unlike the ceremony for David. She tried to persuade him to go back with her, but he couldn't. Not without Katherine.

As he'd expected, Mrs Jenkins was full of genuine sympathy, and she listened quietly as he answered her questions about the accident. But there was something else troubling her, he was sure. When he asked if she was well, she just said, 'As well as can be expected, thank you. Oh, if only we could go home to Wales.' Then she disappeared into her domain, the kitchen.

It was strange. Why should she suddenly want to return to Wales, after so many years? James had always imagined that the Reverend Jenkins would stay in Fivepenny Lanes until he was too old or frail to do the job properly, and there had been no signs of that. For a man of his age, he was very robust and active, and usually quite chatty. But today he seemed to struggle to find a few words of comfort for James, and his mind seemed as far away as his wife's thoughts.

Mary Fitzgerald was kindness itself and didn't intrude while he worked. But as he was leaving, she quietly said, 'If ever you would be needing someone to listen, you know my number. You have a close family, I know, but there are times when they can be too close to help.'

'Thank you.' How kind, he thought, and how perceptive.

Megan was as low in spirits as her mother and, after repeating her condolences and asking after his health, she, too, retired to the kitchen, and didn't sing a little song, as usual. By now, James was really concerned as to what was troubling his old friends, and hoped to God it wasn't a serious illness, or something wrong with the children, but when he enquired after them, she just said that they were all fine.

'Good. I expect Ruthie misses Abigail.'

Megan's hand faltered for a moment as she wrote the cheque, but she merely mumbled something he didn't quite hear.

'I know what it's like to have a daughter living so far away,' he went on, 'so I feel rather sorry for Mrs Burridge.'

To his amazement, Megan's face crumpled, she dropped the pen and ran from the room, rushing past her husband. The curate paused, bit his lip, said 'Good morning' to James, and followed his wife into the kitchen. Their voices were low, but heated. James wasn't sure whether he should leave, or wait, but after a few minutes the back door slammed, and he saw Megan walk across to the patio area, which was at the bottom of the garden, to catch the sun. Then the strangest thing happened. She took hold of one of the wrought iron chairs and flung it into the far corner, on top of the compost heap. It was quickly followed by the other three chairs and a small table, but the larger table proved too heavy to throw, so she dragged it across the lawn and pushed it over, on top of the chairs.

'Oh, dear,' Nigel said. 'Sorry about that.' He hesitated, then noticed the half completed cheque and the pen on the floor. 'Oh, dear,' he said again, 'I'd better finish this, I think.'

James couldn't think of anything adequate to say, so he just said, 'Thank you,' and left.

★   ★   ★

Susan paced up and down the sitting room, watched by Contessa, who sat on one of the elegant Queen

369

Anne chairs — the only one she was allowed to sit upon — her little head turning from side to side as though she were an umpire at Wimbledon. Suddenly, Susan stopped in front of her pet.

'Why are they all so rotten to me?' she cried. 'All of them. First Ralph, with his blonde bimbo of a wife. He didn't even have the guts to tell me he was getting married. And it's only because she's got money.' The little dog's head cocked on one side as she listened to her mistress. 'Then Josh,' Susan went on. 'He's never here when I need him. Why is he spending so much time in Ireland?' He'd told her there were good pickings in some of the old houses, but she wasn't sure she believed him. A good-looking, virile man like him would have the colleens falling at his feet.

For a while, she continued pacing up and down, in silence, then stopped again. 'And now Nigel,' she said, addressing the dog once more. 'It was a mistake to tell him the truth at Percy's party. He must have been lying when he said he'd guessed it was me.' She closed her eyes for a moment. 'But he led me on, let me think it was more than Christian comfort he wanted to give to me.' Her anger increased with the speed of her pacing. 'After all I've done for him, that winter holiday, free use of the beach hut, furniture — God, that patio furniture cost the earth! And what do I get in return? Nothing! Not even a kiss when I ask for it.'

Tired of pacing, she flopped onto the Regency sofa. The gossip was spreading much too slowly for her liking — but she'd only been able to drop hints. There had been one or two comments, but people were reluctant to think ill of the curate. She had to do something, or she would explode.

'I hope he rots in Hell!' she cried. 'Him and his silly, fat wife.' She was bored with the pair of them.

At that moment, Mrs Graham knocked on the door. 'Did you call, Mrs Burridge?' she asked.

'No. I was just — ' A thought occurred to Susan. She hadn't said anything to Mrs Graham. Just a casual remark here and there to her old neighbours at the Grove, and the WI members, about a mythical acquaintance she didn't wish to name. But Mrs Graham was a great spreader of news. She would believe anything she was told. Susan took a tissue from her pocket.

'Mrs Graham,' she murmured plaintively. 'Can you keep a confidence?'

'Of course, Mrs Burridge. I'm the soul of discretion.'

That was a blatant lie for a start, Susan thought, as she motioned her housekeeper to be seated. 'It's just that I am rather upset, and there's no one I can talk to. Not even my husband.' She lowered her head. 'It's such a delicate matter.'

Perched on the edge of her chair, Mrs Graham leaned forward. 'You can trust me,' she said, expectantly.

'I thought so.' Susan thought back to the event. 'Do you remember when we had the bad storm and all the trees came down? We'd only just moved in.'

'That would be five years ago now.' Mrs Graham shook her head. 'But I'm not likely to forget it. I had half my roof — '

'Yes, I know you did.' Susan controlled her

irritation. She had to bring the subject back to herself and Nigel. Taking a deep breath, she went straight on. 'Do you remember what I said when I telephoned you?'

Screwing up her face in concentration, the housekeeper said, 'Not really. It was a very bad line. But you did sound upset. Said the curate had called.'

So far, so good. 'That's right. And I said something else, something about . . . ' Susan paused. It would be better if Mrs Graham remembered herself, with just a little prompting.

'Oh yes. I remember now. I thought you said something about a cuddle, then we were cut off. But I must have been mistaken.'

Holding the tissue to her face, Susan shook her head. 'You weren't mistaken, I'm afraid.'

'Mrs Burridge! You're not saying . . . not our nice curate?' Mrs Graham's eyes were wide.

'I couldn't believe it either,' Susan said. 'He'd always seemed very nice, and I thought he was a friend. But he — ' She paused for just a moment, as though distressed, then went on, 'He tried to take advantage of me when I was vulnerable, and afraid of the storm.'

Mrs Graham sat so still, Susan wondered whether it had been a good idea, after all. But the housekeeper had been thinking, remembering. 'Oh my goodness. There was that other time,' she said slowly, a hand to her mouth. 'A couple of years ago, when you were both in here, and he was kissing you. I remember the gardener saying you were crying when you answered the door, so I thought the curate was just being kind.'

Susan thought rapidly. She had to turn it round. 'I was upset because Nigel — Mr Taylor — had phoned me and said he wanted to see me. That's why I was crying when I opened the door. I didn't want to let him in, but he grabbed me and put his arms round me, so I had no choice.'

'You should have called me, Mrs Burridge. I'd have soon sent him packing.'

'I didn't want a fuss, and I knew I was safe with you in the house. I thought if I talked to him and let him know in what a silly way he was behaving, he'd go away. But he was very persistent, and I must admit I was relieved when you came into the room.'

'Oh, yes. I can see it all now. Oh, dear. How very unpleasant for you.'

Susan nodded, relishing the thought that tomorrow this would be all over the village, but she must shunt the source away from herself.

'Yes, and that's why you mustn't repeat a word of this. Can you imagine how unpleasant it would be for his wife if she found out. She is my best friend, after all, and I would be devastated if anything happened to spoil our friendship.'

'Of course, and you can rely on me, Mrs Burridge. But — why are you telling me now, when you couldn't tell me at the time?'

'Ah. I had hoped it was all over and done with. Let sleeping dogs lie, that's my motto.' The housekeeper nodded in agreement, and waited. 'But I had another call this morning, and I just had to tell someone.' Another tissue.

'I heard the telephone ring when I was cleaning

the bathroom. Was that — ?'

With a sad expression, Susan nodded. 'He wanted to come here and talk to me. When my husband was out, he said.'

Mrs Graham's eyes were round. 'Oh, Mrs Burridge,' she breathed. 'What did you do?'

'I hung up.'

'Best thing, I'm sure. That's what they advise you to do if you have one of those funny phone calls.'

Susan stared at her housekeeper. The woman was brilliant. Slowly and thoughtfully, she said, 'Maybe it was him?'

'Beg pardon?'

'The strange phone call I had last year. Heavy breathing. I must have told you about it.'

Mrs Graham frowned. 'My friend, Mrs Thompson, had a weird phone call like that. I remember her telling me about it, but not you.'

'When was that?'

'Just before Christmas, it would have been. I told her she ought to go to the police, but she wouldn't.'

'That was when I had my call. Oh, God . . . surely he's not a pervert?'

The two women stared at each other, one in genuine horror, the other a very good actress, and enjoying every minute.

'No,' Susan said. 'I can't believe that. Not even Nigel would stoop so low — would he?'

'I wouldn't have thought so, but I suppose you can't be sure. What are you going to do, Mrs Burridge?'

Susan looked the picture of concern as she said. 'I really don't know what to do for the best. Do you think I should just let it go, or what?'

'Well — ' There was a long pause, then Mrs Graham said, decisively, 'I think the bishop ought to know.'

'The bishop?'

'Yes. He ought to know that one of his curates isn't above a bit of hanky-panky with one of his parishioners. And if Mr Taylor is responsible for the funny phone calls, he should be stopped.'

Of course! Why hadn't she thought of it herself? Oh, thank you, Mrs Graham, Susan thought gleefully. Thank you very much. But she maintained her solemn expression as she said, 'And he needs help. It's a sickness, really. You're right, Mrs Graham, the bishop should know.' She stood up, to bring the conversation to an end, but reminded her housekeeper, 'Not a word, mind, to anyone. I don't want people in the village to think I'm a trouble-maker.'

Then she went upstairs to her room and lifted the old portable typewriter from the cupboard. How fortunate that Mrs Graham had heard the telephone ringing. What the housekeeper didn't know was that Nigel had phoned after Susan had left a message on his answering machine, and when she asked him to come over, he had been quite abrupt, said he didn't think it was wise for him to keep calling. Well, Mr Nigel Taylor, nice curate of this parish. Perhaps this will teach you to hang up on me!

When the housekeeper knocked on her bedroom door to say that the piano-tuner had arrived, Susan was half-way through the best letter she'd ever written. It was clear and to the point, but tinged with sadness. There was no address, and she wouldn't sign it, but she didn't want the bishop to think it was just something from a 'well-wisher', so she phrased it very carefully, made sure there was no suggestion of vindictiveness, just a suggestion that all was not well between the curate and some of the ladies in Fivepenny Lanes, and a little unease was spreading throughout the village. Perhaps a quiet word with the curate was all that was needed.

'Tell the piano-tuner I'm busy just now,' she said, 'and I'll post his cheque.'

The letter was almost finished and the piano-tuner was still twanging away downstairs when there was another knock on the bedroom door. 'Not just now, Mrs Graham,' she said, without turning. 'Unless it's really urgent.'

'It is really urgent, Mother.'

Susan swung around. 'Jonathan! What are you doing here?'

'I — I need some things from my room.'

Confused, she stared at him. It was mid-week. He should be in his office. And he looked troubled. Frightened, almost. He hadn't look like that since he was a little boy.

Holding out her arms, she went over to the door and kissed him, then drew him down to sit beside her on the bed. 'Tell me what's wrong, Jonathan,' she said.

'Nothing's wrong. Well, not really.' He pondered for a moment, then went on, 'I have to go away for a while, Mother.'

'Now?'

'Yes, and please don't ask me any questions. It's

business, and confidential.'

'I see.' She didn't see at all, actually. 'This is all rather sudden, isn't it?'

'Not really. The money market has been swinging backwards and forwards for some time.'

'We're not heading for another Big Bang, are we, Jonathan? Only if so, your father needs to know so that he can do something about our own finances.'

'No, Mother. It won't affect Father at all.'

'Are you going to see him before you leave?'

'No time, I'm afraid.' Jonathan looked at his watch and stood up.

Curious, Susan watched from her bedroom door as her son went into his room and pushed the door behind him. She couldn't imagine what he needed. Most of his possessions were in the London flat. He'd only left behind his childhood memorabilia and a few clothes. As his bedroom door swung slightly ajar, she saw him take a sheaf of computer print-out papers from a desk drawer and stuff them into his briefcase.

Suddenly, Jonathan swung round, aware that she was watching. With a cursory glance around the room, he closed the door behind him and came back to her.

'You didn't see anything, Mother. OK?'

'OK, but there's nothing wrong with you taking some papers from your desk, is there, dear?'

For a moment, he looked at the ceiling. Then he said, 'Actually, I'd rather nobody knew I'd been here.'

'What about the housekeeper, and the secretary?'

'They're too busy gossiping over coffee in the

kitchen. I heard them, and they didn't see me come in.'

'There's the piano-tuner. He must have heard your car.'

'He doesn't count. Nobody will question him.'

'Who, Jonathan? Who is likely to ask questions? I wish you'd say, you're worrying me.'

'You needn't worry, Mother. Everything will be fine. More than likely no one will ask you any questions. But if they do, you don't know anything. Right?'

'Of course I don't know anything. You haven't told me anything.'

'Best that way. And Mother — '

'Yes, Jonathan?'

'Whatever you hear, or whatever anyone says about me, don't believe them. It's all lies. Just like when I was at school.'

Susan put her hand to his cheek. 'I know, darling. I could never believe anything bad about you.' She smiled. 'Only about other people.'

He leaned forward to kiss her cheek then, surprisingly, put both arms around her and held her for a moment. Then he said, 'Could you go down to the kitchen for a moment? Just to keep them there long enough for me to get away without being seen.'

26

When James phoned, as usual, to confirm his October appointments, Mrs Jenkins told him that he would be tuning two pianos at the Vicarage: their own, and Megan's. She didn't offer an explanation and he didn't ask for one. But he was curious. There had definitely been something wrong between Nigel and Megan. No doubt they would tell him if they wanted to, and if they didn't — well, it was none of his business.

Mrs Mason said something about the atmosphere in the village being a bit fraught, then continued to attack the paintwork with sponge and disinfectant, and the school secretary merely smiled pleasantly as she handed him his cheque, so he didn't quite know what to expect when he rang the Vicarage doorbell. The vicar let him in, then went straight out. James thought he didn't look well.

'I think it's getting a bit too much for him, especially now he is looking after the almshouses as well,' Mrs Jenkins commented, as she handed James a cup of coffee.

'Oh?' Apart from curiosity, James felt he should make some enquiry. 'Has your son-in-law gone to another parish? You said you had their piano here.'

'In the study it is. The only spare place for it.' Mrs Jenkins remained standing, fidgeting with an ornament on the mantelpiece. 'They've gone down to Cornwall for a bit. You know his parents have a hotel? Well, his father has the beginnings of Alzheimer's disease, and his poor mother has angina and high blood pressure, so they really can't look after each other, let alone the hotel.'

'Oh, dear, that's quite a problem.' But it didn't explain why Megan's piano was at the Vicarage, James thought.

'Yes. Nice people they are, too. But useless now in the hotel and it's been going downhill for some time.'

'Are Nigel and Megan going to take it on — I'm sorry,' James quickly apologised. 'I shouldn't have asked.'

'That's all right, my dear. Actually, they are trying to sell it, and find a residential home for Mr and Mrs Taylor. Not easy, when there won't be much money from the sale. The hotel needs a lot of attention, I'm afraid.'

'It must be quite a worry for you all. But I expect the children are enjoying themselves. All those wonderful beaches, and the weather has been pretty good.'

'The twins think they are in heaven, but Dilys didn't want to leave her secretarial course, so she's staying with us, for the time being.'

'Perhaps it won't be for too long?'

'I'd like to think so, Mr Woodward, but I really don't know.' She sighed, then her tone became brisker. 'Did I tell you that Owen has been accepted by the same theological college as his father?'

'No. That's great news. I didn't realise he was going into the Church.'

'Who would have thought it? Owen, who always

dodged anything that looked like work. And he's getting marvellous marks in all his exams.'

'You must be very proud of him.'

'Indeed I am. And Ruthie's a staff nurse. Going out with one of the doctors, she is.'

James smiled as he began to dismantle the piano. 'Now you can have your physical and spiritual welfare all taken care of within the family.'

Mrs Jenkins nodded. 'Yes. It would be quite perfect if it wasn't for — ' Suddenly she broke off and picked up the empty cup. 'I'd better get on with my cooking, or Hugh will be wondering what's for dinner.'

★   ★   ★

The tea-shop was full to bursting, and James waved to Mary, who signalled him to go on upstairs, and continued to pour endless cups of tea. He'd almost finished tuning her piano when she came upstairs with a tray of tea, poured out two cups, and sprawled in a chair.

'That's the fourth coach this morning,' she said, 'But I'm not complaining.'

'Do you have a dishwasher?'

'Two. One named Sharon, the other named Mary.' They both laughed. 'I'd like one, but I can't afford a commercial one, and the others are useless for a busy trade. The microwave was a good investment, but Sharon and I manage the washing up all right.' She sat up and sipped her tea. 'Are you managing all right?'

'Washing up?' James knew that wasn't what she

meant, so he went on. 'I suppose 'managing all right' is as good a description as any. I manage to get up each morning, go to work, cook a meal, watch a little television, and go to bed. I even manage to keep the cottage clean and tidy, probably more so than Katherine.' He smiled wryly. 'When she died I vowed I wouldn't let myself, or the house go. Sometimes I think I went too far the other way. I can't stop looking for jobs to do.'

'Probably because she's not there to make you ease up.'

'Yes, I'm sure that's what it is. If I was working too hard at anything, Katherine would say, 'Come on, let's go for a walk, or out for a meal.' I miss that.' He was silent for a moment, then said, 'I manage, but it isn't fun any more.'

As they sat silently drinking their tea, he wondered why he had spoken so frankly to Mary. He'd never talked to anyone else like this. But there was something about her that made you feel she could be trusted.

She poured two more cups of tea. 'My father told me that it took a year before he could laugh again, really laugh, I mean. Up to then, he was always thinking, 'this time last year, your mam and I . . . ' But once a year had passed, it became just that little bit easier.'

'Thank you. I'll try to remember that.' James had to change the subject, or he'd be talking about the empty nights. Thinking quickly, he enquired after Brendan.

'He's certainly not your conventional parish priest,' she said. 'The mission stations are all over the place. One minute he's on horseback, the next he's in one of those little planes. Then he has to go to Melbourne regularly for seminars and things.' She waved her hands expressively. 'I'm so proud of him.' Her head drooped a little. 'But I do so want to see him again.'

James's heart went out to this warm-hearted Irishwoman. 'You're the one who is always praying for other people. Isn't it time you prayed for your own wishes, too?'

Mary lifted her head and smiled. 'I always feel guilty when I pray for myself. There's so many more deserving cases. I really have been blessed, with Michael and Brendan. And the bank manager is very pleased with the way the business is going just now, so I mustn't be greedy.' Now it was Mary's turn to change the subject.

'Have you seen your grandson yet?'

James shook his head. 'I'd love to, but somehow I can't bring myself to go on my own.' He glanced at her. 'Perhaps when the first year is over, I'll be able to face it.'

'I'm sure you will.'

He thought of her words as he drove up to Cranleigh Manor. He really should make the effort to go to Australia. Julie sent videos and masses of photos of the little boy and their phone bills were horrendous. But it wasn't the same as a visit. You couldn't hug a letter, or kiss a telephone. And it wasn't fair to expect her to make such a long journey with a toddler. Perhaps he would be able to face up to it next year?

Idly wondering whether the display of daffodils alongside the pond had come from the same bulbs he'd first seen nearly forty years ago, James parked in the lay-by opposite the tea-shop and mused over the morning's events for a few minutes. He'd been surprised to be booked for two pianos at the Vicarage again, even more surprised to learn that the curate's house had been sold.

'It was decided that we didn't need a curate any more, with attendances dropping.' Mrs Jenkins looked and sounded desolate. 'Miss Partridge has bought it.'

'Miss Partridge? The librarian?'

'Retired librarian.'

'Isn't it a little large for a spinster?'

'She has her parents living with her.'

'Oh, I see.' James wondered about Megan and Nigel, but didn't like to ask. He cleared the top of the Obermeier first.

'And my poor girl is living in a slum.' Suddenly, Mrs Jenkins's voice broke, and when James turned round, she was holding a handkerchief to her face. 'And I don't really know why.' Her sobs were muffled. 'Do you know why, Mr Woodward? Has anyone told you anything?'

It distressed James to see her weeping. Gently, he led her to an armchair, and asked, 'Shall I call Mr Jenkins for you?'

She shook her head. 'Hugh is next door, in the church.' Wiping her eyes, she murmured, 'I'm so sorry. I don't know what you must think of me.'

'I think something has happened that has made you very unhappy. But when you ask if I have been told anything — no, I haven't.'

James patted her shoulder and slipped out into the kitchen. There were glasses on the dresser, and he filled one with water.

'Take a sip of this, Mrs Jenkins. Do you want to tell me about it?'

She nodded. 'You've been coming here for many years, Mr Woodward, and I know you're not a gossip. Hugh bottles it all up, but I feel it's better to let some of it out, don't you? He worries me so. They both do.'

'You said just now that Megan is living in a slum. Isn't she still in Cornwall?'

'No, she's in London. The East End of London. And dreadful it is. Really dreadful.' The tears began to flow again. 'The trouble is, nobody will tell me anything. They just say they don't want to worry me, but I can't be any more worried than I am already.'

'Why do *you* think they have moved to London. I assume the whole family are there?'

She shook her head. 'I've still got Dilys, and the twins are with Ruthie, and Nigel and Megan are in this terrible place near the docks.' She sighed a deep sigh. 'I'm not really sure, but I have a feeling it has something to do with Susan Burridge, although I can't put my finger on it.'

'Susan Burridge? I thought they were close friends?'

'Thick as thieves, they were. Did everything together. Then all of a sudden, they hardly pass the

385

time of day to each other. I just thought they'd had a quarrel, the way people do, but then I heard some of the whisperings around the village.'

'Do you have any idea what the whisperings were about?'

'Oh, no. Always stopped when I came into view, they did. But people started looking at me, strange-like, as though they were sorry for me. I asked Mrs Faversham if she knew what was going on, but she just said, 'it's not your fault, Mrs Jenkins', and closed up like a clam.' Mrs Jenkins looked quite indignant. 'Why should it be my fault? I don't even know what the problem is.' She was silent for a moment, staring into distance, then went on, 'The next thing I knew, the bishop had asked Hugh to go and see him. But Hugh wouldn't tell me what he wanted. All he would say was that the bishop was concerned about the falling attendances and felt that Nigel's social skills might be put to better use elsewhere.'

'Had attendances fallen much?'

'Well, yes. That's the strange thing about it. We've always had a lovely congregation, and everybody says what a good preacher Hugh is and how beautiful the choir, especially when our Megan sings a solo. And nobody minded if Nigel took the service instead of Hugh. It worked very well, you see.'

'When did it start to change?'

'About six months ago it would be. When Hugh announced that he was going to spend a couple of weeks in a Retreat, hardly anyone came to church while he was away. He'd done it before from time to time, said it recharged his batteries, you see, and the church stayed as full as if he was here. I thought everyone liked Nigel.'

'I'm sure they do. I've always found him to be a very pleasant man. And he strikes me as being a good husband and father.'

'He is, I know he is. But why has everyone suddenly turned against him? Not only in church, but the youth club. The membership has dropped right off, especially amongst the girls.'

'Oh, dear. Have you talked to Megan about it?'

'I've tried, time and again, but she sort of side-steps me. Says things like, 'Now I don't want you worrying, Mother, we can sort it all out ourselves.' But I know she's not happy in that awful place, looking after those poor down-and-outs. Who could be?'

'Down-and-outs? Are they running a shelter?'

'Something like that, but only for men. It's as though they are afraid to have women anywhere near Nigel. Oh, Mr Woodward, you don't think he's — ?' Mrs Jenkins stopped suddenly, as though horrified at her own thoughts, which were quickly denied. 'No! I refuse to believe that Nigel would ever do anything to harm or embarrass a woman. Kindness itself he is.' She was thoughtful for a moment, then went on, 'But I can see that sometimes he's too kind for his own good.'

'In what way?'

'Well, Nigel has often been known to go out in the middle of the night if one of the residents needs him.'

'But isn't that part of his job?'

'Indeed, yes. But I'm wondering if wicked

rumours have started just because someone saw him out in the middle of the night on his own. Perhaps they thought he had a secret assignation with a lady?'

'I suppose it's possible,' James said, 'Although I would have thought most of the villagers would understand about his work at the almshouses, and certainly the bishop would know. Unless . . . does he ever get called out elsewhere? When the lady of the house is alone, I mean? It's something I have to be very careful about, you know.'

Realisation began to dawn on Mrs Jenkins's face. 'You mean — like the jokes about the milkmen?'

'It can happen, I'm afraid.'

'I hadn't thought of that. Perhaps it might make some women nervous, having a man in their house while their husband is at work.' She looked directly at him. 'Is it very much of a problem for you, Mr Woodward?'

'Not really. It's one of the reasons I rarely discuss anything of a personal nature, and I try very hard not to say anything that might be misunderstood. Once a young woman fled into the garden when I mentioned that the piano had a good frame.' He smiled. 'And another time, I had to beat a hasty retreat myself.'

'Oh! Why was that?'

'The lady came to the door wearing a rather revealing négligé. It was like one of those Benny Hill sketches, but I wasn't taking any chances. So I pretended I'd double-booked my appointments and came back later, when the children were home from school.'

Mrs Jenkins smiled a little smile, then said, 'If something like that happened to Nigel, I don't think he would know what to do. He would be too afraid of giving offence.'

'Exactly. And that's where he could so easily be misunderstood, and it only takes a little bit of suspicious gossip to start the snowball rolling.'

'Perhaps that's why Megan and Susan aren't so friendly. But surely Susan wouldn't believe wicked things like that about Nigel?'

James wouldn't have thought anyone could believe wicked things about Nigel. But then, he had never thought anyone could believe ill of Miss Harding, yet Susan Burridge had. And, worse still, was it more than just a case of disloyalty? Was Mrs Burridge capable of starting malicious gossip? He knew she was capable of deceiving her husband, but what would be the motive for blackening Nigel's good name?

Mrs Jenkins was talking again. 'What do you think I should do about it, Mr Woodward? I pray and pray, but I still can't sleep at night for worrying about it.'

After a while, James said, 'I think you should talk to your husband again. Tell him what you have told me, that the worry is making you ill, and you need to know so that you can all stand strong as a family against the gossip.'

With a relieved smile, Mrs Jenkins stood up. 'I'll do it as soon as he comes home,' she said firmly. 'And thank you for listening. I had to talk to someone, and you are like an old friend. In fact, you have answered my prayers.' Taking his cup, she

389

kissed him on the cheek. 'And let the gossips make what they will of that,' she said, as she left the room.

* * *

James had been looking forward to seeing Mary again, but she was too busy in the shop, and Sharon brought him up a tray of tea and fruit cake. After a moment's chatter about Tom Cruse's latest film, Sharon turned to go, but hesitated before she opened the door.

'Did you think Mary looked all right?'

Startled, James turned round. 'Sorry?' he said.

'She's got something on her mind and she won't say what it is.'

'Oh — but I don't see — '

'It's just that — well, she likes you, and if she's going to talk to anyone, it would be you.'

'Surely it should be her husband?'

'Michael?' Sharon threw back her head and laughed. 'He's probably the cause.' Then she became serious again. 'Although it might be to do with the new roads. Everyone's afraid it will cut off the village.'

'The coaches will still need to stop somewhere, won't they? There's no new services planned in the area as far as I know.'

'But the coaches might stop off at Winchester, or shoot through to the New Forest, and not bother with Fivepenny Lanes.'

James nodded. 'Some might, I suppose. You won't know until the end of the season.'

'Like my mum says, 'No good crying over spilt

390

milk until the eggs is hatched.' But if you get a chance to talk to Mary . . . ?'

'Of course.'

But James didn't have a chance to talk to Mary. Nor did he talk to the next lady of the house he visited. Susan Burridge was away for the day at an antique fair. Mrs Graham left him in the sitting room with strict instructions to be careful with the furniture, it was extremely valuable. Then she took her beeswax polish into another room, promising that Mrs Burridge would post his cheque later.

James wasn't concerned about the cheque. If Mrs Burridge wasn't at home, she always sent the cheque within a few days. Which was more than could be said for Mr Ralph Beresford-Lawson. However, today was one of the rare occasions when he was in residence, so James might be in luck.

Absorbed in playing a few bars of Mozart to test the tuning, James didn't hear the owner of Cranleigh Manor open the door.

'Ah, the piano-tuner!'

James stood up. 'Am I disturbing you?' he asked.

'No. Don't get much chance to play myself nowadays, but at least I know you're keeping the old thing in tune.'

'I've nearly finished.' James tightened the last string a little more, then began to pack up his tools.

Ralph crossed to the window. 'It will all look somewhat different the next time you call.'

'Oh?'

'Yes.' Hands in pockets, Ralph's smile was rather smug as he turned to face James. 'If the red tape

391

buffoons agree, this will be a theme park to outrival them all.'

'A theme park?' James could almost feel the shuddering of the Brigadier's ghost.

'There's a lot of money to be made. Much more than just by guided tours around the old stately home and gardens.'

'Poulton's Park seems to be very successful.'

'Oh, our projection is on a much bigger scale than Poulton's. Deborah and I have been studying Disney, in Paris and the States. They know how to do it efficiently and effectively.'

'So I hear.' James threw the fringed silk cloth back across the piano. 'Do you have a particular theme in mind?'

'Military. The old boy gave us the idea by leaving me his collection of toy soldiers and memorabilia of all the old battles when the stupid sods faced each other in lines with single shot rifles and bayonets. I was going to flog the lot, but Deborah came up with the idea of planning our theme park around it. Wicked!'

At times James had difficulty in keeping up with current jargon, but he gathered the expression was replacing 'Brill!'

'Certainly less trouble than animals, I should think.'

Ralph's laugh was more like a guffaw. He really was the definitive 'Hooray Henry', James thought.

At that moment, the door opened again, and Lady Deborah entered. Easily recognised from the wedding photographs on the piano, she wore jodhpurs and hacking jacket, and raised her eyebrows at her husband.

'Just telling the piano-tuner about our plans, darling,' he said.

'Ah, yes. You must be the first villager we've told. What do you think?'

Her voice was definitely what James would call 'horsy', but she smiled pleasantly at him. He didn't correct her assumption that he lived in Fivepenny Lanes, but he answered her question.

'There's no reason why it shouldn't be successful. It's certainly different.'

'Exactly. I expect a few purists will throw up their hands in horror but, with death duties as they are, it's either that or handing it over to the National Trust. Ralph has, of course, searched high and low for a wealthy American or Arab who would take it off his hands, but they're a bit thin on the ground just at the moment.' She played a couple of notes of the piano, then commented, 'Lovely tone. I'm glad Ralph didn't sell it. Has he paid you?'

'Er — no.'

She turned to her husband, 'Come along, darling. Pay the poor man, then we can go for our ride.'

'I was going to put the cheque in the post.'

Lady Deborah laughed. 'That's what you say to all the tradesmen, and I'm the one who has to deal with it later. Really, darling, you are the limit.'

Five minutes later, the cheque safely in his pocket, James drove homewards, his mind full of unanswered queries. What was the real reason behind Nigel being asked to leave the village? What was bothering Mary? What would the villagers think of Cranleigh Manor being turned into a theme park? And how would Susan Burridge react? After all, the entrance would be literally on her doorstep.

27

Struggling to control her anger, Susan faced her housekeeper. Slowly and carefully she asked Mrs Graham to repeat what she had just said.

'I'm only telling you what the housekeeper up at the Manor told me. Mr Beresford-Lawson is going to turn the estate into a theme park. They were her very words.'

'That's a ridiculous idea!'

'My sentiments exactly, Mrs Burridge.'

'Anyway, he can't.'

'I beg your pardon?'

'He can't turn it into a theme park. My husband is going to develop the other side of the river — he has all the plans and everything. It was promised.'

'Well, I know that's what everyone has been saying around the village for some time. But Mrs Granger has seen the applications in the study and said Mr Ralph is discussing it with the planning people today.'

'They won't agree. Not for a theme park out here. It would change the character of the village too much, and the planners don't like that.'

'I hope you're right, Mrs Burridge. I truly do. But they might say the Manor is far enough away from the village for it not to be a problem?'

'They can say what they like, but my Percy will fight them all the way. You just wait and see.'

After Mrs Graham had gone about her duties,

Susan walked around the sitting room, picking up an ornament here, straightening a painting there, as restless as a tiger, and her thoughts as lethal. Ralph couldn't be allowed to get away with this. Percy would know what to do, if she could get through to him. His mobile was switched off. That could mean he was at a meeting.

Next she tried Josh's mobile. He was just about to go into a saleroom in Exeter and was going on to Penzance afterwards.

'But I need to talk to you, Josh,' she wailed.

'Sorry, Susan. Try again at the end of the week.'

Frustrated beyond belief, Susan went through to the little office where Mrs West beavered away at her word-processor.

'Mr Burridge has a meeting at the Civic Centre this afternoon,' the secretary said, 'but you might just catch him at the site office. Would you like me to try?'

'No, thank you. Just give me the number.'

Michael answered the site phone. 'He's just this minute left, Susan,' he said. 'Would you be wanting me to give him a message when he comes back?'

Susan doubted whether Percy would go back to the site. Those planning meetings could go on for hours. 'No thanks, Michael. It will have to wait until he comes home.' She sighed heavily.

'You sound troubled, Susan. Would there be anything at all that I can do?'

'Not really, thanks. I'm just not having a very good day, that's all.'

'Oh, dear. And it couldn't happen to a lovelier lady.'

Despite her foul mood, Susan couldn't refrain from laughing. 'And aren't you full of the blarney, Michael Fitzgerald?' she said, imitating his brogue.

'But I've made you laugh, and what would be wrong with that?'

'Nothing. Nothing at all.'

It was a long time since a man had made her laugh, she thought, as she replaced the telephone receiver. Percy came home so tired he usually fell asleep in front of the television, and she hadn't seen Josh for two weeks, since they had gone to a country house auction near Andover, and stopped off at a motel for a couple of hours before she drove home. It was the only way they could be together. She couldn't think of a reliable excuse to give Percy so that she could stay overnight with Josh on one of his antique hunting jaunts. Nobody knew where Jonathan was and Abigail was in Africa, so overnight trips to London were out and she hadn't kept in touch with any of her friends in Yorkshire. With both parents dead, there wasn't a soul she could pretend to visit. It would be great to have Josh lying by her side for a whole night. His recovery from their lovemaking was pretty fast, and he would be only too willing to oblige, again and again. Still, she reflected, there was something about their stolen moments that gave an urgency, a wildness that left them panting for more. Each goodbye kiss was a promise, and her need for him, and his for her, was never totally fulfilled.

Waiting for Percy to come home, she wandered upstairs, in and out of the bedrooms, and paused for a while in Jonathan's room. When his boss had telephoned to ask if she knew of Jonathan's whereabouts, she had been able to answer truthfully. Apart from a card at Christmas from New York, saying he was well, she had not heard a thing from her son. She missed Jonathan and worried sometimes that he might have sailed a little too close to the wind. If he had, it would have been due to that bastard, Ralph, she was sure. But Jonathan was clever. He would always manage to keep one step ahead, no matter what happened.

Her reverie was broken by Mrs Graham calling upstairs, 'Goodbye, Mrs Burridge, I've left the casserole in the bottom of the Aga, and the vegetables are all prepared.'

'Thank you, Mrs Graham. Goodbye.' The room felt a little stuffy, so Susan opened the window. The housekeeper was standing by her car, talking to the secretary, who waved up at the window before cycling away. Then they were both gone and Susan felt the quietness of a house with no other human being moving around, only herself. She shivered, and was about to turn away when a very old car with protesting gears turned into the gate.

Oh, God, she thought, I hope it's not some cowboy telling me my drive needs resurfacing. If it is, I'm in the right mood to send them packing with a flea in their ear. But it was Michael who stood for a moment, running his hand through his dark, curly hair. And what a clean and tidy Michael he was! Even more surprising, he reached into the car for a bunch of flowers. Then, as he slammed the door shut, he glanced up at the house and noticed Susan, and there was something in his expression, the vividness of the blue eyes, that was very attractive — and — desirable?

He smiled and waved up at her. 'Me work was finished, so I was able to get away early,' he called out. 'And you sounded as though you needed a little cheer in your life, Susan, so . . . ' He held aloft the flowers.

'What a lovely thought,' she called back. 'And just what I needed.'

As she ran down the stairs, the silliest of thoughts ran through Susan's head. 'My goodness — I have a suitor!'

★　★　★

There was no place left for Mary to search. She'd gone through every drawer and cupboard, twice, and every nook and cranny where it might have fallen, even peering through the floorboards. But the pearl choker was quite large and the rooms quite small, so she would have found it by now if it was still here. That meant only one thing. It had gone to the same place as her beautiful abalone earrings. She would have to go into Southampton as soon as she could get away, and see if she could redeem the necklace back from the jeweller. Wasn't it bad enough that Michael had taken her gift from the canteen manager to pay off his gambling debt? And hadn't he promised faithfully he would stop playing cards for money? It had taken quite a while of arguing and denying before he told her where the shop was, and that had only been because she threatened to tell Percy Burridge. He didn't like the men gambling on the site, said it had caused too many problems in the past, with fights and all, so they were warned when they started work that if they were found drunk or gambling during working hours, they would lose their job.

Mary sat down at the dressing table and studied her reflection. The bruise on her cheek had faded, but not the memory. It was the first time he'd slapped her. Really slapped her. There had been moments when he'd raised his fist, and another when he'd held her arms so tightly to shake her backwards and forwards that she'd had to wear long sleeves for a fortnight. But this was the first time he'd actually struck her, and she hoped and prayed it would be the last. He'd been mortified afterwards, begged her forgiveness, said it was that extra pint he'd drunk that had made him lose control. But she knew only too well how easily, once started, that sort of thing could become a habit. She'd seen it happen to one of the villagers in Ireland, and to women she'd worked with. Once the men started slapping their women about, they never stopped, no matter how sorry they were afterwards.

The only way she could prevent it happening again was to go to the shop herself and redeem her treasured inheritance. Goodness knows how much money she would need. It had originally belonged to great-grandmother, who had married well, so it would probably cost her a pretty penny to get it back. But she couldn't face up to another long-drawn-out argument and the possibility of more bruises. He'd have to get away with it this time. Perhaps it would be safer if she put the necklace in a deposit box at the bank, so he couldn't get his hands on it again.

As soon as Michael came home that evening, he ran a bath and took his one and only good suit from the wardrobe. That in itself was strange, he usually changed into clean but casual gear if he was going out for a drink. And this morning, he'd told her he wanted to watch the Arnold Schwarzenegger film on TV.

'You'll not be going out again, Michael?' she asked.

Immediately he was on the defensive. 'And is there any reason why I shouldn't?'

'No. Only that I thought you were keen to see that *Terminator* film.'

'Oh.' His mood changed. 'Well, actually, me darling, I'm going to watch it with a couple of the lads. You always say you find his films too violent, so you'll be able to watch the tearjerker on the other side and we'll all be happy, won't we?'

'I suppose so.' It was true that Mary hadn't wanted to watch the film, but this was the third evening this week that he'd gone out and she feared that he must be gambling again. 'What about your dinner?' she asked, 'It's steak and kidney pie, your favourite.'

'Oh, and isn't it a pity to be missing such a feast.'

When Michael came at her with the blarney, Mary was even more suspicious. 'Haven't you time to eat before you go?' she asked. 'After all, the film's not on till late.'

'We thought we'd give ourselves a treat and go down to La Margherita's first.'

401

'La Margherita's? Isn't that where we're going next week, for our anniversary?'

'It is indeed.'

'I see.' Mary wondered where the money was coming from, but didn't like to ask. 'So that's why you're wearing your suit?'

'That's right. It's Eddie's fortieth, so we're going to celebrate in a bit of style. Didn't I tell you?'

'No.'

'Oh. Sorry, darling.' Turning to the wardrobe mirror, Michael straightened his tie, then casually asked, 'Would you be letting me have some money? Just till the end of the week.'

'I thought you said Percy was going to give you your overtime money today?'

'Well, that's what he promised, but he's gone up to Yorkshire for a few days. Business or something. So it's left me a bit on the short side.'

'How much would you be wanting.'

'Fifty should do nicely.'

'Fifty pounds! You've got to be joking. That's more than I've got in the float.'

'But you always have a few pounds tucked away for emergencies, you know you do. Come on, Mary. Just till Friday.'

'But fifty pounds just for a meal? Michael — you wouldn't be . . . ?'

'No, we're not gambling. On my mother's grave I swear it.'

Mary was tempted to say, 'And on my grandmother's necklace, I doubt your word.'

'It's not just the meal,' Michael went on. 'We've had a whip-round for one of those kissogram girls to come to the restaurant. Just a bit of a lark. But I can't tell the lads I've not got the money to put in the kitty, now, can I?' He smiled beguilingly into her eyes, and kissed her when he saw the capitulation in her expression.

She had no choice. He knew where she kept the emergency money and would probably help himself anyway.

★ ★ ★

'I'm glad you're in, Mr Woodward.' Mrs Jenkins's lilting accent gave her away before she announced her name. 'It's not easy to put into a letter, and I wanted you to know what's happening, rather than hear gossip from the village.'

'That's very thoughtful of you.' A little apprehensive, James waited.

'I felt I owed it to you to tell you what I know.'

'You don't have to, Mrs Jenkins, not if you don't want to.'

'But I do want to. We go back such a long way. You've known Megan since she was just a girl, and I met your lovely wife and children. It would be unkind to just disappear and not explain.'

'Disappear?'

'Hugh and I are leaving Fivepenny Lanes. Thomas has offered us a home on his farm in Wales. He hasn't remarried, but he has a girlfriend who lives with him. He calls her his partner. Nice girl, but — ' She sighed, then went on, 'However, we felt Megan needed us more. So we're moving into a little flat in one of those tall buildings — highrise, I think they're called — and Dilys is going to stay with Ruthie and the others.'

'It will be rather different, living in London, but I do wish you well. Do you know who is to be the new rector of Fivepenny Lanes?'

'No, but he should be appointed before your next visit. The bishop did ask Hugh to stay on, but we couldn't, not once we found out about the letter.'

James waited, sensing tears were not far away.

'Apparently someone had written to the bishop, accusing Nigel of being — over-familiar was the expression he used,' she went on. 'Of course, we don't believe a word of it, but the damage has been done. The gossip had started before the letter. And the poor boy feels it is his fault because he didn't see the danger and put a stop to it right from the start.'

Quietly, James asked, 'Do you know who wrote the letter?'

'The bishop wouldn't tell us, but we have our own ideas. More than that I won't say, not on the telephone.' She sighed. 'Nothing could be proven, of course, but that was why the bishop suggested it might be better if Nigel moved elsewhere, rather than split the Church down the middle.'

'I can't tell you how sorry I am.'

'I know, Mr Woodward, I know. And I was so grateful for your good advice when you last called. I might be still in the dark if I hadn't insisted that Hugh tell me what was going on. It was painful for him to tell me the truth, but at least we know where we stand.'

'That's true. Are they looking for another curate as well?'

'No. They want someone who will take on all the duties. Shortage of money, I suppose. That's why they sold the house in Susan Close. Which reminds me, Miss Partridge has bought Megan's piano, so asked if you would kindly make an appointment to tune it in October. The telephone number is the same. And the Obermeier will stay here for the next rector, of course, so I know you will continue to look after it.'

'Of course.' James didn't quite know what to say next.

There was quite a long pause, then Mrs Jenkins said, 'Nearly thirty-five years we've been here. It's going to be quite a wrench.'

'Yes, but surely Nigel will be able to apply for another parish before too long?'

'He can apply, but will he be considered, with this stigma hanging over his head? You know what people say about there being no smoke without fire.'

'Well, if it's any consolation, I will never believe there was as much as a flicker of flame, let alone a fire.'

'Bless you, Mr Woodward. You always manage to say the right thing. And at least we can pray.'

'If anyone should believe in the power of prayer, it's you and your husband. And I do thank you for phoning. Hopefully I might be able to scotch a few rumours.'

She laughed. 'You're a kind man, Mr Woodward. Have you thought any more about visiting your daughter in Australia?'

'Oh, yes. I think about it all the time. I just haven't quite plucked up the courage. But now that

Julie is pregnant again, I have a feeling it won't be too long before I book a flight.'

'That's wonderful news. Just what I needed to cheer me up.' She paused. 'I had to take the two dogs to the vets. It didn't seem fair to expect them to get used to a new home at their age, and poor Dylan was quite blind.'

James looked down at Bess, lying asleep at his feet. He'd known for some weeks that the inevitable was about to happen. 'I'm afraid I shall be doing the same with Bess, soon,' he said. 'She has a tumour. The steroids have helped, but it's really only a matter of time, now.'

'But she's had such a lovely home with you all these years. Couldn't have asked for better. Goodbye, Mr Woodward. And God bless you.'

★ ★ ★

Horrified, Susan stared at the television screen. Jonathan's face stared back at her. The announcer's voice told the world that her son was wanted by the police. Something to do with the Merchant Bank. Falsifying figures. Moving money to offshore accounts. It couldn't be true. It couldn't possibly be true. When the plain-clothes officer called the other day, he'd only asked if she knew the whereabouts of her son. And when he mentioned missing papers, she thought Jonathan's London flat had been burgled. But now it looked as though they were accusing him of being an embezzler. They talked in figures of millions. Jonathan would never get involved in something like that. Ralph might, but not her son. Then her mind went back to his last visit, when he'd grabbed those papers from his desk and shoved them so hurriedly into the holdall. And they'd heard nothing from him since, only the Christmas card from America. Not even a telephone call. No, she thought, I can never believe that our Jonathan is running from the police.

The announcer was still talking: ' . . . believed he might be in Brazil, or Turkey, where there are no extradition laws.'

Extradition laws! Were they about to bring him back in handcuffs, like that other banker in Singapore?

She tried to concentrate on the television. Now they were showing a picture of the village. Did that mean . . . ?

Rushing upstairs, she peered out into the twilight from her bedroom window. Yes, there was definitely movement by the gate. And not just one person. Oh, God! One of them had slipped into the garden, and was crouching behind the rhododendrons. Two vivid flashes told her what he was up to. Running from room to room, she pulled all the curtains across, not daring to switch on a light. Better lock the back door, just to be on the safe side.

To her horror, a shadowy figure was peering through the kitchen window, another knocked on the door. They were everywhere, shouting, 'Mrs Burridge! Can you tell us where your son is? Did you know he was involved in — ? Mrs Burridge! Susan! Just one photograph. Mrs Burridge!' They shouted across each other, snapping furiously through the window. For a moment she was frozen to the spot, then she dashed across the kitchen and pulled down the slatted blinds. In her haste, the strings became entangled, leaving a gap at the bottom, just enough for them to peer through and snap through and shout through. 'Mrs Burridge! This way please! When did you first suspect . . . ? Is your husband . . . ?'

'Go away!' she screamed back. 'Leave me alone.' Then she bolted the kitchen door and fled into the hall. Now they were at the front door, ringing the bell, banging on the door. With shaking hands she locked all the security locks Percy had installed, and set the alarm. Now for the drapes in the lounge, the dining room, the study, the office. There wasn't a downstairs window without a peering face and a camera on the other side, even the downstairs cloakroom.

'Percy!' she cried aloud. 'Come home. I need you.' But Percy was in Yorkshire. Another business trip.

Still not switching on the lights, she ran upstairs and into the bedroom, grabbing at the bedside phone. His mobile was engaged. She pressed the code for continuous re-dial and sat on the bed, listening to the commotion in the garden. How the hell did they get here so quickly? It had only just been on the nine o'clock news. They must have spies everywhere. And it would be in all the papers! Oh, God, Percy, get off the bloody phone!

The shrill bleep startled her into a little scream.

'Mrs Burridge. Can we have a quick word?'

She slammed down the receiver. Immediately the phone rang again.

'Susan. Clive Simmonds of the *Daily* — '

After three calls, she left the receiver off the hook. But she needed the line open for Percy. The answerphone! That was it. Not the one in the office. That was a different number and already set. Creeping downstairs, she pressed the record button on the telephone in the hall, which was ringing again. Sliding down the wall, she sat hunched up on the floor, and listened. Five messages were from the media. The sixth was Percy.

'Susan! I've been trying to get through to you for ages. Who have you been talking to all this time?'

'I haven't. They keep phoning me. And they're all over the garden.'

'Who are? Susan. I can't help you if you keep crying.'

But she couldn't stop. 'I'm so frightened, Percy. Haven't you seen the news?'

'No. We've only just finished dinner. What about the news?'

'It's Jonathan,' she sobbed. 'He's wanted by the police.'

'Don't be daft, lass. Jonathan's in New York. Why would the police be after him?'

'I don't know.' Now she wished she had told Percy about the detective calling, but he was away at the time and she had been trying to get out quickly to meet Josh. By the time Percy came home she was so excited about a *causeuse* they had bought, she forgot about the policeman.

'You've got it all wrong, lass. It must be somebody else.'

'I wish to God it were.' Trying hard to control her

tears, Susan told her husband the whole, miserable story.

There was a long, long silence before Percy spoke. Then he asked, 'Are the newspaper people still there?'

'Yes,' she sniffed. 'I daren't switch the lights on, and it's quite dark, now.'

'Right, lass. I'll tell 'ee what to do. Phone PC Plod, or whatever his name is. Tell him to clear them out of our garden straight away or he'll have me to deal with. Then close and lock gates. Put chain round. And make sure those bloody great lights are working in case any of the buggers try to climb over wall.'

Susan breathed a sigh of relief. Percy always knew just what to do. 'Yes, dear,' she said. 'I'll do that right away. When will you be home?'

'I've got an important meeting first thing in morning with county architect. As soon as we've got his agreement, I'll be out of that door and on way home.'

'Can't you come home tonight, Percy? I'm all on my own here and it's like having a pack of wolves baying at the door.'

'I know, lass. I know. But I've worked my backside off to get this contract. Just be patient for a few hours more. Can you get someone to come and stay. Happen Mrs Graham might oblige?'

'She's gone to see *Crazy for You* at the Mayflower with her sister, and they're having a meal after, so she won't be home till late.'

'You could try Mary at the tea-shop. She's a nice friendly lass. Reckon she'd keep you company for a couple of hours, like.'

Over my dead body, Susan thought. She'd never taken to the Irishwoman, and the feeling seemed to be mutual. To Susan's way of thinking, there was always something very suspicious about people who were well liked in the village. Megan had been too popular for her own good, and her pious husband. Still, she'd managed to despatch them into obscurity with very little trouble. Just as she had done with the old headmistress, and the milkman. So Mary Fitzgerald had better watch her step.

'Susan! Are you still here?'

'Yes, Percy. I thought I heard another noise, that's all. Just come home as soon as you can, dear.'

She touched the button lightly and immediately dialled the local policeman. He said he'd ask for some back-up from Winchester and come round straight away. While she waited, Susan switched on the ten o'clock news. It was more or less the same. Then she heard voices outside. Peering through the side of the curtain, she saw three uniformed officers ushering the reporters and photographers out of the gate. Only when they were all out did one of the police officers ring the front doorbell. No way was she going to open the door, not even to the police. It was in full view of the lane and they had zoom lenses.

'Will you come around to the back door?' she called out. 'I don't want any more photographs.'

Opening the kitchen door a fraction, she recognised the village policeman. 'Will they go away, now?' she asked.

'I doubt it, Mrs Burridge. They'll probably camp

out. Is your husband at home?'

'No. I'm expecting him back tomorrow, and I'm really quite nervous about being on my own.'

'Don't be. I'll try to keep an eye on things as much as I can. It'll probably be a nine days' wonder, anyway.'

'My husband told me to padlock the gates, but I'm a bit nervous about going out there. Could you lock up for me?'

He nodded. 'Give me the padlock and keys. I'll lock up and take the keys back with me. Do you have a spare?'

'Yes. In the office. Thank you.'

Susan checked all the locks thoroughly before she went back to the television, just in time for the local news items. To her horror, they were interviewing Ralph. He must be at the Manor.

'Yes, I did know Jonathan Burridge slightly, but only for a short while.'

You lying toad, Susan thought. He lived practically next door to you for years.

His supercilious voice continued to answer questions. 'It is true, we were neighbours at Canary Wharf for a while. I felt sorry for the boy, just starting out in the City, and he did come from my uncle's village.'

The TV reporter asked, 'Is it true, sir, that you introduced Jonathan to one of the bank's directors?'

Ralph's smile was a little thin as he said, 'Ye-es, in a way, although I regretted it later.'

'Why was that, sir?'

'There were one or two doubts as to his capabilities and, if I'm to be truthful, to his honesty.

That is why I severed all connection to him some time ago.'

'But did you not have business and social connections with Jonathan's parents?'

After a pause and another humourless smile, Ralph drawled, 'Mr Burridge wished to purchase some of the estate land for building development, but I was not interested.'

'And Mrs Burridge?'

'What about Mrs Burridge?'

'I understand you were quite close at one time. Before you were married, of course.'

Ralph's laugh was explosive. 'Whatever gave you that idea? Mrs Burridge helped my housekeeper to organise one or two social events at the Manor, and that is all. I have had no need of her services for some time.'

Susan felt like hurling the remote control at the television set, but stopped herself just in time. Instead, she ran upstairs, flung herself on to the bed, and sobbed until it hurt. Then she sat up, hugging herself and rocking backwards and forwards. If only she had been able to get rid of Ralph along with the others. Now it was too late. The ideas for revenge that came into her head would have done credit to Lucretia Borgia. But none of them was fool-proof. She needed someone to talk to, someone who would understand. As usual, Josh was never around when she needed him, and she couldn't even phone him in the peat bogs of Ireland.

Fiddling with the make-up and perfume bottles on her dressing table, she picked up the necklace. It really was rather pretty, and she planned to wear it with her new velvet evening gown at Percy's next Ladies' Night. It would give an authentic Edwardian look to the style and her husband would believe her when she told him she had taken a fancy to it at an antique sale. She glanced at the bedside clock. Was it too late? The media had given up half an hour ago, probably gone down to the Red Lion or the Dog and Duck before 'last orders' was called.

On impulse, she dialled the number, but it had to be Mary who answered, didn't it. Forcing sweetness into her voice, she apologised for phoning so late.

'Not at all,' Mary said. 'I was just decorating the cake for the church fête raffle.'

'I thought the church fête had been cancelled because of — well — you know, the scandal. And no one to organise it.'

'Oh, I wouldn't know about that. I'm doing it for the Sacred Heart.'

'Ah, yes. I'd forgotten you were Catholic.' Susan thought rapidly, then decided it might be better to grasp the nettle and see what the reaction might be. 'Have you or Michael seen the news on television?'

'No. Michael has been out for the evening and I've been down here in the kitchen since I closed up. Why?'

'Well, I expect you'll hear all the gossip in the shop tomorrow, anyway. It's just that there's some cock-and-bull story about Jonathan being wanted by the police.'

'Your son?'

'Yes. It's all lies, of course. But with Michael working for Percy, I wanted you to hear it from me, not from those parasites who've been hanging round

414

my house all evening.'

'Surely you don't mean the villagers?'

Really, the woman was dim. 'No, no. The media. It's been appalling.'

'So I can imagine. Oh, dear. If I didn't have to finish this cake tonight, I'd come over and sit with you for a bit. But Michael has the car, anyway.' There was a pause, then Mary asked, 'Do you want to come down here?'

'No. I'm all locked up and I'll wait now till Percy gets home. I just thought that if they saw a man around the place, they might back off. What time do you reckon he might be home?'

Mary laughed. 'There's no telling. He's been in and out every night this week and not home before the wee small hours.'

Susan was curious. Michael had told her he was working late on the site while there was still daylight, and then he was too tired to do anything but have a bath and go to bed. 'Where on earth does he go? The pubs close at eleven.'

'And wouldn't I like to know as well. He keeps promising he won't gamble any more, but I think he's at it again.'

'Casinos?'

'No. Cards with the lads is more his game.'

'Does he win?'

'If only . . . '

'So where does he get the money from?' It never occurred to Susan that it was none of her business. Michael had wined and dined her quite well for a few weeks and bought her the necklace for her birthday, which must have cost an arm and a leg.

Perhaps he was dipping his hands into the tea-shop till?

There was a long pause, then Mary said, 'I'm afraid he's been — borrowing — my jewellery.'

'What do you mean? Borrowing?'

'Perhaps pawning is a better word.'

'Are you sure?'

'Oh, yes. I got the ear-rings back from the shop last month. And now I have to go into Southampton again to try and redeem my lovely pearl choker.'

Susan dropped the necklace on to the floor as though it was red-hot. Michael had told her he had seen it in Southampton and knew it was just perfect for her.

Mary was still talking. 'I wouldn't mind so much, but my grandmother left it to me. It had belonged to her mother. So you see, I have to get it back. But I'll do it on the QT. You won't say anything about it to Michael, will you? He'd be furious.'

'No, of course I won't.' Susan moved the necklace with her foot. She wasn't going to wear it to the dinner-dance, that was for sure. In fact, she wouldn't wear it, ever. How dare he palm off his wife's things that had been hanging around in some Irish hovel for donkey's years?

'And would you be wanting Michael to come along in the morning before he starts work? In case those newspaper people turn up again?'

'Oh, they'll be there right enough. But Mrs Graham and the gardener will be here first thing, and Percy later on. And the police are giving me protection.'

'Well, phone me if you need anything. And Susan?'

'Yes?'

'I do understand how you feel. Even now, I still worry about Brendan in that faraway country. I'll pray for you.'

'Thanks. Better get off the line, in case Percy phones again. He's a good husband, is my Percy.' And put that in your Irish pipe and smoke it, Susan thought. If you were more of a wife, he wouldn't need to look elsewhere. Percy doesn't. And I won't be pitied by an overweight cook just because she has a priest for a son. And I won't be stood up for a card game, either, Susan thought, as she threw the pearl choker into the waste-paper basket.

28

October 9th. James had so many amendments in his diary, he didn't know whether he was coming or going. First the headmistress had asked if he could possibly come later in the day, as the choir was entering a festival and would be rehearsing in the assembly hall all morning. Next the housekeeper up at Cranleigh Manor telephoned and said the decorators were in, so would he please leave the piano for now. Then Susan Burridge had not so much asked as demanded that he come in the morning rather than early mid-afternoon. She had an appointment with her solicitor at three o'clock, and the housekeeper had asked for the afternoon off. 'Ruddy nuisance,' she complained, 'But I suppose it can't be helped. Anyway, I want to know what you think of my new piano.'

Usually she asked him to look at every new piano she wanted, but not this time, although she had said that the next one would probably be a baby grand. Something more in keeping with the style of the house. James wondered what she had bought.

Now the appointment at the village hall had been cancelled. Permanently. Poor Mrs Mason had looked quite embarrassed when the chairman of the parish council spouted forth. She'd obviously not been told about the keyboard. Might as well phone the new vicar, see if it was convenient to call earlier.

The Obermeier still graced the sitting room of the

Vicarage, but a clutch of small children watched curiously as James unpacked his tools. A bearded young man wearing jeans and sweatshirt with a wildlife logo, had greeted him heartily. 'Call me Steve,' he said. 'Lynne's upstairs, still sorting out packing cases, I'm afraid. Do excuse me, I have a sermon to write. You don't mind if the children stay? Just tell them to shut up if they get on your nerves.'

The children kept up a constant stream of questions, but at least they didn't get in his way. His thoughts went back to his first visit, when the Reverend Simpkins had prayed endlessly and sung hideously, and he smiled. The Jenkins's children and grandchildren had brought life to the old house, and he was glad to see a family here again. But he knew he would miss the friendly chats around the fire with Hugh and Gwynneth Jenkins.

★ ★ ★

Mrs Graham let him into the Dower House. 'Mrs Burridge asked if you would thoroughly examine the new piano and let her have your opinion.' At the door, the housekeeper repeated her usual message, 'And will you please be careful not to put anything on the table. It's Sheraton, and rather valuable.'

James was almost afraid to breathe near the furniture, let alone put anything on it. The new piano looked handsome in the curved bay window.

'I've always wanted a baby grand. And Steinways are the best, aren't they?'

Framed in the door, Susan Burridge wore a

419

white, fluffy dressing gown, her hair in a towelling turban.

'They're not called the Rolls-Royce of pianos for nothing. But it does depend on the condition, of course.'

'It belonged to a concert pianist, so it should be in perfect condition. His widow had to sell it, and Josh thought it too good an opportunity to miss. So I told him to go ahead. It sounds lovely, doesn't it? What do you think?'

Certainly the tone was mellow, although out of tune. But he would need to take it apart. He opened out the huge dust sheet and proceeded to lift off the top lid and the keyboard lid. Apart from talking about the piano, conversation was going to be a little difficult, he felt. There had been so much in the newspapers during the past couple of months, and she must be worried about Jonathan. James hadn't been surprised at the news, but he had been sorry. He would have been devastated if it had been Robert, but then Robert wouldn't have got into that situation in the first place.

As if reading his mind, Mrs Burridge said, 'I'm hoping our solicitor will put an injunction on the media to stop hounding us. I expect you've heard about Jonathan?'

'I never believe anything I read in the papers, but I am sorry you and your husband have been caused such distress.'

'How kind,' she murmured, then poured two whiskies from the decanter, carefully placing one on a silver coaster to protect the drum table near the piano.

'Not for me, thank you, Mrs Burridge. It's a little early.'

'Nonsense. It's never too early or too late.'

'No, thank you. I'm driving.'

For a moment she watched him thoughtfully. Then she said, 'Why don't you call me Susan? You've known me for yonks.'

He answered carefully. 'Exactly. I would find it too difficult now to call you anything other than Mrs Burridge.'

'It wasn't a problem with Megan.'

'Only because she was so young when I first met her.'

'I wasn't that much older than her.' Mrs Burridge's voice took on a slightly petulant tone.

'I'm sorry, I didn't mean — ' Not much point in trying to justify his remark, James thought. He changed the subject. 'You have some very fine pieces of furniture in here and, certainly on appearance, the piano sets off the room beautifully.'

Her attitude softened as she walked around the room, touching the secretaire bookcase, inlaid chest, the new sofa. 'They are grand, aren't they? Who would have thought I could care for anything this much. Me, always chopping and changing, as you know only too well.'

He glanced around the room. 'You have excellent taste, Mrs Burridge.'

'Thank you. And I'm taking no chances. Look.' Pointing upwards, she drew his attention to the intensive fire and security systems. 'It would break my heart if I were to lose my treasures.'

'Very wise.'

She tipped his whisky into her glass. 'Did you hear about the theme park next door?'

'Again, only what I read in the paper. Is it true?'

Her face darkening with anger, she nodded. 'We'll never be able to sell this place — not that I want to — but it's the principle of the thing. When I think of that bastard and all his promises . . . '

James was surprised at her language and glanced in her direction. It was a mistake. She was watching him over the rim of her glass. 'I never really thanked you properly about that time you saw us together, did I?'

'There's nothing to thank me for.'

She still had the freshly scrubbed look of a girl just out of the shower. In a strange way, it underlined her sexuality. If she'd been pouting crimson lips and wearing a clinging robe, he would have known exactly what she was thinking. But this childish image with secretive eyes bothered him. Now her voice was soft. Not exactly seductive. It was almost as though she were playing a game with him. Testing the water.

Delicately tracing her fingers along the arm of her seat, she said, 'Do you know what this is called?'

He looked up briefly, then went back to his work. 'No. But it's a very pretty sofa.'

'It's called a *causeuse*.'

'Really? I didn't know that.'

'If you're romantically inclined, like me, perhaps you would know it better as a love-seat?'

James knew she was still watching him, but he refused to be drawn. That pathway led only to trouble. Look what had happened to Nigel. Then

James's hand stiffened, as he realised that what had only been a very slight suspicion in his mind was actually true. Of course. It had to be Susan. There was no other explanation. Unable to control his emotions for a moment, he stared at her.

Her body didn't move towards him. Only her voice. 'I'd like to thank you properly,' she murmured. 'You only have to say the word.'

With the unwieldy top of the piano in his arms, he was at a disadvantage. Best to pretend not to hear. Look inside the piano. Tune it, and get out. Quickly.

Oh, dear. He stopped listening as he stared into the piano. This was serious. Then his ears picked up fragments of her words again as he examined the piano more carefully ' . . . won't be back until late . . . always felt you were attracted to me . . . different when your wife was alive . . . '

He straightened and looked at her. 'Mrs Burridge.' He fought to regain his self-control, conceal the disgust from his voice. 'In thirty years of marriage, I was never once unfaithful to my wife. And I have no intention of starting now, especially with the wife of a man I respect.'

For a moment, he thought she was going to throw her glass at him. Then she carefully placed it back on the coaster, gave him the most contemptuous look he'd ever received, and said, 'Whatever gave you the impression I'd ever look at you? After all, you're only the piano-tuner!'

As she stood up, the housekeeper came into the room, dressed in outdoor clothes, her car keys in one hand, a lovely pearl necklace in the other.

'I'm just off, Mrs Burridge, but thought I'd better

show you this.' She held up the necklace. 'It was in the waste-paper basket in your bedroom, but I'm sure you didn't mean to throw it away. Shall I put it in your jewel box?'

'No! I don't want it.'

'But what shall I — '

'I don't care what you do with it. Keep it if you want it.' With that, Susan Burridge flounced from the room.

Mrs Graham looked ill at ease as she stood in the doorway. Then she sighed, murmured, 'Well I never,' nodded goodbye to James, and left, still holding the necklace.

★   ★   ★

Half an hour later, James straightened up from the stile at the top of the hill. The woman had taken the bucket back indoors, the Sierra was clean and dry once more, and his fierce anger had abated. He would have to go back to the village, there was still Miss Partridge's piano to tune before lunch, then the one at the tea-shop and the school. As for the Dower House, he would have to find a pretty good excuse for not calling again. Then there was the other matter.

Miss Partridge flapped around the piano like a mother hen. 'I always promised myself that I would take up music again when I retired, but I really began to despair that I would be able to find a decent piano that I could afford. It's a shame that Megan couldn't take it with her. I understand the flat in London is rather poky?' She looked questioningly at James, but he just mumbled, 'I wouldn't know.'

'I've often wondered why they all moved so suddenly,' she went on, 'but I don't know the neighbours well.' Miss Partridge paused, but he didn't respond, so she continued to probe. 'Still, I expect you are aware of the reason. When I asked if you were reliable, Mrs Jenkins told me she had known you for many years.'

James had never been good with dates, but thought it must be . . . yes . . . 'About thirty-five, I suppose. I tuned the piano at the vicarage for the previous vicar. And the one at the Manor.' This was safer ground.

'Of course. I'd forgotten, you played the piano at the Brigadier's eightieth birthday party. The day the caretaker hanged himself.' She shuddered. 'They said it was grief over his son, but I've often wondered if there was more to it than that.' Eyebrows raised, she looked directly at James. 'You were there when they found him, weren't you?'

'Not in the village hall, no.'

'But you were in the Manor house. You must have heard things?'

'No, not really.'

'Oh.' The tone of disappointment faded as she took a new tack. 'And Megan sang so beautifully on that day, too. Not that she's had much to sing about of late, from what I've heard.'

James turned the pliers a fraction, wishing they held Miss Partridge's scrawny neck. 'They are a very musical family. It was always a pleasure to hear Megan sing.'

'Yes, I agree. Such a pity they had to leave under a cloud.'

'I don't think that's quite right.'

'Oh, yes. I did hear there was some kind of scandal involving the curate. It's unlikely that he'll get his own parish, I believe. But I don't think they'd allow him to care for young people in a hostel if it was anything to do with — well, you know — choirboys and that sort of thing — do you?'

James slotted the lid back into place. 'I never heard anything of the sort, Miss Partridge, and I'm quite sure that Mr Taylor has nothing on his conscience. But then, village gossip should always be taken with a heap of salt, as I'm sure you agree?'

'Oh, yes. Yes, of course. Far be it from me to gossip.' Flustered, Miss Partridge took her handbag from the glass and chrome coffee table. Noting his look of recognition, she said, 'That came with the house. Mrs Taylor said she didn't want it.'

James remembered seeing it first in Susan Burridge's lounge, before she had given it to Megan.

'And the wrought iron patio furniture,' Miss Partridge continued. 'Very kind of her to leave it, but what's that saying about an ill wind?'

A thin reedy voice called down from upstairs, 'Edith! Do you have a man in the house?'

Blushing slightly, Miss Partridge called back, 'It's only the piano-tuner, Mother. Nothing to worry about.'

★　★　★

426

The tea-shop was almost empty, and Mary seemed a little down in the dumps. And she had a bruise on her face. Sharon insisted that Mary should sit down while she make a ham and salad sandwich for James, but it was Mary who brought the tray upstairs after he started work on the piano.

'Are you sure you're all right, Mary?' he asked. 'Sharon said you'd had quite a bad fall.'

'Oh, she fusses over me more than my sister,' Mary said, smiling. 'I'm fine. Or I will be if I can make up my mind what to do about this business.'

'Oh?' He took the cup of tea. 'I thought you were happy with the way things were going.'

'I was, until this quarter's figures. Would you mind if I run it in front of you? as the young people say, with all their jargon. I really would appreciate your opinion.'

He listened attentively while she told him what the bank manager had said, and her fears about the new stretch of roadway.

'If I'm to change the image and bring in more custom, I'll need more capital. All I have is the savings I've been putting by so we can visit Brendan. I don't want to touch that, if I can help it.'

'What does your husband think you should do.'

For a long, long moment, Mary stared down at her plate, pulling at the piece of cake until there was nothing left but crumbs. Then a tear rolled slowly down her cheek, followed by another. It was worse than when Mrs Jenkins had wept.

'Oh, Mary. What is it?' He knelt by her chair and put his hand on her arm. When she buried her head upon his shoulder, it seemed the most natural thing in the world that he should hold her close until her tears had subsided and, even then, he didn't move away. Not until she began to grope in her pocket for a screwed up bit of tissue.

'Here.' He handed her his spotless handkerchief, but stayed close. 'Do you want to talk about it, or did you just want to cry something out of your system?'

After a juddering little sob, she said, 'I think I have to talk about it — because I don't know what else to do.'

He waited patiently, still kneeling by her chair, still with his arm around her shoulder. Then she told him.

'I think Michael has left me,' she said, simply. 'We had a terrible row last night, and he didn't come home.'

'Did he do this?' Gently, James touched the bruise.

She nodded. 'I don't think he meant to hurt me quite so much. But he'd been drinking, and when I tried to get out of the way, he pushed me, and I went down the stairs.'

'Is it the first time he's done something like this?'

'No.' She blew her nose. 'When I first found out he'd been pawning my jewellery, he became angry and slapped me, and again last week when I had a go about his gambling. But last night was the worst. I've never seen him so violent, and he wouldn't believe me when I told him the filthy letter was full of lies.'

'What letter?'

Crossing to the sideboard, Mary took an envelope

from the drawer. It was typed, as was the letter. And it was addressed to Michael Fitzgerald. Silently she handed it to him. It was brief, and cruel, informing Michael that his wife had been seen visiting a man in the next village, late at night. An older man who lived alone and had never married. He had a reputation for being weird, and no self-respecting woman would visit him, especially not late at night. The writer felt that Michael should know that his wife was not the sweet innocent she pretended to be.

'It has all the worst clichés I've ever seen,' James said, 'except that it isn't signed *a well-wisher*.' He handed back the letter. 'Why should someone want to write such lies about you?'

'I don't know, James.' It was the first time she had called him James, but he didn't mind. 'I think I know the incident, but it was quite innocent, believe me. Mr Dennison had won my cake in the church raffle, and he was on his bike, so I offered to take it up to his cottage.'

'Where's the harm in that?'

'No harm at all, except that he said he wouldn't be going home until after the darts match, so it was gone ten o'clock when I delivered the cake. I was only in the house for a few seconds to put the cake in the kitchen.'

'Long enough for a dirty mind to put two and two together and make half a dozen, obviously. And you say Michael didn't believe you.'

'Oh, I think he believed me, right enough. But I've heard rumours — '

'What sort of rumours?'

Mary bit her lip and twisted the handkerchief. Her voice was almost a whisper. 'Another woman sort of rumours. And I've been wondering if it eased his conscience to put some of the blame on me?'

'You mean, he feels guilty about his own behaviour, so takes it out on you?'

'Yes.' She frowned thoughtfully. 'I don't think he's been unfaithful to me before, although there's no telling of what went on when I was in Ireland. But for some weeks he hasn't wanted to — ' She paused, and looked away.

'Make love to you?'

She nodded. 'That had never been a problem in our marriage, but suddenly, it was as though he'd gone right off me. I kept thinking it must be just his age. After all, men do have what they call a mid-life crisis, don't they?'

He smiled. 'So I'm told.'

'But at the same time he was getting all spruced up and off out every night. Said he was out with the boys. But one day I noticed a stain on his suit, and decided to take it across the road so it could go on the van to the cleaner's.' It was obviously very painful for her to continue.

'And you found something in the pockets?'

She nodded. 'It was a receipt for two meals at Colleys. On the night he'd told me he was going to La Margarita's to celebrate one of the lads' birthdays. And I could smell perfume on the jacket.' Mary's eyes were still filled with tears as she said, 'Wasn't it bad enough that he was taking my things to pay for his gambling debts? But to borrow money from me so he could take out his fancy woman . . . '

Her expression was so desolate, James wanted to take her in his arms again.

'This time he's taken them to another pawnbroker, and he won't tell me which one. He's denied touching the pearls, but I know it's him, and I want them back.' Another solitary tear trickled down her cheek. 'They belonged to my great-grandmother.'

A chill ran through James. Slowly, he asked, 'What were the pearls like?' He hoped she would say single strand, or double. But she didn't.

'Four rows of beautifully matched pearls, they were, in a choker, with a diamanté clasp. They were very fashionable in Edwardian days.'

In his mind, James saw Mrs Graham clutching a pearl choker with a diamanté clasp. She had found it in Susan Burridge's waste-paper basket. But surely Susan and Michael weren't lovers? They were chalk and cheese. Then he remembered the dealer in Salisbury. Josh, she'd said his name was. And Josh had helped her buy the piano. Maybe Josh was more than an adviser on antiques? And maybe Susan Burridge was the sort of woman who liked what some people referred to as 'a bit of rough'. Katherine had thought there might be more to Mrs Burridge than met the eye but, if his suspicions were correct, she wasn't just an unfaithful wife.

James picked up the letter again from the table. Yes, there were the double letters overtyped, in the words 'village', 'especially', 'innocent', and he remembered Miss Harding talking about her little bit of sleuthing over the typewriter that had been used for the malicious letter that hounded her from the village. Then he opened his briefcase.

There it was. The envelope that had contained Susan Burridge's last cheque. He'd used it to hold some loose stamps. The double oo's in his name were overtyped, as were the t's in Cottage. Brown manila envelope, exactly the same.

Mary looked at the two envelopes. 'Who?' she asked.

'Susan Burridge. And I think I've seen your necklace today at the Dower House.'

Her expression changed from shock to disbelief. 'Why?' she asked. 'Why would Susan Burridge want to hurt me? I thought we were — not friends, exactly, but not enemies.'

James thought carefully before he answered. 'I don't know, Mary, but I very much suspect that this isn't the first time she's written this sort of letter.' He told her about Miss Harding, and Megan and Nigel. Then he remembered another. 'And Mrs Faversham was very distressed over a letter some years ago. I can't remember the details, but the end result was that Mrs Faversham resigned from the Women's Institute and Mrs Burridge was made president.'

Open-mouthed, Mary stared back at him. 'If this is so, James, she must be a very sick lady.'

'Very sick indeed. Pity she doesn't disappear from the face of the earth, like her son. He was an evil little so and so, too.' James looked at his watch. 'I must be getting along to the school, I'm afraid. I'll come back to do the refelting.'

She nodded. 'Thank you, James, for letting me cry on your shoulder like this. I hope you didn't mind.'

He smiled. 'I'm pleased that you feel you can. Listen, Mary. We must put a stop to her before she does any more damage.'

'But how? Brown envelopes and a faulty typewriter aren't much to go on.'

'No, but your necklace might be. Leave it with me. I'll try to get it back, I promise you. There's something I've got to tell her about the piano, anyway, so I'll go up there after I've left the school.'

Standing on tiptoe, she kissed his cheek. 'You're a good man, James Woodward,' she said, but not in quite the same way that Mrs Jenkins had said it. And there was a fragrance to Mary's hair that reminded him . . . it was a long time since he had noticed the sweet smell of a woman.

★   ★   ★

The Mercedes was parked in the drive. Good. That meant the master of the house was home, which would make things easier. James still didn't have a clue as to how he was going to recover the pearl choker, but he would have to think of something. He'd promised Mary.

There was no answer to the doorbell, so he walked around to the back of the house, his footsteps light upon the grass. Through the hedge, he saw Mr and Mrs Burridge sitting on the far side of the pool, heard the ice clinking in their glasses. Percy Burridge had a booming voice at the best of times, now it was amplified by the water.

'Why change now, Susan?' he was saying. 'The fellow's been coming for years. He knows his trade.

433

And I trust him. That's more than can be said for some.'

An instinctive curiosity stopped James in his tracks. He knew he was eavesdropping, but he didn't care. Mrs Burridge's voice was so low, he couldn't hear a word, but her husband suddenly exploded.

'Made a pass at you? The piano-tuner? He's not got it in him.'

This time James caught something about him being a widower and it must have made him peculiar.

'Never! I can't believe . . . you said that about Nigel. Am I to believe they both tried it on? If you're lying Susan — '

Protesting her innocence, Susan began to weep, but her husband was having none of it.

'And you can cut out that sob-stuff right away. You know I can't stand women who turn on the water-works.' Percy Burridge was off at full blast as James turned and crept away. He had to go home and quietly work out a scheme, where the tables could be turned on Susan Burridge. She might have a devoted husband, but Percy Burridge was no fool, and he was beginning to have suspicions as to his wife's character. That would do for a start.

29

Susan would have given anything to blacken James Woodward's name from one end of the village to the other. If she had her way, no one would let him anywhere near their pianos. But Percy had been behaving very strangely since that day. Watchful. Then there was the reporter. Most of them had given up after a few weeks, but this one still hung around the village. She'd seen his car outside most of the pubs. He was obviously looking for a story, and she had no intention of providing him with one. So she'd have to put the piano-tuner on the back-burner for the time being.

The new piano had a magnificent tone and she'd taken to practising most days. There was something rather stylish about sitting in a bay window playing a Steinway baby grand, surrounded by beautiful antiques. Among all the things they'd written about Jonathan, dreadful lies most of them, she'd read one paragraph again and again. It referred to 'Jonathan's elegant family home in Hampshire, the Dower House of the Cranleigh Manor estate.'

Josh had been very comforting, but even he didn't contact her quite so often. Usually she had to phone him — when she was so terribly lonely she knew she couldn't survive another day without him. But he reminded her more and more that he was a gypsy at heart, and wouldn't ever be tied down. And he hinted that he might move to Ireland. The easy-going lifestyle suited him and he liked the people. She'd been tempted to ask him if there was one person in particular he liked? A female? But she dare not. He would be off like a shot. So she had to content herself with rare assignations which left her gasping for more.

Michael was out of her life, for ever, thank goodness. She'd made a few discreet enquiries amongst Percy's lads, and discovered he was living with a pub landlady in Southampton. That was just about his style, she thought, and it had been very satisfactory to notice the bruising on his fat wife's face and know that the letter had achieved its objective: to cause them both grief. Of course, Susan had been the essence of sweetness, expressing her concern and tut-tutting about the staircase. Strangely enough, Mary hadn't smiled back, just nodded and excused herself back to the kitchen. Surely she couldn't have guessed? They'd been too discreet, and she'd never worn the necklace in the village.

Actually, she couldn't care less if the Irishwoman did know they'd had a bit of a fling as long as she didn't spread it around the village. Mary had always seemed to be a cautious woman where gossip was concerned but, if she was jealous, perhaps she would tell someone? The cocky little kid who worked in the shop had stared rudely in the Post Office queue, and the old maid who sat in the shop window had scuttled off on her bicycle when Susan said 'Good morning'.

What Susan really wanted was to leave Fivepenny Lanes. She loved the Dower House, but was bored with the pettiness of village life. The main problem would be selling the house, with a theme park about to be built next door.

Susan was playing the piano when she heard Percy's key in the door. By the expression on his face, he'd had a very good day. She had to wait until he'd poured himself a drink and settled back in his armchair before he made his announcement.

'We're going back to Yorkshire, Susan!'

Too stunned to speak, she stared back at him.

'I reckoned you'd be knocked out cold when I told you.'

Finding her voice, she asked, 'But why? Where? When?'

'One question at a time, if you don't mind.' He laughed, then became serious. 'Why? Because I've always reckoned a man should go back to his roots before he dies.'

'You're not ill are you, Percy?' For a moment she was afraid. If anything happened to Percy, she would be totally alone. Even her children had deserted her.

'No, lass. Nothing like that. But I'm not as young as I was, and happen I should think about the future a bit more serious, like. As to where? Not too far from Bradford. That's where it will all happen.'

'What will happen, Percy? I don't understand.'

'A major shopping mall, lass. We'll put the others in the shade. There's a consortium that's taken me on board because of my experience down here. Not one of them has done as much as I have in that field. Yorkshire folk don't put so much store on degrees and suchlike. They know I have more up here,' he tapped his head, 'than they can learn at any university. There's life in the old dog yet.' He grinned as he put his glass down on the table.

Susan's mind went back to the days when she had worked with him on the budgets before he began each new development. 'Won't you need a huge investment, dear?' she asked.

'Aye. I will at that. It'll take every penny we've got, and a bank loan that will have me holding my breath until the council start parting up with some of their brass. So we'll have to watch what we're spending for a bit. No sliding roof over pool, I'm afraid.'

It still wasn't quite sinking in. 'What about the business down here?' she asked.

'Nowt to worry about there. Frank Griffiths is buying me out and that's going in kitty.'

'We're not going to be poor, are we, Percy? We both had enough of that before we were wed.'

He laughed. 'Of course, we won't be poor, Susan. Happen there'll be plenty of brass coming our way later on. Might even become a millionaire before I snuff it. Always said I would.'

Questions poured through Susan's head, but she was anxious about the table and paused to slip a coaster under her husband's glass and mildly protest: 'If it leaves a mark, it will really damage the wood.'

'For Christ's sake, Susan!' he shouted. 'Can't a man have a drink in his own home, without worrying about your precious furniture all the time?'

'I'm sorry, dear, but it is irreplaceable, and you like me to take care of things.'

After a moment, he nodded. 'You're right, love.

It's just that I've got so much on my mind at the moment.' He went on about units, a whole floor as a refreshment area, entertainment, Marks and Spencer's, Next, Sainsbury's. 'All the big names will be there, Susan,' he said. 'I'll show thee plans later. It'll be grand, really grand. And we should be able to open for business around end of next year.' He handed her his glass for a refill. 'I'll have to move up there for a start, while you take care of things this end.'

'Right. But it might take a while to sell the house.'

'You could have a word with his lordship up at Manor. He'll need somebody living on the spot to take care of things. Hang about, though. He wasn't too kindly about our Jonathan, was he?'

Percy hadn't talked much about Jonathan, although he'd made a statement to the press through his solicitor saying he had total confidence in his son's honesty, and threatened to sue for libel if anything was said that couldn't be substantiated. But Susan knew he had been deeply hurt that Jonathan had never contacted them to put his side of the story. And she knew that, like herself, he was just a little bit afraid that some of the accusations might have foundation.

Now he remained deep in thought for a while. 'Leave Ralph out of it,' he said eventually. 'Just go to the better estate agents, make sure they put photographs and a good description in the *Hampshire Chronicle*.'

'And *Country Life*,' she suggested.

'Aye. Reckon I can leave it all to you.' Suddenly, his face creased into a huge smile. 'Guess who else is putting capital into this venture, Susan?' She shook her head. 'Old Sam Grimshaw.'

'Not the Sam Grimshaw I worked for before I met you?'

'The very same. It's thanks to him that we met in the first place. He's a few year older than me, but still got it all upstairs.' Again Percy tapped his forehead. 'And he sends his very best regards to you.'

'That's nice,' she said, thinking back furiously. Was there anything that Sam Grimshaw knew about her that Percy shouldn't know? No. Only that she hadn't been a secretary, and that wouldn't matter now. But Percy's next words did matter.

'He's gone into partnership with a younger fellow. I didn't know him, but happen you might. Used to be a rep before he set up on his own. Made quite a bit of brass, I believe, and full of ideas.'

There had been many reps calling in at Grimshaw's when she'd worked there. Susan doubted whether she would remember him, or that he would remember her, but she asked his name, out of politeness.

'Dennis Rivers. He would have been on circuit about the time you worked for old Sam, I reckon.'

Susan sank down onto a chair. It would be him, wouldn't it? Dennis Rivers, who'd been the first to sample her virginity — in the back of his car.

★   ★   ★

James was making a list. If he was going to Australia before Christmas, he needed to know what to take.

440

It would be high summer out there so he'd need to buy new pyjamas for a start, underwear, lightweight slacks, and shorts. He'd bought a new pair when they went to the south of France, but perhaps he'd better get another pair? Certainly he would need sun-block, and a good supply of films. A sudden thought came to him and he searched the bureau drawers. Yes, there they were. Just before Katherine had died, he'd finished up the film to put a fresh one in the camera and popped it in the post-box out in the lane when he went out to look for her on that terrible day. When the processed packet had been returned he had put it in the bureau, unable to face the memories. And he hadn't used the camera since.

It was quite a jolt, seeing Katherine smiling back at him. And there was Bess. He missed her greeting when he came home from work. She had been more his dog than Katherine's. Duke was Katherine's pet, and Jaffa belonged to no one. He was still the one who made up his mind whether or not he would please you with his presence, but now he was getting older, he preferred a warm lap to a cold evening's hunting. In fact, he hadn't been into the paddock once since that day. It was though he knew what had happened.

James turned the photographs over, one by one. What a lovely summer that had been. Ah, yes, Salisbury market, teeming with life and colour. It was the first time he'd used the new zoom lens. They were rather good, even if he did think so himself, especially the ones taken from the upstairs window of the pub. Good detail on that bric-à-brac stall, with the couple browsing. The white shorts and top of the woman made a good contrast against her tan, and the way they smiled at each other and held hands, almost secretly, was a nice touch. Funnily enough, he didn't remember seeing them when he'd taken the picture, he'd been focusing on the stallholder and — good God! It looked like . . . James found his magnifying glass and studied the photograph more closely. Oh, yes. No doubt about it. It was Susan Burridge — and Josh.

For a while he sat quietly gazing at the photograph, realising the implications. Sharon and Miss Partridge had been superb channels of little tit-bits of gossip about Susan, but it hadn't been enough to help the people she'd harmed. Perhaps the photograph could be used in some way? Slowly, an idea came into his mind, so delightful, and so devilish — and so right. As he jumped up and punched air, Jaffa screeched and fled to the safety of the kitchen. James was ebullient. 'I've got her!' he yelled. 'At last I've got her.'

30

Susan's hands were shaking as she replaced the photograph in the envelope. How dare he spy on her? To think that he'd been taking photographs of her and Josh. Leaning out of a window. Just like those vultures who'd hung around for weeks. They'd been trying to destroy Jonathan. And this — this — piano-playing git — was trying to destroy her.

Contessa whimpered as Susan pushed her aside with her foot and flung herself down on to the sofa, rapidly thinking of her options. She could tear up the photograph and the letter and hope he was bluffing. No. He wasn't bluffing. He had the negatives. He could prove to Percy that Susan had been more than a little friendly with Josh. And she thought they had been so careful. But why should the piano-tuner care what happened to Nigel and his holier-than-thou Welsh wife? Why not leave them to rot in the slum they deserved? There had to be more to it than that. He said he'd overheard her trying to blacken his own name with her husband. Perhaps if she pleaded with him, promised she would tell her husband she must have misunderstood, so the wretched man's reputation would still be snowy white?

Susan read the letter again. No. He was quite adamant. If she didn't write to the bishop within seven days, one copy of the photograph would go to Percy, and another copy to the bishop — both with explicit letters of explanation. She couldn't risk it. She dare not risk it.

Through tears of self-pity, she slowly made her way upstairs and dragged out the old typewriter. It had never been much good, always scrunching up the keys if you tried to type the same letter twice.

★　★　★

Mary watched James, admiring the shape and gentle strength of his hands, as he played Liszt's Liebesträume. Idly, she studied his face. He had a good profile, with a straight nose, and crinkles at the corner of his eyes. She liked a man with laughter wrinkles. And she liked a man with a good head of hair. Michael had a good head of hair still, but it was rather coarse and his neck was thick, bull-like. Why was she thinking about Michael? She hadn't seen sight nor sound of him for weeks, nor had a penny out of him. And, if she was honest with herself, she didn't want to. Not with his violent nature, his gambling, his unfaithfulness, the endless promises that were never fulfilled. She sighed.

James looked up from the piano. 'What's wrong?' he asked.

'Nothing. I was just wishing — '

'What were you wishing?'

'Oh, I don't know.' She couldn't possibly tell him her dearest wish. 'All sorts of things. It's too long since I've seen Brendan. And I wish I knew what was going to happen to the business. And — ' She shrugged.

For a long moment he was thoughtful, then he

looked back at the piano as he quietly asked. 'Do you ever wish you weren't still married to Michael?'

Mary was so startled, she almost gasped. James had made her think about the one question she had pushed to the back of her mind, again and again. But he had asked an honest question, and would expect an honest answer. So she answered, just as quietly. 'Yes.'

A little smile played around his mouth as he looked back at her. 'I hoped you would say that,' he said.

Her smile was just as tentative as she said, 'But there the hope must end, I'm afraid, James.'

'I know. You certainly have grounds for divorce, but your religion wouldn't allow it.'

'*I* wouldn't allow it,' she said. 'My marriage vows are still sacred to me, even though my husband isn't.'

Sadly, James nodded.

'But that doesn't have to stop me caring for someone else, does it?'

His expression changed. 'Now I'm the one who's wishing.' He reached for her hand. 'And you saying what I think — what I hope — you are saying?'

'To be honest, James, dear. I'm not sure what I'm saying. Too many things are happening to me right now. But I will say this: I never thought I would look at any other man but Michael with such feelings of affection.'

James leaned forward and kissed Mary lightly on the lips. 'And I never thought I would do that to any other woman but Katherine.'

'Do you feel guilty about your feelings?'

'No. Do you?'

'Not about my feelings. Haven't you given me more warmth and friendship than anyone in the world.' Slowly she shook her head and truthfully said, 'No, I couldn't possibly feel guilty, not even — not even if my own feelings do turn to love.'

'Do you think they might?'

She smiled. 'Let's just take one day at a time, shall we?' It was time to change the subject. 'Do you have a photograph of your wife? You say she was beautiful, but I'd like to know what she looked like.'

Silently, James reached into his wallet and took out a photograph of Katherine, with the three children sitting on a farm gate behind her. 'This is my favourite,' he said. 'It was taken the day the *Canberra* returned from the Falklands.'

As Mary studied the photograph, it was like looking at an old friend. Her eyes were misty as she handed the snapshot back to James. 'I was there, too,' she said.

'At Calshot?'

She nodded. 'We'd only just come down to Southampton and I persuaded Michael to drive me out to see the Great White Whale come home. And he pointed you all out to me. You were such a handsome family.'

'And you didn't recognise me when we sat by the pond, feeding the ducks?'

'No. You had your back to me while you were taking the photographs. But I passed your car later and looked in at Katherine. And she smiled at me. I thought she was the most beautiful woman I had ever seen.'

James looked down at the photograph. 'She was beautiful. I wish you two could have known each other.'

'Somehow, James, I think we do.' She stood up. 'Now, I'd better be paying Sharon, or she won't be able to go to the disco tonight.'

After Sharon had left, Mary locked the door and counted the takings, wondering whether it was worthwhile struggling on.

James had packed away his tools, but he had a suggestion for her to think about after he'd left.

'Obviously, you'd like to see your son.' It was a statement, not a question. 'But I would imagine the air fares are a bit prohibitive.'

'Well, yes, although I have a little savings that I managed to hide away from Michael. Almost enough for the fare, but not for the rest of it. Then there's the shop, of course.'

'Would you consider closing the shop for a few weeks? Trade must be falling off at this time of year.'

'That's true enough.' With a wry smile, she showed him the small handful of notes and coins. 'I suppose I could consider it. I haven't begun to take orders for Christmas cakes yet.' She knew there was more to come, and was very curious.

'Would you have to pay Sharon while you were closed?'

'Well, Yvette, who runs the little gallery over on the Romsey road thinks she has talent and has suggested a graphics course at art college. Sharon said she might start after Christmas, if they'll take her on a term late. I'd have to pay her till then, of course, but that wouldn't amount to much. What are you thinking about, James?'

'I'm thinking about the two of us travelling to Australia together.'

'But you're spending Christmas with your daughter.'

'That's right, and there's no reason why you shouldn't spend Christmas with your son at one of his mission stations, is there?'

Her eyes rounded with excitement, then clouded. 'There's nothing in this world I'd like better than to be cooking Christmas dinner for Brendan, wherever he might be. But I really haven't enough money, and the bank manager won't extend the loan for me to go gallivanting across the world.'

'No, but I would be only too happy to top up your savings if you'd allow me to.'

'Oh, James. Aren't you the kindest of men? But I couldn't possibly.'

'Yes, you could. Call it a loan if it will make you happier.'

She knew she was weakening.

'And — ' he went on, 'after Christmas, you and I can spend some time together in Melbourne. Just getting to know each other.'

'On our own?'

'I don't think we need a chaperone at our age, do you? And you can be in charge of — '

'Of?' She knew only too well what he meant.

'Of, shall we say, our emotions? I won't press you to consider any more than that. The ball is totally in your court, Mary, as they say.'

Staring back at him, she knew it was going to be difficult to control her emotions if she was alone with this lovely man. And it might be that she would have something to say at confession that was a little more sinful than impatience and intolerance.

'Would I be able to get on the same flight?' she asked.

'Too right you will.' His laugh was infectious. 'I'll pick you up first thing in the morning and we'll go to the travel agency. Bring your passport.'

★ ★ ★

The huge tree in the hall was decorated with style and good taste. But nobody commented on it. Susan couldn't understand why the secretary wasn't responding to her questions about Christmas. She couldn't be miffed about the job, surely? After all, Frank Griffiths was keeping her on in his own office. She'd have to travel to Southampton, but Frank had given her an increase, and a small company car. In fact, she had good opportunities for running the site offices, and she only had to look at Susan's lifestyle to see where that might lead. Perhaps her husband objected? But that was no excuse for saying she was too busy to talk or have coffee in the kitchen with her employer's wife. She was still staff, until the end of the year, and it was rude, the way she had snubbed Susan.

The house was on the market, but so far there had been no enquiries. Susan had expected that Mrs Graham and the gardener would stay on until she left, even though she had no idea of where she was going to live; certainly not in Bradford. But the gardener had already stopped work, without an explanation, and Mrs Graham had told her today that she would like to leave at the end of the week, if that was all right with Mrs Burridge. It bloody well wasn't all right, but the wretched woman wouldn't be persuaded to hang on until after Christmas. It didn't matter so much about the gardener, at this time of year, but it did matter that she would have no housekeeper to take care of all the extra work over Christmas.

Then again, would there be much extra work? The invitations had gone out for a cocktail party on Christmas Eve, but so far there had been only messages of apology from the doctor, the manager of the golf club, and the bank manager. It just wasn't fair. Perhaps Percy would have a word with Mrs Graham tomorrow. She would have gone home by the time he came home tonight. He was taking the men down to the pub for a farewell drink.

But Percy Burridge was in no mood to discuss the housekeeper when he came home. Brushing past Susan without so much as a greeting, let alone a kiss, he went straight into the sitting room, poured himself a whisky, downed it in one, then poured another one before flopping into an armchair. Then, with Susan watching in horror, he dragged one of the pretty little Victorian button-back chairs towards him, raised one foot, then the other, and rested both on the velvet, still wearing his outdoor shoes, and not taking his eyes off his wife.

Susan knew better than to protest. Something was seriously wrong, and she waited for an explanation. But the long wait was too much, and she had to break the silence.

'What has happened, Percy? You don't usually . . . ' Her voice trailed as she looked down at his feet.

'No, Susan. I don't usually, do I? But tha'll see me doing a great deal of things I don't usually do, from now on.' Still watchful, he took a good swig of his drink.

'Please, Percy. I've not seen you like this before. It's disturbing me.'

'Disturbing thee, is it?' He nodded thoughtfully. 'That must be what they call poetic justice, I reckon.'

'I don't understand.' His eyes, usually so full of warmth and understanding, were ice-cold and expressionless.

'Well, considering how much tha's been disturbing me, you should be the first to understand.'

What had he found out, she wondered? 'Percy, dear. Do you think you might have had just a little too much to drink?'

'I haven't started drinking, yet, Susan.' He walked across to the cabinet and poured a third glass of single malt, still talking. 'All evening I've only had one pint of ale and a couple of cokes. Didn't want to lose my licence on way home, so just sat at bar, chatting to lads and paying for their rounds.' Turning from the cabinet, he faced her squarely. 'Pity Michael Fitzgerald didn't follow my example.'

Oh, God, now what had Michael said?

'Aye. No use denying it, Susan. It's written all over tha' face.'

'Percy — I can explain — what did he say exactly?'

451

His laugh was mirthless. 'When a man's in the gents' cubicle and hears anther man boasting about his various conquests, including the boss's wife, there's nowt to explain.'

Quickly she grabbed at a straw, a weak one. 'Well, that's it, then. He must have been talking about another boss, another wife.'

'The odds on any of the other boss's wives being called Susan Burridge would be — what does tha' think odds would be, Susan?'

She didn't answer his question, just whispered, after a while, 'It was only the once, Percy. I'm so sorry.'

'What? That it was only the once? Or that tha's been found out?' He didn't raise his voice, but his intense anger was apparent. 'And from what I overheard, Michael Fitzgerald wasn't the only man who made a cuckold out of me.'

'Oh, he was, Percy. I promise you, on — on — '

'Your mother's grave? Don't make it worse, Susan. I despise thee enough as it is. And you can tell Josh whoever he is that yon piano is last bit of dealing he'll do with my wife, if he knows what's good for him.' For a moment, his expression was bewildered. 'For Christ's sake, Susan, if I wasn't man enough for thee, couldn't you have chosen better than a gypsy and a brickie? At least Master Ralph had a bit of class, as well as brass.'

Her mouth dropped open. 'How did you — ?'

'I didn't. But I started to put two and two together tonight. Didn't need calculator.'

Trying to force back the tears, which she knew would inflame him even more, she asked, in a low voice. 'What are you going to do?'

'I've made a start by sacking Michael Fitzgerald. Told him that officially it was because of the card games. He'd already had two warnings and Frank wouldn't keep him on, especially now he's got a drink-driving charge coming up. And unofficially — '

'Unofficially?' Susan was almost too afraid to ask, but couldn't help herself.

Percy looked thoughtfully into his glass. 'Unofficially, I think I broke his nose.'

Fear screwed around in Susan's stomach as she stealthily backed towards the door, but Percy looked up and smiled. It was like one of those leering grins one sees in a skeleton, she thought.

'Getting nervous, Susan? Tha' needn't be. I'll not dirty my hands on you.' He glanced down at his reddened knuckles. 'No, happen solicitor will be best one to give tha' come-uppance.'

'Not a divorce, Percy? Not after all these years?'

He shook his head. 'I don't need all that malarkey just to give lawyers extra brass. And it wouldn't go down too well with consortium. Not that I've owt to be ashamed of.'

Susan couldn't hold his stare.

'No,' he went on. 'First there's Will to be changed. Nowt to thee. And nowt to that ne'er-do-well son of ours.' He paused for a moment. 'I used to wonder about Jonathan. But remembering rotten things you said about Nigel, and piano-tuner — I know now where he gets his conniving streak from.'

'But you can't leave me penniless.'

'I can if I want, but you'll not be penniless. I'll

453

make over the house to thee. Sale of that should see thee right for rest of tha' life.'

'What if I can't sell it?'

'Then at least tha'll have a roof over head.' He grimaced as another gulp of whisky hit his throat. 'There'll be an allowance. You'll not have enough for fancy frocks and things, but you'll not starve.'

Susan knew she was trapped, and there was no way out. Even if there was a possibility that once the dust settled, Percy might allow her to live with him in Yorkshire, she couldn't. Not if Dennis Rivers was part of the business scene. Everyone said she hadn't changed much. He was bound to recognise her. And if Percy had so much as a hint that he wasn't her first, he might not be able to restrain from bruising his knuckles again. Another thought brought her back to reality.

'Who's getting your money, then, if not Jonathan and me? After all, we are your next of kin.'

His laugh was incredulous. 'So is Abigail, or had you forgotten?'

'But she's in Africa, more interested in being a missionary than inheriting a fortune.'

'And she'll be one hell of a missionary with some brass behind her. Just think what she could do for those poor devils. Thank God there's one member of my family I'm bloody proud of.' He drained his glass and stood up. 'I'll sleep in spare room tonight and take my things to hotel tomorrow.'

'Won't you stay until — ' She pleaded with him. 'You'll not want to spend Christmas in a hotel ... all on your own ... they'll be fully booked. Please, Percy!' The thought of being entirely alone over Christmas was appalling to Susan.

'I'll not be on my own. Frank Griffiths has asked me over to their place.'

Shocked, she said, 'You've not told Frank?'

'Aye. Reckon he had a right to know.' At the door, he paused and looked back. 'I used to worship the ground you walked on, Susan. Now . . . I don't want to be in same room.'

★ ★ ★

Two days before they were due to fly to Australia, James had a telephone call from London. It was Gwynneth Jenkins. And her voice was bubbling with joy again.

'I just had to tell you, Mr Woodward. The bishop sent for Nigel. Told him that Susan had written to him, claiming she had been unwell when she wrote about Nigel, and had completely misunderstood his intentions. Made out it was all to do with the menopause, a time of their lives when women aren't responsible for their actions, according to Mrs Burridge. But she said she was very sorry if she had caused any distress — *if?* — and hoped the Church would find it in their hearts to forgive her.'

'Sounds like the violins were playing with feeling.'

'Oh, yes. I don't know what caused her about-face, but I can't tell you how grateful I am that someone, maybe someone I know, managed to persuade her to confess.'

'That's all that matters, then, and I'm delighted for you all.'

'Thank you. We won't be able to go back to

Fivepenny Lanes, of course, but Geraint has just heard through a friend that the vicar of a parish on the outskirts of Hereford has been diagnosed as having multiple sclerosis. Very sad it is, and he doesn't think he can carry on for long.'

'Is there a chance that Nigel might be offered the job?'

'Quite a good one, I think. It's a large parish, and some of his social services skills could be very useful. Nigel has telephoned the bishop, who has promised to put in a word. It might be that Nigel could start as curate to the poor man who is ill, then take over when he is too frail to continue.'

'It sounds like the ideal solution for Nigel. And what will you do if they move to Hereford?'

'Oh, we'll move in with Geraint and Melanie. They keep saying that the farmhouse is too big for just the two of them, and they are only just across the border so we'd be able to see Megan's children as often as we wish. Although they're hardly children any longer, except for the twins of course.'

'True. But you'll have a much happier Christmas than you thought, won't you?'

'Indeed we will. Megan and Nigel are staying in the hostel for Christmas Day, making sure the men have a really special day. Then we'll take over on Boxing Day so they can go to Ruthie's. What about yourself?'

He told her about his visit to Australia and how much he was looking forward to seeing Julie again, and meeting the grandchildren.

'Such joy you will have.' There was a slight pause, then she asked, 'And are you travelling alone, or do you have a companion by now?'

He smiled at the guarded words, but decided to tell her the truth, feeling sure she would understand. And she did.

'I'm not sure what the future will hold for you both, with Mary being a Catholic, but she is a good person, and so are you, so I'm sure the Lord will find a path for you somewhere. I'll ask him in a minute.'

'Thank you, Mrs Jenkins.' He chuckled. 'And a very happy Christmas and New Year to you.'

★ ★ ★

The following morning, as James packed Mary's bags into the back of the car, he noticed Sharon chatting to a young man by the signpost.

'Who's the guy with Sharon?' James asked Mary, after she'd locked the front door of the shop. 'Boyfriend?'

Mary followed his gaze. 'No. At least I don't think so. He's the newspaper reporter who hung around after the others had all gone back to London when the scandal broke about Jonathan Burridge.'

They both watched as Sharon got into the young man's car, and waved brightly to them as he turned the car onto the Winchester road.

'Well, well,' Mary said, grinning. 'If he's combining business with pleasure, he might get a story after all. There's not much Sharon doesn't know about the goings-on around the village.'

'Does she know that Susan was behind most of it?'

'I think she has a pretty good idea. And what she doesn't know, she'll make up.'

James laughed. 'Between the two of them, there should be quite an interesting little yarn in his paper before long.'

Mary went back to check the door lock once more.

'There's no risk that Michael could come back and do any damage, is there?' James asked.

'I hope not, but to be on the safe side, I've told the local policeman where I'm going, and that Michael has no legal right to enter the shop, and he's promised to keep an eye on it for me.'

'Good. Then the lease isn't in joint names?'

'No. I was afraid that we might lose it in a double or nothing card game, so I insisted that the deeds should be in my name only. Caused a huge argument, of course, but it was worth it. Anyway, I might just have a customer.'

'Oh?'

'Yes. Yvette came over yesterday to talk to me.' James followed her gaze across the pond to the tiny art gallery. 'Her premises are really too small to display the paintings properly, and she's been looking around, but doesn't want to leave Fivepenny Lanes. And Sharon mentioned that my place might be on the market soon.'

'Could solve both your problems.'

Mary nodded. 'What she has in mind is to keep one side for teas and coffees with just scones and biscuits, and display the paintings on the other side. Sharon would help out at weekends and holidays if it was too busy. I said I'd think about it, and would get in touch with her when we come back.'

'Sounds like too good an opportunity to miss.'

'That's what my gut feeling tells me, but I wanted to talk it over with you first.'

He smiled. 'We'll have plenty of opportunity. It's a long flight. Are you nervous?'

'Not at all. Haven't I got the nicest man in the world to keep me company and hold my hand if I'm nervous.'

'It might be you holding my hand. I'm not that keen on flying.'

'So we'll hold each other's hands.'

As he helped her into the passenger seat, James handed her a small package. 'Here's something you can wear when I take you out to dinner in Melbourne.'

'But it's not Christmas yet.'

'I know. It's not a Christmas present.'

As Mary opened the package and saw the jeweller's box inside, hope dawned upon her face, then realisation. 'Oh, James!' She was quite breathless as she gazed at the pearl choker. 'How on earth . . . ?'

'I tried devious means but it didn't work. So last week I told Mrs Graham the truth. She was shocked, but said of course you must have it back. And the reason I didn't give it to you straight away was because Mrs Graham couldn't find the original case, and I couldn't get hold of one until yesterday.'

The expression on her face was thanks enough, but she leaned across and kissed his cheek. Then a little frown crossed her face as she fastened her seat belt.

'What's wrong?' he asked, sensitive to every change in her mood. 'You're not getting cold feet, are you?'

'About Australia? No, of course not. It's just — meeting your family, and staying at your cottage. Won't they think I'm a terrible sinful woman, still being married and all?'

'Why should they? It made sense for you to stay overnight, with such an early flight tomorrow. Anyway, Robert and Lucy will be there to chaperone us. And they've been living together for ages, so they won't mind.'

'But they are a younger generation. Surely Katherine's parents will resent me trying to take her place — which I never would, anyway.'

'I know, and Katherine will always be a part of my life. But Jean and Ronald understand only too well that because I care about someone else it doesn't mean I do not care any more for their daughter.'

'You're sure?'

'I'm sure. And this trip has taken me off their conscience this Christmas, so they are going off to a hotel in the Lake District. They're hoping for a white one.'

'And your mother?'

'My mother hasn't said very much. She's a wise old bird who likes to make up her own mind, just like Grandma. But once she's met you, she won't be a problem, I promise.'

'I do hope you're right.'

'I know I'm right.' Glancing over his shoulder, James put the car into first gear and pulled away.

'Talking of family, have you told your son about us?'

'Yes. He phoned me to check what time he should meet me at Melbourne. I felt it only fair to put him in the picture, rather than just come off the plane holding your arm.'

'What was his reaction?' James was rather apprehensive. After all, how else could a Catholic priest react, other than with disapproval?

'I think he was more concerned about his father's behaviour than anything else. He just went very quiet, then said he was there to listen to me, but he wouldn't take sides.'

'That's fair enough.'

'And your daughter? She'll be at the airport to meet you, won't she?'

'Oh, yes.' James grinned broadly at the thought. 'And she's tickled pink that I have another lady in my life, as she put it. She doesn't like the idea of me living on my own; has been on at me for ages to apply for a permanent visa.'

'I'm looking forward to meeting her.'

'So am I. And the children. Did I tell you the new baby is being christened on Christmas Eve?'

'Isn't that just perfect? What name have they chosen?'

'Katherine. But apparently her big brother calls her Kate.'

For a long moment, they drove in silence, then James glanced out of the window. 'What a damp, dismal day,' he observed. 'I can't wait to feel that warmth and sunshine, can you?'

'It's like a dream come true.' Mary's sigh was full of happiness. 'Now I know how Cinderella felt. And I'll not be thinking too much about the clock striking twelve.'

'Maybe we can stop the clock,' James murmured. 'Julie says Australia is a great country.'

As he changed gear so that the car could tackle the steep gradient out of the village, Mary suddenly turned to him. 'I've been meaning to ask you something for ages,' she said.

'Ask away.'

'That day, last October, when you were angry over Susan.'

'What about it?'

'You said you had to go back, because there was something you had to tell her about the piano. Was it stolen or something?'

The memory brought a slow smile to his face. 'No. Much worse than that.' Teasing, he made her wait.

'James Woodward,' she cried. 'If you don't tell me what was wrong with Susan Burridge's grand piano, I'll not get on that plane.'

'OK. I'll tell you.' He paused, relishing every moment. 'Inside that beautiful piano, I found . . . woodworm!'

Concentrating on the narrow lane, he could only snatch a glance at Mary's profile. Her mouth was open and she stared through the windscreen.

'Doesn't that spread, in time?' she gasped.

'Through everything.'

'Antique furniture?'

'Loves it.'

'The parquet floors?'

'It'll be like a plague, if it's not treated.'

462

'And won't that make the house even more difficult to sell.'

'Almost impossible.'

After a sharp intake of breath, Mary said, 'Susan must have been absolutely mortified when you told her.'

'I didn't tell her.'

'You didn't tell her?'

'No.'

The engine continued to whine. Then she said. 'Isn't it dreadfully wicked, not to tell someone they have woodworm in their piano?'

'Dreadfully, dreadfully wicked. Will you say a few Hail Marys for me?'

Another glance. She still had her face turned away from him. Softly, he began to whistle. There was a funny sound coming from the passenger seat. Not so much suppressed mirth, as squelched up mirth.

Then, just as he topped the hill and passed the cottage where the blackbird had vandalised his car, Mary joined in his song.

'*And he sang as he watched, and waited till his billy boiled.*'

Hallelujah! She has perfect pitch, was his delighted thought, as they sang the last line together, at the tops of their voices.

'*Who'll come a-waltzing, Matilda, with me?*'

We do hope that you have enjoyed reading
this large print book.

Did you know that all of our titles
are available for purchase?

We publish a wide range of high quality
large print books including:
Romances, Mysteries, Classics
General Fiction
Non Fiction and Westerns

Special interest titles available in
large print are:
The Little Oxford Dictionary
Music Book
Song Book
Hymn Book
Service Book

Also available from us courtesy of Oxford
University Press:
Young Readers' Dictionary
(large print edition)
Young Readers' Thesaurus
(large print edition)

For further information or a free
brochure, please contact us at:
Ulverscroft Large Print Books Ltd.,
The Green, Bradgate Road, Anstey,
Leicester, LE7 7FU, England.
Tel: (00 44) 0116 236 4325
Fax: (00 44) 0116 234 0205

THE UNSETTLED ACCOUNT

Eugenia Huntingdon

As the wife of a Polish officer, Eugenia Huntingdon's life was filled with the luxuries of silks, perfumes and jewels. It was also filled with love and happiness. Nothing could have prepared her for the hardships of transportation across Soviet Russia — crammed into a cattle wagon with fifty or so other people in bitterly cold conditions — to the barren isolation of Kazakhstan. Many did not survive the journey; many did not live to see their homeland again. In this moving documentary, Eugenia Huntingdon recalls the harrowing years of her wartime exile.

FIREBALL

Bob Langley

Twenty-seven years ago: the rogue shoot-down of a Soviet spacecraft on a supersecret mission. Now: the SUCHKO 17 suddenly comes back to life three thousand feet beneath the Antarctic ice cap — with terrifying implications for the entire world. The discovery triggers a dark conspiracy that reaches from the depths of the sea to the edge of space — on a satellite with nuclear capabilities. One man and one woman must find the elusive mastermind of a plot with sinister roots in the American military elite, and bring the world back from the edge . . .

STANDING IN THE SHADOWS

Michelle Spring

Laura Principal is repelled but fascinated as she investigates the case of an eleven-year-old boy who has murdered his foster mother. It is not the sort of crime one would expect in Cambridge. The child, Daryll, has confessed to the brutal killing; now his elder brother wants to find out what has turned him into a ruthless killer. Laura confronts an investigation which is increasingly tainted with violence. And that's not all. Someone with an interest in the foster mother's murder is standing in the shadows, watching her every move . . .

NORMANDY SUMMER/
LOVE'S CHARADE

Joy St.Clair

NORMANDY SUMMER — Three cousins,
Helen, Tally and Rosie, joined the First Aid
Nursing Yeomanry. Helen had driven ambu-
lances through The Blitz, but it was the
Summer of 1944 that would change their
lives irrevocably.

LOVE'S CHARADE — A broken down car, a
mix-up of addresses and soon Kimberley
found she was stand-in fianceé for a man
she hardly knew. What chance had the pair
of them of surviving this masquerade?

THE WESTON WOMEN

Grace Thompson

Wales, 1950s: At the head of the wealthy Weston family are Arfon and Gladys, owners of a once-successful wallpaper and paint store. It had always been Gladys's dream to form a dynasty. Her twin daughters, however, had no interest, and her grandson Jack had little ambition. And so, it is on her twin granddaughters, Joan and Megan, that Gladys pins her hopes. But unbeknown to her, they are considered rather outrageous — and one of them is secretly dating Viv Lewis, who works for the Westons but is not allowed to mix with the family socially. However, it is on him they will depend to help save the business.

TIME AFTER TIME
AND OTHER STORIES

Mary Williams

In this collection of mysterious short stories the recurring theme of 'time after time' is reflected upon with varying intensity, and in several as a haunting reminder of life's immortality. Time itself has little meaning in the wheel of eternity, and it is more than possible that the vital spark or soul of any human being could by chance contact that of another known to him or her in a previous existence on earth. Some stories concentrate on the effect of wandering apparitions about the ether and in all of them can be found love, tragedy, emotional yearnings and sheer terror.